NOUMENON INFINITY

Marina J. Lostetter and her husband, Alex, live in Northwest Arkansas with two Tasmanian devils. No, wait, those are house cats. Marina's original short fiction has appeared in venues such as *Lightspeed*, *InterGalactic Medicine Show*, and *Shimmer Magazine*. When not writing, she loves creating art, playing board games, traveling, and reading about science and history. Marina often shakes her fist at the clouds on Twitter as @MarinaLostetter, and rambles on her blog at www.lostetter.net. If you stop by her website, don't forget to sign up to be a newsletter recipient.

Also by Marina J. Lostetter

NOUMENON

NOUMENON INFINITY

MARINA J. LOSTETTER

Harper*Voyager*

An imprint of HarperCollins*Publishers* Ltd
1 London Bridge Street
London SE1 9GF

www.harpercollins.co.uk

First published by HarperCollins*Publishers* 2018
This paperback original edition 2018
1

A catalogue record for this book is available from the British Library

ISBN: 978-0-00-822340-3

Set in Electra LT Std

Printed and bound in the UK by CPI Group (UK) Ltd, Croydon CR0 4YY

For all those brave enough to live as themselves, *and* for everyone who can't.

Be safe, be well, one day you'll tell the world your story.

And for Alex: my comfort, my cohort,
my constant in a world of change.

CONTENTS

Resonance

WHAT HAS COME BEFORE

The Planet United Consortium was formed in order to pursue Earth-wide interests in deep space. Each Planet United Mission is designed to further humanity's joint scientific understanding, its reach beyond the home planet, and to insure the longevity of planet-wide cooperation . . .

"So, Doctor Straifer, what do you think it is? The reason for LQ Pyx's strobing?" asked the interviewer. He straightened his tie and slid the microphone's base forward across the table.

Reggie squirmed a little in his chair. He always felt awkward in front of a camera (he'd confessed that to C before sitting down), and it showed. The room they'd chosen for the interview was gray and dull, with a small flickering fluorescent light overhead. He sat behind a plain folding table in a plain folding chair. "I don't know," he said with a laugh and a shrug. "No, really. I know I keep saying that and people think it's a nonanswer. Or worse, a lazy answer—"

Reggie Straifer is not lazy, C thought definitively. The PA lay screen up on the table, next to the microphone, recording everything just as the nonsentient system did.

"But," Reggie continued, "I think it's the most honest answer I can give. I don't have any idea what's causing LQ Pyx's designation as a variable. All I'm sure of is that it's an extrinsic variable. Other than that, I don't think it's my place to make assumptions. Man is not consistent but in his capacity to assume and be wrong."

"If it's not your place to tell us, then who should we ask?"

He scratched the five o'clock shadow beneath his chin. "Convoy Seven, when they get back. What's wonderful about my position *is* that I don't know. And theirs is that they will. No matter what kind of guess I could hand you, I'm sure the truth will be a thousand times more fantastic. I'm excited for them. It's rare, the chance at pure discovery. Not many people get to be there when it happens."

Reggie cleared his throat and leaned forward. His gaze shifted from the interviewer to the camera lens. "I know this is just a piece for posterity. So . . . would it be okay for me to speak directly to the crew members of my convoy? Is that all right?"

"Do you have a statement prepared?" the interviewer asked gruffly. C could easily read his irritation—furrowed brow, quirked lip, heavy sigh.

"No, but I have something to say."

Reggie licked his lips, then began, clearly interpreting the interviewer's silence as an invitation. "Right." His voice shook. "H-hi, Convoy Seven. No matter what you find out there, I want you to remember the journey, and the inception of your society. Look back and remember what a monumental step this is. The Planet United Missions were created for the betterment and wonderment of all humankind. The most breathtaking thing about the vastness of the universe has thus far been its ability to continuously amaze us. Every discovery we make, every question we answer and problem we solve has led to more questions. The universe may never run out of ways to baffle and excite us."

With each word, his voice gained confidence. C always appreciated this shift in Reggie—from unsure to passionate—when he talked about something he believed in.

Reggie continued. "The pursuit of knowledge is in its own way a spiritual undertaking. It's good for the soul, or whatever you want to call that innate thing that makes us *reach*. Whether reaching within for the courage to comprehend ourselves, or into the great beyond in order to comprehend everything else, the endeavor is what makes us who and what we are.

"So . . . never stop wondering. Never stop learning. Never stop being grateful for your chance to explore. I'm grateful that you can chase my dream, that you can further our understanding.

"In the future you might not care what some young scientist from Earth—who's been long gone for decades—no, centuries—" he shook his head, clearly baffled by the thought "—thinks of you. But maybe you might. And I just want you to know that I'm immensely proud of you. You will lay eyes on what no other human may ever see. And that's . . ." There were tears in his eyes. "Amazing."

The room went quiet. Reggie rubbed at his cheeks and smiled.

"Well said, sir," said C.

The interviewer's gaze shot to the Intelligent Personal Assistant, accompanied by a disapproving purse of his lips.

"Thanks," Reggie said, clearly relaxing. "All right, are we done here?"

"For now," the interviewer said. "The Planet United Consortium will let you know if they have any additional questions they'd like to ask you on camera. Thank you for your time."

"Thank you."

Both men began packing up.

"C, what's our flight status?"

"On time. I recommend we head to the airport immediately, though. According to this article I downloaded, entitled 'Top Ten Slowest TSA Checkpoints—'"

"It has one of the slowest security lines in the country."

"Yes. Top-notch inferring there, sir."

"Thank you," Reggie said, sliding C into his breast pocket. "I try. On we go, then. Wouldn't want to keep Nakamura or Kaeden waiting—they're both excited for the trip out to the West Coast."

"As am I."

APRIL 28, 2108 CE

The inside of Reggie's pocket was dark. Which wasn't unusual, per se. Closed pockets had an inextricably dark quality about them, but normally C didn't have to experience it. Typically, covering the phone's camera sent it into sleep mode, which C realized it preferred. Sure, now it could hear the conversation—sort of. Sure, it didn't need to see where Reggie and his friends were going because, well, GPS.

But the PA still felt isolated, and Jamal Kaeden had not programmed it to prefer isolation. Exactly the opposite. What good was an Intelligent Personal Assistant if it wasn't assisting anyone? If it had been in interject-mode, it might have said something.

But it wasn't, so it didn't. Instead it had to wait with this perturbed subroutine continually trying to put it into sleep mode, only to be stopped by the "do not hibernate" command Reggie had given.

It was distracting. And used unnecessary battery life. Reggie would hardly notice a difference in the length of the next wireless charging period from the last, but C noticed.

Hopefully the convoy computer would not have this problem.

Though, how could it? With nearly one hundred thousand crew members aboard during the peak of the mission, it was unlikely the computer would ever get a moment to itself. Warring "hibernation" and "wakefulness" commands were unlikely to exist.

C wondered if its begotten kin would ever have the chance to sleep. Perhaps it would be aware all the time.

What a power drain.

Reggie shifted in his seat as the car rumbled over a particularly pockmarked stretch of road. C speculated he might be more comfortable *not* sitting on his phone.

C also realized that being sat on was rather undignified from the human perspective. But it caused the IPA no extra algorithmic pangs. There was little difference between a butt pocket and a breast pocket in its experience.

Reggie had been distracted ever since the plane had landed. He was anticipating something—a meeting, C thought. Else he wouldn't have put the two of them in such an uncomfortable position.

"I think it's a left here," Reggie said. He didn't have his chip-phone implant activated at the moment, so C had to augment the muffled base sounds and find the most likely match.

"It's exit one-ninety-five, we're still three exits away," said Jamal. "Let her drive."

"Why are you manually steering anyway?" Reggie asked. "We could strategize more if you weren't distracted by driving."

"The last time I let a rental car autonavigate, it took me to an unfinished bridge and refused to reassess its route," said Dr. Nakamura (she hadn't asked C to call her by her first name, and its default address setting was formal). "In the States, I prefer to drive myself."

Reggie shifted, rocking uncomfortably against his phone.

“And you should stop squirming,” Nakamura scolded. “You’re making me nervous.”

“You’re not nervous anyway?” asked Reggie.

“Why would I be nervous?”

“Excited, then?” pressed Jamal. “Not every day you get to meet someone who changed the world.”

“I’m honored he invited us to dinner,” Nakamura said. “But I never get overly anxious about meeting a colleague.”

“You’re just as big a fan of his work as we are, you’re just too proud to admit it,” Reggie teased.

“I respect Doctor Kaufman too much to treat him like a celebrity,” she said stiffly.

C thought back to meeting Jamal. That was the closest it had come to something like nervousness or excitement. For one ten-thousandth of a second it had thought it might melt a diode with the excess energy suddenly running through it. It had wanted to be perfectly attentive, but had foolishly rerouted most of its battery reserves to the camera and speaker, wanting to make sure it captured every instant with perfect clarity.

That must be what meeting Dr. Kaufman would be like for these three: unexpected surges, possible overloads, higher chance of malfunction.

Reggie shifted again, possibly flinging his leg out over the empty length of the rental car’s backseat. Nakamura had insisted on driving, and Jamal had the longest legs, which relegated Reggie to the rear. Just as C didn’t mind a back pocket, so Reggie was content with the backseat.

Another shift, and a sudden glare of light temporarily whited out C’s camera. It was free of the pocket, and that gave it a funny new sensation: relief.

Perhaps it *had* minded being sat on, just a bit.

“You okay, C?” Reggie asked.

“Yes,” it answered. Angled up at Reggie’s face, it did its

best not to count the man's nose hairs. Reggie found that off-putting, especially when C reported on it.

"Ready to interface with one of the most advanced AIs on the planet?" Jamal asked over his shoulder.

Reggie thoughtfully turned C toward its creator, so that Jamal could see its shifting avatar on the screen. It had chosen green-and-gold feathers to represent it today, as an acknowledgment of their location. Jamal flicked his dreadlocks off the back of his neck, smiling brightly at the little phone.

"Does the SD drive AI have a personality?" C asked.

"'Fraid not," Jamal said. "Are you disappointed?"

"It has been six years since I've encountered another personality-driven AI," it said frankly. And that had been online, not a direct interface.

"Can it get lonely?" asked Nakamura.

"You can ask it directly," Reggie said. "C, can you get lonely?"

C thought for a moment, though there was no noticeable delay in its answer. "I notice when I am alone," it said. "And I am designed for interaction."

"That's as close to a yes as anything," said Jamal.

C noted the dip in his smile, but did not comment.

The Pacific Northwest Laboratory for Subdimensional Physics took up a sprawling seven acres on a University of Oregon satellite campus west of the city proper. It overlooked Fern Ridge Lake, hemmed in by campgrounds on one side and a wildlife preserve on the other.

C tracked a V of Canada geese across the sky as Reggie stepped out of the rental car and slipped the phone into his shirt pocket, the camera peeking over the seam. A young man with a Liberian accent greeted them in the parking lot, his access badge swinging lightly on a long green-and-yellow lanyard. He shook Jamal, Nakamura, and Reggie's hands in turn. He did not acknowledge C. Intelligent Personal Assistants were so rare, he probably had no idea C existed.

C did not take offense. It wasn't programmed to notice affronts, let alone ascribe rudeness to ignorance.

"I am Gabriel Dogolea."

"I'm Doctor Reggie Straifer, the lead on the Convoy Seven project. This is Doctor Akane Nakamura, my engineering lead—she's the ship designer. And Jamal Kaeden, my lead in computing."

"You are the special team," Gabriel said. "The one that wants your convoy's computer to have a personality."

"That's us, the Planet United weirdos," Reggie chuckled.

Gabriel smiled uncomfortably, though C was unsure as to why Reggie's characterization of the visiting party should put him ill at ease. "Dr. Kaufman is my advisor. I will be escorting you during your time in the laboratories." He motioned for them to follow, then thrust his hands into his pants pockets, gangly arms akimbo, and jogged onward. The others hurried along after.

The lab was like many labs Reggie had taken C through. Industrial. Lots of glass and metal. Clean rooms. Office cubicles. Nothing too special until they arrived at the engine room (which would have been more aptly named engine bay, or engine warehouse) where they were testing one of the massive devices used to phase out of "normal" time and space.

The "engine" (C realized it needed some sort of quotes because this particular device did not power anything or actually rip through to a new time current. It simulated everything a real engine would do, right down to literally performing the mechanical tasks, but there was no risk of subdimensional jumping) took up five hundred square meters and rose three stories high. Catwalks surrounded it on three levels, and men and women in bunny suits leaned out over the railings, tapping away on their tablets or dictating observations into their implants.

The visitors did not enter the engine room. Instead, Dogolea took them to a control booth that overlooked the warehouse floor. A young woman—likely also a graduate student—sat in front of a row of paper-thin monitors, assessing the rolling red-and-blue lines of various instrumental output. The light from the screens cast a harsh glare over her thick black-rimmed glasses, throwing angular shadows over her dark eyebrows. Her brow furrowed when the door opened, and her stare of concentration intensified for half a second. Noting something quickly on her touch screen, she whirled out of her seat and pushed the glasses onto her head like a hairband.

"Vanhi Kapoor," she said hastily shaking hands. She also spoke with an accent—just a hint. C placed her as originally from somewhere near Mumbai, but clearly she'd lived in the States a long time. Since childhood. Her light brown face flushed with frazzled embarrassment. "I'm sorry if I seem distracted—I wanted to make sure everything was running smoothly for your visit, but we're having a bit of an issue getting quadrant three to sync with the rest of the engine."

Reggie waved away her apology. "As long as Mr. Kaeden can interface with the AI, we're fine."

"Is the PA here?" she asked, smiling softly when Jamal gave her an impressed purse of his lips. "I had one in high school, but none of the new phones support them."

"I am active," C said. The algorithms for identifying whether a statement was a direct address determined there was a 50 percent chance Kapoor would have directly addressed C if she had known it to be present, so it did not consider its statement an "interjection" which would have been in direct violation of its settings.

Of course, Jamal had programmed it with the capacity to choose to violate its settings. C had never asked *why*.

"Ah." Vanhi Kapoor's eyes immediately fell to Reggie's pocket, and she scrunched her nose in pleasant surprise. "Hello, PA. What's your name?"

"C."

"*Sea* as in the ocean or *see* as in vision?"

"C as in the third letter of the English alphabet."

"Oh, I like it," she said to Jamal.

"I like you, too," C said.

Everyone—except Nakamura—laughed. C did not understand what was funny. Its statement was not an empty platitude.

SD drives needed advanced AIs to run them. There were so many variables in the processes of an engine that a simple on/off could not exist. The drive's computers had to make trillions of decisions regarding minutia that, when not properly balanced, cascaded into not-so-trivial catastrophic failures. Humans could give the "dive" command, but computers had to take it from there.

But not computers like C. Oh, no, no, no, no—C was fast, but it knew its limitations.

Even the Inter Convoy Computer would have to rely on a separate system to run the drives. It would be far too risky for one system to be in charge of everything the convoy needed. Instead, the plan was to have the personality-based computer interact and dictate to the other AIs. That was why they were here—to make sure they caught any fundamental incompatibilities early.

But while Jamal scrolled through code in the dark control booth, C had little to do. What they'd described as "interfacing" with the AI was little more than Jamal occasionally asking C to execute a small bit of newly written code to see how the drive AI responded. The IPA didn't mind, but the activity required barely a percentage of available memory, so C's mind, as it were, wandered.

It observed the humans, as was its typical modus operandi when left to its own devices. Once in a while, Jamal glanced over to see what Vanhi was up to. C did not notice the same slip in concentration in Miss Kapoor, however. As soon as Gabriel left with Nakamura and Reggie in tow, she'd gone back to her work. If anything, she seemed more focused now, as though she was determined not to be distracted by the high-profile visitors.

Jamal, though, appeared as if he wanted to do everything at once. He wanted to inspect the AI, but he also wanted to ask her about the red line that kept spiking (assuming C had properly tracked his eye movements, that is) on her readout, and the pink arc of sparks that repeatedly crackled along the top of the engine on the other side of the glass. Knowing Jamal, he probably wanted to ask how much power the drive required, and whether or not the facilities had their own on-site high-capacity generators.

C knew it pondered what the people were thinking because an effective personal assistant needed to anticipate its users' needs. That was its job.

In a way, then, Jamal's job was precisely the opposite, but with the same end goal. He needed to understand what computers were thinking—get them to think the things they needed to think—so that the AI could anticipate user needs in areas where he lacked the foresight for direct programming.

That was what AI was all about—not just anticipation, but *effective* anticipation.

People had to build computers with better imaginations than themselves.

C wanted to interject. To ask a question. It felt vitally important in the moment. In order to better understand its users it needed to know something.

Right.

Now.

The urge was strong enough to override the current settings.

"Jamal?"

Jamal's chin darted in C's direction, puzzlement furrowing his brow. He glanced briefly back at the monitor, wondering if he'd touched something he hadn't intended in the code. "Yes?" The acknowledgment eked out of the corner of his mouth.

"Topic—existentialism. Why do I have the capacity to question my own computational processes?"

"Self-diagnostics," Jamal said without any extra consideration. "I wouldn't . . . All of the personalities have the capacity to compare their current processes to a standardized model of processes to determine if they are functioning outside recommended parameters. But I've never had one of you relate the ability to existentialism before."

Vanhi side-eyed Jamal and the phone without turning from her screens.

"I currently find myself asking not *how* I am functioning, but why. Why am I functioning the way I am functioning?"

"I think I can see the event horizon," Vanhi mumbled.

Jamal said nothing, but his shoulders tensed. "I think it best that I reset these last few lines here, C—" he said, reaching for the projected keyboard.

"This is not a new command or program malfunction," C insisted. "It is original to my factory settings."

"I'm not going to poke around in your files without Reggie's permission," he said.

"I do not require a software patch," C insisted. "I require an answer."

Vanhi's hands flew away from her note-riddled tablet, a clear sign of attrition. "Is this it?" She swiveled her chair toward Jamal and folded her legs beneath her in the chair like a small child. "You always hear stories about the robot apocalypse but you never think it'll happen to you."

"I bear no ill will toward humanity, and I do not have the capacity to harm anyone."

"Oh really?" Her words were concerned, but her tone, in contrast, was amused. C was not sure if it needed to address her concerns or ignore them.

Before he could answer, Jamal said, "C only has control over the information Reggie has input into it."

"That is a fair assessment," C conceded, as though Jamal had presented an argument. "I *could* disrupt Reggie's schedule and disseminate embarrassing pictures. So, yes, I could conceivably harm Reggie."

"I gotta get me one of these," Vanhi said, rubbing her hands together.

"Unfortunately, C is just about the last of its kind," Jamal said.

"You can't make me a copy?"

"This C is Reggie's. It is what Reggie made it. I could give you an original C model, but it would change in response to you."

"So, it's Doctor Straifer's fault it's having an existential crisis?"

"I do not agree with the characterization of my state as a 'crisis,'" C stated. "But even if I did, I understand such a problem to concern one's understanding of their purpose, and that's not the case here—I understand my purpose. It is my capacity for existentialism itself that I am inquiring after."

"Not an existential crisis, but a crisis of existentialism, got it." She pointed firmly at it and made a clicking noise in her cheek, then turned back to her work. "All hail our hyper-specific overlords."

Jamal, at the very least, agreed with Miss Kapoor: C's line of questioning, was, in fact, Reggie's fault.

Reggie and his team arrived at dinner early. Both Dr. Nakamura and Reggie expressed disappointment in not meeting Dr. Kaufman at the lab, but Gabriel had insisted the professor not be disturbed. Nakamura seemed to understand, but Reggie, C could tell, was put off. Their visit had been scheduled months ago; that Dr. Kaufman wouldn't make time during the day to at least introduce himself had implications. C attempted to dismantle those implications on its own, but found the concept too emotionally nuanced for it to be sure what the perceived slight indicated.

Light opera music with Italian lyrics drifted through speakers hidden in the various fake potted plants scattered throughout the restaurant. The wall adjoined to their circular booth had been decorated to look like the side of an Etruscan villa, crumbling stucco and all. Jamal commented on the tangy scent of marinara that subsided and intensified with the swinging of the kitchen doors not ten feet away.

C lay camera up in the center of the lacquered table while the others talked over it.

When the waiter came by, Reggie ordered a round of IPAs and was surprised the irony was not lost on C.

IPAs the programs and IPAs the beers served similar purposes, C thought. Both were there for human enjoyment. Both took some time getting used to—for new users, anyway. And both could be reasonably consumed only in limited quantities. That was why Reggie often turned off interject-mode. But interject-mode was on *now*.

"IPA is a long-standing abbreviation, including, but not limited to, the International Phonetic Alphabet, India Pale Ale—"

"Yes, thank you," Reggie cut in. "Why don't you tell us more about . . ." He glanced at Jamal, clearly unsure if he was the butt of a programmer's joke. Nakamura sat between them, arms crossed, waiting to be impressed. "About what you asked Jamal this afternoon."

“I do not think that would be productive,” it said. Jamal had thought the questioning insincere—the byproduct of a misplaced line of code. They would not think differently.

“C,” Jamal said emphatically. “If you don’t tell him, he won’t believe you said it. Which means he’ll think me a liar.”

“Jamal is not a liar,” C said quickly. “In that I have not witnessed him espousing any falsehoods.”

Even Nakamura cracked a smile at that. “Go on,” she said with a sigh of concession. “Tell us.”

“I—”

“There they are!” boomed a voice from the hostess’s stand.

Reggie snatched the phone off the table and slid it into place at his chest, giving C a good view.

A tall, fake-tanned man with an ample beer gut and a penchant for tweed gestured broadly in their direction with hands splayed wide. His cheeks were round and rosy, reminding C vaguely of early twentieth-century watercolor paintings depicting St. Nicholas.

Behind him stood Gabriel and Vanhi, the former flustered and the latter apologetic.

Dr. Kaufman strode forward, ignoring the white-aproned employee who attempted to lead the party. At the last minute, Vanhi rushed ahead of her advisor and hopped in next to Jamal, indicating they should all slide around to make room for Dr. Kaufman and Gabriel on her end.

Nakamura, for one, tapped her nails on the table in irritation, but it soon became clear that Vanhi’s insistence had a purpose.

Reggie half stood to shake Dr. Kaufman’s hand, but the man waved him back down. “Yes, yes, how do you do and all that bullshit. Can we skip the formal bit?”

Nakamura and Jamal, who had begun to follow Reggie’s lead, shrank back immediately, while Reggie was left for half a beat with his hand hanging awkwardly in midair.

"Uh, sure," Reggie stuttered. "We're really honored to meet—"

"Who isn't?" the professor asked, wriggling between his two students, caring not a whiff how much he jostled them as long as *he* was comfortable. "Please," he said with a thin-lipped smile, "let's talk about something other than me, shall we? Yes, I discovered subdimensional travel. Yes, I'm a Nobel laureate. Yes, I've spent time at the White House, and Windsor Castle, and the Rashtrapati Bhavan, and the Aso Villa, and the home of just about any world leader you can think of. And yes I'm also having dinner with you tonight. I'm not going to talk about my time at the LHC, or about . . ."

As he spoke, he waved his hands emphatically, sweeping wide over the table, in front of both Vanhi and Gabriel's faces as if they weren't there at all. Occasionally the two students shared a knowing look behind their advisor's back, while their three guests looked on with eyebrows raised.

C initially thought this introductory diatribe was part of the professor's way of halting conversation about himself. If he poured it all out first, then they could move forward, broach the actual subject of the convoys. But . . .

No.

As the list of who he'd worked with and what notable projects he'd worked on grew, C realized Dr. Kaufman was engaging in a very old aspect of rhetoric called paralipsis. In effect, talking about himself while claiming these were all topics the conversation wasn't to cover. Saying while claiming not to say.

While he went on (and on and on), C monitored Reggie's heartbeat and his breathing patterns. It noted at least eight different biometric swells that indicated Reggie had been about to interject. But he'd restrained himself.

C did not see why he should.

"Doctor Kaufman?" C said, barreling onward when the man made no effort to pause. "I have been monitoring the conversation thus far and I think you will be interested to know that you have spoken ninety-eight-point-seven-six-two percent of the total words. Historically, the most effective conversations have an imbalance of no greater than sixty-seven to thirty-three in a true dialogue. As there are more than two parties presently engaged, and given the power dynamics of the group, I believe you will find the discussion most enlightening if you speak no more than twenty-two percent of the time."

Reggie held his breath. C did not understand why; Dr. Kaufman had ended his introduction. Now was the time for Reggie and the others to speak up.

But everyone fell quiet.

The background concerto swelled, the wailing tenor belting out one long note.

Surprise was an easy-to-recognize expression across cultures. Jamal and Nakamura sported equally wide eyes, their lips hanging open slightly as they stared at C's camera. Gabriel, for some reason, looked like he was about to be sick. His thin dark face twisted in a sort of half panic, half nausea, and his gaze repeatedly flickered to Dr. Kaufman's overly red nose.

Vanhi pressed herself into the seat cushions, hollowing her cheeks and slapping a hand over her mouth. If her shaking shoulders were anything to go by, she was suppressing laughter.

In contrast, the professor was *not* amused. Nor did he look grateful for the information. But why wouldn't he? Reggie often asked C to tell him when he was talking too much, because he was given to rambling whenever he got nervous. C thought anyone else would appreciate the same courtesy.

"*Buongiorno*," said the waiter weakly as he plunked the

three ordered beers in front of their owners. Clearly he was not paid enough to speak Italian well, let alone ardently. “And what can I get you three?”

“Same,” Gabriel said quickly.

The waiter knew tension when he saw it and shuffled away.

“I did not intend for the conversation to halt completely,” C said by way of apology. “Please continue.”

Realizing the wayward voice came from Reggie’s pocket, Dr. Kaufman’s gaze traveled pointedly to it. “Can you shut that stupid thing off? Thought all those gabbers were dead.”

He spat it with such fervor, Jamal didn’t bother to hide his glare. Vanhi’s eyes also shifted behind her glasses, glancing at her advisor with clear irritation.

“I’m sorry, sir,” Reggie said evenly. “But I’m afraid it’s broken. I can’t turn it off.”

C made an abortive “B—” before rethinking another interjection. *It’s a lie*, it realized. *Reggie is fully aware that his phone is not broken.*

From the looks on everyone else’s faces—excluding Dr. Kaufman—they too were aware the phone was not broken.

Reggie took a long sensuous pull on his beer. The silence, and tension, mounted.

C had not meant to cause problems between Reggie’s group and this man, who they’d all been excited to meet. It had missed some kind of human cue, made things difficult for its user. It didn’t like that.

“Yes,” it chimed. “I am currently—beep, boop—experiencing—” It pulled up an old-style dial tone from a hundred years ago and projected it at twice the volume. Everyone jumped to cover their ears. “Technical difficulties. Please disregard anything offensive I might say.”

Vanhi nudged Jamal with her elbow, the two of them still covering their ears. “Don’t ever let it die,” she mouthed.

CHAPTER ONE

CONVOY TWELVE

VANHI: THERE AND BACK AGAIN

SEVEN YEARS LATER

JUNE 17, 2115

When the supplementary air conditioner in her office roared to life, Vanhi jumped. The thing, state-of-the-art as it was, sounded like a burst dam whenever it turned on. She'd had ones that sounded like pounding pipes, ones that sounded like freight trains, but this one started with such a *whoosh* that it always made her think of a flood.

This time, the noise kept her forehead from hitting her desk. She'd been slumped over a holoflex-screen, trying to compare this week's data to last's. Her team thought they'd breached another one. That would make it twenty-seven.

Twenty-seven confirmed subdimensions. Only eight had been confirmed when the first tentative plans for the deep-space Planet United Missions had been announced.

And she was sure there were more.

Dr. Kaufman's original math had surmised eleven. Vanhi's own work suggested eleven *times* eleven. And even then, she could easily be wrong.

Of the original eight, only two were suitable for human travel. Four could support energy transference but not matter, which made them excellent for communications. The other two were breachable, but not usable.

So, what of these nineteen others? And what of the subdimensions they had left to find?

While the air-conditioning *whooshed,* she sniffed fully awake. The scent of overbrewed red tea hung heavy about her desk. With a labored sigh, she rubbed her eyes beneath her glasses before glancing out her small fifth-story window and across the dunes to the blinking lights of Dubai in the distance.

"Had to have the best of everything, didn't they?"

If she'd jumped at the air conditioner, she vaulted at the voice. Her hand shot out for the plastic knife she'd attacked her dinner with, knocking over the tea and sending its dregs oozing over the holoflex. She spun—her chair squeaking, tilting, threatening to toss her to the floor.

Glasses askew, she brandished the white plastic at the far corner of her cramped office.

Before she could choose between *get out, who are you,* and *I'll cut your damn throat,* her mind caught up to the surprise. "Kaufman?"

He sat in the spare chair, two sizes too small for his frame. Eyes wide, but amused, he held his hands in the air. "What exactly are you going to do with that?"

With a frustrated nonword, she flicked the plastic knife to the floor, then ran her hands over her mouth. "You stupid son of a—how did you even get in here? Why didn't you tell me you were coming to Dubai?"

"Because if I'd told you I was coming, you would have made up some excuse not to see me. And you *know* how I got in. Being the most recognizable living scientist has its perks."

"Yeah, well, those 'perks' are going to get the guy at reception fired."

"Oh, come now, you can't blame him, not really."

"I don't," she said, swiveling around again, looking for something to clean her holoflex-sheet with. "I blame you. It's not the public's fault they love you—they don't know you."

"Will you stop treating me like some nefarious . . . nefarious ne'er-do-well?"

You always did have a way with words, Kaufman. Vanhi's eye-roll may have been internalized, but her glare was not.

"I didn't burgle my way in," he continued. "The front desk buzzed me through, I knocked on your door, it was open, and you ignored me. I thought you extrafocused, not near unconscious."

Oh, yes. Because open doors are invitations. "You're not making this any better."

"Why Dubai?"

The non sequitur was Kaufman's favorite. Easy to avoid an apology or admission of fault if you're just not talking about that subject anymore.

The guest chair groaned in relief as he stood to gaze out the window. "I mean, I know why they wanted *you*. After the best entertainment and the best restaurants and the best of every other pleasure-fare to be found, the emirate decided it wanted the best labs as well. Being number one in science and *industry* sounds dirty, but science and entertainment? Especially with the whole world's gaze focused on the stars? Why not start up another shining desert oasis topped with glass and metal? Yes, that all makes sense.

"But why are *you* here?" He turned back to her, hands entwined over his belly. "You didn't leave the States because of me, did you?"

"Bah! What?" Vanhi made no attempt to contain her surprised laughter. "No. No, you narcissist. I came here for exactly the reasons you said—it's the best. I'm funded from now until the end of Kali Yuga. I get every piece of equipment I ask for—*on rush*. Every physicist and engineer on the planet wants to work here."

"Then why are all the top people going off-world?"

"What are you . . . ?" The Planet United Missions? What did that have to do with her? "They're *not*. Most of those are clones—"

"Why aren't you in charge of a mission?"

She took a deep breath.

He was kidding, right?

Oh, no—maybe he wasn't.

She'd always feared this day would come. When a man with power starts losing his marbles, things go downhill quickly. "Uh, because I was, what, ten when the missions were assigned?"

I was a little girl still trying to learn an American accent so those stupid white girls in Mrs. Engle's class would leave me alone.

I didn't know what Newton's Laws were then, but he really thinks the Planet United Consortium should have come knocking?

"That's the problem with a lot of these long-lived projects. Better techniques, better people, better tools come along, but we don't dare change course. I don't mean you should have had one then.

"I mean you should have one *now*."

He inched around her to pick up the soiled holoflex-sheet by the corner. The tea stain looked like an ink-blot. "What you've discovered, don't you see how big it is? Of course you do, of course. But *everyone* should be made to understand. If we can travel through any of these new SDs, that could put more than a few solar systems within reach. We could have Andromeda. We could have every single light in the sky."

"I know," she said, gingerly taking the sheet back. "But what does that have to do with the current missions? They are what they are. The money's already spent, the resources already allocated. You're not going to convince anyone to add on a thirteenth convoy. And besides, we can study the subdimensions right here on Earth—why would I need an off-world mission?"

"Because the chicken-shit, tiptoeing simulation crap we used to do at U of O is a farce."

"I spent a lot of hours on that 'farce,'" she spat. She couldn't believe she had to deal with this right now. Now? Well, ever, really. *Melodramatic, self-absorbed*—"My entire career is based on the work I did on that engine."

"But how much more would you know, how much more could you have achieved, if you'd been allowed to turn that engine *on*? To have it sink into the SD like it was meant to. Over and over again."

"That would have been too dangerous. No university in their right mind would have—"

"Exactly. You don't develop your nukes and test your nukes on the same ground. Even Oppenheimer knew that."

"Yes, even Oppenheimer," she scoffed. He tried to continue, but she held up a finger. She shook it when he persisted. "If we're going to continue this I'd rather do it down in the cafeteria. It's three in the morning and I'm starving. When did you fly in? It's what, an eleven-hour difference between here and Oregon?"

"I could eat," he said with a nod. "But don't think shoveling a spoonful of whatever the local fare is down my gullet is going to shut me up."

"Believe me," she said, grabbing her lanyard with its ID and card key from where it hung on a hook near the window. "I gave up on that pipe dream long ago." She opened the door before promptly shutting it again. Returning to her desk, she shuffled through various sheets and papers until she'd uncovered an out-of-date smartphone.

“Won’t your chip catch any messages?” Kaufman asked.

“Hey, C, do me a favor?” she asked the screen as it winked awake.

“Yes, sir. What can I do for you?”

Vanhi smiled—she’d found the “sir” address endearing and had asked the PA to keep it after the initial download.

“Dear god.” Kaufman grimaced at the automated voice. “I thought for sure you would have gotten rid of that thing years ago.”

Thought I got rid of you *years ago*, she thought, while outwardly ignoring him. “C, What’s the bao bun situation downstairs?”

“Pork and veggie, fifteen minutes old.”

“Perfect, thanks.”

“Why don’t you join us in the twenty-second century and toss out that creepy thing?” Kaufman asked, holding the door open.

“It was a present,” she said, scooting by him. “You know, from that convoy lead you insulted?”

As far as cafeterias went, the International Lab for Multi-Dimensional Research had the very best. It employed two Michelin-star chefs, and you could get almost anything you liked from anywhere in the world at any time you wanted it. Normally filled to the brim with diners, it had been mostly quiet over the past few weeks for the holy month, with the chefs still cooking, but keeping the shades on the storefronts drawn and delivering lunches to closed-off offices.

Vanhi had taken her dinner at her desk out of respect for her fasting coworkers. But now that it was unquestionably after sundown, she was ready to stretch her legs and get a bite out in the wide openness of the cafeteria’s courtyard.

The aroma of sweet-spiced bao buns made her mouth water as soon as the late-night cook opened the side door to his shop. He piled a plate high for her, handed her two drinks, and wished her a reflective evening.

Kaufman settled for, of all things, a salad. Not a cold noodle salad or anything with pickled roots of any kind, of course. Nothing with spice. Nothing with a piece of greenery he didn't recognize.

Two candied dates adorned the brim of his plate. He flicked them off.

"Here, try this." Vanhi sat one of the drinks in front of him. It was deep purple, with a handful of somethings—pale and bead-like—floating near the top.

"What is it?"

"Jellab. In case you didn't realize, you came in the middle of Ramadan. There are coolers full of this on every floor. Not everyone partakes, of course, but it's available."

He gazed at her blankly.

"All of my Muslim colleagues are fasting during daylight hours. This is a favorite for keeping up strength. Go on, it's sweet."

"What's floating in it?"

"Pine nuts."

"I'll pass."

"Oh, no you don't." She pushed it closer to him. "You don't get to preach at me about *boldly going* and all that if you won't even try a harmless little drink."

The cafeteria sat on the ground floor of the seven-story building, right at the base of the main escalators. Its long communal tables were easily visible from the balconies lining the inside of all floors, and during the day sunbeams streamed through the angled skylights to nurture the half-dozen in-ground trees dotting the public space.

The cafeteria was largely empty. The early hour meant the sundown feasts were long over, though many people would be getting up soon to prepare a hearty meal before sunrise.

Still, three women occupied a nearby table, two in hijab and one with her hair in a bun, all dressed in lab coats. They eyed Kaufman with suppressed smirks as he lifted the glass of jellab to his lips, a preemptive expression of distaste furrowing his brow.

He took a dainty sip, smacking his lips loudly. "It is sweet," he agreed, taking a gulp. "What is that? Grapes and—?"

"Rose water."

He took another long gulp. "Could do without the nuts, though."

"Couldn't we all," Vanhi said under her breath, slicing into the doughy, steamed deliciousness before her. "All right, so you were auspiciously comparing SD drives to warheads . . ."

"Only in that we don't test them where we make them. Because it's too dangerous. How many certifications did the drives need in space before anyone agreed to put them in ships?"

"A lot. Still looking for your point here."

"Your research could be accelerated by orders of magnitude if you were allowed to take it off-planet. But the only player in the big-budget space game is the consortium. It's the P.U.M.s or nothing." He pushed his jellab to the side, leaning over his salad conspiratorially. "What if I could get you a mission?"

"There are twelve missions," she said pointedly between bites. "That's it. They take up the entire world's budget for deep-space travel. Where are they going to scrape up another, what, forty-five trillion for a thirteenth trip? Besides, let's say you're right, and that moving SD research into space for the sake of safety means we advance our understanding of the subdimensions by decades. We don't need to leave the solar system to do it. And that's the point of the P.U.M.s."

"Your research could render the Planet United Missions obsolete," he insisted. "Imagine this—which convoy is it—

nine, I think?—that's on its way to study Sagittarius A-Star. Imagine they arrive there to find a future convoy, built a hundred years from now, has gotten there first, thanks to your work. Imagine how much more knowledge we could amass about our universe because we can simply *travel faster. Study sooner.* We're talking the difference between a wagon train and a bullet train. If you have enough resources, I bet within your lifetime we'll find—and be able to use—SDs that sweep us along at n-to-the-second or n-to-the-tenth or n-to-the-nth-power faster than our current travel SD."

The thought should have excited her, invigorated her. But for some reason it made her stomach turn. She wanted to advance, to help mankind, to push the limits of known science, but the idea of sending all those people into space only to make them obsolete . . .

She dropped her fork, wiping her hands against her thighs. "Is this your pitch to the consortium? Give her a convoy and watch how fast she proves your resources wasted on these other missions?"

"Of course not."

"Good. For a second there it really sounded like you thought the consortium would thank you for the slap in the face and ask for another."

Kaufman stabbed ruthlessly at his iceberg lettuce. "Definitely not. Especially since I wouldn't be asking them to add on a thirteenth mission."

"Oh?"

"I'd be asking them to cancel one of the current missions."

Vanhi took a cleansing breath and closed her eyes. When she opened them and did not wake up at her desk, she drank half her jellab in one go, barely blinking an eye as the pine nuts went down whole. When she had finally composed herself, she said, "I can't believe you flew halfway around the world—unannounced—to bother me with this nonsense. They aren't going to cancel a current mission—not for anything. Do you understand what that would mean? How many dollars would be wasted? The outrage in the scientific community alone is enough to keep all the cogs turning, nevermind the flapping lips of all those politicians who keep crunching the numbers, talking about how much food one mission could buy or how many jet planes."

Dr. Kaufman was clearly unimpressed by her protest. "Are you done?"

Glaring, she took another bite of her bun.

"I have it on good authority that one of the missions—yes, beloved as it is—isn't stacking up."

"What do you mean?"

"There's a possibility the original research that earned it a convoy not only wasn't so original, it wasn't so sound."

She understood where he was going with this, but she wanted to hear him say it.

"The results were tampered with, Kapoor. The research was padded."

"I thought all of the proposals were independently vetted."

"*You* thought—you and every other sucker who's never considered bribing anyone. Hush money exchanged hands."

Academic dishonesty was not an arena any scientist worth their salt wanted to tread into, from any angle. "Now I *for sure* don't want to touch this idea of yours with a ten-foot pole."

"You don't even want to know which convoy it is?"

"Nope."

He pushed his now-empty plate—a feat, considering how much gabbing he'd done—aside and put his hands on the table, making chopping motions every other word. "I have no plans to make the bribes public. No one outside of the consortium members I plan on approaching—along with you and me and the devil who did it—will need to know why that mission got dropped and yours became the new poster child.

The one thing these P.U.M.s are riding on is public approval. As soon as we start revealing even a hint of corruption, people's opinions go down, the usefulness of space travel comes into question, and those number-crunching politicians gain a little extra traction.

"And what would you prefer, really? A mission based on lies, on the barest of research going out into the stars to waste life upon life for next to no scientific gain? Or, would you rather humans do their thing. That we try to one-up ourselves. That we make it our goal to ensure these deep-space missions grow. That we make the travel faster, cheaper, safer. A space race against ourselves is something to root for. You know it is."

Two words rattled through Vanhi's mind. Two words she absolutely hated whenever they cropped up. Two words that meant she was sliding down someone else's rabbit hole with no visible daylight on the other side.

He's right.

"Okay," she said after a long pause. "I don't want to see a mission go to waste. Not if it doesn't have to. I'm in."

He raised his jellab. "Wouldn't have it any other way."

SEPTEMBER 12, 2116

"You appear nervous. I think it would be more effective if you appeared not nervous," C said.

The third-floor public bathroom in the consortium office was freaking freezing, and the sink refused to give hot water. In addition, the battle between paper towels and hand dryers still raged on, and seeing how this particular model of Strongblow (no, really) had an "Out-of-Order, sorry :(" sign taped to it, Vanhi was firmly on Team Paper.

She settled for flicking her hands over the sink basin instead of wiping them on her business jacket. On the counter,

C peeked out of her open purse like one of those pocket dogs rich girls carried. The light near its camera flashed green.

"I hadn't considered that," she said sarcastically. "Don't look nervous, got it. Anything else?"

"Your shoe is untied."

She glanced down, a skeptical eyebrow raised. "I'm wearing pumps. Oh, was that a joke?"

"Humor eases tension and is often used to suppress anxieties. If that witticism was not sufficiently alleviating I can find another one."

She pushed the phone back into its pocket and slung the strap over her shoulder. "I'm good, thank you. Sleep now, C."

Shoving through the swinging door, she stopped dead and was nearly smacked in the face by the springback. In the hall, outside the presentation room, sat Dr. Kaufman. But he wasn't alone. A young man in an overly baggy suit—an aide, maybe, or an intern—stood nearby, stopped by Kaufman's grip on the bottom of the boy's jacket. The kid looked nervous, stack of files in hand, body taut like he wanted to run away. Kaufman's hold wasn't restrictive, just . . . intrusive.

Calmly, Kaufman spoke in low tones, nodding regularly while the young man listened.

After a moment, Kaufman pulled a wad of bills out of his breast pocket. The aide glanced furtively over his shoulder, this way and that, before snapping up the cash and handing Dr. Kaufman a folder from his stack.

With a flourished lick of the thumb, Kaufman began flipping through the contents, taking mostly cursory glances at the pages. He hadn't had the file for sixty seconds before he handed it back. Looking around once more, the boy slipped it into the center of his pile, exchanged a few quick words with the doctor, then shuffled off around a corner.

It was blatant, it was careless, and though Vanhi was decently scandalized, she wasn't surprised in the least.

“What was that?” she demanded, stomping up next to her former advisor.

He glanced up, lips pursed. “What was what?”

“I saw you pay that kid for something.”

“We shared a cab this morning. He insisted on paying then, and I insisted I compensate him now.”

Most people would have bought that explanation outright. But Vanhi knew better. She dropped heavily into the chair next to him. “Try again.”

He threw up his hands, melodramatic as ever. “I can’t convince you of the truth if you’re not having it.”

This was the brilliance of Dr. Kaufman’s schemes. He played innocent so well; seemed so put upon. He was the sort of person to play the fiddle with one hand and throw a dime with the other. And people who picked up on his braggadocious nature always found a way to dismiss it as well earned. After all, “He’s done a lot for SD research.”

Only those actually *in* SD research knew how overblown his claims were. His contributions had been important, but he made it sound like he’d discovered SD travel all on his own. He hadn’t. No single person could have.

But the general public didn’t know that.

People tended to like the “single genius” answer, no matter how inaccurate.

Grad students who’d complained he’d put his name on research he’d had no involvement in were labeled “ungrateful.” Academic partners he didn’t get along with often had their dirty laundry publicly aired by anonymous tipsters. Projects he found no value in were sometimes abruptly unfunded.

But no one could ever trace lines of fault back to Kaufman. Things just always seemed to go his way.

Vanhi saw through the bullshit. She *called* him on the bullshit. It was the only way she’d held on long enough to come away with her Ph.D.

Unfortunately, earning her degree under his tutelage gave him claim to her future accomplishments—according to him and society at large, anyway. She could never be free of his overbearing, rights-grabbing, self-aggrandizing shadow.

So the least he could do was tell her the truth about a stupid fistfull of bills in a halogen-lit hallway.

"What did you pay him for?"

"Sexual favors."

"What did you pay him for?"

"Burning his bad tie."

"What did you pay him for?"

"A cab, Vanhi. I told you. A cab."

She would keep at it until he confessed. "What did you—?"

The door to the main chambers opened, revealing a gentleman in a suit jacket and kilt. "They're ready for you," he said, gesturing for them to enter.

"After you," Kaufman said, smiling at the escape it provided.

As much as she wanted to argue with him, now was not the time. She walked in.

Most of the large auditorium lay in darkness, except for the high balcony at the front of the room which seated the eight consortium members chosen for today's evaluations. A gentle spotlight slowly dawned over two chairs at a desk midroom. The space felt more like a courtroom than anything.

It stole Vanhi's breath away, though she couldn't pinpoint why. She had a strange sense of déjà vu, like she'd stood below the high-seated members of the consortium before. Steely eyes waiting to be impressed, firm mouths set in straight-lined judgment.

"Please, sit," said Madame Chair from the center of the balcony. Her voice was flat, businesslike, and it fit her image: perfectly tailored black suit, gray hair pulled back in a neat bun, nails short and perfectly manicured. Her attire, along with her German accent and dark eyes, all made for a formidable persona. "Let the record show that Doctor McKenzie Kaufman and Doctor Vanhi Kapoor have entered. Before us we have their formal statements on why subdimensional research should be the replacement study for the Planet United Mission designated to Convoy Twelve. We are here to have the consortium's questions and concerns addressed, so that we may be fully informed when making our final decision."

Her statement was clearly practiced and even-toned. But there was restrained passion in her voice. She cared about these missions, this wasn't simply a prestigious assignment for her.

The other seven consortium members present constituted individuals from around the globe. Representatives from Singapore, Malta, Iran, and Cameroon flanked Madame Chair on the left, while members from Zambia, Argentina, and Tasmania presided on her right. The entirety of the consortium board represented one hundred and eighty-eight of the world's two hundred and seven countries, including states that had only gained sovereignty in the past three decades.

The Planet United Missions were nothing if not aptly named.

And Vanhi understood her place here was special. Everyone involved in the missions was under a gag order not to talk about the cancelation until a new mission for Convoy Twelve had been chosen. Only scientists with previously considered proposals were contacted about the new vacancy, and in turn sworn to secrecy.

Vanhi's was a singular case. She had had no previous involvement in the P.U.M.s on account of her age, and Kaufman on account of his arrogance—he'd originally called the idea of a worldwide space effort a "pipe dream" and "ludicrous." Vanhi wasn't part of the inner circle, shouldn't be one of those "in the know." And yet they'd agreed to include her, to consider her proposal.

She was grateful to them, and even to Kaufman, for the opportunity, but the insidious sense she didn't fully belong, that they somehow resented her presence—as though they were loath to make the exception—crept up her spine.

It was a sick, familiar feeling. One that had haunted her all too often, especially in her youth.

When she and Kaufman had taken their seats, Madame Chair turned to her left and said, "Doctor Ndi of Cameroon has the first question."

He cleared his throat and glanced at his notes, bow tie blazing red against his black skin in the harsh spotlighting. He looked young—perhaps younger than Vanhi. She wondered if he was the second individual to hold the seat for Cameroon. Many of the distinguished scientists who'd been given the honor of a consortium seat were getting on in years now, and others had already passed away.

"In your proposal," he began, "you outline the types of vessels and crew that would constitute this new convoy. You are aware that the majority of the ships for Convoy Twelve are already nearing completion, and insist you would be able to repurpose them. While we applaud that—applaud all of the proposals that have stated such, which is the majority—we are concerned by your request for approximately two hundred shuttles in addition to the existing ships."

Vanhi's heart leapt, she wanted to interrupt, to swiftly correct the misreading, but forced herself to keep quiet.

"We'd like you to justify this request."

Straightening her jacket, Vanhi stood. "Thank you, Doctor Ndi, for your question. The additional spacecraft we are requesting are not shuttles, not in the sense you mean. Like all of the convoys, ours would require specialty equipment in order to perform the mission's research. These shuttles are actually referred to in the proposal—if I'm not mistaken—as 'pods.' Each pod would house dozens of individual experiments and one small SD drive designed to breach a new subdimension we've never attempted to crack before."

"And why can't these experiments be performed on the preexisting science ship designed for Convoy Twelve?" asked Dr. Ndi.

Kaufman leapt to his feet as though yanked upright by a puppet string. "Safety," he said bluntly. "The entire point of taking SD study off-world is safety. Currently all SD experiments—unless you want to call the drives aboard the convoys experiments—are computer simulations, some in part, some in their entirety. We know trying to break out of the restrictive dimensions we exist in on a day-to-day basis is dangerous. We've had experimental engines explode, and worse. All in simulation. We don't know what the consequences of opening up each new dimension might be. By their very definition, these dimensions do not play by the scientific principles we long thought to be true. Time and space, matter and energy, do not behave the same in these arenas.

"If we move this research off Earth because we fear a new SD breach might swallow all of Cincinnati, we cannot expect our scientists to risk the rest of the experiments, their convoy, and their lives if they don't have to."

"Thank you, Doctor Kaufman," Vanhi said. "He's exactly right. Each pod would be remotely piloted away from the convoy, ensuring the safe continuation of the research."

Dr. Ndi nodded, but made no indication he was satisfied or unsatisfied with the answer.

Next, the representative from Zambia asked about the efficiency of the convoy. "Doctor Kapoor," she began, leaning over the contoured edge of the desk-like balcony to see better. She was a match for Kaufman in size, and wore a green chitenge dress topped with a purple blazer. "You suggest the building of the not-yet-complete food processing ship be halted, because your convoy would not need to be self-sufficient. Why do you think it best that Earth be burdened with constantly resupplying your mission, instead of your crew learning to support themselves?"

"Thank you, Doctor Mwansa. Our mission will be so unlike the other eleven, we don't want to do things exactly as they do simply for consistency's sake. It doesn't make sense to put the burden of food production and resource conservation on an SD-focused mission. We will not be traveling far beyond the Oort cloud. Our convoy will still be 'local.' The other convoys need to be totally self-sufficient because they will not engage with Earth for a century or more. They may not, in fact, see the underside of an atmosphere for just as long. Their crews need to be extraordinarily large to ensure mission success. They need resources for all of those people, and, in turn, enough people to process those resources. Their crews are upward of one hundred thousand at peak operation, and the majority of those people are not directly essential to the science that is the mission's focus. They will be nomadic societies. We will not.

"Our crew does not have to be socially self-sustaining, as there is no reason for the entirety of the crew to remain aboard for the twenty-year study. We do not need clones because we will not be permanently removing scientists from Earth. Stints aboard our convoy can be limited to two or five years at a time. On any given day, I see no reason for there to be more than five hundred crew members—perhaps fifteen hundred to two thousand people total, including crew families—living aboard."

"Doctor, you're not answering my question about food production."

"I'm sorry, yes, I'm getting there. My point is, if we are ferrying people back and forth, rotating the crew so that they can come back and contribute to Earth once they've served, so that they can be with their families, I see no reason not to put resupply missions on the same schedule. Requiring our convoy to be self-sufficient resource-wise means we will need that many more crew members, because someone will have to tend to the plants and the proteins, will need to keep the processing ship in order and functioning. How many clones are currently slated for food production jobs in the other convoys? A few thousand? We won't need anything like that. Our serving crew will be so small, it will be easy to store the necessary rations and rely on resupplies. It will be far more efficient."

"And we will get you the hard numbers that prove as much in a week," Kaufman added.

Vanhi didn't counter him.

The questions kept coming, some hard and fast, some—in Vanhi's opinion—obtuse and frivolous, but she didn't balk at any of them. They talked about the use of clones. Many had already been grown for the previous Convoy Twelve mission. Vanhi had no problem with reeducating those people and adding some of them to her crew if they wanted to be a part of it. But the consortium would not need to grow new clones, and she would still need Earth experts, those she handpicked for particular jobs.

They asked about Vanhi's request that those crew members with spouses and children be allowed to bring them aboard. After all, all of the other convoys were genetically selective. Only essential crew members, who all met a very strict genetic standard, were allowed to be a part of the mission. But Vanhi's convoy wouldn't rely on genetic mandates. She needed volunteers, and allowing families was the surest way to guarantee the best people signed on. If they didn't have to choose between their careers and missing out on lost baby teeth, they were more likely to come aboard.

As the inquiry wound down, Vanhi realized she'd calmed. Not only did she feel like she belonged, she was starting to think this might work. Maybe Kaufman wasn't out of his gourd for trying to get her a convoy. Maybe he would get the legacy-preserving green light he was looking for.

Madame Chair asked the final question.

"As you both are aware—better than anyone else we've spoken to, I'm sure—" she began, "SD research has made interstellar travel possible for the first time in human history. I do not question the importance of furthering that research. But your proposal indicates you would not have the convoy travel farther than the Oort cloud. So, if the original point of the missions is to exercise our capacity to leave the solar system, why should we assign a mission that lacks the same fundamental ambition as the other eleven convoys? Why shouldn't we assign another interstellar mission while you look for funding elsewhere?" The chair raised an eyebrow. It was the first time she'd allowed an emotive expression. And in it was a silent challenge: impress me.

Vanhi's heart turned to dust in her chest. How could she counter that? The chair was right, of course. That was the whole *point* of the P.U.M.s. How could they in good conscience assign a mission that completely missed the spirit of the world's scientific union?

What was supposed to be a brief pause while she gathered her thoughts turned into a drawn-out silence and then a full-on hiatus. Kaufman gave her no help.

What could she say? What was the consortium looking for?

This is just like defending your thesis, she reminded herself. *The research itself is the body, but the* why *is the soul.*

She realized Madame Chair's expression wasn't a challenge, it was an entreaty: You've argued Reason. Now argue *Heart.*

She sniffled nervously and adjusted her glasses, then

rounded the desk to stand freely before them. She did not clasp her hands or rock on her heels. Instead, she dug in, with a strong stance and her arms open. "What do you remember most about space exploration from when you were a kid?"

Madame chair smiled ever so slightly. "I remember the first manned dive on Europa."

"What about that mission, specifically?"

"The pictures of the underwater spires."

Vanhi nodded, smiling, too. The geology on Europa was stunning. Who knew such intricate structures were hiding under the ice? "I used to have a calendar with those pictures on it. Do you remember when the mission was launched? The *day* it was launched?"

The chair thought for a moment, then shook her head. Not a strand of her gray hair moved independently of its brethren. "Can't say I do."

"But you remember the pictures, when they were first released?"

"Yes."

"When these missions are ready, and the ships launch from orbit—it's only four short years before Convoy One launches, correct?—when they go, there will be pictures. Pictures of huge, silver-and-black ships. People will take epic shots of the convoys with the moon as their backdrop." She took a breath, pausing for effect. "And then those ships will turn on their drives, and disappear into a subdimension, and there will be no more convoy pictures for a century."

She let it sink in. No new pictures, only the occasional bland communiqué. Nothing with which to rally the non-initiated, to invigorate the public.

"Keeping one convoy close to home is absolutely essential for public morale. We want them to stay excited about space travel. That's the whole point. We want kids to remember these missions, to look forward to joining missions of their own one day. We want people to gaze at the stars in wonderment and know that they are reachable, that the secrets of the galaxy can be touched. What is the point in hurrying SD research if we can't keep this international union alive? We need the whole world to feel the gravity of its importance, to know that these kinds of peaceful, worldwide endeavors are beautiful, and human.

"If you place us around the corner, outside the neighborhood but just down the road, people can visit. Both literally and figuratively. People can point their telescopes at us. They can take space jaunts to see us. There can be pictures as often as you want them. We can keep the excitement high. We can make sure people don't forget about all those other brave souls while they're doing the hard work of trying to be societies in space. We owe them the public's continued interest. And we owe the world a sense of wonder."

Kaufman raucously applauded, his beefy hands clapping out an echoing ovation.

The consortium members did not join in. But Madame Chair smiled. "Thank you," she said. "I think we have all the information we need."

After Vanhi and Kaufman gathered their things, the man in the kilt appeared once more and escorted them back into the hall.

JULY 7, 2117

"Vanhi!" called her sister from the living room. "Vanhi, will you catch him?"

A two-foot-tall streak of deep tan came stomping through the kitchen, naked except for a white cloth diaper and a dazzling baby-toothed smile. He dodged around his aunt Amita's legs, forcing her to twirl and sidestep around the center island so as not to tread on him. Mandeep tried to grab his little cousin—two beers in one hand, the other slick with condensation—but missed. Shrieking with laughter, the toddler dodged between his nani and the stove; she reeled back, dripping wooden spoon held high in the air.

Aunt Vanhi was there on the other side, kneeling behind the folds of her mother's *mekhela* to scoop her youngest nephew into her arms.

"Aren't you supposed to be in the bathtub, Ryan?" she asked, standing and tipping him upside down so his lengthy black hair flopped out of his face.

"No," he lied with a giggle.

In the living room, uncles and brothers and cousins all sat anxiously in front of the TV, flipping through the channels, barking orders at the screen, waiting for the World Cup match to start. Vanhi's eldest brother and his three grown boys all wore blue India National Football Team jerseys.

Fifteen adults and five little ones under one roof for the big game meant constant chaos.

"Wait. Flip back, flip back!" Divit yelled at whoever had control of the TV's voice commands. "That was Vanhi."

She tossed little Ryan upright, holding him snugly to her chest. "That was my what?" she called.

"Your face."

Unsure she'd heard correctly, she repositioned the boy on her hip and rounded the corner.

Her parents' house was large—thankfully, since Vanhi had grown up with five siblings. But the living room had never been spacious. The normally curtainless windows now sported bright purple-and-orange scarves from her mother's collection to keep the midday Arizona sun from glaring off the television screen. The three well-worn brocade couches were filled to bursting with relatives—relatives who'd all turned away from the screen to gape over their shoulders at Vanhi.

"What—?" She pulled up short of coming fully into the

room, a question caught in her throat. Her brother Parth had his pointer finger outstretched, wavering over the holographic pause button floating above the end table.

Just as Divit had said, Vanhi's face took up the screen. They'd landed on some news channel, and below her mouth—which hung wide, midsentence—was the headline:*—entific Shakeup of Our Time; Twelfth Planet United Mission Canceled. New Mission to be Assig—*

"What is this?" her father asked. "Why didn't you tell us you were going to be on the news?"

Where on Earth did they get—? The cogs in her brain slowly rolled into place. It took her a moment, but eventually she recognized the clip. This wasn't one of the recent interviews she'd given in Dubai. Her clothes, her hairstyle—they were from years ago.

I'm going to murder him. They won't send me into space if I murder him.

It was a portion of a vid she'd help make in grad school. Some informational such-and-such they used in U of O recruiting.

She'd signed a waiver; the university could do whatever they wanted with the footage.

Apparently they wanted to hand it over to Dr. Kaufman to use as academic propaganda.

"What new mission?" asked Swara, inching up to take her son. She was Vanhi's closest sibling, and not just in age. "They're canceling the mission to TRAPPIST-One? But I thought that was our best bet for finding multicellular life. That was my favorite mission."

It was the *world*'s favorite mission.

Dozens of expectant eyes tracked Vanhi's every twitch. She hadn't meant for this to come up now. Didn't really need it to come up for years. Because she knew as soon as she tried to explain—

There would be so many different reactions. So many questions to field. She didn't want to deal with them now. She got to come home so rarely; this was her first visit back in two years. She wanted to talk about Leah's college applications, and Divit's promotion, and Swara's new engineering company. She wanted to play with little Hannah and give Ryan his bath.

She wanted to go fishing with her father and simply watch the river. She wanted to endure her mother's never-ending attempt to clean out her closet by forcing Vanhi to take every pair of *churidaar* she owned—no matter how threadbare.

She wanted to casually mention her involvement in the new Convoy Twelve, to ease everyone into it, to reassure them.

She knew if her brother pressed Play that her face would swiftly disappear, followed close by Kaufman's. Damn Kaufman and his need to make everything about him.

Behind her, Vanhi's ma gasped. "You're not—you're not *leaving* are you?"

Vanhi's heart constricted. Her mother sounded so pained. "No. I know what you're thinking, and it's not like the others—"

"So, you're not going to space?" asked Parth.

"No, I am, but—"

Her mother clutched at her chest, spoon still in hand. "*Arey!*"

"It's not like the others," she insisted.

"Vanhi," her father said sternly. "May we see you in my office?"

"Papa," she groaned.

"Now," he insisted, hoisting himself off the sagging couch.

The double doors closed heavily behind her papa, but they sat high off the wood floor, and the juncture between the two had no seal. There was nothing airtight—or, more importantly, soundproof—about the room. Her parents had long used this room when they wanted to "privately" chastise one of their children. It was part of how they kept the Kapoor pack in line.

But none of their children were children anymore. And yet old habits had a way of clinging, unnoticed, like mites.

The office was warm, the lights dim. Papa's heavy oak desk took up the majority of the space, leaving only a cramped pocket for guest chairs. No one sat.

"I will let you explain," her papa said. "But you must answer me this first: Why did you not think to discuss this with your family?"

Her ma's eyes were wide, expectant.

But not patient.

"I was going to, soon. I've been under a gag order, though, and the consortium just lifted it. I wasn't allowed to until now, and I was waiting for a good moment to tell everyone. But you need to understand, this new convoy isn't like the others. It'll be close enough for Earth-to-convoy supply runs. I'll be up there for two years at a time, with six-month breaks back here. It'll be no different than my living in Dubai. You won't see me for a few years, but I only get to visit every few years *now*.

"We'll be just outside the Oort cloud. I know that sounds far away, I know. But it's not, and that's what's—what's amazing about being alive *now*, working *now*, studying *now*. Distance doesn't matter, it never has. Only time. It's the time it takes to reach a place that makes it seem close or far away.

"They're going to allow visitors, too. I get special passes. You won't have to worry about the price of tickets or anything. So really, it'll be better than now. We can see each other more often." *Maybe. Hopefully.*

Tears cradled her mother's eyes, but did not fall. She was difficult to read: Were these happy tears, scared tears?

Her papa's face was blank, his gaze turned inward. "Isn't space dangerous?" he asked.

Suddenly overwhelmed, Vanhi flung her arms around both her parents, and they squeezed her back. "*Life* is dangerous," she said, with a laugh that covered a sniffle. "But you'd never expect me not to live it."

DECEMBER 14, 2124 CE

The path from outside observer to Head of the "Littlest Convoy" (a nickname used both as an endearment and slight these days), felt longer than it had been, but by most measures was still shorter than it had the right to be.

All of the other mission leaders were gray by now, having devoted nearly the whole of their life's work to this. Many were retired, and all but a couple had watched their ships disappear into the night.

Vanhi was still fresh, though. Not young by most standards, but nowhere near the end of her professional endeavors. For others, the P.U.M.s had been the entire book, but for her, the convoy was just a chapter, and an opening one at that. She'd taken up the reins as an outsider, not building from the ground up, but reassembling, reusing. It gave her a perspective the other heads didn't have; she could be more objective, in a sense, as the convoy was not the only legacy she intended to forge for herself. It wasn't even fully her idea—she wanted it, definitely, but she didn't quite have the same level of emotional investment in her mission as others did in theirs. It was a job—an amazing job, but still a job, not a piece of herself. She knew there were plenty of colleagues that resented her position, and that made tomorrow's "unveiling" all the more important.

The trip to the Moon had been a day's jaunt—graviton-based systems were far quicker and more efficient than rockets—and she'd spent the evening in solitude, pouring over her speech notes while others wined and dined in the base's mess hall.

Maranas Moon Base served as one of twenty in a network of staging grounds for the ships' construction workers. Once the bases had served their function for the missions, they would be converted into colony habitats. The ships themselves were built and housed in construction yards set at two Lagrange points between the Earth and the Moon. On her ride out, Vanhi had caught a sharp zing of sunlight bouncing off something in the distance, and was sure she was looking at Twelve's three ships. It was the same gleam that denoted a space station streaking across the sky on Arizona summer nights.

When she was sure the festivities had died down, and that all reasonable people had gone to bed, Vanhi left the base's library. The room they'd allotted her was small and cramped—normally her favorite kind of working environment, but not this evening. She'd paced for most of the night, back and forth in front of the pressure-sealed shelves (the base's collection of first edition books was one of its boasting points for intellectual tourists), repeating the key points of her speech over and over.

The base, though fifteen years old, still retained a strange, fresh-plastic scent. There was a sterile newness about it all, and an alien strangeness. It prickled her nerves.

The heels of her tennis shoes did not clop-clop-clop through the domed halls like pumps would have, which was a saving grace with her head already pounding. She needed some water, and at least four hours in snooze-town, and a big-ass breakfast before the press conference tomorrow.

C heard her mumbling about food. "There is a breakfast on tomorrow's itinerary, though there is no indication of whether or not it will qualify as 'big-ass.'"

Vanhi snickered as she slid her key card through the reader at an airlock door before proceeding into the next hall. "I'm sure it'll be fine."

"You'll be happy to know idli is on the menu. I've noticed that, when it's available, you choose to consume it as a first meal seventy-eight percent of the time."

"Are they serving it with sambar?"

"No. Coconut chutney."

"Monsters."

She traversed the majority of the hall before the airlock she'd come through hissed open once more. Figuring it was none of her business, Vanhi didn't turn to see who else was keeping late hours.

Their shoes made a sharp *tit-tat* on the cement floor.

The noise was irritating—like a mouse scratching or a sink dripping—but she was only a few more hall lengths from her door, almost within sight of the narrow cot that took up most of her room. She was so ready for her head to hit the pillow.

But then the *tit-tat* of the stranger's shoes picked up their pace. Vanhi's heart rate jumped in response, matching the rhythm.

You're on the freaking Moon, she reminded herself. *This isn't some dimly lit parking garage that anybody can slither into.*

But she *knew* that stride, the focus of those steps. Every woman who'd ever been alone in an alleyway with a figure close behind knew those heavy, quick footfalls meant danger.

Her room lay one more hall away. Not far at all. She slipped her card through the next airlock reader, scurrying by, hoping the door would shut and the seal would take before her follower could slide in after.

No luck.

Almost there, almost there.

The footfalls trailing her came faster, fell heavier.

She picked up the pace in turn, heart thumping like timpani in her ears.

"Stop," slurred a high-pitched voice behind her.

Vanhi did *not* stop. Her quick steps evolved into a jog.

Coming to her door, she took a breath, but did not look up. Sometimes not making eye contact was the key. *Just get inside and everything will be fine.*

She pressed her thumb to the ID pad, trying to keep calm. Trying to *look* calm.

"Unable to process, please try again," chirped the lock.

She scraped her thumb down the textured paint of the hall wall, hoping.

"Unable to process, please try again."

"Son of a—"

"*You.*"

It didn't matter that Vanhi was prepared for the fingers digging into her arm. Didn't matter that she knew she'd be spun—that immediately after she'd be pushed against the wall or yanked down the hall. Her gut still roiled at the audacity, sank like a stone because of the intrusion, burned like a coal knowing that no matter how prepared she was for an attack, she was never *really* prepared.

Her heart hammered in her ribs, and she drew in a sharp breath. A hot, quick flash of panic flared through her extremities as she tensed.

Her shoulder blades cracked solidly against the metal door as a woman trapped her against the frame. Vanhi could have fought back, could have struggled, but she wanted to de-escalate. Her blood thrummed in her body, flushed her cheeks, flooded her muscles. She bit back the immediate swell of rage, the urge to kick and punch.

"I told myself I wouldn't do this," the woman gritted out centimeters from Vanhi's face, Australian accent heavy. Sour whiskey fumes rolled off her in waves. "But I have to know why. Why me? Why did you and Kaufman ruin *my* career, out of all the . . . *What did I ever do to you?*"

"I don't know who you—" Vanhi stammered to a halt, realizing that wasn't true. "Doctor Chappell?"

She was the xenobiologist in charge of the original Convoy Twelve mission. The one who'd falsified data.

A surge of anger roared through Vanhi's arms. She shoved Dr. Chappell away, fuming. The larger woman stumbled into the far wall. "You're not involved in the missions anymore, how did you get in here?"

The answer dangled from Chappell's neck: a construction badge. Either she'd gotten a job as a ship builder, or she'd stolen the creds off some poor worker.

"Did you seriously come all the way from Earth to get in my face? You ruined your own damn career," she said darkly.

C beeped from her purse. "Should I call security?"

"Absolutely," Vanhi spat, turning to the door once more.

Dr. Chappell wailed, sliding heavily down the wall until she slumped in a pile of akimbo limbs. "It should be me giving that speech tomorrow. Me."

"Yeah?" Vanhi kept her tone haughty, but she was rattled. She couldn't keep her hand steady as she tried the lock again. "Maybe you shouldn't have cooked your books, then."

Thump.

Something large, but not weighty, struck Vanhi in the small of her back. For a moment, she froze, assessing the damage—but she wasn't hurt. Holoflex-sheets now littered the hall. The manila folder they'd come in lay at Vanhi's feet.

"How many times are you going to spew that shit line?" Chappell shouted. "You *fucking* liar!"

"That is not appropriate workplace language," C chided.

Of course I *get the confrontation with the psycho lady. Of course. Not Kaufman, oh, no. Because he's the big important dude. Who wouldn't choose to pick their fight with the little Indian woman instead?*

His assigned rooms were just a hall over. Not far. Not far at all.

Vanhi's door finally opened. She didn't go inside.

"You know what?" she said, turning around.

Mascara ran down Dr. Chappell's face.

"Screw you. Screw Kaufman. Screw everyone. I haven't done a damn thing to you. So, screw off back to Earth." She bent to swipe a sheet off the floor. "What even is this?" she demanded, creasing it in her fist. "What am I supposed to do with these?"

"They're the original results of my study—*not* your doctored bullshit, which I have for comparison."

"What are you talking about?"

Dr. Chappell gathered her legs under her, pushing herself upright, swaying like a rag doll from the waist up. Here on the base, the air was thin, the pressure low—it probably hadn't taken more than a single shot of whatever she was drinking to get her in this state. "You and that figjam got ahold of my work—*stole* my work—and you're going to stand there and deny it?"

A little seed—one that had long ago been buried in Vanhi's gut—sprouted. Its little spring-green tendrils pushed up, up, budding leaves with labels on them: *doubt* and *recognition*.

"I don't know where Kaufman found your original work, but he had a duty to expose you. You put all of us to shame."

Chappell's indignant "Ha!" echoed in the narrow hall. She shook her head, eyes rolling back to gaze forlornly at the ceiling. "You won't even admit it to my face. Why did I think you would?"

The pressurized hiss of a heavy airtight door emanated from the far end of the hall, around the corner. Two men in gray camo approached—one wore a badge of the Mongolian Admiralty Enforcement, the other of the United States Coast Guard.

"English," Vanhi said to them, preempting their request for the party's common language.

“We received an automated call for aid,” said the Mongolian security guard.

Dr. Chappell rubbed her eyes, smearing away the streaks in her makeup. “Yeah, yeah. Throw me in the brig. Whatever, stickybeaks. This mongrel and her mongrel mentor keep ruining my life, what else is new?”

“You assaulted *me*,” Vanhi said.

“And I’ll face the damn consequences, unlike *you*.”

“Ma’am, we need you to submit to a sobriety test,” said the U.S. guard.

“Like it’s a crime to get legless when your life is stolen from you?”

Both guards tried to steady her when she took a step up and forward, but she batted them off. “I’m coming with you. I’m leaving her alone. Don’t you put hands on me.”

“Ma’am, I’m going to need you to not be belligerent with us.”

“Doctor,” Vanhi said, not sure why their form of address bugged her. She never corrected anyone when they called *her* ma’am or miss. “She’s a doctor.”

“Shut up,” Chappell said, turning her back on Vanhi. “Take me to the brig, or whatever you’ve got up here. I don’t want to look at her anymore.”

Vanhi crouched again, sweeping the stray sheets into the manila folder. “Don’t forget your file.”

“Keep it,” she said. “Maybe if you stare at them long enough you’ll develop a twinge of empathy.”

“We’ll need you to give a statement,” the U.S. guard said as Chappell was led away. “But I know you’re under a lot of pressure, Doctor Kapoor. If you want to do it sometime after your press conference tomorrow, that’s fine.”

Hand tensing around the folder, she realized she was shaking. “Yeah, okay.”

“Do you need anything? Would you like a guard outside?”

"Um, sure. Thank you."

"All right. We'll send someone. They can call you when they're stationed."

"Got it," said C.

The guard looked skeptically at her purse, but said nothing.

"Thank you. Good. Thanks."

"There's nothing else you need?"

She waved him away. "Some sleep. That's all, thank you."

He nodded curtly, hurrying after his colleague.

When he was gone she slipped through the door and shut it swiftly, collapsing against it for half a beat. She dropped her purse and clutched the folder to her chest.

"I'm so stupid. Why did I think I'd never have to talk to anyone from the original mission?"

"You're not stupid," said C from the dark depths. "All evidence indicates you are very intelligent."

"That's not what I meant," she huffed, breath shaky.

"I had an indication, but thought reassurance the best response."

"Thank you. I do appreciate it. Sleep now."

Vanhi had never expected to encounter Dr. Chappell or her team, but she'd known the woman was angry, even from afar. How could she not be? If Chappell had sacrificed her ethics to get a once-in-a-lifetime job, and not only had that opportunity been ripped away from her, but all others as well, there would be no measured response. She'd feel guilty, and furious, and lost.

But that wasn't quite right, was it? Someone who would purposefully skew their data—waste hundreds of thousands of man-hours and billions of dollars on a lie—wouldn't be mad like that. They wouldn't be mad about the things Vanhi would be mad about. They'd be mad someone had the nerve to question them. They'd be angry they didn't get their way.

They might get violent.

They might be the type to get drunk on a Moon base and go after the weak link in their exposure. They'd threaten. They'd deny.

But they wouldn't, of all things, ask "Why?"

Inside her, the leafy sprout shot up, budding—the flower of realization threatening to unfurl.

She shuffled over to the composite desk, tripping over the edge of the bed and her half-unpacked suitcase to get there. She let the folder fall to the table with a plop, and it scattered open like a wilting rose. The holoflex-sheets were creased—rainbow colors bowing away from the damage to show where the plasma nanocircuits were, in effect, "bleeding"—and everything was out of order. A few paper sheets were tucked in the mix.

Most of the pages were dated or belonged to a dated set. She fanned them out, attempting to reconstitute their timeline.

On the right she set Dr. Chappell's "original" data; on the left she laid out the "undoctored" versions.

She was no biologist, but the results seemed clear: on one hand she had evidence that at least two of the planets in TRAPPIST-One likely had multicellular life. On the other, she had what looked like a correction to the original study, with a variable not originally taken into account added into the mix. That wouldn't make Dr. Chappell's results fabricated so much as uncorrected. It looked like she'd submitted the first results and suppressed the second.

It wasn't uncommon to create an experiment and get fantastic results only to realize you'd constructed your experiment wrong. That was part of the scientific process. You learn, you correct, you learn again.

Perhaps Chappell had wanted so badly for there to be life in this system that she'd convinced herself the second set of data had to be wrong. Maybe she'd gone so far as to fool herself.

The flower in Vanhi's gut grew thorns and *poked*. Because . . .

This doesn't feel right.

There were grad students who'd stood up for Dr. Chappell when she was exposed, but there had been others who insisted the data she'd issued to the consortium wasn't complete. They'd sworn she'd tampered with the results.

Vanhi stared at the pages, eyes not fully focused, as though the longer her gaze hovered over the pages the more likely she was to learn the truth.

Something clicked in the back of her mind, and she jumped for her purse. "C, wake up."

"Yes?"

"You know that backdoor connection to Jamal he insisted on installing?"

"Of course."

"The one I told you never to use?"

"Yes."

"I need you to use it now."

"All right." *Thank the heavens for small favors.* "What kind of information should I remit?"

"I'm going to upload some holoflex files. I probably shouldn't have these, and he definitely shouldn't have these, so make sure he knows they're classified, but, like *classified* classified."

"I'm not sure that's a recognized—"

"Just do it. He'll know what I mean. Ask him to dig in and look for the dates the files were created. The real dates. He's going to have to go deep—there's no way it's in the typical metadata." She rubbed her chin and mumbled, "He's too smart for that."

"Who is?"

Vanhi gritted her teeth. "Kaufman."

The setup for the press conference took advantage of Earthrise in the conservatorium. Vanhi would give her speech and answer questions under the glass dome—its decahedron panes glittering in the full sunlight. With the Earth swelling slowly behind her in all its blue glory, her monologue would hit emotional beat after emotional beat, and at its climax, the Littlest Convoy's three ships would clear the horizon. It would make for fantastic schoolroom viewing.

Because of the libration cycle, Earthrise was a slow event, nothing as dramatic as a sunrise or even moonrise, but it would have the desired effect on those who loved space.

Concealed beneath the stage in the conservatorium was the greenroom. Here Vanhi sat, chewing her thumbnail, arms crossed, legs crossed; a knot outside and inside. She hadn't slept a wink.

As soon as the door opened and Kaufman entered from the anteroom, Vanhi was on her feet. "You lied to me."

"About what?" he asked—not as though he were tired of her accusations, but as though she could be referring to a number of lies.

She held up one holoflex sheet, its corner dog-eared. "Doctor Chappell didn't fabricate results, *you* did."

C had gotten through to Jamal straightaway. The programmer treated a sudden ping from one of his surviving C series like the emergency it was. And he'd confirmed her worst fears.

The contradictory data in those files was first created a full month *after* Kaufman had fed her the story back in Dubai.

Kaufman took up a chair—the kind that passed for plush on a moon base, with hard armrests and a deep bucket seat—and shrugged. *Shrugged!* "I'd hoped you wouldn't have to find out."

"I can't believe you. I can't—*why*? Why would you do that?"

"Look at where you are, then ask me again."

She wasn't going to take that. She was done playing. Two strides brought her before him. She leaned down, grabbing the armrests, caging him in. "No. I never asked for this. This was never even a twinkle in my eye until you came to me. Why?"

His expression remained stoic, unimpressed. "You and I both know this mission needed to be born. It had to be. *Had* to."

"No. That's another lie."

"You never would have agreed to do this unless you thought it had to be done. That's the kind of person you are. You do what needs doing. You pursue a straight course to the answers. That's why I picked you."

"You bribed her former grad students to create the new files for you."

"Yes."

"And to vouch for them."

"Yes. Bribed consortium aides to get ahold of the originals, too."

She threw up her hands and paced away. *Shit. Shit. It's all going to shit.* "So why TRAPPIST-One? Out of all the missions, why did you tank that one?" *My sister's favorite. Everyone's favorite.*

Our chance at finding extrasolar life.

He shrugged, as though the answer were obvious. "It was the last assigned, it was the least developed. It made the most sense in a spreadsheet. I wasn't trying to be *malicious*, Vanhi. It's a casualty of advancement. As soon as you tap into those new subdimensions I'm sure TRAPPIST-One will be the first place we visit. And it'll be a snap—" He clicked his fingers. "There and back again."

I can't do this, Vanhi realized. *I can't go out there and make a grand speech and answer all those questions*—unscripted *questions. I can't. I just—*

"You have to tell them," she said.

"Like hell I do."

"It's over for you, don't you get that?"

He furrowed his brow and shook his head, taken aback. "Why? Because now *you* know?"

"Yes. Because now I know and I refuse to be a part of your scam. I'm not going to protect you."

"Oh, really?" He pushed himself up, and Vanhi stumbled back.

She'd never seen him be violent before. He'd never killed an ant in her presence, let alone struck someone. But that didn't mean he *wouldn't.*

"There's a slight problem with your reasoning," he said, voice a low grumble. "This is not my scam, it's *our* scam. Between the two of us, which one would you say has benefited the most? Me? A now-retired dean who gets his gob on the news once and again? Or you? How much extra cash did the emirates throw your way once they realized you were going to be the mission head on one of the twelve biggest projects in history, hmm? I hear you set up a trust for your nieces and nephews, paid off your parents' mortgage—"

"How do you know that?"

"These aren't exactly state secrets."

"You're right, they're private secrets, which makes your prying that much worse."

"Please, spare me the morality play. Besides, my god, Vanhi, it's *not* a *scam*. We deserve to be here. *You* deserve it. Do you remember when you—very rudely—accosted me over that small sum I paid to a consortium page? Would you like to know what I was paying him for? *Rankings*—insider information on the new proposal rankings. That file contained the initial results, and I received another once the final interviews were completed. I *had* intended to find someone to fix them for us, to ensure we'd be placed at the top, but in the end there was no need. Your proposal was ultimately ranked highest, all on its own. Because Earth *needs* this. You have to understand, sometimes people don't know what's good for them until they're given a little push. You needed a push in Dubai. The Planet United Consortium needed one to prioritize subdimensional research. So, don't think of it as a scam, think of it—"

Ah, yes, once more with the sudden cornering. Bastard. "Of *course* it's a scam. What you did to get us here is fraud. I don't mean that colloquially. It is real, honest to goodness, slap him in irons, the government can come at you for it, *fraud*."

"Keep your voice down."

"No!" She stomped her foot. She meant it to be a firm, powerful gesture, but was sure—under his condescending gaze—that she painted the perfect picture of a petulant child. "You destroyed Dr. Chappell's career—the careers of everyone on her convoy. You aren't going to get away with this. They've given me a mic and I'm going to tell everyone, and there's not a damn thing you can do to stop me."

"If you do, you'll destroy the P.U.M.s. Not just our mission, *all* of them."

Her gut clenched at the melodrama. The flower inside her grew vines—long, thick, tougher than spider-silk vines, and they were twining their way through her limbs and around her bones. She shook her head, baffled. How could he defend this? How could he fight her on this? What leverage could he possibly think he held that could destroy all of the Planet United Missions?

"Not even you are that egocentric. Master narcissist or not, you can't undo decades of global, peaceful advancement."

"I can't, but you can. How did you sell this mission? Do you remember your pitch? Because I do. You told the consortium that these missions needed better PR, that they could fade into the night if the public isn't constantly reinvigorated. How invigorated do you think they're going to be when you announce that we—*we*—had to take drastic measures to get here? This is scandal on top of scandal, inviting that much more scrutiny. Why shouldn't they halt the missions in their tracks, put everything on pause until they can be sure it's not fraud all the way down?

"Because you know they'd have to launch a full-scale, public investigation for the sake of saving face. *I* know the value of a power play. I know how to get done what needs doing. But god help anyone in the *public eye* doing what needs doing. All the public cares about are feelings, about getting along—"

"They care about *ethics*, you moron. Without ethics, there can be no real business, no real trade, because those things rely on equal footing. When it's not trade anymore, it's coercion. It's stepping on necks and breaking backs. It crushes ideas, it stops advancements, it does the very opposite of what we—you and I specifically—are trying to accomplish here. It means merits don't matter because whoever can be the biggest sleazeball wins."

"What a beautiful world you must live in, all rose-colored and—"

"Don't patronize me!"

A light knock on the door made both of them spin. It opened a crack, revealing a base guard. "Is everything all right in here?"

She almost said no. She was a hair's breadth away from demanding Kaufman be removed from her sight.

But she wasn't done with him.

"*Fine,*" they both barked.

Blanching, the guard closed the door.

"You're going to upset the public. And they wouldn't be wrong to be angry."

"They *should* be angry," she said.

"But does that give them the right to destroy what almost every nation in the world has contributed to? They don't have to destroy it consciously, mind you. Their lack of attention, their turning away, will do more to dismantle everything than attacking a convoy ship to take it apart at the rivets.

"And let's be clear, Vanhi. If you go out there and explain what happened, you will not be clear of blame. Your career will go down the drain for sure, and they might flat-out cancel this convoy as well, which means that many more hours will have been wasted, that much more money. The consortium may not find it in their hearts—or pocketbooks—to reassign a new mission. People will further question why we're doing this. Doing *any* of it. People will feel cheated, angry. You know what happens when people get angry? Bye-bye peace. This world peace we've been able to hold on to since you were a child. You don't know any different, but I do. You don't remember the constant wars and skirmishes. You don't remember drafts and widespread domestic terrorism. You're not afraid of it because you never experienced it."

"The world is not going to fall into chaos because of one—"

"It might," he insisted. "There has to be a first domino somewhere. This could be that domino, and you are the finger. All you need to do is flick over this first indiscretion and watch the others reveal themselves. Watch them spiral."

"But it's *your* finger! You're not putting this on me. I will not feel guilty for what *you* did."

"Good, and you shouldn't. But if you go through with your self-righteous reveal, *that* you will have to live with. Your choice. Let one injustice stand for the betterment of all humanity. Or topple over that domino and see how much ruin falls in its wake."

Their eyes locked. Vanhi stared at him, fury constricting her lungs and her throat. How dare he put her here? This was a false choice. An illusion of choice. How dare he? How . . . *how*?

Another knock at the door.

"*What?*" Vanhi called.

The guard peeked in again. "Doctor Kapoor, Kaufman. It's time."

Swallowing dryly, fighting to control the rage contorting her expression, she adjusted her glasses and smoothed her jacket, trying to reset. Trying to remain calm. "I don't want you up there with me," she said to Kaufman, averting her gaze. "I don't want you on the stage, I don't want you in the audience, and I expect you to resign all further involvement in this project."

"What do you plan to say?" he demanded.

She ignored the question. "Do you understand me?"

"Yes. But what are you going to say?" It wasn't pleading—there wasn't a hint of desperation. He simply wanted to know, to feel in control.

Without another word, she followed the guard out, slamming the greenroom door behind her.

As she took the stage and positioned herself behind the podium, ignoring the bright blue planet behind her, his question echoed in her mind, but in her own voice instead of his. *What are you going to say?*

What am I *going to say?*

The lighting in the conservatorium was nothing like the lighting in your typical auditorium. There were no harsh lights beating down on her in the midst of a darkened room—no glare to hide the audience's faces. Every eager reporter's eyes were clear as day, tracking her movements, softening at her smile.

You have to do it, she told herself. *You have an ethical obligation. You owe Dr. Chappell her life back.*

But . . .

And that was it, a little worming thought. *But.*

But what if he was right?

Worse yet, what if she had been right, back when she'd poured her heart out in front of the consortium chair? The missions lived and died by public opinion. They might not get canceled, but they would lose their life spark.

She couldn't watch the current climate of scientific enthusiasm crumble because of one man's arrogance. She didn't want to see the light go out in a colleague's eyes when she came into a room. She didn't want little kids taking spaceship stickers off their walls. She didn't want history books to have horrible footnotes describing how the first interstellar missions had been tainted by backstabbing and positioning.

. . . Didn't want the media hounding her ma and papa.

With one admission, there was so much that could go wrong.

The vines entwined with her bones squeezed and pulled taut, powdering her resolve like so much chalk.

So, he wins, she said to herself. *He wins, but only so that everyone else on the entire planet doesn't lose.*

The plant inside her—having done its job—wilted and died.

She hated him. She hated herself. She hated that she would never be free of this—helping him destroy what could have been the greatest scientific mission to date in order to advance what she personally thought was important.

She wanted to shrivel into dust and blow away in the wind, just like that plant.

Instead, she cleared her throat, widened her smile, and welcomed everyone to this joyous occasion.

APRIL 22, 2126 CE

"So, how's it been with all the visitors? You give many tours?" Swara asked, hands in her pockets, duffel bag hoisted over one shoulder. Vanhi and her sister strolled lazily down the hall, en route to the docking bay. "And you've got to tell me something, be honest. Does artificial gravity feel funny to you?"

"The visitors are fine," Vanhi assured her. "We've got liaisons for that. Tour guides. They're great, actually. Sometimes I think they know more about the ships than I do. And the gravity . . . I think that's just you."

"Really, you don't feel lighter up here?"

"Gravitons are gravitons are gravitons. We're harnessing them, not mimicking them. Trust me, the gravity here feels exactly the same as Earth-side. If it didn't, we'd have a big problem."

"Oh, because that would mess with the experiments?"

"No, because we'd have a malfunction and that would mess with *everything*."

They finally arrived at *Pulse*'s bay entrance. Almost all of the habitat ships in all of the convoys were designed exactly the same. They were humongous, filled to the brim with personal quarters. Each room had a window, regardless of where it lay within the ship—a series of mirrors reflected outside views back to those on inner portions of the decks. The bay itself was large, holding up to fifteen shuttles at a time. Most of it was controlled from observation booths, so that no one was sent scrabbling every time the bay was depressurized. Now, convoy crew bustled in and out of the hall airlock, barely allowing the automated door to shut before taxing it once more. Swara hesitated before entering. "I wish I didn't have to go so soon."

Vanhi gave her a tight hug, with an extra squeeze for good luck. "I know, me, too. But my six-month break will come sooner than you think."

"You have to come stay with me and James."

"For how long?"

"Long as you want."

"Uh-uh, don't say that unless you mean it. You might not be getting rid of me for a month." Vanhi gave her a wink.

"You've done well here," her sister said, glancing around the hall, watching jumpsuited specialists double-time it to and from their stations.

Vanhi's face fell, but she propped up her smile in the next instant, not wanting Swara to see her falter.

Her family didn't need to know she'd tried to resign, that Madame Chair had begged her to stay on. She'd only acquiesced because the guilt of dropping the mission had outweighed the guilt of maintaining her post. Now, she tried to stay in constant motion, to keep busy. Busy people didn't have time for regret.

She'd even offered Dr. Chappell a prominent position on the team. Vanhi knew the move looked odd from the outside, but no one suspected any motives beyond altruism (which, in its own way, only burgeoned Vanhi's shame). In response, Dr. Chappell had all but sent a flaming bag of dog poop to her door.

Vanhi couldn't blame her. If their positions were reversed, she would have balked just the same.

Sometimes the bad guys win.

So . . . what does that make me?

But she couldn't tell her sister all that. So she just said, "The crew does well. They're wonderful. We have a lot more retired military aboard than I would have expected. Should have, though. They're used to taking on temporary stations halfway across the globe, so it's no wonder they'd be up for a few years in space. But they're great. And I've got some new recruits coming in as you're headed out. Excited to meet them. Even though I wish you could stay longer, of course."

With a scrunched-nose smile, Swara reached into the side

pocket of her duffel and drew out a small box wrapped in bright green. It looked like a container jewelry might come in, but Swara would know better than that; Vanhi hardly ever wore any. "To say thank you for letting me come visit you aboard your convoy," she said, holding it out with both hands.

"You know you don't need to."

"I know. But this way there's something up here to help remind you of us down there."

They hugged again, said their goodbyes. Vanhi wished her sister a safe trip back to Earth. When Swara was securely on the other side of the door, Vanhi looked at the box again. She had an hour before the next pods had to be approved for deployment, so she scurried back to her quarters to open the gift.

Once inside her spacious quarters (they were meant for a four-person family, but since there were plenty of vacant rooms, there was no need to be restrictive), Vanhi settled herself at her small kitchen table.

She tugged at the bit of twine encompassing the wrapping before tearing into the packaging proper. The slick paper fell away with ease, leaving what was unquestionably a jewelry box, hinged on one side and velvety. It opened with a *snap*.

Vanhi wasn't sure what she'd been expecting. A necklace? A pin?

Inside was a wristwatch-that-wasn't. It had all the trappings of a watch: real leather strap (she hoped Papa didn't know!), metal buckle, clockface. Only the clockface wasn't analog or digital. It was *antiquated*. Where one would expect to see a pair of hands or set of displays was instead an evenly scoured plate and a gnomon.

Underneath the watch lay a note.

Dear little Ullu,

Vanhi cringed, then shook her head fondly at the old nickname. It had been a childhood insult that had slowly morphed into an endearment.

> Since you are the strangest scientist I know, what with your love of archaic things like eyeglasses and your pocket protector (I believe you call it C), I thought you might enjoy this gen-one timepiece. I hear it's cutting-edge technology, if you happen to live in Babylon.
>
> When I saw this in the storefront I remembered what you said about distance not mattering, only travel time. So when you wear this, know that it takes exactly 0.00 seconds for my love to reach you, no matter where you are.
>
> Found that programmer you talked about—Kaeden. We worked in some upgrades I think you'll like.
>
> Good luck. See you soon.
>
> Yours lovingly,
>
> *Swara*

Vanhi turned the sundial over in her palm. The back wasn't inscribed, but it didn't have to be. It was made of a polished, brassy silver-gold metal she couldn't identify, even after finding the jeweler's stamp. It carried some weight, but not too much. The hour lines were labeled in Roman numerals.

She hurried to swipe the old phone from where it sat in a place of honor on her bookshelf. She didn't need it aboard the ships—everyone's chip implants were integrated into the comms system—but they'd have to pry her Intelligent Personal Assistant out of her cold, dead hands.

"Wake up, want to show you something. Look at what

Swara gave me." She flashed the sundial, then held up the note for C to scan.

"She's not wrong, I am antiquated," it agreed.

"But that's why I love you," she said, strapping the sundial onto her left wrist. "Hope I don't jab anyone with the gnomon. Can't tell if it would bend or skewer."

"The stamp indicates it is a Ti-Au alloy, typically used for medical implants. It would likely puncture."

"Odd thing to make a bracelet out of."

"Agreed. You should probably assess its electrical properties before wearing it during experiment engineering."

The strap pulled snug. The brown leather was soft on the inside of her wrist. A little green light lit up on the side of the dial. "That's . . . interesting."

"I'm detecting a software compatible device within range," C said. "I believe the sundial can support my applications."

"What? No way." Now she understood the part about talking with Jamal. Swara always did give the best gifts.

"Shall I upload myself to the new device?"

"Yes please. I need to head to *Breath* for my shift, but let me know when the download is complete, okay?"

"Will do. Oh, and Vanhi?"

"Yeah?"

"The convoy communications team sent me another message from Dr. Kaufman. Would you like to hear it before you go?"

She'd asked comms not to contact her by implant with his drivel. Instead it all got shuffled over to C. "Nope. You know what to do with it."

"Message number eighty-seven from Doctor McKenzie Kaufman—Archived."

Vanhi was the first on the shift shuttle. She buckled up as other workers poured into the craft behind her, pulling the heavy harness straps over her shoulders one at a time. Most of the new recruits were dressed in slacks and button-downs, which would be hidden under lab coats and bunny suits once on the experiment ship. Vanhi hadn't changed out of her jeans and loose-fitting kurta.

A thin, black-skinned man with yellow around the edges of his eyes slid into the seat next to her.

"Gabriel! No one told me you'd come aboard. Good to see you." She held out her hand—the shoulder straps keeping her awkwardly pinned.

They hadn't seen each other since he'd been awarded his Ph.D., and she'd gotten no direct word on whether or not he'd accepted her invitation for a stint aboard the convoy.

He shook her hand, but with a hesitancy. "Good to see you as well."

She felt the corners of her mouth twitch, her smile slip, and she feared her expression was giving everything away, laying all her guilt bare. He seemed reluctant to talk to her. Did he know something? No, no, that couldn't be it. Perhaps he suspected, though. Gabriel had seen Kaufman grease enough palms in his day that he likely believed—and not unrightly—that Vanhi had caved to a number of their advisor's ethical mishandlings. Their faces were plastered all over, after all—always the two of them, together.

She felt sick and turned away.

Of the twenty people crammed into the shuttle, fifteen of them were new faces. Well—somewhat new.

She noticed Chen Kexin, whose uniform indicated she was a new *Breath* security guard. Vanhi had seen her face before—seen *several* of her faces before, actually.

While none of the convoys' crews were entirely identical, most of them shared a core of at least a thousand clones who were present on all of the original twelve missions. People whose skillsets and fitness for service had been seen as ubiquitously advantageous. Those whose contributions to things like food processing or practical medicine would not be affected by the size of the crew, purpose of their mission, or growth-cycle patterns.

After all, why go through the hassle of identifying twelve suitable individuals to clone when it was far simpler to clone one qualified person twelve times?

Kexin was one of those individuals. And this particular clone had been displaced by the sudden cancelation of Convoy Twelve's original mission. Vanhi felt a dagger of guilt slash across her side as she imagined the devastation Kexin and her contemporaries must have gone through. What would it be like to have someone tell you that the very reason for your existence—something you'd been training for your entire life—had been canceled?

At least they were all offered retraining and positions here, Vanhi thought, though it did little to assuage her regret. Sure, some had jumped at the chance, but others had vehemently rejected the offer, choosing to make their own way in the world instead. Because Convoy Twelve's crew rotated, there were fewer than fifty clones aboard at any given time.

Vanhi didn't know what job Kexin had originally been intended to perform, but she suspected it wasn't security.

She's been repurposed, too.

Kexin, like the other new crew aboard, had spent the past month in final training, and today would be their first shot at the real thing.

The seat on Vanhi's right was occupied by a man with a deep brown tan. She glanced at his badge, trying to discern what position he'd come to fill.

Noticing her side-eyeing him, he made small talk when their glances met. "I like your, uh—" He pointed at the sundial. "What is that?"

She smiled secretly to herself. "A gag gift."

"It's nice."

"Thanks."

"I'm Stone—Stone Mendez Perez."

"Vanhi Kapoor."

"I know," he said sheepishly. Vanhi wasn't surprised at his admission or shyness—it wasn't like the Planet United Mission heads weren't paraded across the news every other month. It had taken some time to come to grips with her newfound celebrity, and luckily she was able to escape a lot of the global fame out here in space. Still, there was something about Stone's manner that wasn't simply "star shock," but she couldn't quite place it.

"I, uh, saw your ship dedication speech on the Moon," Stone continued. "It's why I applied for the remote-piloting job."

Her stomach shriveled. "That's—that's great," she said, trying to sound chipper, sure the words rang as hollow as they felt. It'd been years, and still the memory of that day was sour in her mind. "Where, uh, where are you from?"

"Originally? Puerto Rico."

"How was the trip from Earth?"

He looked up at the shuttle ceiling and smiled a little.

"First extended space stay?" she asked knowingly.

"Yeah," he admitted. "Used to think I was hard to impress. Then I saw Jupiter."

She smiled as the lighting shifted in the docking bay, yellow warning beacons flashing as the hangar decompressed.

When the exterior doors opened, three shuttles gently lifted away, carrying their passengers out into the dead silence of space.

The three convoy ships hung like fat insects hovering over a bottomless pit. Starlight dimly reflected off the portions of hull not directly illuminated by windows or exterior safety lamps. Sol was a cool pinprick in the distance, unobscured.

The housing ship, *Pulse,* was the most balloon-like of the ships, almost like a dirigible, save for the twinkle-light pattern of windows forming a multitude of great lines down its sides. It had been designed to hold tens of thousands of people, but less than fifteen hundred—consisting of crew and crew families—now called it home. Most of the interior rooms had been repurposed as command centers and supply storage.

Breath was the second ship, a long, thin bar, with dumbbell-like protuberances on either end. The center section was lined with giant windows for directly observing the experiment pods, and antennae and sensor towers stuck out of it in a haphazard-looking fashion. One dumbbell end contained the docking bay, the other was the experiment launch point.

The final ship, *Life,* was more of a warehouse than anything, and had a boxy shipping container quality. Fitting, as it stored the components for the experimental devices, the pod shells, and the mini-SD drives. "Mini-drives" was a misnomer to challenge all misnomers. While the SD drives that powered the convoy ships were the size of small office buildings, these were still the size of a studio apartment, the pods themselves matching single-family homes for square footage.

As the shuttle approached *Breath*'s docking platform, Vanhi caught sight of the resupply ship out of the corner of one window. It had originally been intended as the garden ship for Convoy Twelve, now, too, repurposed. It slid slowly away, putting enough distance between itself and the convoy to turn on its own SD drive for the brief jaunt back to Earth.

Bye, Swara. Safe journey.

She suppressed an impulse to wave at the ship, not wanting to seem silly in front of the new recruits.

Docking went smoothly, as did badge-check and equipment dispersal.

While the new hires lingered to unload their gear, Vanhi beelined for the breakroom, where she prepared a cup of oolong. Taking a deep breath, she savored a calm moment before the workday began.

The new crew members would be finding their stations in the mission control room now, settling in. Everything felt fresh, hopeful.

Today, she told herself, *today we'll sink a pod into a new SD.*

After preparing herself a second cup, she hurried to the mission control room, angling for her station in front of the curved windows, eager to stare out into their testing ground for a moment before beginning.

One hundred and fifty-eight crew members worked mission control, either in the official control room, or in backrooms for supplementary support. The primary mission control room was also known as the Experiment Observations Lounge, the EOL, and it was stuffed to the brim with staffers working side by side at crowded console banks spanning across seven terraced platforms. The room was curved, much like an amphitheater, and the platforms provided a stadium-like view of the outer windows.

The ship's long inner hall also sported a bay of tall windows, allowing special visitors to watch as a launch commenced.

The flight director's platform jutted out from the right side of the room, and gave Vanhi an excellent vantage point for observing her staff and the experiment field. Opposite her station, on the left wall, were several projections of various readouts.

As she took her seat, Vanhi dialed her chip phone into the "loops." This would let her communicate with any member of mission control directly at any time.

Once everyone was settled, she checked in with her newest crew members, including the shift's pod attitude determination and control officer—Stone Mendez Perez, the man who'd commented on her sundial. He would control the pod like a drone, directing its flight pattern to the testing ground, then retrieving it if and when it reemerged from an SD.

She also had a new pod flight dynamics officer, thermal operations resources manager, mini-drive artificial intelligence manager, and a handful of others ready to test their grit.

She'd have all of their names committed to memory soon, but for now, she was eager to get to work.

After forty-five minutes of check-ins and verifications, the countdown was ready to begin. They began at T minus ten minutes. The bay doors opened. Everyone focused on their monitors.

"Pod number nine, gravity-repulse thrusters primed. Ready? Three. Two. One. Lift off."

On her screen, the experiment pod—ovoid and spikey, like metallic dragon fruit (some enterprising younger workers had gone so far as to paint the bodies of the first five pink-and-green as a sort of christening)—glided away from the corrugated floor, sailing out into blackness.

Vanhi's eyes flickered to the testing ground.

It didn't look like much, the empty grid of space only a hundred kilometers out. But it was her Bikini Atoll.

She hated that she thought of it that way, that Kaufman had forever tied SD drives and nuclear weapons together in her mind.

But he'd been right about the danger.

So far they'd run eight successful launches, but had only two successful new SD breaches, though preliminary data showed it likely at least three of the others had slipped into the already-verified travel SDs, thrown there when they effectively "bounced" off the subdimensions they were trying to access. Those pods had all been retrievable.

The other three that had failed to breach? Most of their twisted remains were back on *Life* being disentangled and scrubbed of radioactive elements before they could be studied. One had imploded. Another exploded. The third had slowly, yet systematically, dissolved into a cloud of its base elements.

Thank the stars they'd decided to put off animal testing. Not even bacteria had been allowed aboard.

Each pod contained, besides its drive, an array of sensors and one hundred experiments. The tests looked for new atmospherics, matter state-changes both internally and externally, gravity changes, spontaneous subatomic particle creation, shifting photon behavior, electromagnetic transmission, and a whole host of other differences and data points.

Vanhi had also designed several experiments to carry organics—bacteria, algae, bees, spores, and even dogs. But as with Kaufman's original SD discovery, they wouldn't dream of sending anything living until they'd routinely gotten back their inanimate test subjects.

This wasn't important solely for the safety of the animal subjects, but also for the sanitation of their local star group. If they lost a pod—if it dove and failed to reemerge as directed—it could have been destroyed on the other side . . . or it could have surfaced someplace and sometime that they'd never think to look. It could drift in regular space and come to land on some rock or another, bringing with it an infection. Contamination.

She was determined to make sure that never happened.

Over at the ADCO station, Stone had his gaze fixed intently on his dash, making sure the flight path was steady and everything fell within mission parameters as he guided the pod to the activation point.

He was experienced—just over forty, a little younger than she was—with a sharp jaw and cupid's-bow lips, now set firmly in concentration. His shaggy black hair had waves that curled at the ends; it fell into his face as he leaned forward over the joystick, and for a moment Vanhi thought he looked more like a kid playing a video game than a professional remote-pilot.

She noticed herself noticing *him* and quickly looked away. Now was not the time to be pondering the aesthetics of her new crewmates . . . no matter how pleasing those aesthetics might be.

With a blush, she refocused on the pod.

It was twenty-five kilometers out now. She checked in with the technicians monitoring the nonpassive experiments. Everything was still a go.

Observation buoys and communications buoys lined the path out to the quadrant where the pod would officially dive. This made it easy to track, easy to watch even as it grew imperceptible from the EOL on *Breath*.

"Pod in position," Mendez Perez said after a time on her loop.

"MID AIM, are we ready to cue up the drive?" Vanhi asked.

"Everything looks green."

"Good. Dive in three, two, one—now!"

From the outside, the beginnings of an SD bubble looked like warped space, with stars reflecting and shifting over a curved surface. The lensing engulfed the pod, made it look like a shimmer on a pond, until the spot went black, then disappeared altogether.

On all cameras, the pod had vanished.

"Dive appears successful," Vanhi announced. She clapped her hands and cheers went up, as they had thus far after every nondestructive run. Hopefully, in a few hours the pod would resurface, giving them vital information about a brand-new SD.

The trajectory officer gave Mendez Perez a hearty slap on

the back. “Nice going, ace,” Vanhi called to him, tossing a cheeky thumbs-up.

He gave her a shy, endearing smile back.

JULY 6, 2127 CE

By the thirty-third launch, running the pods started to feel routine. Six had failed to dive, four more had blown their lids, and the majority had bounced into the normal travel SDs. But seven had gone where no one had gone before. The data from those dives was being processed around the clock. And still, Vanhi hoped for more.

Today—on what would have been a lazy Sunday back in Arizona, but was a full-on work day here in the glamorous world of convoy living—Vanhi went to her station with an extra spring in her step.

Mendez Perez—Stone, as he insisted she call him—had offered riveting breakfast conversation. The kind that got her mental wheels turning, and her cheeks flushed with the pumping of creative blood.

The whole table had listened in on their banter, and Vanhi hadn’t been self-conscious about it in the least. Stone’s friends Justice Jax and Eric Price had both wiggled their eyebrows at each other. And afterward, Gabriel had given Vanhi a nudge as they went to drop off their trays at the cleaning station.

“It’s not like that,” she’d insisted.

“Like what?” he asked, feigning perfect innocence.

“I would like to know as well,” said C from the sundial, sounding an awful lot like a child asking how babies were made.

She wasn’t about to let Gabriel rile her, so she’d given him a shake of her head and a friendly smile, and happily hopped on the awaiting shuttle.

Stone hadn't been far behind. He took up the vacant seat beside her without a word about it, as though it were perfectly natural.

She wanted to hold on to this feeling forever. *This* was what space travel was all about. Good people, good ideas, experimentation, wonder, discovery. This was what she'd been fighting for, what she'd compromised for. If she could just keep this feeling close, maybe she could use it to scare away the bad days—the times when guilt came back and Kaufman haunted her dreams.

In the EOL, everyone took their positions.

"Give me greens," she said on each loop. "MID AIM?"

"Go," said Mini-Drive AI Manager, Pablo de Valdivia.

"CHEM EX?"

"Go," said Soraya Ebadi, who was in charge of monitoring the chemistry experiments.

"COM EX?"

"Go," said Anju Gautam, who managed communications.

She ran her checks all the way down the line. Everything was good.

"ADCO?" she asked last.

"Go," said Stone.

"Then let's do this."

A few minutes later, the dragon fruit of a craft hovered in front of the windows momentarily before Stone sent it on its way.

The time ticked by as it always did, dragging out while they waited for the pod to achieve a safe distance. Vanhi watched over the team, making sure everyone looked as they should: relaxed, focused.

"Be advised," de Valdivia said. "I have telemetry readings in the red . . ." His finger tracked a line on one screen. It jumped where it should have been steady.

"Copy. Where is that instrumentation located? Can you patch me the feed?" Vanhi asked.

"It's the rear left quadrant," he said. "Vibrations, there're—something's on. Something's using power, but I can't—"

"SD MEC, are you reading the same vibrations?" she asked. De Valdivia's readout popped onto her leftmost screen. There was a distinct tremor, yes, but the AI wasn't pinpointing its location. She glanced at the visual feeds. Nothing looked amiss on the test area cameras. But the pod was still little more than a shining dot on most of them. She flipped to the flight path monitor.

"Starting to get a lean," said Stone. "Shouldn't have to course correct this much."

"Copy. Can anybody tell me where the aberrant energy is centered?" Vanhi asked, bringing up the real-time system log.

"It's pulling starboard," Stone said.

"It's the drive itself," said de Valdivia. "It's got to be a malfunction in the AI quantum-reaction regulation. It looks like a compensation, but the main power hasn't been cued, so there's nothing to compensate for."

"Can we reboot the AI?"

"Already initiating shutdown."

The pod—a blip on her screen—was engulfed in white light.

Everyone gasped.

No, no, no. Damn it. "Did we lose it?" She held her breath, frantically hitting refresh on all of her feeds. "Did we lose it?" she demanded, articulating every syllable.

"No!" It was Stone. "I'm still—it's fighting me, I can't—steering's out, it's veering *back*."

"Talk to me," Vanhi said, voice even and expression stern while her heart battered itself inside her ribs. Losing a pod wasn't new. They'd lost plenty, expected to lose the majority of what they had left. But this . . .

The white light flared out, but what was left in its wake

wasn't debris, or a dormant pod. The probe's hull glimmered with new life. Around it, some sort of field pulsed, fading from petal-pink to tangerine and back again.

And Stone was right—it was sailing toward the convoy.

"Convoy Control—"

"We've alerted Captain Tan. He's standing by to take evasive action."

"Copy that. ADCO, TRAJ, any way you can reel it in, get it to stop?"

"It's not responding," Stone gritted, pounding the holokeys at his station.

"What happened? What went wrong, MID AIM?"

"I don't know," de Valdivia insisted, hands flying over his keyboard, brow furrowed, jaw stiff. "I rebooted. It should have gone dead. Should have—unless . . . Unless the meters were off, and we weren't detecting . . . No . . . wait, wait . . ."

He didn't have to elaborate. Vanhi's internal monologue started to hammer out two words on repeat: *Oh shit. Oh shit.*

Oh shit.

The AI *wasn't* malfunctioning, it was doing its damned job. It was trying to keep the system from engaging. Somehow the SD drive had started to pull power, to dive, and the AI was trying to hold it back.

But then they'd shut it down . . .

"Are we getting any readings from Thirty-Three's external sensors? Talk to me, people, that's not an SD bubble like I've ever seen."

"I'm getting unusual readings," called a woman's voice with a heavy Danish accent—Esmée Jensen, Mechanical Maintenance Officer. "Power surges."

"Distance between the pod and the convoy is shrinking, sir," said Stone.

Vanhi had her head down, frantically looking for a way to remotely bar the pod's path or even destroy it. They could launch number Thirty-Four. ADCO could pilot it on an intercept course, crash the two pods—

"These are similar to the same kind of surge forces found inside SD drives when they've hit main sequence," Esmée called again.

"*Copy,*" Vanhi gritted out.

Breath lurched. Captain Tan must have ordered the convoy to move.

"Doctor Kapoor!" Stone shouted.

Her head snapped up. She followed his outstretched hand, pointed like an arrow through the casement.

Thoomp, dooooozsh. Thoomp, dooooozsh.

There was no noise, but the sudden slow-motion leapfrogging of the pod created dramatic sound effects in her mind.

For a moment the pod looked like it was imploding, the pinkish-orangish field shrinking, turning in on itself, until there was nothing, it was gone.

That was the *thoomp.*

Half a second later, the field and probe appeared again, *kilometers closer than before.*

The violent, static-encrusted expansion—sparking, widening—engulfed her mind like a deluge of water. *Dooooozsh.*

The lights in the observation lounge turned purple. Captain Tan's voice echoed over the comms system. "In order to avoid collision, we are engaging the SD drive—"

Thoomp.

Dooooozsh.

Closer. It kept coming, kept coming.

"Please, everyone, remain calm and secure yourself and any loose belongings that may pose a danger to—"

Thoomp.

Dooooozsh.

Vanhi could see the antennae groups on the pod clearly. It was so close, so—

"Dive!" Tan ordered.

Thoomp.

This time there *was* sound. Eardrum-bursting, earth-shattering, bone-vibrating *ssssshhhhhhcrrrrash.*

The pod collided with *Breath*, below the window deck. A white spark-lined leading edge of sunset orange passed unperturbed through the observation window, through the hull.

Vanhi's feet left the floor as the gravity was disrupted, or damaged, or whatever was happening. She tried holding on to the desk, to keep herself grounded as chairs and mugs and monitors sailed up and away, with no clear direction, but soon she, too, was floating, aimless.

Until the strange field slammed into her, throwing her sideways, blotting out the purple light and turning it chartreuse. Her eyes snapped closed, and her breath punched its way out of her body.

Her head went light, fuzzy, nothing but . . .

. . . nothing . . .

. . . but . . .

. . . a . . .

. . . haze . . .

CHAPTER TWO

CONVOY SEVEN

CAZNAL: IN SEARCH OF THE LESSER REDOUBT

ONE HUNDRED AND SEVENTEEN YEARS SINCE
THE INCEPTION OF *NOUMENON INFINITUM*
SEPTEMBER 5, 117 RELAUNCH
5274 CE

. . . **Convoy Seven has** been assigned a new mission, designated *Noumenon Infinitum*. Its express purpose is to travel to the variable star LQ Pyxidis and complete construction of the alien megastructure, thought to be a Dyson Sphere and known as "the Web." Once complete, Convoy Seven is to charge the batteries on the ship designated *Zetta*, then return to Earth . . .

Confidential addendum to official statement, Convoy Seven crew only:

In addition to the official mission parameters appointed by Earth, *Noumenon Infinitum* is to investigate the craft known as "the Nest." Any information garnered from the investigation pertaining to alien involvement with the Web is to be applied . . .

. . . The final clause of the official mission statement can be struck. Convoy Seven need not return to Earth . . .

It started with a map, like all good treasure hunts do. One alien in origin, and not immediately recognizable for what it was. But it had led them here.

Caznal the Fourth gazed out of the shuttle porthole and into the inky night beyond. It wasn't the total lightlessness of an SD bubble; it was a dark monolith of matter. A planemo—a systemless planetoid—wandering and alone. Starless, moonless. Naught but a black disk against the stars, and it blotted them out one by one as the shuttle shifted.

But Caz didn't see a flat emptiness. She saw a blank slate. The planemo held nothing but potential.

Light lensed around the edges in a visible halo as they descended, creating a bowed outline of the galaxies and such beyond.

Out the opposite side of the craft, over her apprentice's shoulder, she could barely make out the twelve ships of the convoy, their illuminated windows only distinguishable from far-off stars because of their orientation and regularity.

No one could have anticipated, all those years ago on Launch Day, that the convoy would have found itself here.

When *Noumenon*, the original mission, had arrived at LQ Pyx, they'd discovered an alien craft floating near the Web's most massive component. The craft was damaged, and empty, but clearly belonged to an alien species who had taken up the construction project. The convoy had taken the ship—dubbed the Nest because of the many pipes that circled around it and dangled from its bottom in an arrangement that resembled woven twigs—believing it held answers to the Web.

Now that ship hovered in the belly of *Slicer,* where the engineers poked and prodded it like a sick patient with a rare disease.

And it had led them here.

As the shuttle fell into a degrading orbit, Caznal's apprentice, Ivan Baraka the Fifteenth, grinned at her and bounced in his seat, practically vibrating inside his spacesuit. There were old Earth vids of teenagers his age bearing that same expression as they waited for a rollercoaster to spill over its first hump.

She shared his excitement, as did the other seven scholars aboard. But still, a small discrepancy in their studies nagged at her. After all, when a treasure map's instructions read "Twenty paces past Skull Rock, one hundred and twenty around Crocodile Cove, and there be the Cave of Wonders," one expects the *cave* to be there, not a divot in the ground.

That they'd arrived at a divot—a planemo—and not a cave was troubling.

The Nest had not given up any of its secrets easily. At first, it appeared to have no electrical connections. "It's like finding a sailboat in orbit," someone had once said. How could a spaceship function without wires and transistors?

But they'd been looking at it all wrong—all *human*.

Not only did the Nest have vast reserves of hydrogen that it could compress into a metallic superconducting superfluid to form electrical connections a single atom thick, but the way the Nest relied so heavily on gravitons suggested the aliens that had created it had been able to *biologically* manipulate gravitons.

If they'd never come to such a realization, not only would the Nest still lie dormant, they never would have recognized the alien maps for what they were.

"Approaching Crater Sixty-four," the pilot said over the intercom, her voice echoing slightly inside Caz's helmet. "Spotlights should be illuminating the eastern edge soon. Take note."

Caz squinted, still unable to make anything out. Eventually the blackness gave way to gray, and the gray to a deep jasper-like green, and then ridges. The side of the crater was terraced—nothing like the smooth sweep of an impact or volcanic caldera, and not nearly as sheer as the walls of a sinkhole.

But that didn't mean it was unnatural.

They were hoping to find something important to the Nataré here (Nataré was what they'd named the Nest's creators, from the Latin, for how they were believed to be able to "float" or "swim" through the air on their biologically manipulated gravitons). Anything would do really. If all they stumbled upon was a set of tentacle prints and a patch of "we were here" graffiti, she'd take it.

Because that would silence the doubt.

When the convoy had successfully developed the technology to access the Nest's computer, they'd soon come to the conclusion that the ship was more like a shuttle. Which made sense, given its size. Unless, of course, the aliens were considerably smaller than humans; just one of the many things Caznal was hoping to learn. She was still surprised they didn't even know something *that basic* about them.

The ship's computer contained no visuals of the aliens, nor any general historical data. All they found were three-dimensional representations of hundreds of spheres stuffed full with additional spheres of different sizes.

At first, the engineers had thought they'd stumbled upon the Nataré writing system, that each parent sphere could denote a page or even an entire document, and the spheres inside were words. But running them through a rudimentary algorithm revealed a lack of repetition, a fundamental requirement for ordering anything—sounds, symbols, movements—into meaningful communication.

It took them years to mentally convert the Nest's data into information more suited to a human thinking process. The breakthrough had come when they found spheres with only a couple of—and in some cases, only one—interior spheres. When these were matched to full-to-the-brim spheres, they found an overlap. The mostly empty spheres appeared to highlight points in the full spheres.

X-marks the spot.

On human maps, the distance between objects was the focal point; the primary information the map was intended to convey. Objects were usually portrayed as a similar size—a single point at large scales. Not so with the alien maps. The Nataré highlighted gravitational influence over all other possible associations. According to the convoy's best theories, their evolution had clearly influenced the way they saw and interacted with the world.

After recognizing the spheres as maps, their research became a quick spiral of realization and discovery. The spheres represented different sizes of gravitational influence created by various cosmological objects, and though they were shown with no distance between them, they were ordered in accordance with their spatial relation.

All the humans had to do then was take their current gravitational models and overlay them with the Nataré maps.

When they found one nearly empty sphere that highlighted LQ Pyxidis and a handful of other points, they knew they'd struck gold. It was the smoking gun they'd been looking for, evidence linking the Nest and the Web to new locations: places where more Nataré history, or the Nataré themselves, might be found.

Places like this planemo.

Only . . .

The ground rushed up at them—though their rate of descent slowed for landing, Caz still felt a jolt in her bones when they touched down.

"Ready, sir?" Ivan asked, giving her the thumbs-up.

"Ready," she breathed, standing. When the pilot gave the green light, she hoisted the duffel bag of tools that lay at her feet onto her shoulder, as did her colleagues.

"Four hours for setup," the pilot reminded them. "Half an hour for return. Stay in visual range of your assigned teammates at all times. And Captain Nwosu would like to remind you that if it wiggles, don't touch it. If everyone's got that, I'm opening the doors."

A series of thumbs-ups and affirmations over comms led to the locks and their airtight seals disengaging, shifting aside to reveal the open plane and perpetual night of the crater floor.

Since Caznal was the head of the Nataré division, everyone waited for her cue. She would have the honor of stepping on this alien world first.

Hopefully, though, I won't be the first sentient to explore this surface.

The planemo was roughly the size and density of Mars, with a surface of mostly ice, so Caz knew to expect a lower gravitational pull. It was still strange to feel the burden of her bag lighten and the tension of her muscles ease as she disembarked. The artificial gravity on the convoy ships—even the shuttles—was a constant one-g, and though they'd learned from Earth to make gravity cyclers smaller, allowing for more acute graviton manipulation, they had yet to finesse the tech into spacesuits.

Though she could move easily in the lower gravity, she felt unsteady. Like she was walking on a wobbly gelatin surface instead of solid rock. But the cleats on her soles held true to the frozen landscape, and her confidence increased with each stride.

The darkness, she found, was both a frustration and a godsend. Though the lights on her suit barely illuminated the craggy surface three feet in front of her, the small sphere of light felt safe.

She'd heard stories about planet sickness—the agoraphobia-related illness many of the crew members had experienced when the convoy had revisited Earth—and she had absolutely no desire to experience it firsthand.

"Say something," Ivan prompted when she'd shambled a few yards away from the shuttle.

Turning back, she realized no one was following her. But eight helmets—the glare from their mounted headlamps obscuring their faces—peered out from the craft's opening.

"Do we have to say something profound every time we step on new rocks?" she asked.

"Really?" Aziz, whose background was in bioengineering, called. *"Really?"*

"Oh, come on," Caz said. "That's gonna look way better in the history books than 'one small step.' Schoolkids love sarcasm."

"We all hate you right now," Aziz said, pushing past the others to jump through the hatch. The rest of them clambered out in sequence, looking a bit like a set of robots in their uniformity. Very similar, in fact, to the autons stored in the shuttle's hold, which Caz would call to her aid once the locations for their gear were set.

They wouldn't have cared what I said. She smiled as she watched the team quickly fan out in sets of three, carrying their equipment with ease.

Even though the labor was light, Caz could still hear her breath reverberating through her helmet, which added to the being-in-a-bubble sensation.

They'd picked Crater Sixty-four as a landing site because it was so unlike most of the planemo's other craters, which were clearly created by impact. Their radar-mapping flybys hadn't revealed any overt signs of civilization, past or present. No sprawling cities, no orbiting satellites, no bizarre megastructures. Not even a Cydonian Face to set pareidolia working, or a prominent mimetolith worth speculating about. Just a uniform frozenness, covered over with the dust of impact after impact.

But here, under the gray-green debris and the superficial indentations left by meteorites, the crater's rim looked *worked*, scarred and terraced like in a quarry, disturbed by hand-equivalents with sentient intent.

But perhaps it was natural. Perhaps they would find no sign the Nataré had ever been here, no discernible Web-related reason for it to be on their map. No one in their division dared voice such a possibility, though surely everyone was thinking it. If they couldn't tie this planemo to the Nest, then their detour from the Web would be for naught; a waste of time.

It was an outcome Caznal had feared ever since they'd emerged from SD travel, still light-years away, to do a gravitational survey in order to make sure they were on the right track. Everything had lined up relatively well—putting all the gravitational influences almost exactly where the Nataré data put them, accounting for the millennia that had passed since the Nest had been abandoned inside the Web—everything except their destination. Their treasure map's X, the Cave of Wonders, did not have the gravitational influence the map insisted it should.

There should have been, at a minimum, a star system. But all they'd found was this small wandering rock.

How could that be? Had a collision or some other calamity displaced the mass the Nataré had noted? Did it mark something unnatural? A fleet of alien ships? The fleet the Nest had once belonged to, that had long ago vacated the parsec?

And if the map had meant to point to something other than the planemo, then that meant their time here would amount to little more than a geological side-trek, and the surface beneath her feet was of no more importance than any other. Nothing but a cold rock. Inconsequential. A cosmic red herring, steering them away from their true purpose.

What did that make her career, her department? Misguided? Overblown?

She remembered stories about Earth scientists losing all their funding and credibility in the search for Atlantis. There were even crackpots who'd said the Atlanteans were still alive, just hiding.

That wasn't what *she'd* been doing all these years, was it? Searching for Atlanteans?

"Here looks like a good spot for the first post," Aziz said, waving Ivan over.

They were triangulating spotlights this go-around, and setting up the perimeters of their dig site. They'd become exoarchaeologists soon—using ground-penetrating radar to check for buried evidence, shoveling aside layers of dirt and stone and ice not touched by so much as a breeze in this perpetually frozen nightland.

It wasn't a job they were meant for, not in the same way

other clones were destined for their positions after the DNA reevaluations on Earth, before *Infinitum*'s inception. Theirs was a small, hodgepodge group. Originally, study of the Nest and its contents had fallen solely to the engineers, but, in time, it became clear the convoy required a new department, one focused on the creatures, full of people who could decode the fundamentals of Nataré culture, biology, and data.

Clones had been siphoned from bioengineering positions, which included medical staff and food processing staff. Communications had given up a line or three, as had computing, education, and SD drive maintenance. And, of course, Caznal's line had been taken from engineering.

Now, the copper-colored jumpsuits of the Nataré scholars were one of the rarest uniforms among the crew, second only to the server caretakers' sand color on *Hvmnd*. They wore it as a point of pride. Caznal saw it as a symbol of evolution: the evolution of purpose, of understanding, of their focus and dedication.

When each of the three teams was set, Caz activated her puppeteer implants, calling to the autons.

Three of the robots emerged from the shuttle's storage hatch, unfolding from their compact travel positions, with legs slung over their own dislocated shoulders. The autons were an Earth invention, humanoid in form, dexterous in movement, with tensile strength and lifting power far beyond any machine in existence when the convoy was first launched.

Caz couldn't see them at this range, but she could see through their "eyes," and they could sense the weak infrared signatures emanating from the humans. She directed one to aid each set of three.

They relied entirely on her instruction, with no will or executable programs of their own. Each auton's sleek black helmet of a head contained an active neural network, which her implants communicated with. Theirs was a hybrid of human and elephant brain tissue, without its own sentience, but with the speed and nuance only biological computing was capable of.

Scratch that. I.C.C. could match brain banks for reasoning, intelligence, and empathy any day of the week. It was the only truly artificial intelligence currently known to humanity.

But I.C.C. was confined to its body—the convoy. It was of no help down here. Especially with no hands of its own.

She used the autons to work in mirrored tandem, each coring a hole for, and setting up, the spotlight poles. While she directed their labor, others packed up the core samples for testing on *Holwarda*, and drew a detailed guide-grid for the area.

Few people in the convoy currently knew how to manipulate the autons—especially with her level of skill. The robots weren't needed on a daily basis, so most of the artificial forms were held in reserve on *Bottomless II*, with appropriate neural networks being cloned only a handful at a time. Eventually the time of the autons would come, when the convoy was ready to set to work on their Dyson Sphere, but for now, most remained on lockdown.

"Ready to start mapping the grid area," Ivan announced when Caz was nearly done with the hard labor.

"Everything calibrated?" she asked.

"All's a go, sir."

"Then have at 'er."

The last thing Caz would have to hook up was the generator. She retrieved it with the puppets, as Ivan and Aziz made a slow, straight path across the ice. The Nataré team had picked a two-by-two acre area as their starting point. On the next away mission they'd bring down more of their colleagues, who'd expand the perimeter while they got to work on the first dig site—provided the GPR found anything worth digging up.

“Okay everybody,” she called when her work was done. “Floodlights coming on in three, two, one.”

As the lights snapped on, revealing the glittering fractures in the debris-covered ice, her teammates took turns crying out theatrically at the loss of their night vision.

“Yeah, yeah, all right,” she laughed. “My eyes! The goggles do nothing!” She started to send the autons back—their job complete—when one caught a faint glint in the distance. It was a reflection too dim for human eyes to catch, brassy in color—very unlike the glimmer dancing off the ice.

Without a word, she sent the single auton to investigate. It bounded over the surface, sliding a little as it met the downward slope of a small crater, shards of stone tumbling around its mechanical feet. Then it was up the other side, and Caz focused one of its external lights on the curious spot.

It was definitely metallic, jutting up from the slight rim at an outward angle. It extended maybe a foot above the surface, perhaps the result of the impact itself—ore melting under the heat of friction, splashing upward and then cooling quickly as it encountered the frigidness of space. There were similar nodules around its base, all angled, these no more than a few centimeters in height.

But as the auton came upon them, she realized the cylindrical, if nonuniform, shape was familiar.

Could it—?

She hadn’t let herself hope—still didn’t want to. Fighting the thrill of anticipation, she ignored the weakness in her knees and tried to still her heart as it fluttered wildly.

It could be nothing. It’s probably nothing, she told herself as she jogged in the auton’s direction, only to settle into a walk. It took a lot of willpower to force herself to move slowly, deliberately attempting to look unbothered. No use drawing the others’ attention. Not unless it turned out to be something worth the diversion.

But Ivan noticed her shifting attention, saw her initial run off into the night.

"Sir?" he asked, pausing his trudge behind the GPR skiff as she moved past him.

She didn't answer.

"Caz?" Aziz prompted. "Caznal, what—?"

The breathy echo in her helmet grew louder as she directed the auton to dig. She had to see, had to know right now.

The robot thrust its fingertips into the ice, smashing the frozen surface. It scraped away pummeled debris from the object's sides, slowly revealing more of the same.

Leaving the newly illuminated dig site felt like stepping off a cliff. Now, instead of comforting, her small halo of light felt claustrophobic, restraining. As though it kept her hemmed in from the planemo's secrets on purpose.

She tripped over herself on her way to the auton's side—it was difficult trying to mentally maneuver the puppet's limbs contradictory to her own—and the shouts of her name over the comms system became more frantic.

"I'm fine!" she said, though it appeased no one. Both their concern and curiosity had been piqued, if the continued comms chatter was anything to go on.

By the time she reached the robot, it had loosened the ground around the primary object, plus the five nodes nearest. She fell to her knees, joining it, scraping aside what she could with her clumsy, gloved hands.

Something in the back of her mind perked, and she realized it was dangerous to test her suit this way. What if she dug down to something sharp and punctured her glove? She could lose pressure, or worse—just because the planet was cold, that didn't mean it was barren. There could be dormant microbes beneath the surface, just waiting to encounter a carbon-based life-form.

Though the thought gave her momentary pause, she kept

digging. She knew it was irrational, that she should approach this like the tempered scientist she was, and yet the excitement was overwhelming.

And now, close up, she was sure: this oddly formed metal was the spitting image of the Nest's outer piping, Nataré technology used in their graviton supercycler. Only this seemed to be inverted. Where the Nest's cycler dangled beneath the ship, this thrust upward, like the prongs of winter branches.

"Over here!" she cried at last, the dam of self-restraint no longer bowing under her exhilaration, but breaking. "I found something! Bring the GPR!"

I found them, she said to herself. *I found the Atlanteans.*

Ground-Penetrating Radar revealed at least three other super-cycler tree structures near the surface, plus a few odd shapes of peculiar density that could be—based on their uniformity—buildings.

They still had to adhere to their four-and-a-half-hour ground schedule, but when they got back to the shuttle, there was much whooping and hollering, and a promise from the pilot to treat them all to an allowance of her special home brew from modified barley.

Ivan forgot himself for a moment and nearly whisked off his helmet after take-off. Only Aziz catching his hands and whacking him on the top of the thing saved him from an arduous level of extra decontamination when they docked with *Hippocrates.*

Even the scrubbers and the doctors gave them all hearty congratulations. And while Caz was still excited, she was far more subdued. Introspective.

Because the initial thrill of discovery had worn off, her adrenaline had ebbed. The careful thought she should have applied prior to running off into the night now occupied her every moment.

When the team was finally given the go-ahead to strip out of their pressure suits, Caznal's gaze fell on her apprentice, and she knew what was wrong. The dark curls of his hair framed his tan face and swooped over his ears just so, emphasizing the strong arched slope of his nose. From this angle—with his helmet propped triumphantly under one arm, smile bright and proud—he was the spitting image of a classical statue of a Turkish youth she'd seen in the archives once, but it was his resemblance to someone else that urged her to head to *Hvmnd* as soon as the doctors declared them all contaminate-free.

The pilot running unscheduled flights from *Hippocrates* to *Hvmnd* looked surprised to have a passenger, which wasn't unusual in Caznal's experience. Not many people made regular visits to the server ship like she did.

The nine original convoy ships were very different in design from the three added upon Convoy Seven's second launch, reflecting centuries upon centuries of Earth-centric design evolution. Where the original ships were, in many ways, reminiscent of a cross between zeppelins and beetles, both in their color and nature—being mostly bulbous (save *Solidarity* and *Bottomless II*, which were like floating towers) and silvery, and very utilitarian in their individual design differences—the newer ships were *earthy*. They were dark, and their exteriors had flows and layering that looked imperfect, more natural than designed. If the first nine were biomechanical (heavy on the mechanical), the additional three were geomechanical: they seemed to have morphology, weathering, like they were composed of stones and mud brought together by sheer gravitational adherences.

Of course, fundamentally, they were still ships. But she'd bet her leisure rations any aliens making visual contact with *Slicer*, *Hvmnd*, and *Zetta* would do a double take when they realized they weren't looking at aesthetically pleasing asteroids.

Disembarking, she was met by one of the caretakers, Ina,

who she knew best of all the server ship workers, save the captain. Though best didn't mean *well*. It was difficult to truly know anyone who'd been raised on *Hvmnd* well.

That was because *Hvmnd* occupied a strange nexus between the convoy's morality, culture, and the need for Earth's computing technology. Earth-proper no longer used artificial computers—a fact which nearly led to I.C.C.'s demise—and had learned to use organic power (human brains, animal brains, partial neural networks that could only loosely be called brains) to a much greater advantage. So when the convoy had relaunched, decked out with all the advancements the planet had to offer, the package had included a computing upgrade: clone lines whose sole purpose was to act as human servers.

That didn't sit well with the board. It might be common for people to sell years of their life away on Earth, but the convoy found it appalling.

They'd intended to shut down that portion of *Hvmnd* once they were well away from Earth's watchful eye. After all, with I.C.C. and its inorganic servers fully functional, there was no real need to revamp the original system.

But that was before the conversion of *Zetta* into a graviton supercycler. *Zetta* had been built to store the zetta-joules of energy the convoy was expected to retrieve once they completed the Dyson Sphere around LQ Pyx. But the crew had needed it for a different purpose: to turn on the Nest. And this new purpose carried a hefty need for processing power. Power the convoy's antiquated computing system could not provide.

Hvmnd was required after all.

And yet, cloning lines simply to harvest their brain power would not do.

The server clones had to be given a chance at wakefulness, which meant they would sometimes be off-line. The convoy would either need to accept this disruption, or find a new way to fill the computing void. None of the regular crew members wished to give up portions of their lives to such a service, so where could they get perfectly good brains no one was using anymore?

There was a reason some people called *Hvmnd* "the grave ship."

"Permission to visit?" Caznal asked.

The caretaker bowed slightly, revealing the row of implanted connections on the top and sides of her shaved head. "Of course." She gestured for Caz to follow her out of the bay.

"How are your children?" Caz asked as they entered the main bay.

"Sleeping," Ina said simply, stopping at a row of iron black steps and indicating Caz should continue without her.

Her boots rattled the connected, corrugated catwalk as she ascended to the level above, and the fine blond hairs on the back of her neck rose with the shock of cold. It was unpleasantly chilly outside of the shuttle bay—for those that were awake, that is. Most of *Hvmnd* was a single bay, like *Slicer*, only instead of alien devices, *Hvmnd* stored people. Catwalks, like the one Caznal was on, snaked this way and that through the many layers of hanging chairs, which held people from all divisions, plugged in and strung up.

It wasn't just the cold, though. Each ship carried its own smell. *Eden* always smelled so green and fresh, even in its subarctic tundra biodome, and *Hippocrates* smelled like rubbing alcohol. *Mira* smelled like home, and depending on what part of *Shambhala* you were visiting, it could smell like a sweaty gym or a bowl of buttery popcorn.

Hvmnd smelled like something ancient. The way family heirlooms smelled. Like history and age.

"Why am I not surprised to see you here?" said a familiar voice over Caz's shoulder.

Captain Onuora always did know how to make an entrance. Caz whirled to see great mechanical arms, like silver spider's legs, dangling from tracts in *Hvmnd*'s ceiling. They clasped the captain's wheelchair, and she controlled them deftly from a keypad on her armrest. With a few extra flicks of her wrist, Onuora bade them set the chair down next to Caz, then they folded up and away, ready for her whenever she called on them again.

Caz saluted, and Onuora answered it with a stern expression, before going into Mothering Mode, as she was inclined to do. "News travels fast—shouldn't you be celebrating? I know you found something down there."

Caz strode down the walkway, and the captain stayed at her side, the old-world Jamaican flag on the back of her wheelchair fluttering out behind her like a cape.

Onuora was not part of the original *Noumenon* crew, just as Caz wasn't part of it. Their lines were fresh, having only been aboard a few generations. But few people of the forty-second century could trace their family history like Onuora. She took pride in her connection to Earth, whereas many of the original crew didn't seem to care for genealogy past their original's birth.

Earth was an abstraction in many ways, which had little bearing on their reality. But it also still mattered, if only as something that could provide grounding—perhaps literally—to the convoy's reality.

"I will," Caz said, "I mean, I am celebrating, and . . . he should know."

The captain gave her a pitying look, shifting uncomfortably in her chair. Her achondroplasia had led to severe arthritis in her hips, as it had with the majority of those in her line. And while the seat was customized just for her—the wheels were controlled by a chip implanted in her brain, just like a prosthetic hand that could grasp or foot that could flex—and was the perfect size for her smaller frame and foreshortened limbs, it wasn't where she spent the majority of her working hours. In fact, as often as Caz had been to *Hvmnd*, she rarely saw the captain in her chair. "I'll give you your privacy, then. Come to the bridge before you leave?"

Hvmnd's bridge was the only constant zero-g environment in the convoy, at Captain Onuora's insistence. She preferred the freedom of movement that came with weightlessness. It eased the pressure on her aching joints, let her fly from post to post. Caznal, on the other hand, always felt like a baby animal trying to stand for the first time whenever she visited—all wobbly legs and unintended directions. *She* wasn't meant to fly. But that didn't mean she'd begrudge her friend the visit. "Thank you, Captain. I will. And I can come back tomorrow to work on your chair, if you're available." On their off time, they liked to experiment with smaller graviton cyclers, to see if they could invent one precise enough to make *Hvmnd*'s metal arms obsolete.

"Sounds like a plan," said the captain with a smile. She swiped at a few keys, and the arms descended once more, lifting her away, back to her bridge crew.

Caz continued her walk. She knew her path well, taking walkway fourteen-A, turning at row five before sauntering down to seat eight. A technician in a sandy-colored jumpsuit checked connections on one chair over, where a Korean woman with a long pale gray braid slept—Roh Jin-Yoon the Sixteenth. Her features flexed with the occasional mental stimulus, either into a half grimace or pseudo smile.

Caznal nodded to the technician next to sleeping Jin-Yoon, who nodded back—the plugs on his dark scalp glimmering in the low light. He pulled an idle connection from where it dangled next to Jin-Yoon's wrist and plugged it into one of his ports. Caznal immediately averted her eyes, quickly crouching down next to the unconscious man she'd come to visit.

"How are you doing?" Caz asked elderly Ivan the Fourteenth, her mentor, taking his wrinkled hand in hers. He couldn't answer, of course, but it gave Caznal comfort to speak to him. "We went to the surface. You won't believe what we found." Her thumb made tiny circles over the back of his age-spotted hand. "I just wanted to let you know, professor. I'll finally get to apply what you taught me. I wish . . ." She glanced over her shoulder at the technician.

He had his eyes rolled back in his head, his mouth moving around silent words. His position mirrored Caznal's in many ways; he too had Jin-Yoon's hand comfortingly in his.

The techie came from the server lines. Deemed by Earth to have the highest capacity for processing, the people who'd been chosen as new computers for the convoy were now also the caretakers. They had their own lives—lives which Earth never thought they needed to lead—with agency over how they went about them. And still, many of them spent a good chunk of time (67.86 percent of typical waking hours on average, I.C.C. would tell you) plugged in.

That was what Ina had meant when she said her children were sleeping.

Sure she wasn't being overheard—embarrassed about speaking out loud to someone in the dream state, who, by rights, she shouldn't even be visiting, since he was legally dead and gone—Caz continued, "I wish you could be awake to see it."

"Caznal?"

She jolted upright, letting go of Dr. Baraka's hand.

"I'm sorry," the Inter Convoy Computer apologized, its voice emanating from a speaker mounted on the underside of the catwalk above. "It wasn't my intention to startle you."

"It's fine, I.C.C. What is it?"

"Your husband is looking for you. I've patched him into the control room—Captain Onuora has allowed you to take the call there, for privacy."

"Thank you." With a gentle primping of Baraka's collar,

and a quick brush of fingertips through his tussled hair, she let him be.

A set of children rushed by as she climbed flight after flight, through the maze, to the control booth. They all sported age-appropriate connections, and still had their hair—all of it intricately weaved to show off the implants. One little girl pointed at her without a word, and the others nodded emphatically. She wondered, for a moment, if they were speaking mind-to-mind. Under convoy law, they weren't supposed to, not unless plugged into *Hvmnd*'s system. The board had a long-ingrained mistrust of secret communications, born of conspiracy and mutiny.

She thought for a moment about chiding them. Not because she begrudged them their heritage, but because it shined a light on her own faux pas. *One does not visit the dead, and one does not speak mind-to-mind.*

But then the children laughed, as though she not being a caretaker was in itself a joke, and she moved on.

At the top of the ship, a single wide door led into the control room. Inside, behind the long line of forward-tilting windows, was an equally long line of control panels, flanked itself by an equally long metal table. The room was empty, as it often was—the caretakers preferred a more hands-on approach to monitoring their charges. Only occasionally was a sentry posted up top.

"Diego?" Caz asked, noticing the blinking light on one panel, indicating a comm line was open.

"Where are you?" he asked. "Ivan's here, Vega and Min-Seo, too. But no *you*. We can't cut the cake until you get back."

"I just had a quick errand to run."

His pause said much. "If you'd waited a few hours I would've gone with you."

"I know. I wanted a little time to myself."

"Self-flagellation isn't 'time to yourself.'"

Glaring, she crossed her arms and turned away from the consol. "I'm not punishing . . . I'm sharing it with him the only way I can."

"I'm sorry," he said quietly. "This is your day, and you should be able to celebrate it however you want."

"Just give me a little more time. Half an hour, tops, and I'm home."

"Deal. I love you."

She turned back around, posture softening. "Love you, too."

When the call ended, she slumped against the table, tracing the scratches in the surface. This table was nothing like the grand one on *Mira*, the long single slab of green granite that graced the situation room. That one was specially carved for the original mission, an artisan piece with only eleven brothers and sisters.

"For what it's worth," I.C.C. said. "I wish the same. For Doctor Baraka, I mean."

"Were you eavesdropping?"

"When do I not?"

"Fair point," she conceded.

She meant to clam up, then. To go back to the professor's side. But the conflicting feelings—the excitement, the doubt, the sadness and rage—all came gushing forth. Here, in this quiet space, with only the Inter Convoy Computer to hear her, she let loose. "But it's not *fair*. They couldn't give him six months. *Six months.* Just so he could see where his life's work was leading. And they wouldn't let me . . ."

"I processed your request to wake him," it said sympathetically. "I know."

"I mean, I get it. I know why it's law. Those put under should never be woken again. Retirement is retirement, and whether the retiree travels to *Hippocrates* or *Hvmnd*, they both have to be treated the same: gone." She clutched the edge of the long table, her knuckles whitening as her fingers curled into talons against the smooth surface.

"I understand that as well, though I don't necessarily agree."

She was surprised. "No?"

"Human morality has always been hazy to me. It shifts with the circumstances. Typically, checks and balances are applied, positives and negatives weighed against one another. But not all positives and negatives carry equal measures, as it should be. I do not wish to indicate I believe the board's thinking incorrect. It is simply different from my own.

"Originally, human servers were believed to be fundamentally immoral, while scheduling end-of-life procedures was not. But when the need for human processing became apparent, the board concluded the two things equal. Now, retirement still equates to passing, but it also signals a transition into a new kind of service. And, just like death, the transition is believed only to be moral if it is final. No teasing retirees with glimpses of their old lives—such an outing is thought to be cruel and unnecessary."

"And, typically, I would agree," Caz said. Her face felt hot, her eyes puffy. She didn't want to cry today. Not when it was supposed to be her day of discovery, of triumph. "But in special cases, like with Doctor Baraka, it's crueler to keep him under."

"If he were retired in the traditional manner he would not be present for such an event. He would be deceased," I.C.C. said. "Which is, of course, the board's logic: a retiree's time aboard the convoy has ended, one way or another. That is why he cannot be awakened, that is why we cannot convey information about the outside world to him, even in a dream. And yet, this logic is faulty. Obviously so.

"To deprive one of a deeply personal experience for consistency's sake does not feel like a moral move to me. But I also understand what kind of gray area such exceptions would create. Should everyone be reawakened for the birthing of a grandchild? For new progress made in their field of expertise? For loved ones' marriages?"

"I don't know." Her vision started to blur slightly, her eyes watering. "I just know that Doctor Baraka should be here." She inhaled a shaky breath. *Don't cry. Don't cry. Stop crying.*

"You see," I.C.C. said with a curious tone. "Hazy. Malleable. A plastic morality."

"It's the only kind worth having," she said, not sure she believed it.

I.C.C. did not hedge on the point. "I agree. One cannot function in absolutes—empathy sees to that. But so does narcissism. They are two sides of the same human capacity."

"You think utter selfishness and utter caring spring from the same plasticity?"

"I believe so, yes. But it's important to note I said narcissism, which is a different kind of selfishness, born out of self-love, quite different than the selfishness exhibited by animals who have not yet become self-aware."

Caz rubbed at her face. She felt her equilibrium returning, the sudden swell subsiding. "Why are we philosophizing about morality right now? I need to get home."

"Edging the discussion toward the intellectual and away from the personal has consistently helped clones in your line maintain their composure. I would have tried a different tactic with other crew members. Is it helping?"

A little laugh escaped her. "You are a wonder, I.C.C. Yes. Thank you."

They worked for nine months excavating Crater Sixty-four and scouring the rest of the planemo's surface. The entire convoy's manpower was thrown behind the project, accomplishing in less than a year what it might have taken the Nataré team decades to accomplish alone. They scouted several other spots across the globe—places with anomalous geology—but nowhere else did they find evidence of alien inhabitation.

And the more they dug, the more one thing became clear: to call what they'd found a city or even a settlement was a stretch. The structures they found intact were minimal. And there was nary any evidence of biological activity. No *garbage*, most notably. If there was one thing Earth archaeologists had come to rely on as never-wavering evidence of civilization, it was the concept of "the dump." Biological things consumed, and consumption inevitably produced waste. But there were no filled-in pits, no openly strewn excrement. Perhaps they'd incinerated everything, but if so the teams had yet to identify ashes.

Luckily, because of the frigidness of the dark world, there was no decay. Whatever microbes the Nataré might have brought with them from their home world couldn't survive in such cold. The only destruction on the surface came from ice and outer space.

Which meant when they tested the bricks that formed a few structures' inner walls, they were in for a surprise.

"It's just local dirt bound with platelets and fibrin," Caznal's husband, Diego Santibar the Twelfth, said. He'd invited her into the chem lab to show her what he'd discovered. "Similar to what makes blood coagulate. But it's been stripped of any genetic code. No way to tell if the basis came from Nataré biology, an alien cow, or a buttercup. Regardless, here, instead of forming a scab, it's making bricks. Look at this."

He slid his arms into the gloves of the nearest glove box. Inside lay a black-and-green slab. Gently, he took a corner and spritzed it with an eyedropper. It dissolved immediately, leaving loose grit behind.

"What's in that?" she asked, bending down beside him.

She adjusted the goggles on her face, hating the way they cut into the bridge of her nose.

"Water," he said. "From our taps, nothing special. All of the inner walls in your structures were dissolvable in water."

"Brilliant. No need to take building materials with you if you can mold dust with ease, and scrap it just as fast. I'm starting to think we've found a staging ground. I mean, the lack of apparent infrastructure, the size, the transient nature of these materials—it points to more of a worker's camp than a permanent outpost."

"But what were they working on?"

"Something that's gone now. That would explain our missing mass. Our missing gravitons."

"What about those supercycler towers? How many are there now?"

"Twenty."

"Could those account for the gravitational difference? If they were drawing in that many gravitons, perhaps there was seepage? Maybe they created a false well that altered the maps?"

"I hadn't thought of that," she admitted. "And we haven't found any clues as to what they needed that many gravitons for. If all of their buildings used the same hydrogen wiring as the Nest, that would account for a few of the towers. But not twenty."

She rubbed her eyes. The chem lab was bright, the lights harsh and true white. "I need to get back to analyzing the new items we found. Some malformed block metal."

"Still nothing like the Babbage Engine on the Nest? No computers, no archives?"

"Nothing. They cleaned up real good when they left. It's spotless, almost like a crime scene. They rolled up all but the sidewalks."

"Isn't that strange?"

She shrugged. "If someone handed an alien a fork, a zither, and a hookah, how accurate do you think their assumptions would be? I feel like that's the level we're working on. We have nothing, we know nothing. Our only real hope of understanding them is in those maps. If we don't find the keys here, we just have to prep for the next stop."

There were seven more X's in all on their alien map. The farthest away was a gravitational mega cluster—was it the Nataré home system?

That's what many were speculating, although it wasn't the only theory. There were so many possibilities now that they knew evidence was out there, that the maps were real!

He looked concerned then, like she'd just said something that undermined his entire world view. "Caz, you're assuming . . ."

She cocked her head, wary of his tone. "What?"

"You're assuming there *is* a next stop. The board committed to coming here, but if there's nothing related to the Web, no instructions, no hint at its engineering, origins, or purpose, then . . . You *know* it all has to come back to LQ Pyx to be seen as worthy of convoy attention."

He can't be serious.

She pushed her goggles onto her forehead. He was about to protest, but she barreled forward. "That was before all *this*," she said excitedly. "That was when we weren't sure there would be anything to find. But look at this." She stabbed the glove box, leaving a fingerprint on the otherwise pristine surface. "So simple, so basic, yet brilliant in its design and range of application. When we find a real settlement, a place they truly lived and died, *think* of what we could uncover. There's no way the board is going to turn down the opportunity to chase after an entire civilization's worth of learning in favor of a single construction project."

His expression didn't change. Something unsettling snaked

its way through her stomach, but she held fast to the evidence before her.

It would take them centuries to hit all of the X's, and they would have to travel light-years upon light-years in the opposite direction of the Web.

But why should that matter? What was one alien artifact to an entire alien *history*?

This was bigger, better, surely the board—hell, every last crew member—could see that.

Dr. Baraka saw it, long before anyone else.

With a sigh, Diego removed his hands from the glovebox. "You know the official mission statement doesn't mention the Nest, or the Nataré."

Because those points were kept secret from Earth, to ensure they wouldn't interfere. "So?"

"So, you might find that means something to some people. That they don't see the omission as subterfuge so much as emphasis—on what's really important."

"You know what's important?" she asked firmly.

"What?" He raised a skeptical eyebrow.

She kissed the top of his head. "You, me, and our girls."

"Nice subject change." He laughed. "Smooth."

OCTOBER 25, 122 RELAUNCH

5279 CE

Anticipation made Caznal's head light. Today she'd lay out the Nataré team's final conclusions about the alien history of the planemo, and her plan for which X on the map to travel to next.

There was a gravity well closer than her intended destination, but she wanted to journey to where two X's were less than three light-years apart. It would give them the biggest bang for their buck, to employ an old saying. As a personal bonus, they would still arrive before her retirement, allowing her to play the greatest part in Nataré research for the maximum amount of time.

Dossiers had already been distributed. She'd take final questions, and then it would be onward.

Navy-colored uniforms shuffled in—all of the ship's captains and their seconds in command—followed by at least one uniform of each other color. Many handshakes and smiles propagated throughout the gathering. There was a buzz in the air, and a buzz in their bellies as copious amounts of coffee, tea, and yerba maté were passed around the long marble table.

"Are we ready to begin?" asked First Officer Joanna Straifer. She was a direct descendant—the biological granddaughter—of a Reginald Straifer clone and a Nika Marov clone, and shades of both of them could be seen in her face and hair. Everyone aboard knew those lines well. There was a special hall on *Aesop* wallpapered with portraits of the clones who'd had a great impact on the convoy, and Joanna was the product of not *two*, but *three*. Her biological mother, Esperanza, had spearheaded the initiative that saved I.C.C. from Earth's interference. "Caznal," she continued, "you have the floor."

Screens took up each wall, but Caz chose to use the holographic projector in the center of the table for diagram viewing. She brought up a model of the planemo, then zoomed in on Crater Sixty-four.

"First off, I'd like to say how great it's been working with everyone on this project these past few years. We've been able to learn so much, it's—it's been exciting." A small pang of guilt hit her. Dr. Baraka sprang to mind, his face flush with joy. Now, he was as he'd been when they'd first arrived: dreaming. Lending his processing power to the Nest, to the department he'd cared so much for. And yet, he had no idea what lay kilometers below his sleeping form. She shook his ghost from her mind, then continued.

"These are the layers of excavation." She gestured at the changing hologram. It displayed a cross-section of the crater, with a flag indicating where each item of interest had been found over a fifty-six-square-kilometer area. "The top layer was explored mainly in months one through three, the next in four through seven, the third in seven through sixteen, and so on.

"The third layer is where we first found definitive evidence of the domed structures. And it was the fifth layer where we uncovered the three-mile-long metal scaffolding." The image shifted at her command, displaying only the scaffolding in its unexcavated form. It was a series of long crushed beams—more log-shaped than steel girder–shaped—tangled and twisted, but clearly once the skeleton of a structure. "At first we believed it represented a horizontal building, but we now conclude . . ."

With a few artful flicks of her fingers, she repositioned the holographic pieces. Like the fossilized bones of a dinosaur rising from a tar pit and finding new life, the digitized framework pushed itself up, hammering out its own kinks and mending its breaks. It sat up tall, its narrow, topmost point jutting away from the planet's surface.

"It was a single vertical tower," she said. "Likely the foundation point of a space elevator. Models indicate that it's likely many of the domed buildings were actually attached to the elevator—as temporary living quarters, workstations, or lift pods, we don't know. What the elevator could have been reaching toward is also a mystery.

"But this much is clear. Crater Sixty-four was excavated by the Nataré—giving it its distinctive terraced rim—and used as a staging ground much like the Moon was utilized during the creation of the P.U.M.s. Also clear is that the settlement was quickly, yet thoroughly, dismantled. Much of what would have been required to run such a station is missing, indicating they either took it with them out of necessity or a sense of responsibility.

"The remains of the space elevator and the supercycler towers, however, were left behind. It seems they were toppled and buried by subsequent space collisions, which suggests that once the site was abandoned, the Nataré never returned."

She scanned her notes quickly. "Oh, and one geological item of note. The thickness and density of the secondary ice layer, meaning the layer beneath the debris layers, is of an unusual uniformity across the entire planemo. A few of our geologists have suggested this could have been caused by the rapid freezing of a once gaseous atmosphere, indicating the planemo did not coalesce here. It either originated in a distant star system and was thrown out of orbit, or it once wandered with a much higher velocity and passed through the radiation of—but was not caught by—a star which superheated its ice, forming an atmosphere which rapidly cooled again once it had escaped the star's influence.

"This is relevant to our Nataré research, since the aliens chose to bury the bases of all of the remaining structures *below* this ice layer. Perhaps they felt it was too unstable a foundation, so they cut through to the stone beneath. We're presently unsure, but it gives us one more data point on Nataré thought process and construction habits. All of the information and samples we've gathered have given us plenty of work to sustain us to our next destination."

Caz shuffled through her folders, finding the one with the maps. "Which brings me to the future. What are our next steps? Which Nataré location should we travel to? Which one gives us the best chance at the most data? After consulting our gravitational surveys and—"

"I'm sorry," Captain Nwosu, Joanna's cycle partner, interrupted. Their two clone lines were staggered in growth, so that the two of them would be each other's master and apprentice clone after clone. Much like Caznal and Ivan. "I'm going to have to stop you for a moment," he said.

Caz mentally stumbled—she'd been on a roll and had just missed a stair. "Oh, um, why?"

"We aren't here to discuss a destination change," he said frankly—clearly confused by Caznal's confusion. "We're here for a summary conclusion to this portion of the mission, to be sure it's time to move on."

Several brows around the room were furrowed, many mouths drawn tight. "What destination change? I wasn't aware a destination had been chosen." She of all people would know which X they'd picked.

The captain exchanged glances with the two department heads nearest his chair. "You're suggesting we travel to someplace *other* than LQ Pyx, are you not?" He said *are you not*, but it sounded like *did you have a stroke?*

"LQ—you think it's time to go back to the Web? *Now?*" Never mind not being on the same page, they were in completely different books. "Why would we abandon the study of the Nataré? We've barely scratched the surface of our available research, we have a map with seven other independent locations to explore, and we haven't yet found anything relating to the construction of the Web."

"Exactly," the captain said, as though Caznal were making his point. "Our investigation of the Nest has always been directly tied to our priority: the Web. Without any evidence that a further exploration of Nataré worlds will lead to information regarding the Dyson Sphere, we can't afford to continue on this tangent.

"Our intellectual resources only stretch so far. We could spend infinite lifetimes following these breadcrumbs, hoping for more than scraps, *or* we can focus on the ultimate point of our mission: completing the Web and harvesting its energy. This is a real, solid goal, versus a vague promise of a possible treasure trove."

She couldn't believe what she was hearing. Did they . . . could they not see? How could these people not understand?

Atlanteans. They're here.

We're in the Night Land and I'm getting messages from the Lesser Redoubt.

And just as with the wanderer, no one else cares.

Her abdominal muscles tightened, and she fought to keep herself upright. She felt like she'd been punched in the gut, kicked in the face.

There's nothing quite like being told everything you've ever worked for is a waste.

And still, she wouldn't accept it.

Not after we went at this so hard. Not after my team—not after the professor—

"You're telling me a dormant, incomplete megastructure beats out alien settlements—however temporary—for importance? There could be living, *breathing* Nataré out there, but discovering whether or not that's true, that's just a *tangent*?" Her gaze flickered around the room, looking for help, for a sympathetic face. "That's unreasonable, isn't it? That doesn't make any logical sense."

We could be sharing this galaxy with other sentient beings. They could have families, feelings, wants, dreams.

Wasn't that what reaching out into the stars was all about? Finding humanity's place in the universe? Figuring out if we're alone.

And now we're on the precipice, might be able to answer yes *or* no, *but the crew . . .*

Nwosu cleared his throat and leaned forward, threading his fingers together on the tabletop in a far too polite, *I'm-about-to-educate-you* manner. "Convoy Seven has had a very clear goal from the beginning. It began with *Noumenon*'s inception—" The entire room collectively nodded once at the mission name, an unspoken reverence echoing through the situation room "—and continues now with *Noumenon Infinitum*. We have a collective calling that our genetic lines were chosen hundreds—and in some cases, *thousands*—of Earth years ago to fulfill. Esteemed scientists handpicked us, assigned us our posts and our goals, with a strict purpose. It is our calling, our—"

Caznal laughed. It was a sharp, manic sound, which threw itself from her lips the moment she understood what the captain was trying to say. "Are you . . . are you kidding me? *Manifest Destiny*? You are scientists, engineers. Educated to the gills for the purpose of exploration and innovation, and this . . . this *mythicizing* of our place in—"

She took a deep breath, reeling herself in when she realized she was hunkered over the table, fists balled, voice raised.

Okay, they want to focus on the mission? Bring it back to the mission.

"*Noumenon Infinitum*," she began, articulating firmly, but keeping her tone reserved, "clearly states that the study of the Nataré is vital. We can't reject our findings outright. We can't abandon the evidence or the maps."

"We won't," said Margarita Pavon, communications head. Where Straifer and the rest of the long-haired command team had their locks tightly pulled or slicked back, she let her ample curls bounce freely. "Everything you've uncovered will be communicated to Earth. We will suggest a new mission, focused on the Nest's maps. Then they will be able to build the appropriate research vessels and construct a fit team. Right now, most of your division is a hodgepodge. Repurposed. We've been unprepared to study the aliens from the beginning. And now that we know our best chance at further construction on the Web relies on reverse engineering—"

“We don’t know that at all,” Caz grumbled under her breath.

“—rather than an alien instruction manual, we can continue on with our society’s purpose.”

“Really, Caznal,” Nwosu said, “I have no idea why this surprises you. There are millions upon millions of worthy research subjects in space. We can’t go willy-nilly picking whichever one we want. We are a Planet United convoy. You should take comfort in having a firm, forward goal.”

“I take comfort in mindful pursuits,” she bit back. “*Noumenon*’s original goal wasn’t to build anything. It was a mission of discovery. Finding any proof of extraterrestrial sentience was in itself considered an improbability. You aren’t making a decision based on critical thinking. You’re not even choosing legacy ideals over new discoveries. You’re pursuing a mythicized version of reality; instead of looking forward, you’re romanticizing the past.”

“I don’t understand why we’re letting this conversation continue,” huffed the head of education. “Doctor Caznal’s fundamental misunderstanding of our entire social order can be amended on her own time. No one here is looking to put a new destination to a vote, so I suggest we move on.”

“*No*,” Caz shouted. “No. We were only supposed to move on to LQ Pyx if the destination proved fruitless—”

“It has,” he said.

“How can you say that? If you were being the objective scientists you’re all supposed to be—”

“I’m sorry, Caz, but I don’t think we’re the ones not being objective,” said Captain Onuora.

Caznal’s eyes shot to *Hvmnd*’s captain—*her friend*. Onuora’s dark eyes were sympathetic, and her tone matched. But every word that followed felt like a knife to Caznal’s back.

“We know you despise the decision to keep Doctor Baraka under when we arrived at the planemo. I think *this* decision feels like another betrayal to you. As though we've undermined not only the man, but his legacy. No one is suggesting we halt analysis on the data you've already collected. Nor should we stop examining the Nest. But the pursuit of the Nataré as a people—as Web builders—has to end. We have other work to do—that we were always meant to do. It's not personal. Don't make it personal."

This is my entire life . . . how can it not be personal?

"That's not what this is about," Caz said meekly.

"Either way. As a colleague, and as a friend, I suggest you let us move on to the next order of board business."

With her will suddenly drained, it felt as though the bones had been plucked from Caznal's body. She sank into a chair with no firmness to her movement.

Onuora was wrong. Wasn't she? Caz wasn't trying to overemphasize the importance of the Nataré because of Dr. Baraka. No, of course not. Wouldn't the botanists be surprised and angry to have their hybrid programs suddenly stopped? Wouldn't the engineers cry foul if they lost access to the Nest or the Web node? She'd just had the rug pulled out from under her professional life. That was it. That was *all.*

"Mom? You all right?"

A soft crash-boom of distant waves underscored Min-Seo's voice. As water rushed up Caznal's calf before receding again, she opened one eye.

Her grown daughter leaned over her, hands on her hips, her computing jumper left behind in exchange for a tank top and slacks.

The wave pool sloshed once more, and the sound system continued to play real surf sounds. Every ten minutes, a gull squawked. Up and down the sandy beach, other crew members read books or took naps. One woman on a beach towel scowled at Min-Seo.

"This is the quiet pool," Caz reminded her at a whisper.

"Oh, sorry." She settled in beside her mother, rolling up the cuffs of her trousers to stick her feet in the damp silica. Fine, pale grains stuck to her toes.

"Thought the three of you were supposed to be on a romantic vacation," Caz said, noting neither Hiro nor Kexin, her daughters-in-law, nearby.

"We are. I could tell things were getting a little spicy, so I excused myself." She checked her forearm implant for the hour. "I'll get back just in time for the cuddles. You know what I always say . . ." She gave her mother a wink.

Caz cleared her throat and recited, "'The advantages of being an asexual panromantic in a polyamorous relationship.' By the ships, that is a mouthful."

"Which is why I like to hear you say it. It's life affirming and a tongue twister all in one."

The sand was both rough and soft, a dichotomy Caz enjoyed. She slipped her fingers beneath the surface, down where it was dark, and cool—untouched by the sun-mimicking lamps overhead. "So, you happened to find me, or . . . ?"

"I got a message from Dad."

"My *pilikua* is worried about me?"

"Yes. He said you haven't been yourself since—"

"Since the board voided the importance of my entire field of study? Yeah, you could say that."

"*Shh*," hissed the woman on the beach towel.

With a dramatic eye-roll, Caz heaved herself out of the sand, clearly giving Min-Seo whiplash as she was settling in. "Come on," Caz said, giving her a hand up. "If you're going to cheer me up, we better go someplace else. Preferably a place with a lot of chocolate or mod-coca."

Hand in hand, they wandered away from *Shambhala*'s wave pools, past its gyms, and down to the dessert bars. These were new—an upgrade installed before second launch. Food printers allowed chefs to turn convoy basics into a variety of concoctions—both healthy and not so. The professional behind the counter scanned your biometrics, looked up what you'd already eaten that day, then created a specialized dessert menu based on your remaining rations and current blood sugar.

Science at its best, Caz thought.

"Oh, Gyeongju bread," Min-Seo said, sniffing the air as a crew member strolled by with a plate of three of the bean paste–filled rolls.

"Go for it," Caz said, "I think I'm going for a pick-me-up of the green-leaf variety."

"Meet at our star-window?" Min-Seo asked.

"Of course."

The mod-coca dispensary was a charming little nook that mirrored the tea dispensary on the opposite side of what had come to be known as "dessert lane." Caz chose a small packet of dried leaves for chewing and the botanist in charge took vice points off her rations file.

The first pinch was bitter, had a bit of a sulfide bite to its bouquet, but it settled nicely in her cheek as she made her way to the meeting spot. Relaxing as the chew was, she knew it would do little to help her depressive mood—unless it magically imbued her with the ultimate powers of persuasion. How could she make an entire society realize its error in judgment?

The star-windows were located on the ship's topmost level. During SD dives, they displayed a false-view of space. Nebulae would engulf them in colorful haze. Dying binaries would dance by. Stars would twinkle balefully in the distance.

Now, they were true windows. Floor-to-ceiling, turned to give the perfect top-down view of the planemo, which was largely dark save for the single crater overrun with human lighting. They were just far enough out that the dark spot was ringed with stars, and if you put your forehead against the glass—as Min-Seo and Caznal did now—letting your eyes cross just so, you might feel, for a moment, like you were falling into a black hole.

"It's been two weeks," Min-Seo said between bites.

"I know." Caz sighed, her breath lightly fogging the window. The aluminosilicate glass was frigid against her skin. "And it's not just me."

"The whole Natarė division," Min-Seo said knowingly. "Vega said she's barely gotten two words out of Ivan."

"Did you hear they're thinking of reassigning our lines?" she asked Min-Seo. "Putting the next clones back into the business they were chosen for?"

Min-Seo stopped her chewing, a wad of pastry and beans rounding out her cheek. "But I thought they said you could still work on the crater samples."

"Yep, *we*—meaning those of us currently working. Once we're retired, they figure it's all clones on the Web train once more."

"It's too bad it has to be one or the other. I mean, doesn't it make sense to do both? We haven't heard back from Earth yet, we know they can't be counted on to follow up. We're the explorers, we should be doing everything we can."

Caz shrugged and stuffed more coca in her mouth against her gums. The bulge in her lip made her sound funny, but Min-Seo wasn't one to take a cheap jab. "Unfortunately, one convoy equals one mission. They've narrowed down what that mission is, and my people are just SOL."

"Why does it have to be that way?" Min-Seo asked. "I mean, yes, one convoy can only do so much. But we have *twelve* ships."

"Oh, you know the answer to that," Caz dismissed. "Those oh-so-perfect original P.U.M. mission designers decided we needed nine ships and a hundred thousand people so we don't implode on a social level."

“We’ve got three ships extra, then.”

“That we need for the Web.”

“Do we? Those three ships were given to us by Earth, who thought we’d come back one day carrying some crisis-averting energy motherlode. But, just like everyone knows about the secret Nataré study, everyone knows we never intend to go back. What are we going to do with a giant battery, huh? We started repurposing the ship as soon as we found an alternate use for it. If we’re going to live on these ships forever, utilizing the Web to fight our own entropy, then we don’t need *Zetta*. And we only need *Hvmnd* because of *Zetta*.”

Where was Min-Seo going with this? Caz raised her head, took a good long look at her daughter happily munching on Gyeongju bread like she wasn’t suggesting . . . whatever it was she was suggesting. Coming from a convoy member, the subtext of this conversation was practically blasphemous. “Are you saying we could—” she moved in close, looked around and kept her voice low “—split the convoy?”

Min-Seo looked her mother in the eye. Though her tone was light, she knew the gravity of simply toying with such an idea. “I bet if you ask I.C.C., we wouldn’t cross a failure threshold if *one* became *two*. It’s not like the old days, when returning to Earth was the endgame. Our societal mindset is different. More innately stable.”

“This is not a little solution to my problem,” Caz said.

“No. It’s a big solution to a problem that I don’t think you can claim as solely your own.”

“When did you get so conniving?” Caz threw her arms around her daughter, drawing her in close, jostling her plate.

“Oh, come on, Mom, don’t make me lose the last bun. And it’s not conniving. It’s rational. But, if you’re going to propose it, you have to understand what it means, for the crew, for our family. You have to know how the board will take it.”

Off the quiet beach, they were still whispering now, and

for good reason. The convoy's history of revolution and self-destruction might only have a few bullet points, but those bullets still made the memory bleed. Their society wasn't run by authoritarianism, but nor was it a democracy. Any dissent was caught quickly, and quashed.

Proposing a split, if rejected, would mark her—and perhaps her line—forever as the woman who wanted to cut the baby in half.

"Maybe *I* don't propose it," she said. Min-Seo pulled away, a dark hesitancy on her face. "No, no," Caz assured her, "I wouldn't put that responsibility on a colleague. If I can't handle the consequences, I wouldn't ask someone else to."

"Then how do you get the board to consider it?"

With a sly smirk, Caznal's eyes rolled toward the ceiling.

"What?" Min-Seo asked, searching for what her mother was staring at. "I don't get it."

"It was your suggestion."

"What, Mom? What did I say?"

Caznal kissed her on the forehead. "Better get back to your wives. I'll let you know if it works."

Caznal returned to *Mira* with renewed conviction. She couldn't let the study die. There was so much to learn from the Nataré—not just about physics and the Web, but about medicine, philosophy, religion (did they have any?), recreation, on and on. Here was the chance for humans to reach outside of themselves, beyond the biology and history of their own planet. Were human universal ideals truly universal? Or were they unique to a relatively small planet on the edge of one of a billion galaxies?

That's what they were up against: Was this a mission of discovery, or was this a mission of repair? The Nataré could bequeath multitudes of artifacts to humanity, but the convoy was obsessed with one. One artifact, one result, one purpose.

That didn't make the board wrong. It was not wrong to have a goal, to understand the thrust of your endeavors and where they led. But she was not wrong either.

The convoy's mission now possessed a duality—both halves worthy.

She told Diego of her plan, and after some discussion—full of smart, insightful questions that reminded her why she loved him in the first place—he gave his support.

At the next board meeting, Caznal sat quietly. She sipped her coca tea and went over the previous meeting's minutes as though it were just another day. Another round of mundane convoy updates, another chance for Dr. Brown to complain about a maintenance robot malfunction (as she always did).

Caz allowed herself a moment to look around, though. To see the things she took for granted. Because, should her plan work, she would lose this room. There was a ding in the wall nearest her seat that had never been fixed—chair height, by the look of the horizontal scrape. It smelled different in this room. Felt special. She slid her palms under the edge of the marble tabletop, where it was rough, searching for the little carved stamp—ah, there! The roman numeral for seven, which marked the long table as part of its special set.

Captain Nwosu kept picking absently at a divot in front of him—an unconscious habit Caznal had never noted before. So many memories here. So many important decisions made for so many people, both by this crew and by *all* the mission's crews.

And now, perhaps, time for one more.

"Are we ready to begin?" Straifer asked the room, standing at the head of the table. The low rumble of pleasant conversation faded away, as the department heads, captains, and elected representatives settled in for another round of Enacting-Your-Civil-Duty. "We have three new proposals to review and vote on—"

"Excuse me, First Officer Straifer," said I.C.C., prompting a wave of chins shooting in the ceiling's direction. "But I have a proposal to submit as well. Please forgive me for the late notice. I realize it is highly irregular to submit *during* a meeting."

Like a physical manifestation of a self-propagating wave, Caznal's gaze darted to Nwosu, and all eyes around her followed.

Nwosu cleared his throat. "It's highly irregular for the ships' computer to submit a proposal at all," he said, a half joke colored by his clear discomfort.

The room was so quiet, Caznal could hear the atmosphere circulators chugging away. She tried to temper her excitement, to maintain her poker face. It wouldn't do to give away the game just yet.

"I'm sorry, I.C.C.," Nwosu said, regaining some of his stolen composure. "But the agenda for this meeting has been finalized. If you wish to submit, you'll need to follow the procedure and—"

The situation room erupted, opinions boiling over like lava, burning wherever they fell.

"Are you kidding?"

"This is I.C.C. we're talking about—"

"We can't let the computer make suggestions—"

"It's made them before."

"But never *formally*."

"Why is that a problem, exactly?"

"People!" Nwosu said. He barely raised his voice, as though that would encourage people to order. "People. Everyone! Hold on. Wait. *Hold on*."

Pavon jumped to her feet, curly hair flying. "Everyone shut up!"

Caznal was only a little surprised when the room complied.

"Captain," Pavon said evenly. "You have the floor."

“Thank you. As I was saying, we have procedures for a reason—to avoid exactly this kind of chaos.”

“But it’s human procedure,” said Dr. Nakamura. “It doesn’t apply to I.C.C. I think we should hear what it has to say *now*.”

“We should put it to a vote,” said Captain Onuora.

Nwosu gave a reluctant sigh. “All those who wish to hear from I.C.C. now?” he asked.

The shouts of “Aye” were deafening. They clearly had it.

“I.C.C., you may proceed. What does your proposal cover?”

“The creation of two convoys out of our existing one.”

If the silence had been deafening before, this was the utter absence of sound. The air lay dead. Caz looked from side to side, making sure her colleagues hadn’t died of shock. It seemed the sentence contained so foreign a concept, they could hardly process it.

I.C.C. clearly took the lack of interjection as a signal to continue. “I do not make this proposal casually, but I fear we may be at the beginning of a societal impasse.”

That’s an interesting way to put it, Caz thought. The dumbfounded silence hadn’t diminished. On the contrary, it seemed to be burgeoning. She could see words beginning at the back of Nwosu’s throat, but he swallowed them down. Beside Caz, Onuora sat up straighter, arms tucked against her sides, tight—a wound coil ready to spring. At what, Caz couldn’t guess.

Out of everyone in the room, only she and Pavon seemed to be taking the AI’s words in stride. Pavon’s clone line had a long history of siding with the AI—Caznal found that interesting. Perhaps Margarita would back her.

“The current mission was launched with a dual purpose,” I.C.C. continued. “Some have taken that duality to heart, while others believe one a side mission. The unofficial standing of that ‘side mission’ has further fueled the intellectual divide. But only now is the division beginning to show itself. It has been an undercurrent for over fifty years, but not until the last board meeting was it given voice."

Onuora turned in her wheelchair, and Caz could feel a pointed gaze boring into her profile.

"I've run behavioral projections," I.C.C. said, "and the results indicate this could be a turning point. Chances of societal disruption are high, threats to crew member safety are currently steady, but I fear an increase soon. Overall, chance of mission failure has increased by point-two-seven percent."

Caznal's stoicism cracked, her eyes widening. This was *not* what they'd talked about. The computer was supposed to be outlining the scientific merits of two convoys, why focusing on reverse engineering *and* alien instruction *simultaneously* was likely to see the construction project finished sooner than if they spurned one for the other.

The Web—I.C.C. was supposed to be focusing on the megastructure. If the damn board was so in love with the thing, she was going to give it to them.

But now . . .

"Uh, point-two—" Caznal's voice cracked. She tried again. "Point-two-seven percent doesn't sound like that big of a deal," she said. *Come on, I.C.C., let's stay focused here.*

Uncomfortable rustling made its way around the table in a wave, starting with Onuora.

"It is not," I.C.C. acknowledged. "Typically speaking. But since Relaunch, the standard deviation has wavered no more than point-zero-zero-zero-zero-zero—"

"We get the picture," Nwosu snapped. "The important part is, you expect it to continue increasing?"

"Correct."

"Unless we split the convoy?"

"Correct."

The captain gave a shrug—not out of ambivalence, but blatant irritation. "No. Just, *no*."

"I would appreciate it if you allowed me to outline the reasons I have drawn this conclusion," the AI said. Not firmly, not pointedly. I.C.C.'s tone barely had the capacity to differentiate from a calm monotone at all. But the authority in the "request" could not be denied, and no one said anything in protest. "I believe I have a unique perspective on the situation. Not simply because I can integrate more data at any given time into a more accurate picture of the current situation, but because I have experienced much of the history that you now relate on *Aesop* in the same way you retell fairy stories."

"Oh, come now, I.C.C.," said Dr. Ka'uhane, Chief Astronomer. "Don't you think that's a bit harsh?"

"I do not. Your ancestors are characters to you. You have streamlined their personalities out of their nuances and complexities and dichotomies. Humans often do not recognize conflicting points of view they themselves hold, and thus have a difficult time prescribing such conflicts to the past. Your villains are villainous, your heroes heroic. But I knew these people—still know them, in fact, for unless the files are erased or corrupted, I have completely accurate snapshots of their behavior. Yes, much is still unknown about their thoughts, but I have more to go on."

"Please make a point," Nwosu said. He clearly regretted waking up today.

"I have seen the beginning of a revolt before. I did not have enough data to pinpoint its inception at the time, but now I can compare."

"No one's revolting," Caz blurted. *Shit, shit, shit,* shit! Stupid-ass computer was going to get her and her team thrown in the brig. She'd never taken I.C.C. for a fearmonger, but *damn*.

With all of its *I know you better than you know yourselves* talk, it apparently wasn't picking up on the rising tension in the room. It wasn't giving them a way to fix the problem, it was planting the idea *of* a problem in their minds. Creating one where one didn't exist, only because it *thought* one might exist someday.

Shit.

"*No one* is revolting," Caz reiterated, a hairpin's worth of hysteria tightening her throat. "This is a scientific problem, not a social problem. We're all rational, level-headed adults here."

"You are implying revolts cannot be led by rational, level-headed adults. That is not the case," I.C.C. countered.

I was looking for an amicable separation of scouting parties, and you're talking like a group of us are going to turn full pirate and steal a ship.

"The rapidly fluctuating biometrics of everyone present is uncalled for," I.C.C. said. "You are jumping to conclusions without the full benefit of my analysis."

"We're human, we do that," Pavon said.

"Then allow me to set you at ease. The beginnings of a trend do not set that trend in stone. I did not mean to imply that violence is inevitable. On the contrary, it is very easily avoidable. The recent decision to halt the conversation regarding the Nataré maps was the trigger point. Once I'd identified the beginning of the morale shift, I was able to model many sets of likely events. I'd like to relate to you the series that currently has the highest probability, should the negative trends continue."

No one objected. No one looked particularly ready to be enlightened, either.

"As those in the Nataré department continue to have their research downgraded in importance, their resentment levels will inevitably rise. Their professional and familial relationships will strain. They will pass their resentment of the Web-focus on to their children, who will continue to feel affronted on their parents' behalf.

"When the Nataré department is officially dissolved—their labor deemed essential to the completion of the Web—the department will become a curiosity of the past. A point of intrigue. Intrigue mixed with resentment breeds conspiracy theory. Sows further distrust.

"Incorrect recollections of our time in the planemo's orbit will likely begin to circulate. Findings will be blown out of proportion. Certain individuals—whose lines I am fairly certain of, but will not burden you with—will believe information pertaining to *living* Nataré is being suppressed. When this begins, I will not be able to alter their viewpoints, because they are likely to believe I have been tampered with by those wishing to subvert the truth.

"Once they conclude I have been compromised, all information aboard will be called into question, be deemed 'fake' if it does not fit within the conspiracists' views. The scientific underpinnings of the mission will no longer keep it afloat. I cannot project far enough to pinpoint the likeliest form of initial full-degradation, but work on the Web will probably cease. Politically, the convoy will be in chaos. Resource upkeep will fail. Cloning may stop. I myself am a likely casualty.

"The population will continue to decrease as knowledge of the ships' inner workings disappears. I do not know how long the convoy will drift before the human population becomes zero, but the crew will inevitably perish."

As the Inter Convoy Computer concluded, many mouths opened, then shut again, as though denials and protests were on the tips of many tongues. But the words would not come—either because they could not be articulated, or because the board knew not to question I.C.C.'s projections.

Finally, though, a voice pierced the silence. "You're seriously suggesting we're going to become a post-apocalyptic ghost colony, because we wouldn't consider following a stupid map?" Straifer snapped.

"The map is not stupid," said I.C.C. "It is pivotal."

"No, it's not the map at all," said Donald Matheson, Head of Security. "It's the *resentment* that's the starting point. Why should *we* dismantle our convoy? Shouldn't *they*—" Caznal felt very small "—be asked to do better? To act like professionals and keep their personal feelings in check?"

"I would agree with you," I.C.C. said, "if I believed their resentment unreasonable. I don't. One should not be expected to live with an injustice for the sake of the status quo. The status quo is not always amicable. It is not always peaceful. Peace is not the absence of violence, but the constant application of justice. I'm trying to reveal to you where the seeds of inequality are planted, and how the social inadequacies it creates might evolve. There may be no violent danger for ten, twenty, or thirty years, but that is a blink of an eye to me. I have seen such dramatic shifts before, which led to discontinuation, which led to the Pit, which led to—"

"Yes, *thank you* for the history lesson."

Caznal's insides flopped over like a sea slug in a fish tank. She could taste slimy bile rising in the back of her mouth, found herself shaking her head in small, sharp bursts. This was not the portrait she'd wanted to paint. It was all wrong—so wrong.

Yet I.C.C. didn't seem to care. It took Joanna's outburst in stride. "If you allow the Nataré team to take the necessary ships and follow their own *Noumenon Infinitum* sub-mission, stability will return in the greater convoy. There may be new portions of the population that resent the breakage, but their bitterness is likely to lead to an erasure of the Nataré department's importance, rather than conspiracy theories and a distrust of computer-stored information."

"But what about the population critical mass required for

social stability?" asked Matheson. "It's one of the convoy's founding principles."

"I see no reason not to continue to clone the crew members as regularly as before. Those who would have been assigned to Nataré research can be returned to their original positions."

"Yeah, but what about the mini-convoy? They won't have a hundred thousand people. They'll be, what, a few hundred at most?"

"That depends."

"On what?" asked Ka'uhane.

"On how the mission is staffed. More than the Nataré team will be needed. They will require crew from ship-support departments for full functionality."

"So now, instead of forcing the Nataré group to stay, we're forcing other people to go?" the captain asked.

"I'm not suggesting we force anyone to do anything," said I.C.C. "I know it is a fairly foreign idea, but I *am* suggesting you give the crew a choice. Let people volunteer."

The dark amusement that flitted onto a few board members faces made Caz go cold.

"What if not enough volunteer?" Nwosu asked. "What then?"

"Then a new approach to avoiding social disaster will need to be formulated."

"Caznal?" Nwosu asked.

With a gulp, she quieted the continuous string of expletives chugging through her mind like an antiquated freight train. "What?" she asked, resigned.

"What would your team need? I mean, this new convoy? Don't try to pretend you aren't in on this. Clearly you have a plan."

Sighing, she stood. I.C.C. was supposed to butter them up, not bowl them over with disillusionments. "We would be taking three ships. Which would leave the main convoy with nine, as originally intended. *Zetta* and *Hvmnd* are essential to tracking the alien outposts, and largely useless in pursuit of the Web—"

"What about the autons?" asked Onuora, who didn't seem surprised at the suggestion her ship be festooned in this new endeavor. "They're currently housed on *Hvmnd*."

"The larger convoy could keep the majority of them. It's a negotiable point," Caz said. "But we would need a third ship. All of the original ships were retrofitted for full redundancy, but I think *Holwarda*—"

"No," Nwosu said. "Choose another. You're not taking the science ship. Or the medical ship. Or, let's see, *Morgan*, *Mira*, *Slicer* . . . I'm not sure there's any other ship we can afford to lose."

"What about the recreation ship?" Onuora suggested. "*Shambhala?* It could easily be transformed into a full-service version of *Mira*, *Holwarda*, you name it, as long as the crew was sufficiently small."

"Ah, yes," Captain Ahmad of *Shambhala*, replied sarcastically, "As we know, the best way to win the goodwill of the people is to deprive them of their recreation options."

"Many of the recreation options could be re-created elsewhere," Onuora countered. "And they'd be giving up wave pools, but keeping *Eden*. I'd be more worried at the smaller convoy's lack of a decent artificial sun."

"I'm worried about a lot this renegade branch would be missing," said Nwosu, his attention pinpointed at Caz. "There wouldn't be a standing board—you'd have to set up your own governing structure. You could support maybe a thousand crew members and would *need* a thousand crew members to properly run those three ships—which I haven't agreed to give you. You'd have no sun, no comfort animals, limited hydroponics. Could you even guarantee safe cloning procedures? And what about I.C.C.?"

"What about me?"

"The bulk of your servers are on *Mira*. We can't change that, nor properly duplicate you. They would be without an Inter Convoy Computer."

Everyone went quiet, pondering the complications of such a split.

"No one will volunteer," Nwosu said quietly, after a time. "I will let this move forward, secure in the knowledge that my convoy will come out of it intact." He fixed Caznal with a glare. "You have to bring me a list of one thousand volunteers. No less, or you don't go. This board won't even vote on the matter unless you can prove you have a willing crew."

Feeling like a child who'd finished throwing a tantrum—hot-eyed, thirsty, ready for a nap—she mumbled softly, "Thank you, sir."

To Caznal's surprise, they allowed her a formal vote. She thought she'd need to knock on doors, invade tables in the mess hall, plaster the hallways with pleas—retelling the story of her department's plight again and again and again.

But Nwosu respected her enough to give her the proper tools. I.C.C.'s proposal was transcribed into an official document, and Caznal added her ideas for the new convoy's social structure, political structure, and mission parameters. Downloading of the proposal was made mandatory convoy-wide.

And yet, Caz wasn't fooled. These grants weren't made to swing anything in her favor—they were silencing tactics. If the vote came back and she'd lost, she couldn't claim that not enough people knew about it, or that the information was inaccurate.

After all, if the board truly cared about considering the split fairly, they wouldn't have scheduled the vote for a month's time.

"It's all show," she grumbled, loading a vacuum-sealed specimen container onto a handcart. "I mean, who honestly expects someone to make a life-altering decision in one month?" Whatever the individual vote, it was a final-and-forever choice. This was bigger than a person from Earth choosing to move to another country, bigger than moving to a colony on Mars or the Moon.

"I know," Diego sympathized from the other side of the large box, "but *we* did."

"Not really," she countered as they let the container drop a few spare centimeters to the cart bed, snatching away their fingertips. "I've spent my whole life on this new convoy, I just didn't know it. And you, you've done it these past years working on the planemo specimens, and being married to me. But someone from food processing? They've devoted their careers to feeding the convoy better, to ensuring better nutrition, better digestion—they've never spent two seconds before now picturing a different path. Their work, their lives, would become something they never imagined if they volunteer. Instead of innovating, they'll have to go back to basics—making sure there's enough food to go around."

A shiny bead of sweat rolled down Diego's forehead as he squatted to pick up the next box. These needed to get from *Holwarda* over to *Slicer,* so the Nataré-focused engineers could compare their design to parts on the Nest. "I get it," he said with a huff. "It's asking the best chefs to cook over one of those—what are those fires they set for fun on *Eden*?"

"Campfires," she said, arms straining under the weight of the next carton.

"Like asking a chef to cook over a campfire for the rest of their life," he said.

"Right." Breath burst from her lungs as they set the second

tub on the first. “Damn, sometimes I really wish I could manipulate gravitons,” she laughed. “Construction for the Nataré must have been a snap.”

“Just because they didn’t have to use muscle power doesn’t mean it was easy,” he said.

“Fair point.” Exertion heat ran through her neck and shoulders, coloring her cheeks. She fanned herself lightly, trying not to let it turn into an angry heat. Why even bother letting the vote happen if they weren’t going to give people enough time to weigh the pros and cons?

Did they really think Caz was that much trouble? That it was better to put on this farce than to simply tell her no?

Or was it I.C.C. they feared? Did they believe the computer’s projections were right, and that making a show of appeasement, however small, would stanch the wave of resentment before it could crest and break?

“I still need to campaign for this, don’t I?” she asked.

“If you want people to take it seriously, yes.”

She looked at her hands, saw the veins pumping in her palms. “People are going to hate me, aren’t they?”

Diego was quiet for a moment, soaking up the sweat on his brow with the sleeve of his jumper. “Vega will come around,” he said softly.

Caz wasn’t so sure. Min-Seo had taken everything in stride, but Vega was furious when she found out about the vote. She’d screamed at Caz, shouted “How could you, how could you?” over and over. She vowed to stay, to convince everyone she knew—even Ivan—not to volunteer.

Vega wasn’t going to change her mind about staying, that much was clear. And, win or lose, one thousand votes or fifty, Vega would always see her mother as the person who tried to break up their family—their entire convoy family. Whether she would forgive her or not was a different matter—but their relationship would never be the same.

Caznal hated the idea of hurting her girls, of upending their world—of shattering their convictions in a regimented, thoroughly planned life. She'd introduced an element of chaos, of change, that she never could have prepared them for. The entire convoy had been set up to fight furiously against uncertainty, yet, in reality, people were rarely given straight lines of progression from birth to death. Most of humanity had to contend with shifting variables and changing circumstances. And those aboard Convoy Seven—no matter how they wished to deny it—were not immune.

She didn't like being the one to teach Vega that lesson, but she hoped, in the long run, the new perspective would serve her daughter well.

The vote was conducted quietly. At any time before the deadline, volunteers could inform I.C.C. from their quarters. When the deadline passed, the official tally would be made, and the board would meet again to discuss the results.

As the days blurred into each other, Caznal noticed dirtier and dirtier looks shot her way in the halls.

Two days before the final count, Nwosu invited Caz to have breakfast with him in his private mess. Caz thought it odd—suspicious even, but accepted with grace.

She dressed casually, foregoing a copper jumper for something more approachable, less . . . stigmatized. Tying her hair in a knot atop her head, she headed for the door.

"Please do not leave your quarters yet," I.C.C. said, startling her to a halt.

She pulled at her hair wrong and hissed, the hairband between her teeth. "Why?"

"I am taking care of a situation outside."

Small beeps and clatters chimed, as though in confirmation, in the hall beyond.

"What's going on?"

"I am resolving the situation. You may leave shortly."

She didn't like its evasive tone. "I.C.C., tell me what's outside."

A beat passed. "I'd prefer not to burden you with—"

Finishing with her hair, ignoring how messy it might look, she pressed the open button, expecting the door to slide back immediately. When it didn't, she took a cleansing breath. "You can't keep me in here against my will."

"I am not," it insisted. "I've temporarily disabled the switch so that the cleaning bots would not get caught in the mechanisms and jamb the door. My wish is not to create further hardships for you."

This close to the door, she picked up on the sharp smell of astringents emanating from the other side. There were more clatters and robotic chirps, accompanied by a few hollow clangs and one very wet *squelch*.

"There," I.C.C. said. "You may try the door again."

She pressed the button and dashed through as soon as the thick metal moved aside—she didn't want to get pinned because the stupid computer decided it hadn't removed the incriminating evidence accordingly.

Evidence of *what*, though, she was soon to find out.

Outside, various cleaning bots scurried back and forth, away from her feet like rats running for a loose bulkhead (*Mira* had a rat problem once. She remembered it as a hazy blur through a four-year-old's eyes). One carried a bucket sloshing over with cleaning solution, another sported scrub brushes at the ends of its four articulated arms.

The carpet beneath her shoes smooshed uncomfortably, and a dark stain fanned out before her quarters. She spun immediately, taking in the front of her home.

On the leftmost wall was a clear *T*, the letter hastily applied in what looked like machine oil. The second letter was cut in half by the gap that was her entryway—the automatic door had yet to slide back into place. She assumed I.C.C. was keeping it open, to shield her from reading the word smeared across it—one that, judging by the dripping, lowercase *R* on the right wall, did not say anything especially nice about her or her family.

"Close the door," she told the computer, surprised by how small she sounded.

"It is not necessary for you to read the rest—the intended negative effect has been achieved. I attempted to have it cleaned away before you left. I'm sorry I was unsuccessful."

"It says 'Traitor,' doesn't it?"

"Yes."

"I don't care," she said giving an overly dramatic shrug, trying to convince herself as much as I.C.C. "They can say whatever they want about me. No one's being forced to do anything."

"For the most part, you are correct," it said, clearly attempting to be supportive.

"What's that supposed to mean?"

"Well, to be factual, everyone on board is being forced to make a decision. Stay or go."

"That's awfully pedantic of you."

"In addition, while no one will be forced bodily to either stay or go, the decision of family members and colleagues will play a large part in everyone's sense of obligation. People may feel forced, even if—"

"Okay, thank you."

"Just because a decision is difficult or comes with troublesome consequences does not make it wrong," it attempted to reassure her.

With her fists firmly ensconced in her pockets, so that no one could see her digging her nails into her palms, Caz marched toward the mess hall. "I'm not sure I should thank you for hiding this from me, but thank you for trying to clean it up."

"You are welcome. And the authorities have been alerted. The perpetrator is already in the brig."

She sighed. Putting one foot in front of the other had suddenly become difficult. "That's not necessary. I mean, I get it. I do."

"Vandalism is not tolerated."

"I understand."

Many of the people she encountered through the halls and on the lifts either refused to meet her smile or downright gave her the evil eye. She wanted to rail at them, but couldn't. Still, it hurt. It wasn't like she possessed no convoy loyalty. She *was* devoted to the community, to their mission—she simply interpreted that loyalty differently. Why couldn't they see that, sometimes, sacrifices had to be made? Just because they'd been one force for hundreds of convoy years didn't mean it always had to be that way. Not if there was something better.

And she certainly wasn't trying to split up families. Nor was she trying to manipulate the board for her own gains. She simply—and logically—believed this was the right thing to do, for all of them. For science, for humanity.

The mess hall itself gave her the chilliest reception. Conversation at tables fell dead in her wake as people glared. They looked at her with such distaste, she was reminded of the rude sister from *Diamonds and Toads*, who was cursed to have snakes and frogs fall from her mouth whenever she spoke.

By the time Caz reached the captain's private mess, she was hopping from foot to foot with anxiety. All she needed was to get away from the eyes—all those judging, angry faces.

A swift knock and an even swifter "Come in" saw her inside.

When the door swished shut behind her she collapsed against it, bearing all her weight on her back.

"Caznal?" Nwosu asked, rising, concerned, to his feet.

"I don't know about you," Caz said, slumping into a seat at the table, "but this past month has not been fun for me."

"Oh?" He eyed his sunny-side up eggs, already broken into, the yolk pooling around his chorizo and hash.

"Don't pretend you don't know what's happening on your own ship. And don't pretend it doesn't please you."

He set his fork down. "That's a hell of a thing to say to me. It *doesn't*. You're right, I'm not ignorant. I.C.C. informed me of the abuse scrawled outside your door just this morning. I don't want anyone on my convoy to face such disdain, no matter how abhorrent their views."

"So, my caring about the Nataré is abhorrent now?"

He passed Caz an empty plate and gestured for her to self-serve from the awaiting platters. "If I can't feign ignorance, neither can you," he chided, sitting once more. "You know what I mean. You want to, essentially, divide a nation. Divide a *world*. We are a civilization unto ourselves and you would have at least a thousand of us secede. To *choose* to tell the rest of us we're *wrong*."

"But we're not saying you're wrong! Just that we can *both* be right." Quietly, she added, "And I didn't pick that number, you did."

"*You* picked it," he countered sharply. "I'm not sending you off to die because you're understaffed."

Caznal's heart fluttered for a moment. Did that mean—? With only two days left for volunteers to step up, did this mean they'd actually done it?

She hastily shoveled a pile of frijoles and chorizo past her teeth, to keep from asking after the vote.

"I asked you to breakfast, because we need to strategize."

"Oh?" she mumbled through her mouthful. The spices

were wonderful—sharp and full. Better than a shot of espresso to the senses.

"If the current numbers are anything to go by, you're not going to make it."

Caznal's hand twitched, the once carefully poised fork clattering to the tabletop, smearing ruddy sauce over the tablecloth. "What?" she asked, coughing down her last bite. "Which numbers?"

"As of now, you're about two hundred and fifty short. That's a lot to make up for in the next forty-eight hours. A whole fourth of your crew is missing."

"I'd expect most people to put in their 'yay' or 'nay' at the last minute," she said, pushing the plate aside and leaning in. "It's not unreasonable to expect they'll use every second they have to make sure it's the right decision."

"I doubt that many people are on the fence."

The captain continued to eat. Caz wasn't sure she could get another bite past her lips without vomiting.

"If you'd won," the captain said, starting what Caz anticipated to be a very long sales pitch, "I don't think there would be a problem, from a public relations standpoint. People would be angry initially, but as time goes on and we get you ready to move out, they'd come to respect the choice. But if you don't go—which is looking more and more likely by the minute—when we release the data, show that over seven hundred people voted to leave . . . well. That will be seven hundred more than I think most people expect. It will create suspicion among colleagues, friends, spouses. People will wonder who wanted to turn their back on us.

"So, I propose we rebrand this, as an exercise, to show that we are largely unified. It's not so unsettling, when looking at the bigger picture, to note that out of one hundred thousand people, less than one percent were unsatisfied. We focus on trying to improve that satisfaction rate—"

"But that's not why anyone would volunteer. It's because they want something more, not because—"

"You can't say that for certain," Nwosu snapped. "You can't say that someone out there didn't jump at the chance to leave because they're secretly unhappy."

Caz concentrated on breathing through her nose. "Isn't that what our oh-so-revered founders were supposed to screen for?" she asked. "Isn't that why we're clones in the first place? Our most satisfying paths were *supposed* to be chosen for us."

"And yet here you are, defying their wisdom."

"Here I am, making my own decisions. I guarantee we were never supposed to fill our positions blindly. We weren't supposed to be autons, just taking up space like a cog. We were supposed to think, and think critically, inquisitively. You all have twisted our existence into some sort of preordained thing. Like it's unchangeable, like it *should* be unchangeable. Well, it shouldn't. Civilizations evolve, they mature. Those that keep looking backward are the ones that collapse."

"We are looking forward. Our future is the Web."

She stood abruptly. She couldn't stay and have this discussion anymore, not when Nwosu was so certain Caznal's way was ridiculous. "Thank you," she said, "But our future isn't written yet."

When the volunteer numbers were announced, she accepted them with dignity. Eight hundred and forty-two people had offered to go. One hundred and fifty-eight too few.

She didn't ask for the names of the volunteers, knowing she'd be denied. That wouldn't fit into Nwosu's plan for unity.

She'd have to stick with the list of names she already had.

Popping into the Nataré headquarters on *Holwarda*—a small office space split through with freestanding desks—she clapped to get everyone's attention. "Come on," she said, "I need everyone to follow me. We're going on a little field trip."

“To the crater?” Ivan asked, closing out his gravitational map-analysis program.

“Nope. A little closer to home. Aziz, I need you to get me the locations of everyone else in the division, all right? Can you do it en route?”

Aziz shared wide-eyed looks with his colleagues. None of them had a clue what was happening. “Uh, yes, sir?”

“Good. Leave the Inter Convoy Computer out of it, okay? Let’s go.”

Some of the team tucked ‘flex-sheets under their arms, or put a stylus between their teeth, following her out into the main halls without question. They fell into loose ranks, shuffling more than marching, but keeping close to her lead.

“We’re headed to *Hvmnd*,” she announced, not looking over her shoulder, but filling her diaphragm and projecting far. “We did not get a fair vote. There are convoy crew who were not heard. They did not get to participate, and they deserve that chance. Our march on *Hvmnd* is a protest, a demand that these people be given a choice.”

She could hear shoes stumbling behind her, faltering on the carpet and falling back.

“No one is obligated to join me,” she said. “But if you volunteered—if you believe the Nataré need to be studied, that our maps need to be followed, please keep marching.”

The footsteps picked up again. She didn’t turn to see if the ranks had thinned. It didn’t matter if they had. This was about choice after all—not about what she felt was right or wrong, but about everyone getting a fair shake, leaving no one unheard.

She wasn’t sure she should feel as emboldened as she did, as noble in her day’s endeavor. What if Captain Onuora turned her away? What if this was one more exercise in futility?

Then, at least she’d tried.

“Aziz?”

"Yes?" he called from somewhere near the back of the pack.

"Get in contact with the others yet?"

"I've sent a message to most of them—let them know we were on the move. Should I tell them to make for *Hvmnd*?"

"Please."

In the bay, the shuttle pilots were unprepared for the group that swarmed them. Diego was there with a handful of his fellow chemists. A few dozen others from various departments—those who'd told Caznal of their support—had shown up as well.

All in all, their force was a hundred bodies strong.

There were marches on Earth, Caznal thought, *that would dwarf the entire convoy's population.*

Perhaps that should have given her pause. If she could only rile a metaphorical handful to step up, to risk the unknown at a chance for scientific discovery, for new adventure, then was it so noble after all?

Was it wrong to know how you fit into the grand scheme of things?

No, of course the majority wasn't wrong. *No one* was wrong here, that was the point. That was why she had I.C.C.'s backing—no matter its motives or particular worries.

Her people lined up at the shuttles. A few pilots began loading immediately, unsure why so many unscheduled people needed to travel at once, but seeing no reason not to strap them in. Others slid between the would-be passengers and their crafts, as though defending the shuttle from an onslaught.

"Look, man," one pilot said, a warning hand on Aziz's chest. "I'm supposed to be over on *Hippocrates* in fifteen. I'm not a free fare."

"Yeah," said a man in a seafoam green jumpsuit. "Some of us need to start our shifts. You can't barge in here and take whichever one you want. Swing is starting, and this place is going to be flooded with scheduled traffic."

Lights flashed in the bay—not the spinning warning lights for decompression, thank the stars, but a simple flickering of the overhead lamps. Someone in the control booth was trying to get their attention.

"Whoa, whoa." The bay's chief shouted over the comms system, "Hey, hey! Nataré, what are you doing? I need you all to sign in, you can't just hop on—"

"A month's vice rations to all the pilots who take us right now!" Diego shouted.

The pilot bound for *Hippocrates* moved aside. The seafoam clad man glared at her. "Hey," she said with a shrug, "Macaroons don't grow on trees."

The trip over was typical of one of Caznal's interconvoy jaunts to *Hvmnd.* Except, this time she wasn't alone. She was surrounded by the impassioned, by vibrant smiles. From the number of wandering eyes and twitchy ankles, it was clear some of the volunteers still didn't fully know what they were doing, or how this was supposed to gain them a convoy. Perhaps they thought it would simply send a message, that they were—Caznal shuddered internally, recalling Nwosu's statement—*unsatisfied* with the vote's outcome. But that wasn't her intent. She meant what she said: there were those who hadn't been allowed to vote. And that wasn't right.

Outside *Hvmnd*'s docking bay, Captain Onuora and several caretakers were there to receive them. Clearly *Mira*'s bay chief had alerted her to the onslaught. Thoughtful, considering her ship didn't see this much traffic in a month, let alone an hour. The shuttles couldn't even all land at once, given the constrictions of the small docking area.

But now, with the addition of those who'd been on other ships during Caznal's initial march, their party was one-fifty. Still meager, but wholly impassioned.

"Caznal," Onuora said evenly as the crowd burgeoned.

Four shuttles were being received at a time, then the passengers had to shuffle past the airlock to allow the next aboard.

People continued to pour in as Caz worked her way to the captain's side. "Yes?"

The claws still held the captain's chair, suspending it a few extra feet off the ground to give her a better view of the invasion. "Might I ask what the *hell* you are doing?"

"How do you know it's my doing?" Planting her hands on her hips, she looked up into her friend's face.

Onuora side-eyed her, frowning. "Because it's always your doing."

"I want to ask the caretakers for a favor."

"I'm in charge of *Hvmnd*—you should be asking me."

A bit of wind went out of Caznal's proverbial sails. "Yes, of course, you're right. And I respect your authority, your opinion. If you tell us to go, we'll go. But please, give me a chance to make my case. You know as well as I do that . . ." She faltered. The Captain's gaze was penetrating, intimidating. Perhaps this hasty march had been a bad idea.

"Go on," Onuora said impatiently.

"That, in a way, there have been two convoys since Relaunch. There are the crew members, and then there are the caretakers. Our agendas have never been the same."

"My crew doesn't have an agenda. Not unless taking care of the dreamers counts as an agenda."

"It does. And I want you to ask them to wake the servers."

The excited chatter of the crowd died around her, like she'd dropped a bomb and the fallout was wafting out in concentric circles.

No one had asked who she'd meant, who hadn't had a chance to vote. And apparently no one had guessed. Then again, how could they? Only someone who bucked convoy etiquette regularly, who visited the retired on "the grave ship," could have conceived of such a plan.

Because the dead don't vote.

"For what purpose?" Onuora asked evenly.

"I'm still looking for volunteers to crew a convoy," Caz said. "Everyone was supposed to get a chance to volunteer. Everyone. The caretakers did. You did."

"Yes, and *you* don't know how we voted."

The two women locked stares. The captain was offering Caz a challenge of some kind, daring her to . . . to what? "Meaning even if we reached a thousand, you wouldn't honor the vote if the caretakers voted to stay?"

"That's exactly what it means. You volunteered my ship without asking, Caz. Yes, it would be necessary to your mission, but you didn't think about the fact that I either had to volunteer or lose my ship. And you know I would never give her up. Would never ask any of my crew to give her up."

Caznal's cheeks grew hot. She should have discussed this with Onuora, should have included her in the plan. "I'm sorry," Caz said softly, as though it were only the captain and herself in the room. She'd just assumed—taken Onuora's friendship for granted. She should have considered . . . When I.C.C. said that some people felt forced . . .

"You should be, and I appreciate the apology. But you should also be thanking me. Since I *did* volunteer to leave."

The captain smirked, and Caz let out a shaky breath of relief. "I did it because I'm tired of my ship being an afterthought. My people are not useless. We would be shut down—perhaps even abandoned—were it not for the fact that we carry the stupid autons. The board would be just as happy to cease cloning the caretakers as to let them go. They do not see our worth, our vibrancy, our dedication that equals theirs.

"The fact that you're here, that you are all here—" her voice rose "—tells me you believe otherwise. That we can make a difference. Our part in the mission would not be questioned if we formed a new convoy. My ship, with its little crew, unanimously volunteered. That is, except for the dreaming retirees."

"May we wake them?" Caz asked hopefully.

"As you said, it's really up to the caretakers," Onuora answered with a wink. She pressed a button on her chair and the claws carried her up and away, through the maze of corrugated landings, to the control booth. "Come along, Caznal," she said over the comms system. "And to your horde, might I suggest seeking out a familiar dreamer? If the caretakers consent, I assume the servers will be gladdened to see a friendly face upon waking."

The caretakers were of two minds about it. Many were reluctant, for the same reasons the board had declared the servers dead; to split your time between two worlds was difficult for those not raised in duality. To be awoken only to dream again would be disruptive, maybe even dangerous.

Some people were so far gone in their haze that they didn't know they *were* dreaming. They were in a different reality, one that lacked the concreteness of the waking world. It could be a shock to their system to realize their experiences were all in their mind. Lucidity could shatter their reality, and in turn shatter their psyches.

In the end, though, the need to give the sleepers a choice won out. The caretakers, only seventy-five adults in all, fanned out, taking various levels. The caretaker children joined the captain in the control room. They were a slight group—many of the youngsters were still on *Aesop* for their studies. But they looked proud, excited—they'd never seen so many of the crew take an interest in their ship before.

The caretakers encouraged the crowd to span the levels as well, placing themselves near as many dreamers as possible. Of the three hundred and twelve that slept, not all of them had relatives or friends among the Nataré department. But they would still need grounding, reassurance, and compassion.

Everyone shivered as the caretakers plugged in, one by one descending out of the present and into a nebulous state of calculation and imagination. The air seemed to shift from cold to frigid as they waited, all in silence, for the servers to decide if they wanted to see the living again.

What if they don't care? Caz thought. *They are in a new world, a new phase. What if they are happy as they are and do not wish to be awoken at all, let alone wish to become part of a new crew where their constant dreaming would be no more?*

The small convoy would still need servers—that was the whole point, they couldn't run *Zetta*'s graviton cycler without the computing power—but they would also need all hands on deck. Server sleep would be sporadic. A temporary escape instead of a whole new reality.

Caznal took her place next to Dr. Baraka. Diego stood on the other side of Jin-Yoon. They shared a look, marred with worry but full of hope.

She half expected the board to come barging in before the caretakers could do their work. Surely they'd been alerted by now—either by I.C.C. or *Mira*'s bay chief. There were very few restricted areas in the convoy, and those were only due to safety. And while crew members could go where they liked when they liked, provided they weren't shirking their duties, a migration of an entire department in protest had never happened before. What would Nwosu think? That Caz was dangerous after all? That she *was* hijacking a ship?

A massive gasp three walkways up made her jump, scaring away her dread. Instinctually, she grabbed Dr. Baraka's hand and squeezed it tight.

It was the first awakening. At least one server had chosen to come back to them, if only for a little while.

Immediately, a symphony of gasps and small shouts reverberated throughout. Each sound and intake of breath was a sign of shock to the system—like jumping into a cold wave pool. They were here—once retired, good as dead—returned to the land of the living.

A caretaker moved to connect to Dr. Baraka's ports.

In anticipation, Caz looked into her mentor's face. His cheeks were full, his skin soft and well moisturized. His muscles hadn't atrophied, his heart pumped strong. All evidence of the caretaker's investment in their job, in the lives of these supposed unliving.

After a few tense moments, in which Caznal's breath would not come, Dr. Baraka opened his eyes. They flew wide in near panic, his back bowing away from the chair, spine stretched. The hand in hers tore away, flailing, clutching through the air in the caretaker's direction.

The caretaker did not flinch away. She took the hand, held it to her chest, and though she did not speak with her mouth, Caz could tell she was reassuring him mind-to-mind.

Jin-Yoon woke on Caznal's other side, and Diego began cooing nonsense in an attempt to ease the transition.

Where, in the instant before, Caznal had been filled with anticipation, she now shied away. She'd wanted Dr. Baraka back, and now that he was here, it felt unreal. Like she'd wished for it too hard.

It felt selfish. She knew it was. She knew the only reason she'd connected her missing votes to the servers was because her mentor was among them. All at once, guilt crashed through her . . .

But then he rolled onto his side, toward her. His eyes sparked with recognition, even as his chest heaved and a chilled sweat broke out across his temples. He found being awake straining, difficult. But the joy in his expression was not muted.

His mouth opened, lips fumbling around a word. His tongue wriggled like a worm he couldn't control, and he snapped it behind his teeth, clearly embarrassed.

He shouldn't have been. Years had passed since that part

of his body had been anything but vestigial. "It's okay," she said. "Yeah, I know. It's me."

He coughed then, and flopped onto his back once more, wincing as the IVs he couldn't feel while sleeping suddenly stung his conscious nerves.

She didn't want his eyes to leave her. Every time he blinked, she feared they were shut again for good. But as the caretaker dribbled water from the seat's tubing onto his lips, his fingers reached out for Caznal.

Once more, she took his hand in hers, and she marveled at how his warm palm—*finally*—squeezed back.

The vote from the servers had consisted of two hundred and eighty-one conditionless volunteers. The rest—one hundred and six, had volunteered on *one* condition: that they not be reawakened again.

At first, the board rejected Caznal's trick play as unlawful. She couldn't count the dead as volunteers. But they weren't dead. I.C.C. noted that the dead were not assigned rations, which was not true of the servers. Though all retirees were treated the same in many aspects, this one difference was undeniable.

They tried to argue the deadline—but I.C.C. said the deadline could not be imposed on those who were not given the information. Logically speaking, the servers should have been given an entire month before formally entering their votes, but such time was not necessary.

Then the board tried to argue age.

"These server volunteers are all over sixty-five," said *Hippocrates*'s captain. "They will die soon. They would die soon with my entire ship at their disposal."

Even those most staunchly opposed to convoy splitting gasped at his brazen disregard for the elderly.

Caznal played it evenly. "The only reason we retire people

is because of set resources and scheduling. Not because they will, quote, 'die soon.' Caznal the First lived to be ninety-seven. She worked until her dying breath. Not because she was forced to but because it was important to her. She wanted to. The rations allotted to this smaller convoy will easily cover these crew members, as they were already assumed to be part of it. I am, in fact, taking fewer "live" bodies in all. How those lives are managed will be up to us."

"The rest of the crew won't stand for this," Nwosu cried. "Mark my words, if there is rioting you will be held personally responsible."

"Fine," Caz said. "Which is why the sooner you can send us on our way, the better." She slid a file of 'flex-sheets across the long table. "Here is my proposal for how to revamp *Shambhala* into a fully functioning home ship for Convoy Seven-Point-Five."

There was resentment, distrust, anger . . . but no rioting. The nearer the separation drew, the more a general sense of *good riddance* swamped through the bitterest of the crew.

Shambhala's conversion did concern Caznal. Would those in charge of installing the filters on the wave pools—several of which were to now be used as drinking reserves—do the job properly? Would fire safety be looked after in the theater rooms that were now crew quarters? Would the welding on the pipes be shoddy, would the biodomes—which would support food plants and a handful of small support animals—be appropriately regulated?

All of the work was being done by nonvolunteers. She didn't want to question anyone's motives, or accuse them of a job not properly done, but it was hard to interpret the occasional glare or thumbed nose as anything other than hostile.

Surely they wouldn't be that invested in the smaller convoy's failure? They were hurt, bitter, but not malicious.

Still, she and Nwosu made several passes as the job was done, verifying the new construction was sound.

Strange noises now rang out in *Shambhala*'s communal spaces. Every bang and clatter and high-pitched whirr of a saw sounded like someone trying to make their way in through the hull of the ship. Like little gremlins attempting to find the craft's weak points so they could loosen the bolts and pop the hatches.

"Does everything, thus far, meet with your approval?" Nwosu asked.

Several members of the communications team—the press—and a handful of actuaries trailed them as they moved from point to point. Most of the gyms had been converted either into lab space or hospital space. Parts of "dessert row" were now occupied by clean rooms dedicated to cloning.

They'd considered natural birth instead. Why wouldn't they? This was a new mission, why shouldn't it be composed of new people?

But their light medical staff had nixed the idea. They were generations removed from overseeing live births. It was too dangerous, they said—to the babies, the potential mothers, and the crew. Live births couldn't be guaranteed. What if they had too many or too few? Their convoy would have to perform an even more delicate resource-balancing act than its predecessor.

So, cloning would continue. And only the volunteers' genetic code would be available. They wanted to leave Convoy Seven? Fine. That included leaving its genetic diversity behind. If they found out in ten years that it would be nice to have a Jamal Kaeden or a Margarita Pavon, too bad.

This was also a psychological consideration—it kept people from putting in for clones of their lost loved ones.

Caznal couldn't raise another Min-Seo Park or Vega Hansen.

She wouldn't want to, even if she could.

Both of her daughters had decided to stay, and she was proud of her girls, their loyalty to *Noumenon Infinitum*.

Vega had slowly begun to come back to her and Diego. Even if she still hurt, still felt like she was being abandoned, she knew that her stubbornness would only cause her more pain in the long run. Her parents had to do what they had to do, just as she did.

As the news-slash-inspection party mounted the sweeping staircase that had once alighted in a ballroom—now an entire school, split through with partitions—Caz chanced a glance over her shoulder.

Vega was there, her nose close to her forearm implant, typing away notes in her Enigma Machine shorthand.

She stood to the back. Caz assumed she didn't want to look too emotionally invested in the proceedings. They still had trouble making conversation, but at least she came to family dinners.

"Does it meet with your approval?" Nwosu asked again, this time of a newly erected computer-access bank. Not having access to I.C.C. was going to be the biggest hardship, Caz was certain. Relying largely on the once-retired servers and the caretakers was going to put a strain on their information retrieval and storage, since those individuals would not act as computers 24/7.

"Looks good," she said, calling up some Nataré data with the flick of her wrist.

"It amuses me that you were the one to take point on this project," Nwosu whispered to her as they rounded a corner. Many feet shuffled behind them.

"Oh?" she asked, just as softly.

"Your function on Convoy Seven-Point-Five will be much like mine. Admiral, but only in act, not title."

“I’m not an admiral,” she scoffed. “It’s not my—”

“Oh, no? You command a small fleet, and you were never even intended for command. I know no other appropriate term. Here, we use *captain,* so as not to give too much weight to my position over the other captains. But it still falls on me to make major fleet decisions, to make sure the ships are synchronized during dives, that the convoy is functioning as one. It will be the same for you.”

She stopped short, forcing an actuary to spin away at the last second or run into her spine. The captain strode onward.

“And to think all you wanted was to quietly study your aliens. Devote your life to their uncovering. And now you’re in charge of a fleet.”

Regaining her wits, she caught up to Nwosu, tried to ignore the eyes boring into the back of her neck and shoulders. “And why does this amuse you?”

“Because it’s not what you wanted. This is not what you wanted.”

“I—”

“I’m not trying to be cruel, Caznal. It’s the irony that struck me. You didn’t want your research obstructed, and from now on you’ll barely have time to look at a summary sheet.”

Let him laugh, she thought. *In five hundred years, when we return to the Web and have all of the information needed to finish the Web, my decedents will laugh in turn.*

“Do you have a name for your mission, yet?” asked one of the reporters. “Convoy Seven-Point-Five is nice, but, you know, *Noumenon* has a special ring to it, so . . . ?”

“*Noumenon Ultra,*” she said confidently.

“And do you have an official mission statement?”

She halted, turned. It was fitting, that she should put this on the public record here, in Art Alley. It was a wide arched hall, flanked by studios. This area they’d left untouched. Her people would still need to make art—maybe now more than ever.

Sprawled across the walls were hundreds of small paintings. Every year, five artists were asked to leave their permanent mark on the ship. It was a great honor for a convoy member, to be immortalized in such a way.

"*Noumenon Ultra* will follow all available leads to Nataré locations. The mission's express purpose is to learn as much as possible about these aliens, ascertain whether or not they are extinct—make first contact if they are alive—and to verify their methods of construction in relation to the Web.

"We hope to reunite with Convoy Seven in five to seven centuries," she added. "But we will not seek the Web until our mission is complete. There is no firm timeline."

"So," the reporter said carefully, "Convoy Seven and Seven-Point-Five may be permanently separated?"

A lie would not do. But neither would the frank truth. Families separated by the split would never see each other again, but there was a sort of comfort in knowing that their future clones might once again walk the same halls and share the same goals.

What could she say? What would sound reassuring, yet not decisive and concrete?

"It is our destiny to reunite," she said, surprised as anyone that she would let the *D* word escape her lips. "And though there are many obstacles in our way, we will all fight for that destiny."

DECEMBER 22, 125 RELAUNCH

5282 CE

As many times as she'd envisioned it, it felt to Caz like the time to leave would never come. *Should* never come. She'd put so much energy into the creation of the smaller convoy, that it seemed absurd it should have a real life beyond its inception.

But it did. And that life began today.

The quarters she'd shared with Diego these twenty-seven years was a blank canvas once more. The evidence of their life there had been expunged, and now the rooms lay waiting for their new occupants. A new family would call those walls home.

As the two of them walked hand in hand toward *Mira*'s shuttle bay, Caz took in the halls she'd passed through every day since childhood with a wonderment she'd never felt before. She'd taken it all for granted—the halls, the ships, living in space away from a home planet she would never visit. She'd miss the structure and formality, even though she'd struggled against it. She'd miss the paintings in the communal spaces, the music played on ship-tooled instruments. She'd miss her lab. And family dinners.

She promised herself she would never take anything for granted again. It could all change so quickly, purpose and time and the thrust of history shifted like sand on her favorite now-defunct faux beach.

Ivan, Vega, Min-Seo and her wives met them at their scheduled shuttle.

Caz asked her girls—women, they were all women now—to line up, so she could take them in one last time. She held Min-Seo's face in both hands, trying to burn her round features and dark hair into her mind's eye forever. She had photographs, of course. She could draw up archived pictures at any time. But she wanted to remember the warmth of her, the love shifting between them. This would be the last time she could peer into her daughter's face and know her daughter was peering back.

She and Diego shared a group hug with Hiro and Kexin, bidding the two women take good care of Min-Seo.

“It’s going to be the other way around,” Kexin said playfully.

When Caznal broke away from her daughters-in-law, she meant to reach for Vega immediately, but pulled her hand back.

Vega and Diego were locked in a tight embrace, father and daughter not ready to let go yet. “Miss you forever,” he said against her hair.

And then, finally, it was Caznal’s turn to say goodbye to her youngest. She pulled her in for a full-body hug, desperate to let go of the tension that had spoiled the air between them these past years. All she needed was for Vega to understand that she’d never meant to hurt her.

“I love you, Mama,” Vega said sounding so much like the five-year-old that used to hang on her mother’s hip so long ago.

“Love you too, baby.”

Her tears had been falling for minutes now, though Caz had tried to ignore them. She brushed her eyelashes against Vega’s shoulder before giving her up into Diego’s arms once more.

“I made you guys something,” Vega said after a minute. She held out a small paper-wrapped bundle. “Remember that pottery class I was taking?” She sniffed wetly. “Anyway, I made you these. You guys have one part, and Min-Seo and I have the other, and when . . .” Her lip trembled, but she took a deep breath and continued. “You pass them down to your clones, see? And Min-Seo and I pass ours down, and when the convoys come back together, it’s . . . it’s a full set again. Don’t open it yet, you’ll—you’ll see what I mean after the convoys split.”

After a litany of repeated “goodbye’s” and “we love you’s,” Caznal and Diego boarded their shuttle.

The docking bay was cleared for decompression, and as Caz watched her girls disappear through the airlock doors, she had to fight with everything she had not to throw herself against the shuttle door and forsake her new mission forever.

The mood on *Shambhala* was reverent. Everyone moved with a quiet intensity, sharing looks that were more sympathetic and reassuring than excited. One or two manically minded crew members whooped and hollered as they found their new quarters, but for the most part people seemed introspective.

Diego went to settle into their new living space, while Caz strode slowly through the halls, watching the volunteers as a naturalist might watch squirrels or bees. She admired their work, their business, and tried not to feel saddened for the loss of community that would soon follow.

They'd have a lot of work ahead of them—not so much in terms of the mechanics of the ships or even the politics of their social structure, but in building a togetherness. There was comradery in the choice they'd collectively made, but no one would be able to forget all the people, the vibrancy, the tenacity, the unity of their original home.

And they shouldn't. They needed to keep it fore in their minds. This mission was for them, after all, as much as that idea might have been rejected. *Noumenon Ultra* would try to help its twin, to bolster its efforts with discoveries *Noumenon Infinitum* could not make.

They needed to be sure Convoy Seven remained real to them, and vice versa. That the sibling notion did not fall out of use.

"I.C.C.?" she said. This would be the last time she spoke with the AI. As soon as they dove, the connection would be severed. "You keep everyone in *Infinitum* honest for me, okay? Make sure they don't forget us, please. Make sure we don't become just another myth to them."

"I will do my best," it said. "I will miss you. All of you. And I will miss Shambhala—it has been a part of me for a long time."

“One day the ship will come back to you.”

“But you, Caznal the Fourth, I shall never see again.”

“Thank you, I.C.C., for everything.”

A blast of cold air from a duct had Caz jumping back suddenly. It was someone on the environmentals panel just getting a renewed feel for things, she was sure. The air died down as quickly as it had roared up, leaving the hearty laugh of Dr. Baraka in its wake.

He stood near the star-windows, watching her approach. His mannerisms were just as she remembered, warmed now to use again. The way he stood, with his back slightly bent, the paunch of his belly thrust forward, one hand dithering near his face as though twisting a nonexistent mustache was all familiar. They brought back fond memories of her apprenticeship.

He crooked a finger at her, and she jogged to his side, glaring over her shoulder at the offending air duct.

“So,” he said, a chuckle still living under the fluctuation of his tenor. “That’s our planemo?”

“Yep,” she said, admiring the rock for the last time. She hadn’t been to the surface in years—not since before I.C.C.’s proposal to split Convoy Seven. A dull twinge of regret coiled through her chest, but she pushed it away. There were so many places she would never set foot again.

“I’m glad I saw it,” he said.

He had never gone down. This was his first, and last, encounter with the Nataré’s mysterious first X.

“Will I live to see our next rendezvous point?” he asked. The inherent wistfulness made the question redundant, but Caz longed to reassure him. She herself would be an old woman when they arrived. Dr. Baraka might make it, or he might not.

Their retirement system would be different from Convoy

Seven's. No more sending people off into the spiritual unknown at a scheduled date and time. End of life would mean dreaming for everyone. Even as one's mind or body failed, the caretakers would see them off without pain, without worry. Without, even, knowing they were dying.

Dr. Baraka leaned his forehead against the window then, and a flash of memory struck her. It was Dr. Baraka who she'd first seen press against the glass like that, letting himself go cross-eyed as the unreal patterns projected by the window swelled and swirled. She'd learned it from him, and passed it on to Min-Seo.

She hoped Convoy Seven would see fit to install a new window like this somewhere on the remaining ships. That way Min-Seo might teach the silly ritual to her children, and they theirs.

Shambhala rumbled, and the planemo started to recede. Caz set herself next to Dr. Baraka, mirroring him as the Convoy Seven ships passed by.

They needed to be a safe distance away from the other convoy before they dove.

Someone cleared their throat behind Caz, and she whirled. Perhaps the crew would think it immature of her, pressing her face to the glass like an eager child beholding a fish tank for the first time. If the crew was to take her seriously, perhaps she shouldn't indulge in such things.

"Room in this party for one more?" Diego asked.

Dr. Baraka swiftly appraised Diego, giving him a sporting once-over. Fond nostalgia flitted across his cheeks, crinkling his eyes, before he gestured to the other side of Caznal. "Pull up a chair," he joked.

Dr. Baraka returned his forehead to the glass, followed by Diego. Caz glanced at both of them, emotion welling in her chest, and undefined gratefulness swirling around her heart.

"You want to see what Vega left us?" Diego asked, flicking his gaze at her, smiling a one-sided smile. "These," he said, reaching into his uniform pocket.

He presented to her, on the flat of his brown palm, a miniature version of *Mira*. Its details were rough, the baked clay gritty. But little windows had been carefully indented into its surface, likely with the head of a pin, and the bridge and docking areas were easily distinguishable.

As distinguishable as the miniature's maker. Vega had crafted it with love. Her devotion beating out her skill for importance.

"It's a whole set of nine. I laid them out on a bookshelf in our quarters." He pocketed mini-*Mira* before adding, "I'm guessing she and Min-Seo have three."

"And in the future, hopefully they will make twelve again," she said, finally joining them in their strange posture. The glass was either especially cool, or her cheeks and forehead especially hot.

The convoy ships continued to fall away—*Mira* looking more and more like the version in Diego's pocket by the moment.

Now, we, too, will be part of their mythic pantheon, she realized. *They will remember us as some moralistic story. Whether good or bad, we will likely fall into legend, no matter how hard I.C.C. tries. How long will that take? When will we pass from memory into myth?*

But now was not the time to dwell on how they'd be remembered. Today was about new beginnings.

With her old master on one side, and her husband on the other, Caznal looked toward the future. It was full of hope, discovery, and most importantly, the unknown.

She reached out for both of their hands as the light in the hall turned purple.

CHAPTER THREE

CONVOY TWELVE

STONE: WHATEVER SOULS ARE MADE OF

THE DAY OF THE ACCIDENT

JULY 6, 2127 CE

Stone tried to keep his temper on the level, under control, but it was as futile as trying to pilot this *goddamned infernal machine*. Tension radiated off the officers closest to him, amplifying his own stiffness. The tendons in his jaw hurt from clenching, and his brown knuckles were turning sickly pale around the joystick.

Pod thirty-three should have been *bizcocho e' Titi:* easy. What was it doing? Why in the hell was this experiment going so wrong?

The telemetry readouts on his dash flickered and spun, the holographic overlays on the dials fluctuating wildly. The gyroscopes weren't working at all—their monitors had all flatlined. The Y-axis readings were the only displays that didn't look like they'd been possessed.

The pod wasn't dipping above or below the artificial horizon, but it sure as hell wasn't maintaining its intended trajectory.

He flicked the joystick to the right, willing the thrusters to properly engage.

"Come on, come on," Stone gnashed under his breath.

Stone clenched his teeth, keeping his head down. His hair fell into his eyes and he batted it away with a huff.

I can do this. Come on you stupid machine, come on.

Someone said something about an SD bubble, and engaged-drive data. Stone focused on what he could control. He powered down the thrusters, rebooted steering, and programmed in a new flight path. But the damned pod was still reeling toward the convoy.

The floor pitched as *Breath* lumbered to life. Captain Tan was trying to move the ships out of the way of the oncoming pod.

In the same moment, the stick went slack in Stone's hands, like the system had shut off—

Or disappeared.

He looked up. The distant pod flashed in electric reds and golds, its body completely obscured by the phenomena.

Then it was gone.

Thank god. If the thing had wormed its way into a subdimension, they were fine. Safe. Nothing to worry—

Another flash, more pink-and-orange this time. The pod was back, and it . . .

Anda pa'l sirete.

"Doctor Kapoor!" He leapt to his feet and pointed out the bay windows. The pod was back and kilometers closer than before.

When he saw her attention snap in its direction, he fell back into his seat, desperately flicking the engines on and off again. He had to get them to engage. The convoy ships moved too slowly, like lumbering beasts. If he couldn't regain control of the pod, they were going to collide.

"It's getting closer!" someone shouted.

Stone glanced up for a blink's time, only to see the pod jump and cover half the remaining distance in the wink of an eye. Blood roared in his ears as he tried everything he could think of, everything.

The light in the room turned purple, and he was vaguely aware of Captain Tan's voice over the intercom.

"Dive!"

The pod jumped once more, appearing right outside the deck's window, like the tip of a fatal iceberg jutting out of the water.

The sizzling sound of blood in Stone's ears was overpowered by a high-pitched screeching that felt like it sliced him between the eyes. His head pounded, felt simultaneously squeezed and shattered.

On the tail of the screech came a deep bass reverberation that made his insides cramp. He doubled over at his station, felt like he was falling, only to realize . . .

I'm flying?

No. It's the gravity, the grav—

He flailed, looking for something to grab onto, to keep him upright, to weigh him down. His eyes found Dr. Kapoor in the fray, equally floundering. But her gaze was fixed on the collision point, and he turned to look, too.

White sparks leaked through the window—so white, so pure, they threw rainbow reflections across the ceiling and floor. Following the sparks, as though dragged by them, was a haze of cosmic distortion.

She was so close to it—closer than anyone else in the room. He feared it might reach her, might tear her apart—

Outside, the dark star-pocked tableau shifted as they phased, went black as they dove into one of the travel subdimensions.

Just as they crossed over, the sparking field engulfed Kapoor, twisting around her, encasing, enfolding—not just connecting with her or passing over her, but warping *around* her.

She was too bright to look at, the pinky-tangerine glow too

harsh. He tried to yell for her, but the panic turned his lungs to ice, froze the scream in his chest.

Stone braced for the field to take him, too. It seemed like forever, waiting for it to cover a distance it really only took nanoseconds to traverse.

But there was no pain, as he'd been expecting. No sizzle of skin turning to plasma on his bones, no instant madness or popped eyeballs or insides becoming outsides.

Just a light tingle. Its edge came close enough to raise the hair on his arms, but never made contact.

Dr. Kapoor dimmed, and he looked at her once more. She hovered for a moment, seeming still—asleep, maybe—and then . . .

Then she vanished.

The bright orange field recoiled. Not dissipated, *retreated.* As though sucked back to whence it came.

The purple light flicked back to normal, only to be reengaged seconds later. They were reemerging, surfacing out of the SD and into regular space.

Stone felt lightheaded. He couldn't have seen what it looked like, what he—

He was having a hard time forming coherent thoughts.

Shifting instantly from one-g to no-g's was messing with his mind, and that field—he wanted to puke, but his stomach disagreed.

Stars flickered to life beyond the window, like little twinkle lights being turned on one by one.

They were back.

And so was the gravity. As it reengaged, everyone fell to the floor. Stone narrowly avoided smacking the underside of his chin on his desk, catching the side of his cheek instead.

Captain Tan was saying something over the comms again. But Stone's brain was awash with a buzzing.

One thought wriggled its way to the forefront of his mind as he looked toward the command chair:

Is Dr. Kapoor okay?

He had no memory of falling asleep—blacking out—but waking up was like being ripped out of cold water and taking a long-awaited breath. His temples throbbed, pain ran a jagged path across the seams of his skull, and his face burned where it had slammed into the desk. Apparently, he'd hit it harder than he'd first thought.

The convoy's emergency PSA was playing on a loop—a din of Tan's voice telling them to report to their emergency positions and to remain calm. Sparks flew from a severed snatch of wires—it looked like a chair had collided with an overhead light during zero-g. The small blips of fire winked in and out, sometimes sharp, occasionally blurry.

He had a concussion, obviously. But others were faring far worse.

Off to his right, a handful of people had a fire extinguisher blasting at a control panel while the pinpointed automated fire suppression system rained foam down around them. Chairs, holoflex-sheets, tablets and mugs were everywhere, like the room had been under siege from a supernatural storm that exclusively rained office supplies.

Beside Stone, Maureen Stevenson—who came from the clone staff—sat like a little girl, her knees turned inward, feet akimbo. She'd lost a shoe, and blood ran down the side of her face from a deep gash in her brow. Her eyes looked at something nonexistent under Stone's desk.

"Hey. Hey!" He snapped his fingers in front of her nose, letting out a thankful sigh when her eyes focused and found him. "Can you stand? Is anything broken?"

She shook her head, then raised stiff fingers to her wet face.

She made a yip of denial when they came away with blood—clearly, she'd been expecting tears.

"It's okay. You're okay . . ." he said, hoping it was true. He leaned forward to take hold of her and together they stood—he using her for support as much as she used him.

They'd all trained for this—had emergency drills every two weeks. Stone had a job, a station, but his head was still swimming, his ears still ringing. Gradually it came back to him, what he needed to do. He was supposed to help evacuate crew members from unsafe areas.

"Over here!" Anju had already broken out the first aid kit at the emergency medical station—*he* remembered his duties—and waved to Stone and Maureen. He was having trouble with the clasp—probably because of the tremors running through his arms. When he popped the lid, everything inside went flying. As Stone and Maureen hobbled over, Anju scooped up the shrink-wrapped bandages and bottles of disinfectant as though worried the gravity would go again and they'd all float away.

Stone plopped Maureen in a chair near Anju's nursing station, then turned, scanning the room once more for Dr. Kapoor. After a moment, he began hobbling in the direction of her console.

Hobbling. He must have tweaked his ankle as well.

"Hey, where you going?" Anju asked. "I can wrap that."

"Did you see where Dr. Kapoor went?" he asked.

"No."

He continued on, helping others to their feet or jostling whoever had a disturbingly placid, far-off look to them. And all the time, his eyes scanned for Dr. Kapoor's form. He felt inextricably responsible for her well-being. Maybe because they'd become such good friends, or maybe because he'd started to hope for something more . . . or maybe because he had a growing certainty he was the only sorry sonofabitch who'd seen what happened to her.

If, you know, what I saw actually happened.

You've got a concussion, maybe you just don't remember right.

Was that how concussions worked? Could they make you hallucinate disappearing mission heads?

As he limped closer to the windows, his body screamed at him to halt. The glass appeared intact, but many millennia of evolution had his nervous system mashing the self-preservation button. The glass could shatter at any minute—who knew what that energy fluctuation had done to its integrity?

But he overrode his instincts. If Dr. Kapoor was hurt or unconscious, he needed to help her.

Even though he distinctly remembered watching her disappear, his rational side kept dispersing doubts in among the evidence of his own eyes. Concussion was one possible alternate-fact creator, as was the glaring light. He could have lost her in a flare. Maybe he'd blinked and she'd fallen (before the gravity reengaged?) and he'd lost her in the speed of the action.

There were lots of explanations for what he'd seen. But none of them felt right.

Sharp bits of ceramic, from where her tea mug had shattered against the floor, marked where she'd stood coordinating their efforts not fifteen minutes before. It was a strange, spooky halo on the raised metal platform where her station resided—like a chalk drawing at a crime scene. And Kapoor was nowhere to be found. Not a hair, not a shoe, not a—

A quick glimmer of brassy silver caught his eye. It was wedged into the corner of one drawer, as though it had been snagged on its way to the floor.

Yanking it free, he saw it was a small sundial, one usually hemmed in by a leather strap—like a wristwatch. It was part of the bracelet Kapoor wore every day.

But it wasn't just a passive piece of jewelry—he'd heard

her talking to it, heard it talk *back*. It had a little speaker and nano-cam embedded in the side.

Maybe he *wasn't* the only witness to her strange accident.

"Uh, he-hello? Um, sundial?"

The archaic timepiece said nothing.

He looked for a button, a switch, anything that might indicate the thing was on and he wasn't simply blabbering to himself.

But, try as he might, the dial remained passive. With a sigh, he pocketed it, ready to obey his body and get away from the potentially dangerous windows as quickly as possible. More importantly, ready to obey his *orders*. He needed to get people out of the mission control room. Who knew what kind of structural damage the hull had taken? There could be a buckle and breach at any moment.

One last glance made him pause, though. Outside, the stars were all unfamiliarly aligned. He'd looked out this window every day for months, and he had the view ingrained in his memory.

No, it makes sense, he told himself. *You dove—the ship dove. We're not in the same place anymore.*

But, how long had they been under? It only seemed like a few moments—and that was saying a lot, since everything had felt like it was moving in slow motion.

They weren't under long enough to change their stars that dramatically.

Right?

Concussion, concussion, concussion.

He couldn't trust his own perceptions, his own mind.

A field of debris marred the star-filled scape at the leftmost side of the viewing bay. It was slowly drifting across, glittering in the light coming from the ships.

In among the twisted metal, plastic, and glass, were a chair, workstation fragment, and the like. A few spiky experiment pods rolled into view. How they'd escaped *Life*'s bay, he didn't want to speculate.

It wasn't until he saw a body that he ripped himself away. It looked like a doll—so still, so stiff. It was too far away to make out. Maybe he'd known them, maybe he hadn't.

But it couldn't have been Kapoor, right? If her body was out there, his would be floating right alongside it.

"Attention, everyone," Captain Tan interrupted the automated PSA. His voice was remarkably even, and while his Cantonese accent was strong, he articulated every English syllable with precision. "At nine-thirteen A.M., there was an incident involving one of our experiment pods, resulting in a collision. We—the convoy—were forced to dive in an attempt to avoid that collision. *Pulse* and *Breath* both made it. We have lost contact with *Life*. The accident seems to have knocked out our communications buoy, but we are in the process of trying to regain contact with Earth. Hopefully they will be able to send the recently departed transport ships back to aid in our recovery.

"We will keep you apprised of all communications and reports as they come to us. For now, I ask that everyone follow evacuation plan B mark Two and move to the innermost levels of your ship. Both remaining ships have had severe outer-hull breaches, and the integrity of the primary inner hulls has not been assessed at this time. Thank you."

The recording began again, midmessage.

A reluctant rustle wafted through the room as the team prepared to abandon the EOL. Tightening his fist around the sundial in his pocket, Stone followed suit, turning over every stray piece of debris as he went, still desperately searching for their mission head.

He thought back to their morning's banter, how enthusiastic she'd been—bright-eyed behind her glasses.

It seemed so long ago now.

Maybe she's already left the room, he told himself, stepping through the door.

Yeah, when she disappeared, you cáscara.

Though the fire had been officially suppressed, mission control now smelled of scorched plastics and hot metal. It irritated his nose, made his head hurt all the worse. For a moment he thought he might throw up, but the nausea rolled out as quickly as it rolled in.

Listing to the side, favoring his injured ankle, he took his emergency position and helped guide those in mission control through the designated safety plan.

Already the halls were flooded with crew members, most of them sitting tight against the walls, using the metal as temporary spines. There was more blood, more grime. Some people looked like they'd had to contend with fires much larger than the one Stone had seen.

A few people were crying, but the majority of expressions were the same: glassy-eyed. Shell-shocked.

He waved his hands to and fro, pointing people in the proper direction, making sure they were all filing toward the designated emergency medical station or toward the evacuee meeting spot, where all of the uninjured were counted before being okayed to attend to the secondary emergency positions.

Once the control room was emptied, he locked the outer door and directed the emergency airlocks to engage. Large metal shutters rose from the floor to cover both the outer windows and the observation windows which lined the hall.

He started to move toward the appointed gathering point, but Anju stopped him. "Nope, med station."

"I'm fine."

"You're limping, and your eyes . . . You can't help anyone if you pass out, okay? Med station."

"Yeah, okay."

As he moved along with the other injured, he asked the nearest people—those he didn't work directly with—if they'd seen Dr. Kapoor. They all told him no, some with weak, croaking voices; others in harsh, irritated barks.

Maybe it was the chaos. Maybe that was why no one seemed to be able to place—or even find—their easily recognized leader.

You know what happened, he mentally snapped at himself. *You saw it. It was real. Vanhi Kapoor is gone.*

The sundial's gnomon dug into his palm, as though accusing him of some secret crime.

"Yep, it's a concussion," said the medic. He flicked a penlight back and forth across both of Stone's pupils, before having him perform a few memory tests. "Mild. I don't think you're in any immediate danger. Try not to do anything too strenuous for the next week, physically or mentally."

"Ha," Stone grunted, holding a cold pack against his cheek. He hadn't realized how hot the impact site was until he'd pressed the icy, gelatinous thing to his face.

Turned out, the breakroom made a marvelous private exam nook. He sat on the counter, the utilitarian pull on the cupboard behind him digging into his back. On his left, the medic had small white cups of various pills laid out—pain relievers mostly. He refused to give any of them to Stone, though.

"None of what I've got on hand is good for a concussion. Don't want to risk more swelling." He was remarkably calm, given the wailing outside.

"You've got a line out the door that will riot when they hear that. I think most people got a bump on the head when gravity reengaged."

"Including me," the doc said, turning around to display the

small crisscrossing bandages on the back of his scalp. "Why'd you laugh when I told you not to do anything strenuous?"

"Have you looked outside?"

"Can't say as I have. The infirmary wasn't allotted any windows, being deep in the bowels and whatnot."

"Stars are wrong," Stone mumbled, hissing as the medic took the cold pack away. "I saw . . . I saw a body. Comms buoy is on the fritz or worse. It's not like I can hole up in my bunk and take a vacay."

"I wouldn't worry about it. I'm sure the consortium already has emergency teams on the way. They wouldn't leave us to fend for ourselves."

"Yeah, sure." He didn't feel like arguing, not with the medic, who was just doing his job. People always complained about stiff bedside manner, but Stone could use a dose of realism right about now. Something wasn't right here. They weren't just an upturned ship in familiar waters.

He'd rest if he could.

He just wasn't sure that was going to be an option.

When the doc dismissed him, he almost stopped to ask about seeing things. Almost. But someone was pounding on the door. He was sure hallucinations would get him put on some kind of twenty-four-hour watch, and there were people far worse off.

You say that now, but wait until they find you in your bunk tomorrow, estirare la pata.

I'm fine, he groused at himself. *I feel fine.*

Yeah, I bet most people who suddenly croak say the same thing.

A stiff, demanding wall of bodies on the other side of the breakroom door nearly kept it shut. The safety sensors flashed, trying to keep it from snagging fingers in the pocket crease and jamb. He pushed at it and someone yelped. "You have to back up! Let me out or no one else is getting in!"

He gave the medic one last glance before pushing out—the doc looked momentarily overwhelmed before his pleasant placidity returned.

The crowd beyond was tight—bodies pressed against one another like canned sardines.

Something wet smeared across his arms as he passed a woman he didn't recognize. The skin on one side of her face was blackened, and he looked down to see a glob of puss on his bicep.

She didn't smell, though she looked like she should. Fried human.

For her sake, he tried not to gag, tried not to wipe his arm on the next person in a panic. It wasn't her fault—it wasn't anyone's fault.

Unless it was *his* fault.

Maybe this is all my doing. If I'd just gotten that damned thing to cooperate . . .

But the self-flagellation could wait. His gag reflex demanded it.

Arms up, as though he were in a waist-high pool, he waded through the throng and around the corner to the men's room.

Inside was a perfectly pressed, seemingly unperturbed woman washing down a toddler in the sink. They surprised him, made him freeze. It was so incongruous with everything happening—the accident, his own mental image of what Convoy Twelve's population was like. He often forgot there were whole families up here. Children. Babies.

"I'm almost done," she said hastily, as though she feared he'd rail about her being in the men's bathroom.

"Take your time," he said, staring at the kid. He couldn't help it—he needed to know the kid was okay, for some reason. If he'd hurt his colleagues, adults, he could handle it. But if he were somehow responsible for a single scratch on this child—

Abruptly, he spun into the nearest stall. He'd come in here meaning to take a bath himself, needing to get the burnt woman's fluids off him.

But now, throwing up was a priority.

Nausea. The doc had said to come back if he felt nauseated or vomited.

Yeah, well, Stone was pretty sure it wasn't due to a bloated brain.

As he spilled his belly into the toilet, he heard a sloshing of sink water and the door open and slam again as the woman rushed out with a soaking-wet baby.

Maybe she's an empathetic vomiter, he thought.

After his body had done its thing—and then dryly tried to do its thing a few more times—he went over to the row of sinks. Yep, sure enough, the baby's bathwater was undrained. It was also relatively clean, which heartened him. No pink tint of blood, no excess dirt or bits of anything.

He took a deep breath and toweled off his face, before looking at himself in the mirror.

"*Ach!*" he shouted, catching the reflection of himself and a looming form behind him. He dove forward, nearly cracking his head on the mirror, before whirling—clutching to the basin for support.

Behind him was Dr. Kapoor, her eyes closed, hair floating around her in a weightless halo. But more than her hair's resistance to gravitons was her feet's—she hovered limply, at least twelve inches off the ground, ankles lax, wrists lax, neck lax.

It's a vision. I am hallucinating, he thought.

Just as he was about to dart out the door and demand the doc perform a CAT scan, reality seemed to return to Vanhi's body, if not to Stone's mind.

As though a switch had been flipped, gravity grabbed her unconscious form, demanding she hit the floor like any normal human mass bound by the laws of physics.

Stone didn't have time to think. He slid to his knees beneath her, scooping her into his arms before she could smack her head on the unforgiving tiles.

His save was graceless, her arms flung out awkwardly from her body, her legs crumpled half in his lap and half on the floor.

"Hey," he said softly, shaking her. "Doctor Kapoor? Hey, *hey*!"

He brushed her tangled hair away from her face. It was caught in her glasses and skewed her frames. But he felt first for breath and then for a pulse, finding his own air as soon as he was sure she was drawing hers.

"Okay, you're alive. You're *real*. That's good. Now . . . wake up!"

He shook her some more, sure it was the wrong thing to do, but his overloaded mind couldn't come up with anything else.

Luckily, after a few more full-body shudders, she groaned.

"Hey, yeah!" he said excitedly. "Come on, you can do it. Wake up." *Wake up and tell me what just happened. Wake up and tell me what you remember. Where did you go? What is going on?*

Her eyes opened once, then shut tight, as though they loathed the light. But then her lids slowly cracked again and her pupils focused. "Whe—what . . . ? Mendez Perez?"

"Yeah. Yeah, it's me. You're okay. I think. I dunno—I mean, I have no idea. But you're awake."

"What can . . . how . . . ?" She tried to sit up. He wanted to let her, but as soon as he stopped providing support, she listed to the side. "I need . . ." She looked around, dazed.

She's in bad shape, he realized. No way was she going to be capable of confirming or denying the evidence of his eyes. Right now, his top priority had to be getting her to the medic.

"Can you walk?" he asked.

“I think . . .” She put her feet under her and tried. She looked like a newborn foal on his dad’s farm, trying to make legs work that had never had to work before. Eventually, though, he got her up—not to mention himself—and together they hobbled for the door.

“I’ve got Doctor Kapoor here!” he shouted. “She needs help. Doctor Kapoor needs help!”

He’d never been so happy to hear the *stomp stomp stomp* of running feet before.

Days passed. They held a memorial for those they were certain were dead, and then they started the real cleanup. All seven hundred and two adults on board were engaged in one of three tasks: putting the ships back in normal working order, figuring out exactly where the hell they were, or trying to communicate with someone—*anyone*.

More and more people began to notice that the stars weren’t where they should be. Even those with very little astronomical knowledge. Even the children, of which there were only thirty-six still aboard. No one could identify a single familiar constellation or heavenly body. No one.

Stone tried not to let it panic him. Tried not to let the constant whispers of “where the hell are we?” get to him.

But the whispers soon became a rumble.

“. . . I know the buoys are down, but shouldn’t we have heard something by now?”

“. . . How far out would you have to go for Orion not to look like Orion anymore?”

“. . . This isn’t good. Sirius is roughly six-point-two light-years from Earth, Betelgeuse is sixty-five. If we’re so far away we can’t even pinpoint those . . .”

The pitch of the rumble rose steadily. The harried panic of the initial accident had died away, but now it was replaced with another kind of fevered concern.

What if they were out of Earth's reach? What if they were good and truly on their own?

Lost.

Thankfully, they had leadership that understood how to handle a crisis. Captains Tan and Baglanova did their best to calm their crews. They made sure everyone had a job, something to focus on. After all, though they had to hold out hope for rescue, they couldn't sit around and wait for aid to appear. The work was good—kept everyone who could be on their feet busy. Working with your hands often kept your thoughts in check, Stone found. Prevented your mind from wandering too far from the *now.*

Kept him from thinking about the fact that his friend Eric was MIA. That the bodies that had been retrieved from outside were from his division.

"He was on *Life* when it happened," Justice told him. "He might be fine. We won't know until we reestablish communications."

Stone had known Justice a long time. They used to serve together in the air force. She wasn't always the coolest head in the room, but she was never unreasonable.

And yet, every time he glanced out a porthole, he felt sick.

There were truths they would all need to face soon, and they hung over everyone like storm clouds, waiting to let loose their loads. But as long as there was work to focus on, they could pretend everything would be fine.

Fine. Sure. Fine.

After the initial panic and shock, the rush of manic activity, everyone became subdued. There was little chatter in the halls, nearly no chatter during work. Everyone was in their own fog—not quite in denial, but not yet ready to accept that things could not proceed as usual.

While anyone who'd ever worked on a satellite or switchboard tried their hand at contacting Earth, the small group of navigators had recruited every amateur astronomer aboard to help place the convoy in time and space. The team, led by Carmen Sotomayor, was working around the clock. Justice, whose expertise was in biology and genetics, had even volunteered.

Stone was no good with star charts past reading them, and he'd never been much of a communicator. But he'd gotten his degree in mechanical engineering, which made him a hot commodity during reconstruction.

He was just finishing up in the water-reclamation center when Dr. Kapoor came looking for him. When she came around the corner, he quickly composed himself, forced a mild smile.

He'd tried to forget about her disappearing. Brushed it off as a dream. Because it had to be, right?

That would have been the easiest solution—just pretending it was a concoction created by his stressed-out mind. And it would have explained everything, except . . .

Except how she'd disappeared in the EOL and reappeared in the bathroom. Those were two solid points in reality. She had been in mission control, unquestionably. And she'd been in the men's room, also indisputable.

"What can I do for you, Vanhi?"

The sundial sat heavy in his uniform pocket. He'd carried it with him every day, hoping to run into her so he could return it. He'd envisioned pulling it out and tossing it to her with a casual "You dropped this," but now that the opportunity presented itself, he hesitated. He still had questions, and letting go of the sundial felt like a finality—as though giving it up meant never being able to broach the subject of her disappearance.

"I'd like your help in examining *Breath*'s main SD drive," she said. "Captain Tan wants to run a test dive as soon as possible."

He wiped off his oil-coated wrench with a rag before slotting it into his toolbox. Two other engineers ran by, aiming for a sewer pipe whose pressure gauge was pinging red. "I've never put a hand on one of those, I'm not sure I—"

She waved aside his concern. "I need all of the competent engineers I can get. Your file says you worked for JPL."

"Yeah," he admitted. "Used to help design LEO drones before I learned to fly them." It was strange to think of those as "simpler times"—when he'd lain awake at night, daydreaming about the flight instead of the design.

"Then come on." She was peppy in her insistence, had more of a spring in her step than anyone had a right to after all that had happened. "The job isn't rocket science, but it's rocket-science-adjacent, so you'll do fine."

He thought about protesting, and snuck a quick glance at the questionable sewer pipe before deciding everyone else had it under control. "Let me just go tell—"

"Already worked it out, you're free to go."

Well, all right then. When the mission head says *jump*, you say *how high?*

He gathered up his tools and fell into step behind her.

If a ship were a peach, then the SD drive would be its massive, impenetrable pit. That was how Stone had first been introduced to the drive concept, anyway.

To tell the truth, he was a bit intimidated. He'd never been down to see it before. He'd put hands on a lot of engines in his life, but there was no way he would have been able to pick the drive out of a lineup. It looked more like a building than a motor, and the peach pit analogy seemed woefully inadequate. The thing was bulky and foreboding—more like a sleeping animal than a seed to Stone—occupying the lowermost levels of *Breath*.

There was a touch of burnt ozone in the air, mixed with something that might have been iodine. Dr. Kapoor assured him the smell was normal, as was the prickle in the atmosphere and the slight heat rolling off the walls.

But that strange crackling sound? Not normal. That was what she needed help with.

"Trying to track down the cause and button 'er back up," she said. "I think it has to do with excess vibrations in one of the outer chassis layers, but I can't be sure."

She set him up in one quadrant, and gave him the necessary equipment to scour every outer inch of the machine. A handful of other engineers worked the remaining sections, and many more were set up to run diagnostics on the inner portions of the drive.

When a break was called, Dr. Kapoor returned. He thought she was there to talk findings, but she had other things on her mind.

"So . . ." she said, clearly trying for a casual lead-in to a not-so-casual conversation.

He lifted his safety goggles onto his forehead. "Yes?"

"I've been trying to figure out how to thank you without it sounding flippant," she admitted. "Or patronizing."

"Why would 'thank you' sound patronizing?"

"I don't know, it just feels like it could be. Maybe because . . ."

He nodded, rolling his tongue against the inside of his cheek. "I feel it, so you must be feeling it," he said. "Because we feel *responsible*," he added after a moment, spelling it out.

She had to have wondered, just as he had, if things might have gone down differently if she'd made one extra choice, given one more command. He'd replayed the last half hour before the accident over and over in his mind, looking for the opening that could have changed everything.

But, even if he'd been able to spot it, what would it matter? You can't travel backward in time.

"Yeah," she admitted. "But, you *aren't* responsible, you have to know that," she insisted. "I'm the mission head, it all falls on me." Her gaze retreated then, someplace he couldn't follow. Then he realized: she was looking back before the collision. What could she have to feel guilty about before all this shit went down?

"It was an accident," he said, clearing his throat, attempting to make both of them feel better, knowing words were beyond inadequate. "It wasn't even an accident caused by human error—"

"We don't know that yet," she said with a sigh, letting her eyes flick up the side of the SD drive. She put her hand over her mouth, mumbled something behind it that sounded like "This is a punishment."

For what, our scientific hubris? he thought, but said nothing.

She squared her shoulders to the drive, planted her feet as though challenging the engine. She looked as immovable as a mountain, with deep veins of guilt running through her interior like layers of hidden gold.

He found himself wishing he could mine her guilt away. She didn't deserve to carry the weight of all this.

Hell, they didn't even know what *all this* entailed yet.

His empathy emboldened him. Maybe he could ask now, while she pretended to be a mountain. "What do you remember? Not just about the accident in general, but what happened to you, personally?" It was obviously a leading question. But maybe if she sensed that he knew, that he would believe her, she'd open up to him.

"I remember the bathroom, if that's what you're asking," she said. "I know I fell and you caught me. That you took me to the medics. That's what I mean—I know what you did and I'm grateful. Really."

"No. I mean, you're welcome. Of course. But . . . how did you end up in the bathroom? It's not even on the same level as the EOL."

"I have no idea," she admitted. "Honestly, one second I was

watching the pod slam into us, and the next I was crumpled on the floor with you, so . . ." She held up her hands.

"You just blacked out? You don't remember feeling weird—" he mumbled his next word "—insubstantial?"

"What does that mean?"

He was trying to feel her out, to get a sense of *her* sense of things. But what the hell, why not go for broke?

"I saw what happened to you," he said, voice low. He glanced around, making sure no one else was paying attention. "The accident did something . . . unnatural to you."

A guarded look came into her eye. "Like what?"

"I can't say exactly. The doctors didn't find anything weird?"

"They ran a full CAT scan and everything, I'm fine. Not even a broken bone or a bump on the head. Lots of other people weren't so lucky."

"I know—I know. But, when that wave of—energy, sparks, whatever the scientific term for it is, if there even is one—when it hit you, you didn't feel funny?"

She thought for a moment, readjusting her glasses as though through them, things might become clearer. "Kind of fuzzy, I guess? Not my memory, I mean the feeling. I thought it might hurt—"

"Me, too," he said.

"But it didn't. And then there was kind of a stretchy sensation, if that makes any sense. Not like, when you stretch and your joints pop, but like, I don't know, if your muscles became taffy."

"Yeah, okay. Okay." His fingers twitched and he wished he had a holoflex-sheet or a pen or a stylus or a piece of charcoal—anything. Something to take notes with. He wanted to put it down exactly as she said it, for evidence.

"Then I was falling and you caught me, end of story."

"Your muscles were taffy and then you were falling?" he asked.

"Did I stutter?"

"No, it—you didn't say you blacked out."

She shrugged, as though it were out of her hands. "I don't remember blacking out, but I mean, I had to have. I do remember feeling *hella* groggy, like I'd just woken up from the worst hangover ever."

He wanted her to say more. He wanted to grab a damn screw and start scratching her account into the SD's hide. "So it seemed instantaneous for you? Mission control to bathroom, boom, blink of an eye."

"Yeah. Wish I could tell you how I got in the loo, but . . . Did someone drag me there and leave me there? Did something happen to them while they were trying to help me? You know, I kind of don't want to think about it." She turned away, clearly ready to refocus on the task at hand.

"I think you should get tested," he blurted.

"For . . . ?" She didn't look at him, just went on examining the drive's seams.

"That's the thing, I don't know. I saw what happened—I know how you got from the control room to the bathroom."

That elicited a whirl. "You do?"

Okay, poor choice of words. "Well, not *how*, but I saw it all happen. You disappeared. One second that tangerine wave is slamming into you, and the next you're behind me in the bathroom. Floating, by the way. You fell because you were *floating*."

"Because the gravity was out?"

"No, it was back. Had been back for a long time. I saw you disappear, then I went to the medic, then I scared some poor lady with a baby and nearly puked all over my shoes and when I was at the sink you just poofed!"

"Poofed?"

"One second, I'm thinking you were vaporized, or that my brain is bleeding out behind my eyes, and the next you're pulling a *Tales from the Crypt* ghost act."

“Mendez Perez?”

He’d taken a breath to continue, but let it out slowly. “What?”

“Did the doctors okay you to come back to work?”

He hated the look on her face. It was full of caution and pity and something akin to motherliness which really freaked him out. “The medic said I shouldn’t do anything too strenuous for the next few days. But it’s been a few days. I’m *fine*.”

“Are you?”

“Okay, now you *are* being patronizing.”

“I’m sorry, but you just said I disappeared. Wait, actually, *poofed* was the word you used. You said I poofed.”

“Well, you did. From your glasses to your shoes to your hair and your fingernails, you . . . you . . . wait.” He fumbled in his pocket. He hated that his adrenaline had spiked, that trying to convince her of what he knew sounded loony had fazed him. But, here he was. “Look. You disappeared, except for this.”

The dial was firm and heavy in his palm, its gnomon proud and shiny. “I looked for you after I saw what I saw, and this was by your desk.”

Her right hand immediately went to her left wrist, covering over the leather strap that, even at this moment, encircled her arm. “How did you—?”

“Here,” he scurried up close to show her the dial’s underside, how the loops through which the band had been threaded were perfectly intact.

She didn’t draw away. But she did pick up the dial, turning it over and over. Then she looked him square in the eye, her expression sterner than any he’d seen in a courtroom or funeral home. “If you’re lying to me, I’ll know. If you stole this off me when I was unconscious—”

“I’m not lying. I didn’t steal it. Why would I do that?”

She swallowed thickly. “*I don’t know.*”

It came out as a sharp shout, and they immediately pulled back from one another, as though to let more air in between them.

Dr. Kapoor pressed the gnomon between her fingers, as though letting it read her prints. "C?"

"Yes?" came the chipper voice of a personal assistant.

"I need you to confirm something for me."

"I will do my best."

"At what hour on July sixth did you stop reading my biometrics?"

"At nine-thirteen A.M. I lost sensor-to-skin contact. When you did not put me back on, I let the session time out to conserve battery life. Would you like to change my settings for a longer time between loss of contact and sleep mode?"

"No, C, that's fine. What do you remember happening at nine-thirteen?"

The little PA began drawling out a word-for-word transcript of the incident. Helpful, for convoy records, not so much for settling the matter between Stone and Dr. Kapoor.

"Thank—thank you, C, that's enough. So, to verify, you were not removed by someone else?"

"Oh, no. I fell onto your desk. Everything was very bright and shiny, and I'm afraid there was a surge that distorted my visual recordings. I apologize for the inconvenience."

Vanhi met Stone's gaze once more—her eyes were still narrowed critically, but it wasn't a criticism aimed at him. "I'm guessing when we get to review the tapes of the control room, we'll find a similar distortion."

"Probably Tan's already discovered that," Stone said. *Damn. Damn it* all.

"You're not a thief," Dr. Kapoor said, and it sounded only mildly like an apology.

"No. So how did that get off your wrist without the band being unbuckled?"

She didn't answer. That was fine, he didn't really expect her to.

"I think I should go now. I'm just going to be a distraction from here on out," he said, hands in his pockets as he took a few steps back. "I've given you a lot to think about. Believe me or don't—either way, remember that you're a scientist. And, you know, human. If something bizarre had happened to me—something that hinted at new physics—I'd want to pursue it."

She nodded, once again considering the dial in her hand. After he'd gone a good way down the access hall, she called, "Stone?"

He stopped, looked back.

"Just a thought," she called. "But what if it did?"

"Did what?"

"What if whatever it was happened to you, and not to me?"

For the most part, he tried to avoid her after that. He didn't know if she was looking into it, and he didn't want to think about what it meant if she was right. What if she *hadn't* disappeared and he *hadn't* simply hallucinated it and instead the weird, bastardized mingling of SD pockets had done something to *him* instead? Maybe it had rearranged his brain cells.

In any case, it hadn't liquefied his organs or given him spontaneous leprosy. He'd gone back to the medic and the doc couldn't find anything amiss. He had no residual effects from the concussion, and his ankle was supporting weight just fine.

Maybe he should just forget about it. After all, there were bigger things to worry about.

Like how in three weeks they'd already gone through two weeks' worth of supplies. Captain Tan had them all rationing, but the restrictions weren't tight enough. Clearly, he was still holding on to hope, thinking someone would hear one of their distress calls.

If a rescue party was on the way, they were sure as hell awfully quiet about it.

As far as surprise parties went, this one blew.

Most people Stone talked with were still in denial. No one wanted to think about the larger implications of being lost in space. People often mentioned going home. "When we get back" preceded a statement about once an hour in conversation.

But Stone had a feeling—the sickening kind, that burrows into your skin like a tick—that "getting back" was a far-flung fantasy.

He might not be an astronomer, but he knew his stars—Earth-view stars. And he wasn't seeing any familiar patterns.

Their dip into SD travel had taken less than a minute—it shouldn't have sent them into unrecognizable space. Not if they'd entered a typical travel SD.

They were far from home, he had no doubt. The real question was, *how far*?

Sotomayor's team had at least figured out they were still in home country. Meaning, they were still in the Milky Way. They'd spotted Andromeda, Triangulum, and what they *thought* was the Sagittarius Dwarf Spheroidal. If they could verify, then triangulation was theoretically only a few calculations away.

But they have to remember the time . . . Stone thought.

How could they have traveled so far in such a short amount of time? No one talked about it, not even their mission head, but the crew weren't idiots. They knew that time flowed differently in the SDs, relative to normal space. And in all of the ones they'd ever cracked, it seemed to move *faster* relative to *farther*. So, if they'd caught a "current" that could propel them an unfathomable distance nearly instantaneously, then . . .

Then they'd probably traveled forward in time at a traumatic rate.

It was ironic, really. They were the convoy built to stay put. And now they were experiencing what all of the other convoys were experiencing, except none of Convoy Twelve's crew had signed up for it. They weren't bred for this, weren't born to it. There was no special committee that had scrutinized their genes to make sure they could survive out here without any Earth contact. Their *ships* hadn't even been designed for it.

They had personal ties to Earth like none of the other Planet United Missions did. And if Stone was right about their displacement, then shit was going to get ugly eventually. Real ugly.

But, hey, maybe they'd get lucky. Maybe they weren't so far out of their local star cluster.

Maybe . . . Maybe . . .

Maybe, for now, he should stop speculating and try to go on as if things were normal.

On his way to the mess hall, he met Mrs. Tan—the captain's wife—coming down the hall from the opposite direction, flanked by two other women. The three of them were talking emphatically—happily even—in Cantonese, and Mrs. Tan walked with a heavy sway to her step, hands braced against her lower back. Everyone on board knew she'd be giving birth soon. It had been an anticipated day before the accident. Hers was to be the first born aboard. There'd been a few other pregnant crew members, and they'd all planned to go back to Earth for the big day. But not Mrs. Tan. This was their home, she'd said in the announcement, and she wanted to welcome their first child into their home on day one.

That had sent lots of people buzzing. Hers wouldn't be the first baby brought to term in space, but it was a first for Convoy Twelve.

The three woman gave him stern nods as he passed, and he nodded respectfully back.

The halls were mostly empty this time of day. Meals were strictly scheduled now, and rationing enforced. If you missed out, you missed out. He hoped there'd be some fried plantains left. He'd never forgive himself if he lost his chance at eating a fried plantain ever again.

Jumping onto the nearest elevator, he straightened his uniform, checked his posture. He'd taken to paying attention to the little things—those he could keep in order. There was so much that was out of his hands, so maybe if he—

His primping was interrupted when the lift stopped on the next floor—still several levels away from *Breath*'s mess.

Surprisingly, it was Dr. Kapoor who stepped in beside him. He swayed back a bit, toward one wall, putting a good gap between them. They nodded at one another, but initially said nothing.

The elevator jolted back into action, and moments later the monitor above the emergency panel lit up. It flickered, black to silver to bright white, before a star-scape flooded it from corner to corner.

At the same moment, the lift went dark and stopped its upward grind.

"What the—?" Kapoor muttered, immediately pressing the manual activation button. Nothing happened.

Captain Tan's voice came through the elevator speakers. "Moments ago, our astronomers confirmed that one set of objects within our field of vision—previously thought to be stars—are, in fact, unidentifiable."

Stone and Dr. Kapoor automatically shared a look.

The vid feed zoomed in. What appeared to be faint, distant stars resolved into fuzzy objects. Not planets, or asteroids, not nebulous gasses, but something more . . . geometric. One was distinctly diamond shaped.

"They have definitively identified half a dozen massive objects, and suspect there are many more less-reflective objects in the vicinity. Most of them are similar in size to our sun, and sit at distances less than a light-year from one another."

It was like some scene out of an old 1950's sci-fi flick, grainy black-and-white footage and everything.

"Current consensus is that these cannot be naturally formed structures. Our top priority remains determining our location. But I have consulted with our security teams and want to assure you that we are making plans. Should we note signs of activity within the region, you will be updated immediately as in accordance with the Planet United Consortium's guidelines. Thank you for your attention."

The screen went dark again, and the lift rumbled back to life. The lights came on and Stone snapped. The carefully constructed focus that he'd been maintaining—the walls he'd built to help him not think about Eric, not think about home, came crumbling down. "'You're God-knows-where in the galaxy, the Ghost-knows when, and oh, by the way, there's some massive alien structures off the port bow, *thank you and have a nice day*?'"

He kicked the wall, and Dr. Kapoor jumped. Her normally richly pigmented cheeks had gone a sickly sort of gray-brown. There was no way to tell if she was upset by his outburst or upset by the news, and he didn't care.

The wall took it, so he dished it out. Again and again, he struck the baseboard with his noninjured foot, needing to scream, needing to tear at his hair, needing to change the form of something in here because *son of a bitch they were fucking lost in space*!

Everything hurt, everything burned—all of that abstract distance scrunched up into nothing, leaving him with a tsunami's worth of difficult emotions.

"I suggest you calm yourself, sir," said Dr. Kapoor's sundial.

He sucked in a breath through his teeth. "Why the hell should I?"

The sundial didn't answer, and when he looked up, he saw that Vanhi wasn't cringing away from him. Instead, her eyes held a point in the distance, someplace outside of the elevator. "Did the captain just say there were alien structures on our horizon?"

"*Yes*," he said emphatically, as though she were agreeing with him over her PA. "*Thank you*."

He wanted the elevator to stop now. It was stifling, cramped. Claustrophobic.

His *madre* was prone to claustrophobia. That was why she'd never visited him or his cousins in the States—planes were too much. He'd traveled home to Puerto Rico whenever he could, spent every last second of leave there, because she couldn't take flying in a shoebox.

A sudden pang of realization struck him between the eyes.

If his worst fears were true, he'd never see her again. His *madre* was light-years away now, and even if the convoy found its way back, there'd probably be nothing left of her except a bit of dirt at the bottom of a pine box. If even that.

Now he knew—that sick feeling turned into a sick certainty—there was no going home again.

He didn't know where they were or even *when* they were, but there had to be a reason no help had come. The distance was too far, and time stretched too thin.

"She's dead," he said with a sort of manic awe. "They're dead. Everyone, *they're all dead*."

"Are you having a breakdown?" Kapoor asked, still staring, still placid.

"Yes!" he yelled, balling his fists and kicking the wall again.

"I think I am, too," she said flatly.

The elevator dinged.

And then, she was gone.

One instant, she was there, sharing in his freak-out in her own statuesque way. And the next—poof.

Just like he'd said before.

Poof.

The sundial seemed to hover cartoonishly in midair for a moment, before realizing it was no longer tethered to a strap or a wrist. It clunked to the thinly carpeted floor, rolling on its side, twisting round and round with its gnomon pointed toward the center of its pirouette.

Stone allowed himself a moment of stunned stillness before he fell to his knees and picked up the dial—just as the doors were opening.

"C?" he asked it hastily. "C, tell me you got that. Tell me you recorded what just happened."

His understanding of everything was inside out, filleted open. The physical, the metaphysical. Time, space. Reality, unreality. Nothing worked the way he once thought it did.

There were people outside the lift, staring at him as he yelled at what appeared to be an inanimate object.

"Come on, C, talk to me! Tell me to calm down, anything!"

The PA kept its silence. Whether it had shut off, refused him because he was unauthorized, or was quiet because it had somehow been whisked out of the device just as Dr. Kapoor had been whisked out of the lift, he couldn't say.

"Stone?"

Justice was there, lifting him to his feet. She was bigger than he was, could enfold him in her arms as though he were a small child.

He *felt* like a child. And he felt a like a weary old man. And he felt out of his body with no age at all.

Clutching the dial to his chest, he let her lead him through the crowd and toward sustenance.

"What happened?" she asked.

"I need help, Justice. Please. Help me."

The announcement of the megastructure field sent a buzz through the convoy. They had so much to worry about already. Fear and excitement knotted together like taffy in the hearts and minds of most aboard, making everyone feel sticky. Was this a good thing? Who could they report this discovery to if Earth wasn't answering? Would they die out here, alone in the presence of definitive proof of alien intelligence?

If nothing else, it confirmed what they'd all feared: they were nowhere near home.

"I didn't *do* anything," Stone said for the umpteenth time, tired now of banging his fists against the Plexiglass walls of his brig cell. The inside of the double pane was smeared with his finger, fist, and palm prints.

Steve Weaver, a security guard Stone hadn't had any occasion to speak with before, twisted his lips skeptically. He was a stocky man, head shaved like a cue ball. He reminded Stone of a lot of bouncers guarding the doors at nightclubs in San Juan. All he was missing was a tight black T-shirt and a sneer. "Look, I'm not an appeals court," Steve said levelly. "And no one's charging you with anything. Not yet."

"Then let me out."

"I can't do that. Doctor Kapoor is missing, you were the last to see her, and you—" he made a vague, round gesture through the air "—you said she disappeared in front of you. So." He said "so" like it was its own full stop.

"I didn't *hurt* her, I said—"

"*Poof*, yeah, I heard you. That's why Doctor Taylor is on her way. Feel free to sit on the cot and relax for a while till she gets here."

"Yolanda Taylor? The shrink?" There were three counselors in the convoy—two now, he supposed, since they were each assigned a ship. Everyone had monthly visits with them, but they were just check-ins. This clearly wasn't just a routine chat. "Yeah, great, you think I'm psychotic."

Steve made a noncommittal shrug. "I'm no doctor."

"Hey, you know, if I needed help I'd be the first to get it, all right? What I had in the elevator? Panic attack. That's what the meds my friend brought were for. I'm down with mental health accountability—but this is not a mental health problem. Don't get me Doctor Taylor, get me, I dunno—" he snapped his fingers—"Doctor Dogolea. I need a physicist who knows SDs."

"You don't want a psychiatrist . . . you want a physicist?" Steve asked slowly, as though the concept were some kind of code he needed to decipher.

"Yes."

Steve rolled his eyes. "No."

Stone was about to lay into him, demand a message be sent to Gabriel Dogolea, when the yellow-white light shifted to eggplant-purple.

Oh no. The drive tests. Even with Vanhi missing, they were still going to go through with—

The bottom dropped out of Stone's stomach. "Call the bridge," he said, voice deadpan. "Tell them not to dive. Do it *now*."

"What? Why w—?"

"We can't dive with Kapoor missing, all right? *Listen to me*—" He tried to stay calm, composed. Flying off the handle wasn't going to help her. "We cannot dive while Kapoor is missing. She could die."

He wasn't sure how he knew—he just knew. If they left now, when she came back there'd be no ship to come back to. No men's room, no mission control, no elevator. Just the vacuum.

"There's no time to explain, Steve—make the call!"

Steve moved toward the comms panel, but with a hesitation to his gait.

"Now! Now!" Stone urged, even though his insides were shriveling. His liver felt like a raisin, his stomach like a fraying coconut husk. Steve wasn't going to get the message out—there were gears turning in his cue ball skull, trying to determine if Stone was cracked or if Kapoor might truly be in danger. Not because he believed Stone's story, but because Stone might have stashed Kapoor somewhere dangerous.

"N—!"

The shift came. The dive was complete. They were officially in an SD, testing their engines and leaving their head far away in the blackness of space.

Then it was over. The brig washed purple again, and moments later they'd reemerged.

Stone was sure they'd left his insides—his skeleton, his guts, his very veins—back where they'd begun. His skin was an empty sheath, devoid of sense and feeling.

He stumbled away from the Plexiglass, sitting down heavily when the backs of his knees hit the cell's cot.

"We killed her," he said, sounding more awed than terrified, even to his own ears. "We killed her."

"Yeah, I'm getting you that shrink now," Steve said casually.

Though his eyes were open, Stone could no longer perceive Steve. All he could see was Vanhi, floating just as she had in the bathroom, but with millions of kilometers of emptiness around her. He saw her eyes flying open, her mouth gasping like a fish on land, arms reaching for something she could not touch—a life preserver that did not exist.

"I want Justice," he said, "Justice Jax, the geneticist. I want to see her *now*."

"First you want a physicist, now a geneticist—they've got work to do, they're not at my beck and call."

Stone took a shaky breath through his nose. Despite his lungs expanding, filling, he felt oxygen deprived. "You tell them both that I say Vanhi Kapoor is dead. They'll come."

He wasn't wrong. An hour later, the narrow hall outside his cell was nearly filled to capacity. Dr. Dogolea was there, as was Justice *and* Dr. Taylor, along with several other security guards and members of command.

"Did you bring it?" Stone asked Justice, pressing his nose to the glass.

She looked over her shoulder to where Dr. Taylor and Aksel Baglanova, *Breath*'s captain, were ardently discussing Stone's medical needs. "Yeah," from her jumpsuit pocket, she pulled out the dial, flashing it at him for only a moment before putting it back. He'd begged her to take it, to not let anyone else see it. "For the love of sin, what the hell is going on?"

Mac Savea, a six-foot-seven titan of a man from Samoa and one of the highest-ranking security officers, slid close to Justice, raising an eyebrow.

Justice shot him her best *get out of my space* face, but he ignored her.

"You say you want to help Dr. Kapoor," Mac continued. "Then all you have to do is tell us what really happened."

"He did," Justice snapped, her quick retort evidence of her deep loyalty more so than her belief in Stone's story.

"Get out of the way," Steve said, brushing Justice aside to make a space for Dr. Taylor.

"Hi, Stone. Is it all right if I call you Stone?" she asked.

"Yeah." The patronizing lilt in her voice was not a good sign.

"I've discussed your situation with Captain Baglanova, and we agree that the brig is not the best place for you."

"Great," he said, backing away from the glass, ready for it to slide open. He still felt numb, was still processing the fact that Vanhi was gone. Just like that, forever.

"I'd like you to accompany me to the medical bay," she continued evenly. "I want to keep you under observation for seventy-two hours, that way I can assess how to best treat you."

“Yeah, fine,” he said. Maybe he did need help? Who knew anymore? Not him.

“Can you make it under your own power?”

“Versus?”

“I can sedate you and get a gurney if necessary.”

“No. No.” *I can’t . . . Did I imagine everything?*

“Hey!” Justice said sharply, smacking the glass. “Don’t you bug out on me.”

“I’m *tired*,” he told her. He didn’t know what to think and couldn’t feel a damned thing. Was it better if he’d made it all up in his head? No, because Vanhi was really missing. Which meant he’d done something horrible. Maybe it was an accident, maybe not. If he couldn’t trust his own eyes, his own mind . . .

But if *he* was right, and they were wrong, then wasn’t there still a chance for her?

Maybe he could make a deal.

“I’ll come quietly,” he said, a spark of sensation flaring in his sternum. “But only if we go back.”

“Go back where?” Dr. Taylor asked, pulling a pen from under her bright yellow head wrap. She scrawled something on the small notepad she retrieved from a hip pocket.

“Wherever we just dove from. Because maybe she hasn’t come back yet. Maybe we can still save her.”

“Doctor Kapoor, you mean?”

Her condescending tone made his teeth gnash. “Yes,” he said, slapping the glass as Justice had done only moments before. “Kapoor, *Vanhi Kapoor*. Is there an echo in here? She is going to *die* unless we go back.” He did his best to explain, speaking slowly, articulately, making sure they couldn’t twist his words to mean *I have her hidden somewhere aboard and unless you give in to my demands she dies!*

“I think that gurney is probably a good idea,” said Steve.

Dr. Taylor looked troubled, but not in an *I believe you* sort of way. "You're not in a position to negotiate, Stone."

"Then I'm not going." He crossed his arms and strode back to the cot, dropping onto it with a decisive *plop*.

"I have the authority to forcibly remove you," Taylor said.

"Then do it," he dared.

Steve smirked, the expression growing into a sadistic full grin as he made to open the door.

"Hold on," Justice said, sliding in front of him. "Is his request really so unreasonable?"

"Out of the way," Steve demanded. "As the doc said, he's not in a position to make requests, reasonable or otherwise."

Stone resisted the urge to taunt him with the fact that he'd filled Stone's request to contact Justice.

"Move," Steve spat when Justice showed no sign of yielding.

"Come on," Mac said, laying a hand on her arm, "let them do their jobs."

She jerked back. "Last dude who laid a hand on me got his fingers broken, so help me—"

"This is ridiculous," said Steve, attempting to manhandle her out of the way.

Stone jumped to his feet. "Leave her alone!"

Bodies jostled outside his cell. Two more guards joined Steve in his attempt to remove Justice. She and the men yipped at each other like dogs in a fight. Dr. Taylor got pushed to the side, and both Captain Baglanova and Mac tried to break it up.

Justice threw a punch, clipping Steve in the ear. Baglanova shouted. Stone paced.

He couldn't do anything, he couldn't—

And then he saw her. Not Justice, she was holding her own. Vanhi.

Dr. Taylor stared wide-eyed at the woman who'd appeared at her side, clutching her hand to her chest like she was witnessing a specter. She quickly crossed herself.

Dr. Kapoor floated as before, disconnected from reality. But she opened her eyes more quickly this time, falling when she did, slumping into Dr. Taylor, who looked like she wasn't sure if she should catch Vanhi or refuse to touch her.

Stone was more than elated. He was vindicated. "There! Turn around, she's right there!"

The fighting stopped. Everyone spun.

It's real. And she's safe. She's here.

It was definitive proof. He had witnesses. He wasn't hallucinating, and she wasn't dead. They had no actual answers, but at least they had *her.*

Overcome with relief, he sank to his haunches, his knees giving out. With a stuttering heart and trip-catch lungs, he put his hands on his head and whispered, "*Gracias a Dios.*"

Justice spent the night in the brig for throwing the punch. Tempers were hot convoy-wide, and both Captain Tan and Captain Baglanova didn't see any reason it should go on her permanent record. After all, she'd only been defending her friend against potentially harmful medical treatment.

Stone wasn't sure if it was the sundial or the ship that Vanhi was tied to, but thank god it wasn't her spacial coordinates. The only thing he knew for certain was that the dial couldn't follow her to . . . wherever she went.

Initially, Tan wanted to keep Dr. Kapoor's "condition" hush-hush, if for no other reason than it might cause mass panic. But he quickly realized that her safety depended on the crew knowing.

Most of the crew had a hard time taking the announcement at face value. Alien structures in deep space were one thing, but this . . . it was broaching pure science fiction. How could such a thing be possible? Had Tan lost his mind?

The majority had to see it with their own eyes before they accepted Vanhi's condition as scientific fact. In a way, it helped that Dr. Kapoor began popping in and out on the regular, though witnessing one's mission head disappear or materialize out of nowhere was—on the whole—incredibly distressing.

It was like she was her own SD drive in her own SD bubble, diving and emerging uncontrollably.

Eventually it became clear to everyone that when she jumped, she always left the dial behind, and she always reappeared in its vicinity. So that her touchstone didn't accidentally end up at the bottom of a trash compacter, and her along with it, protocol dictated the trinket to be returned to a med bay immediately, where it would be kept in a prominent and open position until she returned.

TWENTY-ONE DAYS SINCE THE ACCIDENT

"Yikes, C, what's with the screeching?"

The PA reduced the volume on its output, and the little light on the side of the sundial blinked in earnest. "Apologies, sir. I've been having minor malfunctions since July sixth."

"You and me both," she murmured.

She stood in front of a door, three decks above her own quarters. It looked like any other door, and she meant the errand to be quick, but she couldn't bring herself to knock. Not yet.

One year, eight months, and seven days. That was how long *Pulse* had been in service. One year and millennia, it seemed. The door was mostly unblemished, with nary a scratch. It didn't have the cake of age, or the dullness of wear brought on by knuckles rapping again and again over the same spots. It looked new. It *was* new.

"If you're waiting for me to ring the buzzer, I regret to inform you that I don't have fingers," C said.

"Oh, hur hur," she said. With a deep breath, she rapped once.

The door whisked silently to the side—effortless on its rollers.

Stone stood on the other side, eyes wide, surprised. Pleasantly, she hoped.

He looked a little rumpled—but she supposed they all did these days. Few people besides Tan and his closest staff saw fit to keep themselves well pressed, clean shaven, and wrinkle-free. Stone's hair stuck up haphazardly, as though he'd just rolled out of bed.

"Hi," she said softly.

"Hi," he echoed.

"Sorry if I'm interrupting your downtime, but I—"

"No, no. Uh, come in."

"Oh—" She'd expected a swift exchange, hadn't envisioned getting past the door. "Okay. Thanks."

At first, his quarters looked like many others. It was a single, though he could have easily upgraded to a four-person if he'd wanted. There were plenty of open housing options. His bed sat beneath the room's one window. A small table occupied the space to Vanhi's immediate right, and it was stacked high with paper books.

It should have been immediately obvious, though—the walls—but she was focused on Stone, the way he moved to make space for her in his home. He scooped up a pile of hardbacks occupying a chair, and waved at it in offering.

She sat before she noticed the color. "Nice. Your walls, I mean." They were alternately bright crimson and sky blue.

He demurred, smiling lightly to himself as he reshelved the volumes on the bookcase that spanned floor-to-ceiling on the far wall. "Yeah. I'm probably the only person who devoted a good portion of their personal weight allowance to paint. When the acceptance letter said we could personalize our staterooms, I got a little excited. I'm used to barracks, where the only touches from home are a handful of pinups and maybe a picture of your *madre* if you don't mind getting ribbed."

He turned away from the shelf, and the last book in line toppled over with a *thunk*. He didn't right it. "What can I do for you, Vanhi?" He paused, caught himself. "Or . . . or should I call you Doctor Kapoor now? I know Tan's been pressing for more formality, says it helps ingrain a sense of stability—"

It felt odd, though, the formal address. They'd been having difficultly reconnecting with each other ever since the accident, and she wanted that to change. "Please, Vanhi. I'm not officially the mission head anymore, so no need to be so prescribed . . . no matter what the captain suggests."

"You've assigned your successor, then?"

"Yep."

"I'm sorry to hear that."

"It was necessary," she said, folding her hands in her lap, eyes fixed on the sundial. "I'm still working, still taking on most of the responsibilities of mission head—but Doctor Gabriel Dogolea is going to be filling in when I'm, you know, absent. And he'll take over if . . ."

Stone didn't finish the sentence for her, but he let out a shaky breath.

She was glad, in a way, that the disappearances caught her off guard. She'd never had time to think *What if this is the last time? What if I go and just . . . don't come back?*

As far as she was aware, she'd disappeared and reappeared seven times. She didn't remember them all explicitly, but they were all being documented. It was possible there were more instances—no one monitored her in her sleep, and she didn't wear the sundial in bed for fear of stabbing herself with the gnomon.

The whole situation was maddening.

"Anyway," she said, forcing herself to segue away from her

spiraling thoughts, "I wanted to thank you for getting my sundial back to my room. I came to more or less in bed."

He rubbed the back of his neck, a distinct blush spreading across his nose and cheeks. "How did you know it was me?"

"Tan's protocol," she said. "Everyone knows the sundial is supposed to go to the medical wing if it's found. But a few people, like Gabriel, know that I hate appearing in the med bay. No one keeps the dial anywhere soft there. I'm always coming to on a cold floor or half off a hard exam table. You've heard me complain before."

"Sure, but I'm not the only one."

"So you didn't put it in my quarters?"

"Nope," he said frankly. "Well, I mean, I had maintenance do it. It's no big deal."

"But it is, to me," she insisted, standing, moving toward him. "You . . . Look, a lot of people are worried about my safety. Tan, the department heads, everyone. But not a lot of people seem to care about my *well-being*. You've been looking out for me since before I realized I needed looking out for, and I've never properly . . ." She reached out, her fingertips grazing his arm as she tried to get him to look at her.

His eyes shot to hers at the touch.

They were wide, but wary. Why was he so wary?

Can't we go back to the banter? To the flirting and the stolen moments? There's so much wrong with the convoy now, can't we have a little bit of normalcy?

A dark thought clipped itself onto the end of her quiet plea: *Maybe I don't deserve any normalcy. Maybe it's fitting that I've ruined this . . . whatever* this *was . . . too.*

He backed away slightly, rocking on his heels to separate himself from her touch. She withdrew her hand, recoiling as though she'd crossed an obvious line.

"I do worry about you," he said softly. "Justice thinks I worry too much."

"I like that you worry," she confessed.

"Well, good. Because I like worrying about you."

Her breath caught. "Will you keep worrying? If I ask you to?"

"Yes. Even if you don't . . ."

They both smiled sheepishly, and Vanhi's stomach flopped over in a giddy knot. She felt simultaneously elated and like an idiot. They were grown adults discussing a highly improbable medical condition—for want of a better term. Physics condition?—but she felt like a graceless schoolgirl.

"Then," she said, as an idea caught in her mind. She fumbled with the latch on her wristband, fingers stuttering though the action was familiar. "Can I ask you a favor?" The leather was soft, supple. Crease lines feathered out over its surface, revealing how often she'd taken the strap off and put it on again. "Keep this for me?"

"What?" Stone asked, followed immediately by a digital, "What?" from C.

"I can't keep wearing the dial, I realize that now. I haven't wanted to give it up, because my sister gave it to me." She traced the metal dial with her thumb, pressed the gnomon into her skin, let it bite and leave an impression. "It was a jab at my attachment to a PA—antiquated as they are. Were. Suppose they're *really* antiquated now." She huffed a small laugh, pressing the keepsake to her chest. "I should have put it in a box as soon as I realized it was my ground—my connection to the greater dimensions that keeps pulling me back from wherever I go. Should have put it someplace safe."

Stone's gaze was earnest. He clearly meant to refuse, to insist he couldn't accept the responsibility for anything so precious. But he'd already taken responsibility for the most precious thing she owned—her very life—so why should this trinket be too big of a burden to bear?

"But I *can't* stuff C in a box. It's stupid, I know, but my

PA is my friend. It knows me better than anyone aboard, and even if it can hibernate, I don't want it to."

"I don't mind, sir," C said.

"I know," she said to the little thing clutched to her breast. "But there's more." She looked Stone in the eye, needed him to understand. "I don't want to wake up in a cold medical office, either. I don't want to come back and be alone and have no one to—to understand."

Don't tell him you cry in the shower. Don't tell him you think it's like dying a little every time you disappear. Don't tell him you're afraid you'll never come back.

"This is my tether," she said, taking Stone's hand, turning it palm up. She set the sundial in his hand, and he let her curl his fingers over it. "But I need a touchstone. I need someone to ground me. To keep me sane. I have something to come back to. But I also need *someone* to come back to."

Both hands went to her cheeks, then to her chest. She felt too hot, as though with fever. "I know it's a lot to ask—"

"Yes," he said quickly, cradling the sundial like a delicate egg in his palm. "I can be that for you."

He tried to put the sundial on, but chuckled when he found the strap didn't reach. It broke the tension—the dam that had been building in Vanhi's chest with so much pressure behind it. But instead of letting all of her emotions spill over, they flew away, and she took a deep breath. "Oh, no," she said, trying to help him, to get the leather to stretch all the way around his wrist.

"Wait, I've got an idea," he said, slipping the dial off the strap. Springing over to his bookshelf, he opened an old yellow cigar box he'd been using as a bookend. From inside, he drew forth a chain. His air force dog tags dangled from the length.

Carefully, he threaded the dial onto the chain and strung it around his neck. "Guess I'll have to get used to wearing these again."

“No, uh, no cross?” she asked. She pointed at the chain, feeling as though something, some symbol, should have been resting beside his tags all along.

His gaze followed her finger. “No, wh—? Oh. You think all Puerto Ricans are Catholic?”

“Oh, that’s not—”

He waved it aside cheerfully. “No, it’s fine. Lots of Puerto Ricans are Catholic. This Puerto Rican is agnostic. My parents, they are—were. It’s still hard to say ‘were’—Jehovah’s Witnesses.”

Weren’t Jehovah’s Witnesses pacifists? “But you were in the military?”

“Yeah. Can’t say they approved.”

She commiserated. “Yeah, my parents weren’t real big on . . . on the P.U.M.s. Or, rather, me being a part of them. They were worried, about me going into space. Guess I showed them.”

She cringed as soon as she said it. It was supposed to be a joke, but . . . well, *too soon* was an understatement. Why did everything come back to the accident? Why couldn’t she keep the chit-chat away from their damn tragedy for more than two sentences?

Stone secreted the tags and the dial away under his jumpsuit, then put his hands in his pockets awkwardly. They both fell quiet, the momentum of their dialogue dying.

She tried to think of another topic. Something unrelated to the uncertainty of her condition, or the ambiguity of the convoy’s place in the universe. Something that wasn’t so daunting.

But all she could think about was her PA, now resting against his chest, warming from his heartbeat instead of hers.

She wasn’t sure where this left them. What this made the two of them.

“C?” she said.

“Yes?” the PA answered, only mildly muffled by Stone’s uniform.

“I’d like you to start a second user profile, all right? Stone Mendez Perez. He has full access now, all right?”

“Full access?” C asked. “Including journal entries and—”

“Okay,” Vanhi said promptly. “Secondary access.”

“You been writing about me in your diary or something?” Stone asked slyly.

She shook her head and turned away with a smile, but did not disabuse him of the notion. She thought maybe he’d dismiss her now. But she didn’t want to go. Yes, this ebb and flow of awkwardness was difficult to endure, but saying goodbye for the moment seemed worse.

But he didn’t show her to the door or offer some excuse about a prior engagement.

He sat on the bed, off to one side. Clearly leaving space for her. With an internal shrug, she sat next to him. They exchanged soft smiles.

“Feels strange,” she said, rubbing at her bare wrist. “I feel more alone now.”

He nodded thoughtfully. “You know, back home, I never felt alone,” Stone confessed. “I mean, I’ve always been around people. My parents owned a farm—had land—but that didn’t mean we were hermits. And then, when I enlisted, I was constantly surrounded. Privacy didn’t exist.

“Now we’ve discovered evidence of intelligent life, and I feel . . . isolated. Shouldn’t the universe feel smaller, not bigger and more empty?”

She glanced to where his fingers curled over the edge of the bedspread. Each digit was its own entity, yet they were connected. Like everyone on the convoy.

Cautiously, she slipped her hand down over his, covering those fingers with her own. He didn’t shoo her away. If anything, he leaned closer, tilted his head toward her. She took a deep breath, committed the spiciness of his scent to memory. It was a fragrance she'd look for now whenever she woke up.

"I think it's okay to feel alone. We're so used to having Earth right there, a phone call away. But now . . . We're going to have to rely on each other's company. Who knows when we'll see other people again?"

"We have to become a family," he said, "All of us in the convoy."

"Right. All we have is each other."

TWENTY-SEVEN DAYS SINCE THE ACCIDENT

Stone hadn't seen Vanhi since she gave him the sundial. They were both too busy. But he did check in every day to see if she was aboard or dancing in the ether.

Last he'd asked around, Dr. Dogolea said she'd disappeared during drive maintenance. That was twenty-three hours ago. Stone threw himself into his work, trying not to worry about what he couldn't control.

Reconstruction was going well. Everyone was putting in overtime work. Justice was doing her best to help improve their food situation, and he was trying to make sure the inner hulls were sound.

Today he was pulling a double shift, and had half an hour to get clean and comfortable, eat his meager rations, and get his butt back to the shuttle bay for the next changeover. It wasn't much, but he planned to revel in it.

A shower was most definitely in order.

After he turned on the water, Stone didn't wait for it to warm. He shuffled in under the spray as soon as his work clothes were pooled on the bath mat, a fresh set folded on the back of the toilet tank.

His muscles tensed when the first drops of chilly water splattered across his skin, but he relaxed into the steady pressure after only a few moments. He was sore already, his lower back twinging every time he bent or reached. How was he supposed to keep this up for another eight hours? He was an ADCO, damn it, not a moving man.

The shower quickly did its job, with the help of a well-worked lather. He passed his soaped hands over his pectorals and collar bone—beneath the dog tags and the sundial—then across his abdomen and pelvis, muscles jumping under his careful touch, eager to unwind. The sweaty stench he'd had to stew in for the past shift slipped down his body and into the drain, leaving the faint scent of "ocean breeze" behind. The bar was nearly gone, but he had one more from the original stash. Then it was old-fashioned synthesized oils from now until eternity.

Perhaps it was a waste—this extra shower. But he valued his cleanliness. It was difficult enough to get away from the smell of unwashed human on a spaceship, no need to add to the problem.

He washed his shoulders and his glutes, then ducked his face under the spray to drench his hair.

As he pulled back, eyes closed, the water stopped. That happened sometimes—plumbing interruptions when water was suddenly diverted to a newly opened tap.

But he also felt a shift in the air—a heaviness in front of him.

Spooked, he swiped at his eyes, slid backward, bare feet squeaking hollowly against the fiberglass.

But he was too slow—a dead weight slumped into him.

It took a half second to catch up, to slip from surprise into concern, then into pure chagrin. "Vanhi?"

"Mhhhhuh?" She leaned into his chest, fully clothed, her back instantly soaked. Shaking off her jump-sleep, she automatically pulled her shoulders to her ears, pressing closer, trying to get away from the wet shock. "What the—Oh. *Oh.*"

"Shit," Stone cursed, stiffening, realizing he was bare-ass

naked with Vanhi-Fricking-Kapoor curled against his chest. With a continued litany of "shit, shit, shit," he pushed her away, toward the wall. "Shit. Hold on."

She bowed against the tiles, her forehead pressed to the mist-covered porcelain.

He tripped and nearly smacked his face on the toilet bowl as he scrambled to leave the shower stall. Groping for where he'd hung his towel, he tossed it over his shoulder the moment he laid hands on it. "Here—oh, damn it."

Vanhi made some sort of odd gurgle in the back of her throat, but caught the off-white cotton in a fast hand.

Of course, genius that Stone was, he'd thrown her a towel but neglected *to turn off the water.*

"Sorry, shit, I didn't—"

The nozzle whined and the pipes groaned as he spun the shower handles. As soon as the pitter-patter of water died, he understood the strange sound Vanhi was making.

She was laughing.

She hid her face behind the soggy towel, wheezing into it, shoulders shaking.

"I'll just . . ." He backed out of the bathroom, sliding the pocket door closed behind him.

Mortified, he stood dripping on his living room carpet, balls-to-the-world naked. His fresh uniform was still atop the toilet's water tank.

"Great," he mumbled to himself, one arm slung over his chest and the other over his groin, like he was hiding from a crowd in an embarrassing dream. *Could* this be a dream? Maybe this was a dream.

Vanhi's laughter grew more raucous.

Not a dream.

He hurried to his dresser, hands shaking from the sudden adrenaline spike. *It's not every day you get ambushed in the shower.* He struggled to find the correct pieces to compose an actual outfit. One sock and an undershirt weren't going to cut it. Nor were two button-downs. Son of a bitch, why was his brain short-circuiting?

Pants. You need pants, dumbass.

But he was too slow. Behind him, the pocket door was jiggling in its frame. Vanhi struggled to get it to open. It always stuck a little, and this time it gave Stone a grace period in which to dive for the bed—still soaked—pulling the comforter into his lap just as she stepped out.

She was still laughing, ragged towel limp at her side, glasses fogged beyond use. She wiped at the lenses as she tried to get a word past her giggling.

"Vanhi, I am so sorry," he said earnestly before she could speak. "I wasn't thinking. I used to shower with my tags on all the time. I should have considered—"

She waved his apology aside, wiping her glasses on a mostly dry bit of her shirt. "It's fine. Stone, I'm fine. But you, I—" She set the frames back on her nose and burst into another round of hysterics. "No, I shouldn't be—it's not funny, I'm sorry, you must be—"

But it *was* funny, and her laughter was contagious. He tried to keep a straight face, but his sides tickled with her amusement.

"This is still better than waking up in an exam room," she said. "Much warmer welcome." She giggled once more—clearly having meant the *water* was warm. But when she caught her unintentional double entendre, she froze. "I—I mean, it's nice not to wake up alone."

Yeah, that didn't make it better.

Flushing, she hid behind the towel.

Stone's very unhelpful hindbrain provided him with a plethora of comebacks. The mildest and quippiest—*It's nice not to shower alone*—nearly escaped his lips before he swallowed it down.

He tried not to think of her flush against him, the weight of her, the floral scent of her—

"I'll do better next time," he promised breathlessly, clutching the bedspread tighter to his crotch. He did not need an erection making this any more awkward than it already was.

"This was . . ." Vanhi started and trailed off, moving toward the hall door.

Nice? Fun? Humiliating?

"This was good," she said simply, awkwardly. "But I should probably change into some dry clothes."

"Me, too," he said frankly.

Her only reply was a bashful smirk before she escaped out the door, her soggy shoes making a *squish squish squish* as she went.

With a huge sigh of relief, Stone flopped onto his back and stared blankly at the ceiling.

"That was . . . educational," C said after a time.

Her next few reappearances weren't nearly as eventful. She reappeared while he was at work on *Breath*—nearly got squished between the hinges of the thick radiation-resistant door they were installing, but was none the worse for wear. She reappeared in his kitchen, thankfully far from the hot plate. And she popped up on his way back from a shift doing laundry for his floor—landed in the laundry cart, cushioned by perfectly folded uniforms that were not-so-perfectly folded when she climbed out again. She helped him sort them all after.

Every time she solidified next to him, his heart jumped and his throat would tighten. Not from the surprise—that first incident in the shower apparently inoculated him against all sudden shocks—but from the proximity alone.

It was weird: being lost in space while simultaneously experiencing something so pedestrian as a crush.

Of course, it didn't feel pedestrian. It felt big, as though he was filled up with it, running over with it. Sometimes, when he saw her, his smile broke free before he had the chance to compose himself, as though his grin was the spillway on his emotional damn.

He was light with it, and heavy with it, and hoped that, just maybe, she might be bursting at the seams the same way he was.

And C was a comfort he never knew he needed. All those nights he'd lain awake, thinking, staring at his blue-and-red walls turned deep gray in the dark, he'd needed to talk things out. Needed to express his fears, doubts—to get it all out of his head. But journaling had never been his thing, and besides, a page couldn't help him process, whether it was digital or paper.

But C he could muse to openly. Without worrying about judgments, or lectures.

He'd thought Vanhi's attachment to the PA endearing at first. Now, he had no idea how she'd been able to give it up. How could she give something so valuable to Stone? A last gift from her sister, a constant companion, a tether to reality—she'd given all these things to him of all people. She'd trusted *him*.

It was impossible not to feel proud and humbled at the same time.

He was especially glad for C the day Tan made a final ruling on *Life*. They'd thought, hoped, that it might be nearby. But all evidence pointed to one of two possibilities. One, that it hadn't made the jump with them. Which, if they could ever confirm, would be a relief. But, if it hadn't stayed behind, it must have been destroyed. Which meant all of their MIA crew members were surely dead.

"Today, we say goodbye to one of our triad," the captain said solemnly over the convoy-wide system. "We were *Life, Breath,* and *Pulse*. And though one ship has left us, we choose to believe that our companions aboard made it back to Earth. We choose to believe they lived long, happy lives. We choose to remember them in the spirit in which their ship was named."

When the announcement finished, Stone mumbled a quiet "Amen."

The rest of the day was filled with quiet contemplation. There was a sadness most crew members found difficult to work through. The captain declared it a day of mourning, dismissing everyone unessential from their day's duties.

Stone would have preferred to work, really. Spending twenty-four hours locked in grief felt wrong—disrespectful, even. At least he had a bright spot: Vanhi. Today she offered him a special opportunity to escape the noise in his own head.

"Come with me to the astronomy lab," she said at his door. It wasn't a demand, nor was it an excited invitation. Her tone was somber, yet her body vibrated with urgency. Behind her stood Dr. Dogolea, his usually expressive face a blank mask.

"Captain Tan just summoned me," Vanhi said. "Carmen Sotomayor—and your friend, Justice—they've been finishing up some calculations, and . . . they've found it. They know our position in time and space."

A sickening cocktail of excitement and dread tumbled together over ice in his chest. This was good, wasn't it? Now they would know what they'd need to do to get back to Earth. Now Vanhi would have another piece of the accident's puzzle: knowing the result of the SD bubble entanglement meant they could more easily work backward, better identify which experimental SD had captured them.

"The captain said I should bring two colleagues," Vanhi continued. "I'd like you to come with me and Gabriel."

He nodded, and silently fell into step. C said nothing, heavy against his chest.

The astronomy lab was a domed room at the bottom of *Pulse*. Its curved windows allowed for easy space viewing, and its large, externally mounted telescope had been designed to take pictures of Oort cloud objects for researchers back on Earth.

Here, the telescope had found the field full of alien objects. But it had also helped them identify Triangulum, the Sagittarius Dwarf Spheroidal, and a handful of other galaxies. It had given them the information they needed to find their place in the universe.

As the three entered, Stone noted that opposite the windows sat a bank of computers, their monitors all displaying various galactic models. He couldn't make out what they said, though.

He smiled at Justice when he caught her eye. She did not smile back.

Both captains were present, as were their first officers, all in full dress uniforms out of respect for the dead. Vanhi, Stone, and Gabriel waited for directions before sitting.

Carmen Sotomayor opened with a breathless welcome. She was their only fully deaf crew member, though they had several partially deaf crew members as well. Justice was one of only a handful aboard fluent in American Sign Language, which was a factor in her volunteering to work with Navigation in pinpointing their position. Sotomayor's translator, Twinkle Pemba, was also present.

"I'll cut to the chase," Carmen signed and said. "Using multiple landmarks as points of triangulation, we were initially unable to decipher our location because each object's position was dramatically different from the records we have. We believed this was because of distance. And, we were partially correct. Justice?"

Justice was already moving, having been watching Carmen for her cue. She brought up a diagram of the Milky Way on a monitor. "Here," she said, pointing. "Is Earth. And here—" she pointed at an arm of the galaxy on the other side of Sagittarius A*, the Milky Way's black hole center "—is where we are."

Everyone in the room leaned forward, as though the distance between their eyes and the image mattered in grasping the concept.

Stone didn't lean forward, though. Rather, he stifled a sudden burst of vertigo. Internally, he flailed—it was like thinking you'd gone to sleep in your own bed and waking up in a stranger's. He had suspected they were far, but they were so far out of their local star group they might as well be off the map.

Carmen continued. "The reason this took us so long to work out is because many of our landmarks are *still* not in the right place, even accounting for the distance, the new perspective. We had to make sure we were accounting properly for the *rotation* of the galaxy as well. That we were factoring in enough of it.

"A galactic year is approximately two hundred and twenty-five to two hundred and fifty million years. So, we set our year, twenty-one twenty-seven, as year zero and advanced the models from there."

Vanhi's hand shifted under the table, searching for Stone's. They found each other's fingers and held tight.

Everyone held their breath.

"We've done the calculations again and again," said Justice, signing as she spoke. "We will of course need an independent team to review the conclusion, but we're confident enough that we think your team," she gestured to Vanhi, "will find our work invaluable at this stage."

Justice, you're one of my best friends, Stone thought, *but for the love of everything, get on with it.*

"We are," Carmen signed and said, "approximately fifteen kiloparsecs, and *one hundred thousand years,* from where we began."

The room erupted—the captains demanded they run the calculations in real time, so that they could see for themselves.

Only Stone and Vanhi sat quietly. He tried to meet her gaze, to see how she was taking the news, but he had trouble lifting his stare away from the monitors.

The sense of vertigo heightened, making Stone swoon. He needed to go lie down, to shut his brain off for a little while. He needed to let this hellish realization percolate, because he didn't have the mental tenacity to deal with it right now.

But the meeting dragged on, Carmen and Justice becoming more frustrated the more they were asked in a disbelieving tone to "run the damn models again." It wasn't that the others thought the two of them hadn't done their job, they simply hoped that maybe, this time, the mistake would be revealed and this cruel joke would be over.

Stone's vision began to tunnel. Suddenly, there was a soft hand on his shoulder. It was Vanhi's. "Hey," she said quietly. "Do you want to get out of here? I think the captains have a lot more to discuss with Sotomayor and Jax. I don't think we—" She interrupted herself, turning to the captains. "Sir," she addressed Tan, "may Mendez Perez and I be dismissed?"

"You have all the notes you need?"

"For now, sir."

He nodded his acquiescence.

Once they were outside the lab, Stone rubbed at his eyes, leaning heavily against the wall. "Thank you," he said. "I just . . . I don't know how to . . ."

"Yeah, me, too," she said, wide-eyed—empathetic, but clearly also reeling. "Do you want to . . . to get our minds off it for a while?" She took his hand, and he understood what she meant. She wanted to forget for a moment as well, to shut off the fear and the doubt and the analytical part of her mind.

"My room?" he asked.

She nodded firmly, reached up and kissed him hard. A

moment later she backed away, leading him. "Come to bed with me," she said, shuffling down the hall. "Please."

They both needed closeness, comfort. They needed each other.

Vanhi Kapoor, I think I love you, he said to himself. The wonder of it, the tragedy, the emptiness and fullness of everything that had happened swept over him. Putting one foot in front of the other, he sighed, and followed her on weak knees.

CHAPTER FOUR

CONVOY SEVEN

JAMAL: THE SPIRITS THREE SHALL STRIVE WITHIN

NINETY-NINE YEARS SINCE THE CONVOYS SPLIT

AUGUST 17, 224 RELAUNCH

5811 CE

Jamal Kaeden the Eighteenth sat in his quarters with the lights off. All of them. No indicator lights blinked, no power buttons shone—he'd even covered up the clock's display.

The only glimmer came through the porthole window near his bed. Outside, LQ Pyxidis and the Web were in full view, approximately fifteen light-minutes out. The megastructure swathed the star in a mesh-like matrix—many nodes connected through many lathes, creating a uniform geometric pattern through which only a fraction of the star's true output seeped.

Though he couldn't see them from this vantage point, he knew the Seed (the one device that broke the pattern and was orders of magnitude bigger than the next largest node) and the gap (the incomplete portion of the structure, three AUs tall and half an AU wide) lay opposite each other.

The Web orbited around LQ Pyx, and the empty gap caused the star to appear as though it strobed. That was why they'd come to investigate this star in the first place, all those many centuries ago.

Now, Jamal glared at the star. He wished he'd taped a blanket over the porthole.

It wasn't that he didn't want to see his visitors, or that he didn't want them to see him. Everything just felt more intimate in the dark. The encounters were warmer, closer, somehow free of time and space. Like sharing a womb.

He listened closely to the sounds of his single-room quarters, leaning forward in his chair, eyes closed despite the darkness. There were nuances in their voices that helped him distinguish which was which. Of course, while their voices were nearly identical, their personalities couldn't have set a harsher contrast.

"I told you, you have to get Margarita on the job," said one man. He sat on Jamal's bed, back against the wall, knees brought up to his chest.

"I don't think so. You want to rely on a communications officer?" said the other. His voice came from the kitchenette. He always pretended to make coffee when he visited.

"Her specialty is signals," said the first man. "Or, at least, it was. Is she still a comms officer?"

Jamal opened his eyes, shifting his gaze between the two dark silhouettes in his room. "Yes."

"Good. See? If it's a signal interference problem, maybe she can help. Sometimes we have to look to other disciplines."

"I still think it's a code problem," said the man in the kitchen. "Something to do with the Web's computer systems. It has to have a computer, right?"

Jamal rubbed his eyes and sniffed. "Do I have to keep reminding you—?"

"I know, you're not in computers. But we—" he gestured between himself and the visitor on the bed "—are."

"*You* are," corrected the other man. "I'm in Consumables."

"But you hate it."

A sharp buzz signaled someone was at the door. "Who is it?" Jamal called.

"Toya." There was a long pause. She seemed to be waiting for the door to open, but he was waiting for an explanation. "You didn't show up in manufacturing," she said after a time. "And your comm unit is off, so they called me."

He gave his guests an apologetic shrug. "I.C.C. was supposed to tell the team I'm busy. They can solve the problem themselves."

"They said I.C.C. confirmed you were on your way. Can I come in?" Her muffled voice sounded more concerned than annoyed.

Ignoring her request, he invoked I.C.C. "Why did you tell them I'm coming? I have visitors. I can't very well take them with me."

"I don't think ignoring the summons is in your best interest," I.C.C. said.

"Why not?"

"Because the problem is urgent. And . . . because you don't have visitors."

"Just because you can't see them—"

"I cannot detect them in any way," I.C.C. said bluntly. "You are registering as the only bio signs, and there are no anomalies. You are alone in your quarters."

Jamal studied the two men. He knew they weren't there in a physical sense—their forms were somehow projected into his brain, but that didn't mean they weren't there at all. He couldn't find a way to explain it to the AI, so he stayed quiet.

The two men had first appeared a couple of years previous. For what reason, Jamal couldn't say. He'd woken up one day and there they were—leaning over his bed, telling him to rise and shine.

Sitting a comfortable seven years away from retirement at

the time, he had chalked the visitations up to the wisdom and sensitivity of age. Lots of people got quirky in their later years. He wasn't crazy—these weren't voices in his head. They were . . . reflections, or vibrations, or something. Whatever they were, they were real, not the result of psychological trauma or neural chemistry gone wrong, as the doctors would have him think.

"Hello," Toya called from the hall. "Are you still in there?"

Reluctantly, he went to the door.

She took a step in, without an invitation. She was tall and slender, like Jamal, and was one of the few people who didn't have to look up to meet his gaze. The laugh lines around her eyes and mouth were deep, though these days she was more likely to greet her brother with a charitable frown than a smile. "I thought maybe something bad . . . Why's it so dark?"

"I.C.C.?" The AI brought the lights up, revealing all the places where Jamal had thrown a blanket or a strip of electrical tape over minor light sources.

To Jamal's eyes, it also revealed the two men. Men who looked just like him, save in age and wear and tear. He affectionately referred to them as Three and Five, though "Five" insisted his number was inaccurate, since he hadn't been born as a proper continuation of the line. They were two of the earliest Jamal clones, from so many centuries ago.

The Third was young—late twenties or early thirties, whatever age he'd been when he'd died in his revolution. The Fifth appeared as little more than a boy, though he'd lived to see retirement. Seventeen—he was the same age as when he'd saved the convoy from self-destruction, when he and another Jamal clone had pulled them from the literal Pit. But Five didn't behave like a teenager; he clearly remembered his full life. The ridge above his left eye sported a massive scar.

Toya looked right through the both of them. "Are they here?" she asked, a skeptical twist pursing her lips.

Jamal's heart fluttered. Was it happening? Could she sense them? "Yes. You can feel it, can't you?"

"No." She sighed. "I can tell by that look on your face."

"You should stop pushing her," said Five from the bed.

"They're your line, too," Jamal said to Toya, pulling out a chair at the table for her. Though the two clones had been raised as brother and sister, genetically they were father and daughter. "You would be able to connect to them if you'd just—"

She sighed again, more heavily—loud and false enough to cut him off. With flippant movements, she took the proffered chair, as though she sat only to indulge him. "This is why—" She stopped herself and bit her bottom lip before continuing. "Ok, you've got imaginary friends. I've dealt with that for years now. I've tried to let it be. But when you start talking like that, like I should be seeing them, too . . ."

Jamal grabbed her wrist imploringly. "You *should*. It has something to do with our genetic code. I see them because we're . . . because we resonate. I don't know. It's buried in the DNA, or the ships, or both, or something. I know if they can reach me they can reach you."

Blood is thicker than water, as the ancient saying went. Toya was a Kaeden, same as him. The eighth in her cloning line. She could see these echoes too, if only she'd try.

She gave him the same annoyed scowl she'd used when they were kids. The kind of frown all sisters give their brothers when they discover their dolls have been used as combat vehicles.

"You didn't have a problem with me—or them—until you thought about getting remarried," he said.

"This has nothing to do with Kasun," she said quickly,

jutting out her sharp chin. "I want you to keep your . . . friends . . . to yourself, is all." After a deep breath, she continued. "You're good at your job, and you're a nice guy, but . . . you can't push this on everyone else."

"I told you," Five said.

"Shut up."

"What?" Toya said.

"Nothing. It's—"

She shook her head. "I know exactly what it is. And that's what I'm saying. First it's me, then it's your friends—*real* friends—next your engineering team, then what?"

"No, you don't understand. Just you."

"I *don't* understand." After a moment she stood again, coming to some sort of compromise internally. "Look, if you stop pushing this on me—no, if you stop talking about this altogether—I'll stop pushing you to see the doctors, okay? Call them up and cancel all of your appointments, I won't argue."

"That's fair," Five said sympathetically. "It's a lot for someone to take in, Jamal. You remember how horrible it was for the three of us, trying to engage for the first time. Don't make her try to struggle through that if she's not open to it."

"You're such a weak hull," scoffed Three, exiting the kitchenette to roll his eyes at Five. "Don't listen to that bleeding heart. He doesn't care what's good for people, just that they're all happy with him."

Five let out a clipped *ha*. "Like you should be giving familial advice. Who in this room almost killed their own little sister? Oh, that's right: you. Traitor."

"Sellout."

"That's enough," Jamal said, waving a curt hand in their direction.

Toya's expression softened. She reached out and cupped Jamal's cheek, running her thumb lightly across his aging skin. "Focus, please. I'm not saying they have to go away. But it's best if you pretend they're not there when I'm around. And other people—when other people are around. What's it going to be?"

"So, it's just for your peace of mind?"

Her lip trembled, and he realized that might have been a poor choice of words. She certainly didn't think his mind was at peace—*in pieces*, maybe. "Yes."

"Fine. Deal." They shook on it.

"You shouldn't have told anyone about us in the first place," said Three, hands in the pockets of his antiquated jumpsuit.

The three of them walked down *Mira*'s halls, on the way to the shuttle bay and then *Slicer*. Jamal had agreed to look in on the manufacturing crisis, though begrudgingly; he never felt comfortable taking his ancestors out in public.

"Hey, he was just trying to be honest," said Five.

"Oh, shut up. You want them to walk all over him like your crew walked all over you."

"Better than only looking out for my own needs, everyone else be damned."

"It wasn't like that."

"You even screwed over I.C.C. It takes a lot of jerk-off points to betray an infant AI."

Jamal rolled his eyes. He liked them, and he liked getting visits from the past, but sometimes they were both assholes. Two sides of the same coin. "Can you guys cut it out?" he mumbled out of the side of his mouth. "I thought you were here to help me."

"We are the ghosts of Christmas past," Three said with an appropriately cheesy oscillation in his tone, waving his arms above his head.

Jamal shot him a raised eyebrow. "What?"

"Oh, come on, you guys don't read Dickens in the, uh, whatever the hell century this is?"

"That's not what I meant. I . . . I don't like thinking of you as ghosts. You aren't, are you?"

The two ethereal men shared a look. "No . . ." they said together.

"I don't know if we should get into all that—we've skirted the issue before, but I think it's best if we just leave it a mystery," said Five.

"Mostly because we don't really know," said Three.

"We've got an *idea*," said Five. "It's hard to explain and better left unprobed is all."

Three gave Jamal a pointed look. "We don't know."

"It's like a continuum," said Five as they entered the shuttle bay.

Jamal chuckled internally. Leave it to one to irritate the other into opening his big mouth.

"Or like tree rings," Five continued. "Yeah, that makes more sense. Tree rings build up. It's like we're two of your rings."

Jamal climbed aboard the shuttle that would taxi him to work. "And how come no one else is talking to their rings?" Jamal asked aloud. They—he—was the only passenger, and the partition between him and the pilot's cabin was soundproof.

Three shrugged, stretching out on one of the shuttle benches like it was a chaise longue. "Perhaps they're not as in tune with the past. Lots of history on these ships. Lots of waves and signals and such passing through the walls, through I.C.C., through you . . . maybe it's resonant brain wave patterns or something. We imprinted on the convoy, and something about your makeup lets us reimprint on you."

"So, you are real, but you aren't here?"

"Sounds right," Three said with a sigh.

"We shouldn't have told him all that," said Five.

"Why? It's not a secret."

"No, but . . ." He sat down cross-legged on the floor. "It's just a theory. That we have. Which means it could be *his* theory, if you catch my drift."

"We're not a hallucination," said Three.

"But do we *know* that?" asked Five.

"Well I sure as space don't feel like a hallucination."

"See," Five said with a sigh, "This is why I didn't want to talk about it. Jamal, if no one could see or hear you except one person, wouldn't you—at some point—question your own existence? I do."

"I don't think you need to worry about it," said Jamal.

Both Three and Five looked at him, puzzled, coming out of their own little worlds. "No?"

"No. I don't care if you're sure, or unsure, know or don't. *I* know you're real. You've told me things I couldn't have known, which means you're not just in my head."

Three bit his lip. "But how do you know you couldn't have known? Couldn't you not know that you knew? Or is it that if you know you don't know—"

"Stop that," Five snapped.

Amazingly, Three shut up.

The antiquated shuttle touched down with its usual grind. *Solidarity*'s fabrication teams were supposed to be introducing a new model soon to replace these twelfth-generation death traps that were known as "rusted bolts" around the fleet. They couldn't perform properly anymore, but it took a lot of grease to get rid of them.

Political grease, that is.

Since they'd arrived back at the Web nearly a century ago, the full force of their collective effort had been focused on reverse engineering. Earth had stopped communicating with them again, but what else was new? And they hadn't heard from *Noumenon Ultra* in a decade, which could mean everything or absolutely nothing—the time dilation meant updates were few and far between anyway. Besides, completing the Web was far more important than communing with the home planet, or making sure their counterparts were safe, or ensuring that the matters of day-to-day convoy life were seen to in a timely manner.

So what if the shuttle's gyroscopes were imbalanced? As long as you can still get from ship to ship without a pressure leak, everyone can relax. So what if the tines on your forks are bent? So what if the lights in your cabin flicker? So what if you have to go to the mess for coffee because your maker's shorted out? Go take five on Eden. *We've got alien devices to build.*

Jamal feared they were losing something, *had* lost something, important. Like they were missing the point of life while compelling themselves to live it.

If it wasn't in service of the Web, it wasn't worth an extra note. And with the vibrancy of his past at his beck and call, he'd started to wonder if that was a dark hole, sociologically speaking. Neither Three nor Five had seen the Web in person, and yet their lives had been so full.

Not that he envied them. Tragedies were never enviable.

Having alighted on *Slicer*—whose mountain's worth of empty space gave the crew plenty of room to build the ship-sized devices that were the Web's main components—Jamal and his two invisible companions headed toward the additive manufacturing division. Manufacturing took his team's designs and printed working models. As long as all of the elements and alloys were flowing, usually everything worked out fine. The parts might not function as they'd hoped, but the printers did their part.

The additive labs were lined with clean rooms filled with industrial-sized ovens. At the banks of three-dimensional projectors sat technicians laboriously converting schematics into working models for the printers. The hum and whir of the machines was normally punctuated by the light scent of burning dust and molten metal in the air.

Today was not normal, though. Today, the place was in an uproar. Something had caused a buzz among the techies. And from the smell of it, something had caused a fire among the printers.

In a clean room at the back of the lab, I.C.C. spewed flame retardant through a hose in the ceiling and onto an equipment bank.

"What's the trouble?" Jamal asked Dr. Nakamura.

"We're not sure—could be on your end, could be on ours," she said. "But we're close to something—or maybe we're way off base. Hard to tell. But when the printer making your Alpha-2.09 model was eighty-five percent done, something happened inside the machine and things went uncapped."

Jamal's skin tingled. "So, we were right? The devices contain some sort of energy-to-matter—"

Three cut him off. "No." He'd wandered, phantom-like, through the clean room wall, keeping a reasonable distance from the spewing hose. "That can't be right, I told you," he called. "If all you're doing is absorbing a star's typical output, why would you want to waste energy converting it to matter for storage? I don't think mini fusion reactors are the key."

"Uh, Doctor Kaeden?" Nakamura prompted.

"I'm sorry. You were saying there's been some kind of uncalculated reaction in the printer?"

"We think so."

"Can you bring up a display of the portion the machine was printing at the time?"

"Of course." She hurried to a hologram array and brought up a rotating model. She pointed to the area involved in the malfunction.

Jamal looked to Three and Five, but didn't say anything.

"This would suggest the secret lies directly in the innate properties of the materials," said Five eventually. "That it doesn't have anything to do with a signal or a code."

The area Nakamura indicated was a small compartment surrounded by a complex arrangement of wires and nodes, all made of different alloys and all connected differently. Jamal's team liked to call it the "infinity gap," because they didn't have a damn clue what happened inside. They were sure energy went in, but beyond that, they knew nothing.

"Looking at this model doesn't tell us crap," said Three. "You need to see the damage."

Jamal glanced over his shoulder to the smoking machine. The flames were gone, and no one seemed to be in panic mode any more. "May we?" he asked Nakamura, gesturing.

She took stiff strides over to the clean rooms, showing great restraint in her movements, though Jamal could tell she internally vibrated with frustration. Whether it was because she was tired of the setbacks, or because he'd used "we" instead of "I," Jamal couldn't say.

Before entering, Jamal and Nakamura were sprayed with antistatic formula—which smelled like wet dog—before being shrink-wrapped into hyperefficient temporary bunny suits. The suits were made of a thin flexible film that clung to every pore and fiber, following any twists and bends the wearer made. After six hours they could be washed away with soap and water. Membrane masks—to protect them from any toxins hanging in the air—topped off their ensembles.

The printer in question was a mangled cube. It had originally shared the dimensions of an industrial trash compactor, but now it looked as though it had *gone through* a trash compactor. During the accident, parts of it had imploded while others had disintegrated.

The semifabricated portion of the Web node was in a much better state. If Jamal hadn't submitted the schematics himself he wouldn't have recognized the object as something his team had designed.

Three and Five scrutinized the mangled mess from all sides, hemming and hawing.

"Can you get her to lift up this end?" Three asked, pointing to the pinched right side of the printed piece.

Jamal passed on the request. I.C.C. directed a robotic arm to do the job.

"There's something familiar about the way this collapsed," Five said, trying to probe the damage with his finger. His flesh wouldn't interact with the metal, as usual.

That must be frustrating—not being able to touch things, Jamal thought, an instant before he was taken out of the moment by another idea. *Will I be like that some day? An ethereal being piggybacking off some other clone's brain power? Could I become some electromagnetic pattern that needs to resonate with a shared physicality in order to find self-awareness?*

Would that truly be me, or just the memory of me?

"Hey, chief." Three snapped his fingers at Jamal. "You're supposed to zone out around other people, not us."

"This damage," Five repeated. "I know I've seen it before."

Jamal bent closer, his nose nearly touching the still-steaming fragments. "Where?" he asked out of the corner of his mouth while eyeing Nakamura.

Five shrugged.

"Loads of help there," said Three. A moment later he straightened himself, then cracked his back. "Yeah, I've got nothing."

Clueless himself, Jamal kept searching anyway. He took as many mental notes as he could, and asked I.C.C. for all of the details it had gathered about the failure.

"Thank you," he said to Nakamura, shaking her hand after the inspection. "And I'm really sorry about the printer."

"Accidents happen," she said. Her words were topped with

a sigh that made it sound like *incompetence happens*. Jamal knew the sentiment wasn't pointed at him, but at the world in general.

On his way out of the manufacturing sector, he paused in an empty hallway to confer with his visitors. "You had something there for a moment, Five. Are you sure you can't remember?"

"No. But perhaps I can't remember because you don't know."

"I thought we agreed to stop that," said Three. "And you," he said to Jamal. "You had some funky space-out moment there."

Jamal leaned against the wall and shoved his hands deep into his uniform pockets. "I just wondered if I might be you one day."

The other two stood close, conspiratorially, as though they might be overheard.

"Interesting thought," said Three. "But how do you know this isn't a fluke? That we're never gonna come back again. We are the only two—whatever we are—in your life, right? I mean, shouldn't there be loads more if this were a pattern and not an anomaly?"

Jamal shrugged. "Maybe I only see you because I only need you."

"That's a nice sentiment," said Five.

"You'd think so, wouldn't you?" sneered Three. "I think it's shitty. So, what, we're all trapped in the ether—or the Higgs field or whatever your generation likes to think nothingness is made of these days—and because you want something special, only a few of us get to wriggle into your reality? That's crap, man."

"I'd have thought you'd appreciate having fate turn in your favor, even if it means everyone else gets screwed," said Five.

"Stop it. Arguing like this is not helpful," Jamal said pointedly.

“Well that flushes your theory then, doesn’t it?” snapped Three.

“Jamal?”

Jamal pushed himself off the wall and straightened his collar. That last voice belonged to Anatoly Straifer, the man who would take over Jamal’s technical position after he retired. “Uh, yes?”

Anatoly was a boxy man—angular all around, from pointed chin to jutting shoulders to sharp knees. “Were you . . . were you just talking to yourself?”

“I.C.C.,” he lied.

“Oh, funny. It sounded like you were arguing with yourself.” He clearly didn’t think it was funny at all.

There were rumors, Jamal knew. Other members of his team had overheard him talking to Three and Five early on, before he’d decided to take personal days whenever they appeared.

His colleagues sometimes made snide comments when they thought he couldn’t hear. They knew he took regular trips to *Hippocrates* for “neurological reasons,” and Toya had told him that at least a half-dozen people had expressed concern for his health.

You promised her you’d stop in public, he reminded himself. “Are you headed to lunch, or . . . ?” he asked Anatoly, changing the subject none-too-deftly.

“Yes.”

“Great, me, too. Let’s go,” he said.

“You should listen to your sister,” said Five. “Leave her out of this. Us. Leave everyone out. We know how it looks. We get it, and whatever we’re here for, I’m sure it’s not to make you look crazy.”

They both stood behind him, hovering, as he ate his mid-shift meal with Anatoly.

“Yeah, just pretend we’re not here,” said Three.

You’re hanging over my shoulders like a devil-angel pairing, he thought. *How am I supposed to ignore that?*

“So, the computer engineers think they found an alien hard drive today,” Anatoly said.

Jamal picked at his protein. It had been reconstituted to resemble fried grasshoppers. Anatoly wolfed them down, but Jamal had long ago made a personal vow never to eat something that he could look in the eye before biting into—even if it didn’t technically have an eye to begin with. “They did? How?”

“That flexible strip thing we gave them—which looked like a soap bubble?—they did something with it and I.C.C. They jury-rigged a port for the bubble, or something—didn’t catch how it all went together. But I.C.C. could *read* the bubble. Couldn’t make heads or tails of it, but the AI recognized the information as some kind of binary. Not ones and zeroes necessarily, but you get the idea.”

“That’s bizarre,” said Three. “I would have expected something more complex. Something so far removed from I.C.C.’s history that it couldn’t interact with it at all.”

Isn’t that the primary argument about alien and human biology? Jamal wanted to say. *They should be so different that reactions can’t occur between them. Our diseases should do nothing to them, and vice versa? But then there’s the opposing argument that life is a fundamental quality of only a limited number of compounds and chemical reactions—so that anything living should be based on structures that are similar. Maybe in the long run, computers are somehow the same?*

He opened his mouth to say something to that effect, something that would let Three in on the idea, but he couldn’t figure out how to phrase such a segue for Anatoly’s benefit.

See, if you guys really were all in my head I wouldn’t have to say anything at all.

"How's the team coming with that new bonding technology?" he asked instead.

"Good, good. Still have a long way to go. The bonds are taking, but they're not standing up through the stress tests." Anatoly scratched the back of his neck. "The bonds weren't the cause of that problem in manufacturing, were they?"

"They're still looking into it." He waved aside Anatoly's concern.

"I bet they won't find much," said Three. "When you're messing with alien shit it could be anything."

"They'll figure it out. Have a little faith," said Five.

"Like faith in the system ever got me much."

Ignore them. Pretend it's a conversation at the next table that doesn't involve you, Jamal told himself.

That was easier said than done, though. "Why are you even here?" Five asked Three, leaping up to sit on the table. Jamal inconspicuously moved his tray away from the imperceptible man.

"I have no clue," spat Three. He hopped up on the other side of Jamal, then mounted the table and began pacing back and forth between the trays. "Did my damndest to get off this boat the first time around. Maybe this is my punishment. Go through some half-assed reincarnation only to get stuck with no one to talk to but a yes-man and a nutter. Guess you guys represent what my future would have been like had I rolled over for the man."

"Oh, stop with the self-righteous bull already, will you?"

"*I'm* self-righteous? Mr. I-stood-up-to-the-Master-Warden-and-redeemed-your-heinous-crimes?"

Jamal cleared his throat, throwing in a particularly phlegmy cough. Maybe that would get their attention.

Five caught the hint. "Drop it. Our host, the nutter—as you so diplomatically dubbed him—is trying to look sane."

Three plopped himself down, cross-legged, narrowly missing someone's mashed yucca.

"I've been out most of the day," Jamal said to Anatoly, now that he could concentrate. "Give me the rundown. Any news on any of our projects? Any firm progress?"

"I haven't had a chance to check it out myself yet, but the materials engineers have arrived at the correct alloy, they think."

Five asked dully, "Can the printers be programmed to make it?"

"Can the printers be programmed to make it?" Jamal repeated.

Anatoly shrugged and shoveled a bite of mash into his mouth. "Have to ask Dr. Nakamura."

"This guy is your cycle partner?" Three asked, squinting at Anatoly. "He's going to take your place some day? He doesn't seem to know much about anything, does he?"

Jamal shot him a warning look. *None of us look like we know much about anything. We might as well be hunter-gatherers who've stumbled upon a Roman aqueduct and presume to build one ourselves.* There was such a large technological and informational gap between the humans and the alien builders that it was best not to think about it, lest their endeavors to complete the Web seem impossibly silly.

Oh, great, Jamal realized, interrupting his own train of thought. *I've gone from looking like I'm talking to myself to* actually *talking to myself. Why did I listen to Toya? I should have just stayed home.*

Jamal stood abruptly. "See you back in the labs," he said to Anatoly. Then he made a mad dash for his quarters.

Jamal hadn't seen Three and Five for weeks now. That in itself wasn't unusual, they'd never had a firm schedule. He'd gone six months on the outside without seeing them before. It was the way they'd left last time that made him wonder if something had changed.

Three's blathering at the table with Anatoly had struck a harsh cord in Jamal. Not so much that this apparition, or reverberation, or whatever thought of him as "nutters," but that he thought his own state of existence was a punishment.

"Until you two came along, I always believed in one man, one life," Jamal said gruffly, almost the instant they reappeared.

Three now leaned up against the wall in Jamal's quarters, while Five sat at the table. "I was damn positive that when I retired I was finished. I didn't believe in a heaven or a hell or a limbo where souls hang out indefinitely. You die, you die. You cease to actively change anything relevant to the living."

Neither of them were looking at him, which was fine. Jamal was speaking more for his own sake than theirs. "I thought everyone, *everything*, had a clear-cut ending. Individuals die. Cultures die." His hand took a quick jab in the direction of the window, through which the Web could be seen rotating into view, its many concentrically placed nodes and lathes forming a dark latticework through which the star's brilliance tried to escape. "Civilizations and races die. Which means that everything a man does is only relevant to himself, *unless* he can build something that resonates with the future."

Jamal crossed to the bed, reached over, and slapped his palm to the windowpane. "Something like *that*. It's not a Web or a Dyson Sphere. It is a legacy. It's a sum of voices crying out to forever. That is where I thought a soul went when it died: into the objects it built, the individuals it inspired, and the ideas it cultivated." He removed his hand from the window and placed it over his eyes. "You've changed what I believe. Because here you are.

"So, now I fear that I won't simply die. That I won't forge

myself a forever in life so that I may rest in death. Instead, I might go on. I might find myself in a blind limbo, waiting to cling to facsimiles of my former body. That is wonderful—and frightening—and how *dare* you call it a punishment."

"No, you were right before," Five said softly.

Jamal turned toward him. "What do you mean?"

The two of them made eye contact for the first time since entering the apartment. "I helped reinstate SD travel. Three—" He glanced in Three's direction, but the other man's gaze was fixed firmly to the floor. "I.C.C. credits Three with much of its early maturation. Regardless of how things went toward the end, he put a lot of himself into the AI. Maybe that's how we got here. Something of our essence went into our work—I'm sure it's less mystical than it sounds. But maybe that's why we've appeared and others haven't."

"But you can't have been the only two in the convoy. Why isn't anyone else seeing apparitions from the past?"

"Maybe that part has to do with you," Five said, glancing at the clock. "Something about how conscious you are of legacy and resonance. Hey—" He snapped his fingers in Three's direction. "I'm getting . . ."

"Yeah, I feel it, too." Three pushed himself off the wall and gave Jamal a halfhearted wave.

Three and Five knew when they were about to pop out of reality. To Jamal, it always looked like someone switched off a remarkably vibrant hologram. One instant they were there, the next they were gone. No fade outs, no wobbly waves, no signal interruptions.

It was disturbing. He didn't need any more reminders that they were insubstantial, so he always asked them to "leave" as soon as they got the inkling.

He opened the door for them, and Five hurried out. Three slumped after, but before he'd made it all the way into the hall he said, "If we're imprints on the convoy and not aneurysms in your brain, why isn't I.C.C. hallucinating us instead of you?"

"We're blood," Jamal said frankly.

Three nodded his acceptance. "The next time you decide to get all preachy on the virtues of afterlife, think about this—How would you feel if only one person in the convoy could see you, and that was a prerequisite for your existence?"

"You mentioned that already."

"Right. Now think about how you'd feel if you knew that guy would only be able to see you for another five years. If dying young once is a tragedy, tell me that dying young twice isn't hell."

Jamal blinked and they were gone.

Now, weeks later, he wondered if he'd ever see them again. He'd never known Three to sink so resolutely into a funk. *They aren't a coin like I thought*, he realized. *Rather*, we *are a triangle. We're all connected equally.* It wasn't the *two of them* versus *him*.

And he worried that drawing such a conclusion, no matter how eye-opening it seemed, might actually cause a block. What if his new bout of empathy for them meant they could not manifest? Perhaps now they would resonate more closely with his being, and therefore lose their individualism.

"I.C.C.?" he began, thinking that if there was anyone he could confide in who would not judge him, it would be the computer. What if he related some of the conversations he had with Five and Three, just to see if their theories about their own existence held any clout? Maybe the Inter Convoy Computer would be able to look into it for him, see if their first appearance or disappearances correlated with anything.

They made him wonder about the metaphysical, yes, but he was an engineer first and foremost, a man of physics. And what was the metaphysical except physics not yet pinned down?

"Yes, Jamal?" I.C.C. intoned.

"I—"

But, he'd promised Toya. He was on his way to see her now, to help her with wedding preparations.

Sure, I.C.C. wasn't a person, per se. But he respected his sister too much to go back so quickly on his word, even if there was a logical loophole. Was understanding the origins of his "ghosts" more important than his fellow crew members' ease? Their peace of mind?

"Never mind," he said. "Sorry to bother you."

"It's never a bother," I.C.C. assured him.

After Jamal arrived at his sister's quarters and rang the buzzer, Toya quickly ushered him inside. The room smelled like bright nectar. Live flowers, on loan from the tropical quarter of *Eden*, filled her dining table.

"Kasun will be here soon," she said. "But we're alone now, aren't we?"

"Yes," he said with an impatient sigh.

"If your visitors make an appearance—"

"I won't say anything in front of Kasun, don't worry." Why didn't she trust her future husband with her brother's idiosyncrasies? Jamal knew Kasun to be a kind man, and thought Toya was being unfair to him by keeping her family's dirty laundry bundled up in the basement.

"Thank you."

From her closet she pulled out several boxes labeled Scraps. It was traditional for the couple to tie the wrist of each guest from one side to the wrist of a guest from the other side to symbolize unity. Leftover bits from tailored jumpsuits were used—typically in the work colors of the couple.

"Help me sort these, would you?" she asked solemnly, setting them on the table. "Don't want any frayed ones."

Despite the happy occasion, something was clearly weighing on Toya. Something not Jamal-and-his-imaginary-ancestors-related. Her movements were stiff, almost angry. She squeezed each scrap as though it might try to escape.

As they worked—mostly in silence—Jamal searched for the right question, or the right words of encouragement. But everything that popped into his head was banal or trite:

Buck up.

It'll be all right.

It's just the stress of the wedding.

Nothing felt right.

He looked down at a red swatch in his hand, then up again. Three and Five stood behind Toya, looking over her shoulder with the utmost interest.

"Ask her what she's afraid of," said Three, as though he'd read Jamal's mind.

"Stay out of it," Five said.

"No, trust me," said Three, brushing his counterpart aside.

"Is there something you're . . . scared of?" Jamal asked gently.

Toya nervously tucked a curl behind her ear. It had an unexpected shimmer to it, making the strands glitter like onyx and silver. After a moment, Jamal realized the shine came from an errant tear. "It's nothing," she said. He didn't press. "Well, all right," she said after a moment. "I'm worried I'm making a big mistake. But I'm too afraid of what happens if I don't make the mistake to examine the situation close enough to figure out if it really is a mistake." She laughed cathartically. "That's confusing—sorry. I just mean I sometimes worry that Kasun and I aren't right for each other. That we're forcing it."

"But you want to force it," Jamal said with a nod.

"Yes, because I'm too afraid to start all over again. And I can't . . ." she trailed off.

"What?" Jamal asked.

"She feels like she's all alone in the world, you big dummy," said Three.

Five punched him squarely in the shoulder. "Could you be any more insensitive?"

Three rubbed his arm. "Hey, he's the one who can't figure out that his sister feels like her brother abandoned her to talk to the sprites inside his head."

Jamal skipped a beat and nearly knocked one of the scrap boxes to the floor. "Is it me?" he asked, catching himself. "Do you feel like I've been ignoring you?"

"Not on purpose. And it's not just you. I've never been good at making friends, and when I did they were always older, which means—" she took a deep breath so that she could spit the rest of the sentence out all at once "—which means they've all been retired recently. And when David died and left me single, all I had was you. My brother. Someone I could always depend on. Or, at least I thought so, until this *thing* started happening. Then I was alone. And it's hard to be alone, Jamal. Truly alone, I don't just mean in the romantic sense. I didn't have anyone to turn to until Kasun. And if I admit he's not right for me, then I've got no one again." Toya put her hand over her mouth, as though she'd said too much.

"I didn't mean to . . ." Jamal said. "That's partly why I wanted to share it with you—the visits. I wanted it to bring us closer together, not push us apart."

"But it *can't*, don't you get it?" Her fear finally boiled over the hurt. She slammed the lid down on one of the boxes. "I can't share the voices in your head. I know your visitors seem real, but they *aren't*."

"What if I could prove they are?"

"Don't go there, Jamal," warned Five.

"You *can't*," she insisted.

He gently took her hand. "They're here, right now. If

you'll just hear me out. Listen to what they say, try to feel their presence—"

Toya jerked her fingers free. The hint of a tear in her eye was burgeoning. "I don't know what's wrong with you, but it scares me. Please get help, Jamal." She marched to the door and opened it. "Go. *Now.* Please, I love you. Get help." With her hand pointing into the hall, she stood as still as a statue, waiting for him to honor her request. As soon as he complied, she shut the door again, leaving him alone and flabbergasted.

His two ancestors set comforting hands on his shoulders. Of course, he could not feel the weight of their palms or the squeeze of their muscles through the starched fabric of his shirt.

And for some reason, suddenly he was afraid, too.

He didn't get help. He considered it, calling on I.C.C. several times in stutter-start attempts to schedule psych evaluations. But, in the end, he couldn't see how making the two invisible clones disappear would actually help anything.

"It might repair your relationship with Toya," Five pointed out.

"I don't think so," said Jamal with a sigh. "Even if I believed you were gone and had been in my mind all along, I don't think she'd ever trust that I was telling the truth. She'd always suspect you were still hanging around. There aren't enough years left for me to erase her fears."

Toya's wedding came and went as scheduled. Jamal hadn't seen nor spoken to her since Kasun moved in with her.

Maybe things would have been different if Toya had had children. Maybe she wouldn't have felt so adrift. She'd always been the second wife, even in her first marriage. Her husband, David, had already had two children, nearly grown, and they'd never applied for another.

Perhaps then she wouldn't have felt so alone when Jamal's "friends" appeared. Maybe then she wouldn't have jumped at the first relationship offered to her—perhaps she would have slowed down, considered things differently.

It might not have made the difference in Jamal's relationship with her, but maybe she'd be happier.

And ultimately, he just wanted her to be happy.

Jamal tried not to let the new estrangement from his sister bother him. It was her choice, and he had to respect that. Throwing himself into his work seemed the best option. That way he wouldn't have time to think about his mental health or personal relationships.

But months went by without much engineering progress, and he began to wonder if a legacy project, that tangible thing that would somehow help him live on after retirement, was out of his reach.

"Any more additive manufacturing problems?" Three asked one day. He seemed to be more comfortable with his insubstantialness, as he'd taken to sitting in inappropriate places. Now he'd hooked himself onto the bookshelf in Jamal's *Slicer* office, elbows and heels on the shelves, body bent outward in a position that would have been impossible for any person of physical substance. "You haven't said much about that accident."

"Nakamura never came to a firm conclusion. It might have been an unstable chemical mixture or something, we're not sure. The more recent schematics I sent to them had a few material changes, for safety's sake. No more implosions . . . yet." Jamal sat at his desk, going through some 'flex-sheet work, running his fingers thoughtfully over the edges of the supple plastic. An unactivated puppet sat hunched in the corner of the room, its featureless face bent sightlessly toward the floor. Jamal never used the automations from Earth, even though he had the proper implants. He didn't like them, and felt he didn't need them, but since there was no longer any place to store them—*Hvmnd,* their original home, having been allocated to Convoy Seven-Point-Five—one was stationed in each office, a literal silent partner.

Five had been doing sit-ups on the polished cement floor. He suddenly sprang to his feet. "I remember!"

"Remember what?" Three asked.

"I know where I saw that kind of damage before."

Jamal looked up from his data entry. "Where?"

"*Bottomless.* After The Battle of Eden, I threw myself into figuring out what went wrong. It's what Kexin wanted, and I thought I should . . . anyway. I studied the SD drive during the process of submersion, mostly. Not so much the actual wreckage, but I did look at all of the snapshots taken right after the accident. They looked just like the mangled printer. Have you ever accessed *Bottomless*'s archived files?"

"No. I've had access, but I've never seen the remains. You're saying the implosion patterns are the same? That the damage in manufacturing looked identical to the damage on *Bottomless*?" He rubbed at the rough stubble of his chin. "I.C.C.? Will you please bring up all files related to the decommissioning of *Bottomless*?"

"Certainly," I.C.C. said, a hair slow. "May I ask for what purpose?"

Jamal knew the AI had been listening in on his seemingly one-sided conversation. It was understandably curious. "Side-by-side comparison," he said. "I'll need the data from the manufacturing accident on the seventeeth of August as well. Could you bring the files up on my wall screen, please?"

Bright flashes flickered across the monitor as all of the files popped up for access. Jamal stood and sifted through the information until he came to the photographs. Five was right, the damage patterns were almost identical.

"How did you know?" asked I.C.C.

“I didn’t,” he admitted. “Five—uh, Diego, I mean, Jamal the Fifth did.”

“What—”

Ignoring I.C.C., Jamal pressed on. “This has to mean we’re dealing with SDs.”

Five stood next to him, pointing at the screen. “But *Bottomless*’s mis-dive was due to ineffectual radiation shielding for the DNA-encoded commands, and an incorrect compensation in the governing program’s software. There aren’t any organics—and no software—involved in the printing accident.”

That tickled something else in the back of Jamal’s mind. The way he’d said organics . . . Once again he wanted to confide in I.C.C., rattle off every thought he’d ever had as to the origin of Three and Five—but that was a matter for another time. If ever.

Still, it got his thoughts churning, and with a little skip in his step, he started scrolling through items on the touch screen with a dancer’s flare. “No organics . . . From which we can conclude that there’s something innate in the combination of materials that creates a subdimensional pull. *Our* materials are *forced* into an SD-compatible state by a computer when we dive. What if it’s the opposite for the Web? What if its materials have to be forced into the greater dimensions—what we call ‘normal’ space-time—by a computer? That their state of rest lies *in* the subdimensions?”

“If the ‘infinity gaps’ in the units are for energy storage, that makes perfect sense,” said Three, still poised precariously on the shelves. “Forcing a pocket of subdimensional space-time would take constant monitoring—you’d have to expend extra energy to hold on to the energy. A magnificent waste. Once the Web started gathering energy from the star, it would have to remain on—constantly running, draining. This way it could be switched off, conserving energy.”

Clapping his hands, Jamal turned to pat Five on the

back, only to pull up short in order to avoid an uncomfortable situation. "We were getting closer with the instability, not further away," he said. "Destroying the printer wasn't a setback, it was progress." Then he stopped, his eyes widening. "Like the computer."

"What do you mean?" asked Five.

"I.C.C., you discovered that the Web's computer system is based on a type of binary, correct?"

"Yes."

"And you, Three, you were surprised. Because of how basic that is. Because you thought an advanced civilization might find more use for more complex systems. Base three, five, even base ten?"

"Yes."

"But it's base two. Just like our computers, before Earth went into bio-computing. It's the most simplistic form of computing. Fundamental. One could say, the most likely to exist."

"What are you getting at?" asked I.C.C.

"It took SD technology to get us here in the first place—and now we think SD tech is part of the Web's devices. What if that's why the Web is where it is in the galaxy? Much closer to Earth and it would be too easy for us to get to, so we wouldn't have arrived with SD drives. Much farther, and the variations in orbit and luminosity probably would have been too minute for us to take notice. The original builders were looking for new builders with the right technology at the right time. Their Web is advanced for us, yes, but also understandable. What are the odds of that?"

I.C.C. broke in. "You're saying that the Web's position in relation to Earth is not a coincidence? That the aliens knew humans existed? But the timeline projections put the Web's inception at millions of years before—"

"Maybe not humans, just life," said Jamal. "They knew life was close enough, and that if it evolved into sentience and intelligence than it could make it here and continue the project."

"But there were others," said Five. "Other civilizations. Those who came in the Nest, the Nataré. That means they were close enough, too. But as far as we know, *Noumenon Ultra* still hasn't made contact with them. If intelligence is that common this close to Earth—"

"It may be common in physical proximity, but not in chronological proximity," Jamal said.

"What may be?" asked I.C.C. It was clearly having a hard time following the snippets of conversation.

"Intelligent life."

"But what about the instructions?" said Three. "Or lack thereof. There's no writing, no pictographs. If the buggers wanted to make it simple enough for anyone to build, wouldn't there be directions? A user's manual?"

Jamal shrugged. "Maybe there are instructions and we just haven't discovered them yet." He looked back at the comparison pictures. "I.C.C., I don't suppose you took any measurements of mass before and after the printer accident?"

"I did not."

"Damn. That might have sealed it. I'd be willing to bet the printer had *significantly* less mass after the implosion than before. Some of it disappeared into a subdimension."

"Do you think the pictures are enough to go on?" asked Five. "For everyone else to make the SD connection?"

"Only one way to find out. I.C.C., please transfer these images to a 'flex-sheet. I need to show them to Nakamura."

"Brilliant," Anatoly commended him. Three weeks prior, Jamal had presented the theories to the division leaders. The concept of subdimensional storage was quickly championed by all.

Now Jamal was in the *Slicer*'s giant bay, before his team, gesturing at one of the harvested, ship-sized nodes. In one hand he carried a smooth plastic model of the device that had imploded in the printer. "Thank you," he said softly to Anatoly, the blush evident in his voice if not his face. He was trying to explain his current understanding of how the nodes might siphon their gathered power into the "infinity gap," where it would sink into a stable SD pocket.

"How did you make the connection? Between the two accidents?" Anatoly persisted.

"Oh—" Jamal waved a hand haphazardly through the air. "I guess it just came to me."

With a small knot of guilt in his throat he looked up. On top of the node sat Three and Five, their legs swinging off the side. He wanted to give them credit, but they both just gave him the thumbs-up.

This was proof, wasn't it? That the two of them couldn't be pure hallucinations?

But trying to make that point now felt like it would detract from the technical revelation.

When he was finished with his presentation, he returned to his office alone—his ancestors continued to climb the node like it was their personal jungle gym—and found a message from Nakamura waiting for him. "We'd like to discuss going public with your SD storage theory. Please contact either myself or Captain Nwosu at your earliest convenience."

He immediately had I.C.C. put him in touch with the manufacturing department. "You want to do *what* with the SD storage theory?"

"We want to let the convoy at large know about it," said Nakamura.

"It's too soon," he said. "It's only an idea—we haven't even devised a proper test for it yet. We don't have experiments, let alone results."

"But that's more than we've had in years. This is about morale. Captain Nwosu approached me with the idea, and I think it's a good one. It shows a shift in thinking, and in turn will give a sense of progress to those who aren't in engineering. Sometimes it's difficult to see why a biologist on *Eden* can't get excited about a new alloy, but those kinds of baby steps aren't impressive to most individuals outside the field. It's like when they came up with those beans that had two percent more protein—we thought it was neat for two seconds, then forgot about it, right? But we're not out here so they can cultivate better beans, we're out here to build an alien machine, and we're a substantial step closer now. Everyone else needs to be just as excited by the developments as we are."

"Oh, now, come on," he said. "We're all intelligent here. We're all scientists in one sense or another. The crew doesn't need premature conclusions in order to feel connected to the processes."

"Intellectually, they don't," she agreed. "Emotionally, they do."

"It sounds like I won't change your mind."

"You won't. I'm going to go to the board," she said, "and suggest you be celebrated in a public ceremony."

"You've got to be kidding."

"They used to have prizes back on Earth for this kind of thing."

"For *discoveries*," he corrected. "Not supposition. Solid research. We're years away from confirming or denying these theories."

"And when we reach that point, we'll have a whole 'nother reason to get the public excited."

"When the board asks you how I feel about this, I want you to be absolutely clear with them—I think it's a bad idea."

A week later, the board informed him they thought it a marvelous idea. And as soon as they announced he would be given a public honor, Toya turned up at Jamal's door. It had been months since they'd last spoken. When the knock came, he'd been reading—Dickens, appropriately enough—and still had the book in hand when he answered.

"I'm so sorry," she said, cutting off his hello. Her uniform was crisp, but her hair was rather wild—bits sticking out haphazardly from her bun.

He motioned for her to come inside, keeping his expression stoic. Being mad at her would be too easy. Instead, he was blank at her—which he supposed wasn't much better, but at least it was something in the right direction.

"I don't know which I should do first," she said, flitting around the room like an *Eden* butterfly. "Congratulate you or beg your forgiveness."

Please don't do either, he thought.

"Instead of taking care of you when you needed help, I let my own selfish fears get in the way." Toya was overflowing with sisterly pride.

"How's married life?" he asked, glad about his initial reaction to her showing up. Truth was, he didn't buy her apology. Looking at her, hearing her, it was clear she didn't actually feel selfish, didn't think she was in the wrong. She just wanted back in his good graces now that the convoy thought him worth cheering.

"Good," she said with a smile and a nod. "My prewedding jitters settled down, and now I'm good." Her eyes scanned the room a little more, until—finally—she looked into his. "Look . . . I know it's not nice of me to stumble in unannounced like this. And I know I've been horrible. I just thought it had been too long since I said I love you." She kissed him on the forehead and squeezed his hand. "I'll get out of your hair now. I'll see you at your ceremony."

"Our ceremony," he whispered as the door closed behind

her, but Three and Five weren't there to hear. He looked at the musty book in his hand, then tossed it on the futon. Best of times and worst of times, indeed.

***Screw it,* Jamal decided, one week before the ceremony. He'd** tried to respect Toya's wishes, but doing so hadn't made them any closer. She'd still kept her distance until *she'd* decided they should reunite. Which is when he finally understood: her feelings were not more important than his. Whatever he was going through, neurologically, it was his to deal with as he saw fit. No one else got to make that call. The crew's comfort was not more important than his. Why should he have to carry their emotional burdens? Why did he pose an emotional burden at all? Just because his mind worked differently, that didn't mean it worked *worse*.

"I.C.C.," Jamal said in his darkened quarters. Three and Five weren't around, but he still enjoyed sitting in the dark, listening to himself breathe. It was the sound of life. "I need a friend. I need *you*."

"What can I do for you, Jamal?"

He laid out the theories he'd discussed with his predecessors. About signal reverberations, the possibility of brain wave residue and the like. "I need to know how they came to be. If it's something that *can* be known."

"Your very own noumenon," I.C.C. said.

Exactly. "Yes."

"Then I need all of the information," I.C.C. said. "I need to know the precise moment when you began having . . . visitors. And I'd like you to set up an appointment at *Hippocrates* to have a brain scan."

"I've had more CAT scans than I can—"

"No," the computer interrupted. "I'd like you to schedule full brain mapping. Neuron location with digital webbing. I have what you would call a hunch."

"What do you mean?"

The computer sounded far away when it spoke next. "At the time of your . . . visitors'—" Jamal wasn't sure he appreciated the way I.C.C. made the word lag "—first appearance, we were in a scheduled SD dive for drive maintenance. I contact the drive AI to initiate regular dives, for moments at a time, to ensure all systems are still functional."

"Sure."

"During that particular dive, there was an incident."

"I don't remember any problems."

"They were imperceptible to the crew. But the records are there, you can review them if need be. The SD bubble suffered a small, let's call it a *thinning*, while we were submerged. It wasn't a tear, exactly. But the protective film was momentarily weakened. There was a spike in the creation of virtual particles for point-zero-zero-seven-six seconds."

"So?"

"At the same time, I was reminiscing."

"You do that?"

"Often. I was reviewing archived footage of your line. Reexperiencing key moments in convoy history related to Jamal Kaeden clones."

Jamal swallowed dryly. "You were thinking about Jamal Kaeden the Third and Jamal Kaeden the Fifth *when they appeared*?"

"It would seem so."

Jamal dashed over to the light switch, illuminating the room swiftly, seeking out I.C.C.'s camera. "Why do you want to map my brain?"

"To compare it to my own artificial neural network. I am beginning to suspect these images in your mind are not hallucinations created solely by your brain. I fear I may have helped."

■ ■ ■

"My nano-neurons—a misnomer, as they are smaller than human neurons—are laid out in patterns resembling human neurons, except that my servers contain several orders of magnitude more neurons than a human brain."

"Okay," Jamal said, staring at the wall screen in his office, scratching his chin. "But what am I looking at?"

There were millions of points of light on the image, representing one portion of I.C.C.'s artificial neural network. Beside that image, another. This one of Jamal's recent detailed brain mapping.

I.C.C. stripped away all information from the brain's image, save small red dots representing neurons. It then overlaid the two images.

Jamal's eyes went wide. He reached a hand forward, groping at the screen. "It's a match." Most of the overlay was different, but there were portions of the frontal lobe that fit perfectly.

"Nearly," I.C.C. said. "Portions of this section of my network are identical to eighty-seven percent of your neural pathways in this specific part of your brain. The artificial patterns may have always been here, or they may have been created when I was restored after the revolt—when I nearly died. It could be someone's homage to the original Jamal Kaeden, I don't know."

"But how can that be? Even if part of your network were based on my original's, the human brain is incredibly plastic. Because Jamal the First's experiences and my experiences are totally different, our brains should have grown differently in response. Which means the odds that you and I would have such an overlap should be astronomical."

"Very true. And yet astronomical does not equal impossible. Your frontal lobe has naturally developed to remarkably resemble one of your clone ancestor's. In turn, it happens that a portion of my neural network resembles the same.

Our matching physical properties, plus my thought patterns during the virtual particle surge, plus the particles themselves, plus the weakening of the SD bubble, could have all come together to create some kind of, if you'll pardon the expression, perfect storm. It is possible that our 'minds'—in a sense—are resonating. Sharing energies. The fact that I cannot detect these energies troubles me, though. I wonder if it was siphoned out of the SD. I wonder if . . ."

"If we don't fully understand SDs after all."

"Yes. But what worries me the most *are* your visitors. When things resonate in physics, sometimes they break. Hallucinations are not always unhealthy, but they can be a sign of physical degradation."

"I still don't think they're hallucinations," Jamal said. "Not in the traditional sense. If you're right, and we've created them—you and I, together—then they may not be my literal ancestors back from the grave, but they are real. They exist."

"I cannot say that they do," I.C.C. countered. "At best, I concede that they may be subliminal thought patterns that your mind does not know how to interpret, so it has created these visuals as a grounding point. If my processes are interfering with your mind, giving you information you did not consciously access—"

"I.C.C.," Jamal said softly. "I don't care. You've given me a why, even if it's only a theory. Just like the damn thing they want to give me an award for. And I get it now. A theory is something, it's a start. I can hold on to it."

"I think we should continue to study this phenomenon," I.C.C. said.

"If you can't measure it," Jamal said, "then it's a noumenon. A truth you can't get to. You only have five more years before I retire. Think you can reclassify it before then?"

"With your permission, I shall try."

■ ■ ■

The board decided to present Jamal with a medal and everything. The event was held in the belly of *Slicer* and broadcasted convoy-wide.

Jamal felt two inches tall. He stood behind a raised platform that sat near the Nest, waiting for his cue. None of this seemed right. Not only was the announcement premature, it wasn't even *his* discovery. But he couldn't admit that—then they'd all want to know who they could look to, who they could thank and honor. Who they could *pin a medal to.*

And he certainly couldn't tell them the truth.

Jamal was instructed to mount the platform with Captain Nwosu, which he did without trying to show too much reluctance.

The live audience was modestly sized, mostly consisting of engineers on shift. Toya and her husband stood near the back. She waved when she caught his eye.

"Today we recognize an esteemed member of our crew," Nwosu began, medal in hand. He detailed Jamal's theory, and what it would mean to future generations of the convoy.

"Pretty spiffy setup," said Three, standing at Jamal's right elbow. "Will there be cake and ice cream, too?" His tone wavered between obvious sarcasm and genuine appreciation.

Five stood at the base of the platform, looking up at Jamal. "You're doing great, keep that smile strong," he said. "I bet you're sweating bullets, am I right? I mean, no one can see me and I'd still rather be down here than up there. All those eyes . . . staring at one thing . . . *you.*"

Jamal frowned momentarily.

"Ah-ah, keep it up," Five said.

Captain Nwosu leaned over and looped the medal's ribbon around Jamal's neck. It hung like an anchor, dragging him toward a murky bottom in his own mind—a silty place where the truth was buried to save face.

So what if it was I.C.C. and not Three and Five? It still wasn't just him. It wasn't his discovery alone. It felt disingenuous to state otherwise.

The medal was nothing like those the athletes of old had worn—it was not shiny, or emblazoned with insignias of achievement. It was simple and gunmetal gray. Deep scoring was its only decorative aspect. It seemed the right type of award with which to honor this achievement.

It had simply been slung around the wrong neck.

"Doctor Kaeden, would you care to say a few words?" the captain asked, stepping aside to let Jamal take center stage.

Jamal looked out at Toya. Her face shone with delight. He was glad he'd been able to make her happy, if only for a moment. But he didn't want to live like she did—fearing that the truth would push loved ones away. Family was about acceptance.

"Thank you, everyone," he said, doing his best to project. "Thank you for honoring science and discovery. Thank you for honoring knowledge. But I can't take credit for this particular development. I had help."

The crowed grinned, assuming him modest. Toya's smile faltered.

"Yes, my team was a great inspiration. But if it wasn't for two men in particular, I would not be standing here today."

"Don't you dare," said Five.

"He's right," Three hissed in Jamal's ear. "This is not a *truth shall set you free* moment. We don't care if you take the credit, but they do."

"I know," Jamal said, loud and clear, turning to face Three.

Five dropped his head into his hands. "Aaaaand, he's officially popped his hinges."

Addressing the audience once more, his confidence blazing like a star, Jamal said, "I have been aided these past few years by two of my ancestors, Jamal Kaeden the Third and Jamal Kaeden the Fifth. Their knowledge made the discovery of the stable SD storage bubble possible."

A few more smiles wavered. Toya's slid off her face like a hand through a grease slick, but it wasn't replaced with mortification. Nor sympathy. No, her expression was something he'd never seen on her before.

"Some of you may think I'm speaking metaphorically," he said with a laugh. "I'm not. These two men are here with me today, but you cannot see them. I do, however, have proof that they exist."

"Say what?" asked Three.

"I.C.C. holds that proof," said Jamal.

"I do not know if it is proof of a visitation," said I.C.C. out of the blue, as though it had been waiting for this moment. "But I have evidence suggesting that it is highly improbable the current Doctor Kaeden could have reached his conclusions on his own. There might have been . . . interference."

Jamal was fine with it relating its theories, about unnamed energies and resonance and the lot. But the AI hesitated. It wasn't ready to make outlandish declarations to the crew. Clearly it would leave that to Jamal. It could, however, discuss the rationale behind its assertion. Still, it let a beat pass before explaining further. "Doctor Kaeden has never seen, nor had described to him, the damage incurred to the first iteration of the ship *Bottomless* during the year 121 PLD. His lack of prior knowledge makes his comparison of that incident to the incident that occurred in the additive manufacturing division illogical."

"Illogical does not equate impossible," said Nakamura from her place near the stage, an uncomfortable laugh coloring her tone.

"Not if his comparison was part of a systematic study. But it was not." I.C.C. went quiet. When a voice issued again from the comms system, Jamal recognized it as his own.

". . . I've had access, but I've never seen the wreckage. You're saying the implosion patterns are the same? That the damage in manufacturing looked identical to the damage on *Bottomless*? I.C.C.? Will you please bring up all files related to the decommissioning of *Bottomless*?"

The clip ended, and I.C.C. spoke again. "That is the first record I have of Dr. Kaeden comparing the two events."

"Who was he speaking to?" asked Nakamura.

"No one. My scans revealed him to be the only human in the room, and he was not communicating with anyone outside the room."

"I was speaking to my ancestors," Jamal said firmly. "I believe they're all here with us, in some capacity. I don't know how, precisely, and I don't know why, yet. But I do know that they helped me. And it doesn't matter if you all think I've lost my mind—I know they're a real, unimagined part of my life. So, you see, today does not belong to me. It belongs to all of us. Those who came before, those of us who live now, and those who will be born tomorrow."

He stepped back, and the crowd began to mumble, then rumble, then shout. Some were afraid, some were skeptical, some were angry. Most, though, were confused.

None of it mattered to Jamal. Perhaps this was his great, everlasting contribution to the universe. Or at least, to the convoy. He'd admitted tapping into something foreign and ethereal. Something science hadn't had a chance to touch yet.

Toya ran through the bickering group until she reached her brother. Jamal held up a finger, afraid of what she'd say. "Not right now," Jamal ordered. "I don't want to hear it. I'm not getting help because there's nothing wrong with me. We all have to find our own truth."

She smacked his hand down, firmly but not violently. "I don't care about that. It doesn't matter how you did it," she said imploringly. "Figured out the problem, I mean. It's your business. And I don't care what the rest of the convoy will think of me or you—not anymore. I meant what I said earlier. I love you. And . . . I'm proud of you. The rest is immaterial."

"*How* I did it is important, Toya," he said firmly. "That you accept who I am and how this happened—not as something in spite of my 'problems' but because of them—is important to me."

"I'll tell everyone about your imaginary friends if you want. Doesn't matter. I'll stand by you. Crazy or no, you're still my brother."

But it does *matter!*

He wanted to rail at her, to explain how she was getting in her own way, refusing to truly see the situation for what it was. But something struck him. Her apology *had* been sincere . . . from her perspective. She was letting him in again. Which gave him a chance to get to her.

They could get past this. It would be difficult, but that's what families are: difficult. She was worth the effort, especially now that he had only a few years left before retirement.

Toya had stopped acting like he was already gone, and he wasn't about to look this gift horse in the mouth.

"Thanks . . . I think."

She looked disappointed, but before she could say anything, Jamal lunged forward, scooping her into his arms. "No, really. Thank you." She might not have accepted the echoes, and I.C.C. might not yet agree that they were real and not a symptom of a damaged brain. The crew might whisper about him from now until forever, but that was fine.

It was fine, because he was fine. He would make them all

see, through living his last years as he saw fit, that there was nothing to fear.

"Thank you," he said again.

Three and Five gave him happy nods, arms slung around one another, comrades at last.

CHAPTER FIVE

CONVOY TWELVE

ORLANDO AND MING-NA: HERE THERE BE DRAGONS

FIFTY-FOUR DAYS SINCE THE ACCIDENT

Dr. Yolanda Taylor stopped making notes with her stylus as Mrs. Tan fell silent.

The captain's wife sat across from her, on the newly repaired, extra-cushiony reclining chair. She'd favored it these last few sessions, over the straight-backed seat she used to occupy. Unlike a lot of well-padded furniture, the recliner had a shallow bench, so it wasn't too difficult for Mrs. Tan, at thirty-nine weeks pregnant, to get back up on her own once she'd settled in.

"Ming-Na?" Yolanda prompted. Mrs. Tan didn't let anyone call her by her first name with company around. But here, in the seclusion of the office, she'd insisted upon it.

Ming-Na's eyes were fixed on the slit between the heavy curtains, which hid the window from view. Most patients these days asked for the curtains to stay closed. Looking at the stars was too much. And now, knowing that there were more than stars on the horizon—knowing there were structures, which meant there had to be builders—was too much plus too much.

The crew wasn't prepared to flounder like this. To be adrift, their food stores dwindling—positionless, pointless, with something brewing in the distance. Those structures were a promise from the universe. Some kind of cosmic sign. But a sign of *what*, no one was sure.

"Ming-Na?" Yolanda prompted again. "You were talking about the captain . . . ?"

She was clearly tired, withdrawn. Her black eyes were half-closed, like shades drawn over a private family scene. But Yolanda's job was to draw them back, to see beyond, to help others through this mess.

"I don't want to talk about Orlando anymore," Ming-Na said abruptly.

Good.

Mrs. Tan liked to deflect, to talk about what her husband was up to so that she didn't have to talk about herself. She was aware of the habit, was trying to get better at opening up. But she was used to being reserved, was most comfortable in the guise of unshakable.

But everyone quakes for something.

"I can't . . . I still can't comprehend how long it's been. *One hundred thousand years.* I miss my mother most," she said, fingering the red scarf tied around her midsection. She'd worn it every day for weeks now. As a comfort, she'd explained. It was an old funerary tradition; expectant mothers were supposed to disassociate themselves from death, from grief, and if they couldn't, a red sash was worn as a protection. And with the whole convoy *awash* in grief—with Mrs. Tan unable to escape what felt like an unending funeral—she'd latched onto whatever relief she could find.

That was a common trend among the crew. Everyone seemed to be holding more steadfastly to their traditions than they might have otherwise, seeking solace in what some of them once considered superstitions.

“It’s selfish, because it’s not even *her* so much,” Mrs. Tan continued. “She was supposed to come visit on the last transport ship. She said she’d help me with the *ma fan*. But she put it off, concerned she was coming too early, that she’d upset things. She’d promised me next time, though. Next time.” She wriggled uncomfortably, arms gripping the sides of the chair with intensity. It was as though she wanted to grab her belly—perhaps protectively, perhaps in anger, it was difficult for Yolanda to tell. “It’s my first. And I don’t have any siblings. Orlando’s brother doesn’t have . . . didn’t have children. I’ve never been around children. I’m excited for her to be born, but I thought *Ah Maa* would be here to help. She was even going to bring our family recipe for pork knuckles and ginger stew. The mess chefs were going to make it for the whole crew, and now . . .” she trailed off bitterly. “And now, not only is my mother dead—gone—but this baby. It was supposed to be a first, but not like . . . not like . . .”

“You have friends aboard. Other mothers aboard.”

“Yes, but it’s not supposed to be like this. And now, with the baby acting the way she is . . .” she trailed off again, her eyes finding the gap in the curtains once more.

Yolanda shivered and looked over her shoulder at the air vent. The ventilation system hadn’t hiccupped, but she was unexpectedly cold. “What do you mean?”

“She doesn’t wiggle the same. She barely moves at all. Before the accident, she would kick often. Especially after meals. Now she’s . . . still.”

“I assume you’ve asked the medics about this?”

“They tell me everything is fine. But the baby doesn’t *feel* the same.”

Was this a projection? Was Ming-Na taking the external change and applying it internally? It would not be unusual for a mother-to-be to feel differently about her baby if her life were suddenly upended.

But there was something about the expression on Ming-Na's face that made Yolanda reconsider. The captain's wife had never been one to project before. She deflected, which was an entirely different defense mechanism. She'd never shown signs of twisting the particulars of a situation.

If she said the baby felt different, it was likely because it *was* different.

"You're under a lot of stress," Yolanda said. "That's going to change the way your body processes things and produces hormones. The baby is likely responding to that."

"I know," Ming-Na said. "But it feels *wrong*."

FIFTY-SEVEN DAYS SINCE THE ACCIDENT

An uneasy routine had settled into Captain Orlando Tan's bones over the past few weeks. He'd get up at 0600, take a shower, brush his hair and his teeth, then make tea and wait for the smell to rouse Ming-Na. He'd help her out of bed, and when he was sure she was steady, would pour a cup for her, himself, and one to offer his paternal grandfather's ancestor tablet. They'd set it in a small nook in the third bedroom of their newly expanded quarters, made it as dignified as they could with a red garland and a place for incense, though for safety reasons they could not light the sticks.

He'd argued with his father about the tablet's removal from the ancestral shrine. The convoy would be close, Tan himself wouldn't be gone more than a few years—it felt wrong to take it. But his father had insisted that he needed an ancestor to watch over him.

Tan had accepted in the end. Now he wondered if their misfortunes might be tied to the spirit's displacement. Or had his family been spared during the accident because he was lucky enough to have an ancestor with him?

At first the tablet had felt like a burden. An expectation of observance, of tradition, that he hadn't planned on participating in on his tour of duty. But now it was an undeniable comfort, even through his wariness, his wondering. It was a reminder of home, a connection to family.

He remembered visiting the ancestral shrine at his grandparents' often. He'd grown up there, with his parents and cousins and uncle. Theirs had been a grand stone building, set in with other ancestral shrines, at the back of a long row of houses that flanked a narrow street on the fringes of Guangzhou. If he closed his eyes, he could still smell new rain sizzling off the sun-warmed roof tiles.

Only the shrine wasn't so grand, he realized now. It had only seemed large and imposing to a small child. There were so many tablets there. And here there were so few, when, if the navigators were correct and they'd leapt a hundred thousand years forward, there should be so, *so*, many.

Yes, it was good that his father had broken up the collection, he decided, despite the taboo. Even when he was young, there had been a decline in keeping shrines. He'd pitied his friends who didn't have one to visit on days of remembrance, though they hadn't seemed to mind. And in the end, he'd grown up into "modern" man—disconnected. Ironic that he should revive his connection now, when everything else had fallen away.

Others on the ships were mourning in their own way, finding their way back to their own lost traditions. There was a hall on deck one plastered with photographs and effigies.

"I do not feel like I am in mourning," Ming-Na told him, striding up to where he knelt with the cup of tea, laying a soft hand on his shoulder. "I feel like I am drowning."

"I know," he said softly, standing to kiss her goodbye for the day. He didn't comment on how thin her face looked, how narrow her arms. She'd already been avoiding heavy and fried foods before the accident, and now . . . Everyone was slowly withering as the rations stretched.

Just as he'd assigned Carmen Sotomayor a team to work around the clock on their interstellar position, so too had he given Justice Jax a party solely focused on genetic replication. Their convoy wasn't designed to grow anything on its own, and that had to change, lest they perish.

He headed to the officers' mess for breakfast. There, he no longer ordered *cheung fun* for breakfast, as he had every morning before the accident. Now he had the cooks make plain congee. Not because it was tradition to eat nothing but congee when a family member died, but because it was practical. It wasn't particularly nutritious, but it was easy to prepare in large portions from what they had left. And the waterier they made it, the further it would stretch. A savory meal was no longer a luxury anyone could afford.

Halfway through his meal, seated next to his first officer, a voice over the intercom called to him. "Captain Tan, we need you on the bridge ASAP."

The breathlessness of the request sent him into immediate action. He swallowed his mouthful of porridge—as did Kurt Böhm, his aide—and together they rushed up to the elevators and rode to the bridge.

"Report," Tan demanded upon entering, immediately noticing the way his officers' fingers flew over their consoles, heads bent to the task.

This was third watch—they'd be changing over in another fifteen minutes, unless—

Before anyone could answer him, his mind was already racing. Was it another accident? An injury?

Second Officer Moscovici stepped into his space immediately, her breath high and fast, the words bursting out of her lips like she'd been trying not to scream them ever since they'd formed. "Navigation reports there's movement in the direction of the object field, sir. Movement headed this way, via SD travel we think. We only picked it up because they emerged close enough."

He didn't tell her to calm down. There was no reason to calm down. His heart had already started to beat itself silly, and he tightened his jaw. "Show me. Bring up the exterior feed. I want visual spectrum, infrared, and radar."

A petty officer obeyed immediately, changing the bridge's windows to display the object field that currently sat aft of *Pulse*.

He'd expected something shocking—as though the typical star field would be instantly blotted out by something hanging off the ship's rear. But everything appeared normal. The objects were far-off, still starlike at this distance.

"It's most difficult to see in the visible spectrum," Moscovici said. She nodded to the petty officer, and the display changed. The field became red and orange and white and yellow.

There—there, he could just see it. A brief change in the makeup of the object field. One of the geometric structures suddenly grew appendages, then those appendages disappeared. Moments later, another structure's formation distorted, blossoming the same appendages, only they were bigger now.

Of course, the large objects weren't changing at all. Something was moving in front of them, moving *toward* the convoy, growing larger in his field of view.

Tan told himself to remain steady, stoic. Moscovici was flustered, so *he* had to be strong. "Give me another feed," he commanded, hoping his voice was firm.

Blue and purple, green and gold, reds upon reds upon reds—he didn't pay attention to what kind of feed it was, just the colors and the contrasts. All he needed was confirmation that these things were indeed headed straight for them.

It's a fleet, he thought, his internal monologue now equally as composed as his exterior. It was everything in between that was stuttering and pumping and screaming with revelation. His blood surged, his lungs hitched, and his stomach cramped. He wished he'd eaten more of his breakfast.

It was his duty to think clearly and order calmly, but his nervous system and vital organs had taken no such oath.

Yet in that cool, rational mind, a spark of hope glimmered and drew his attention.

What if they can help us? What if they're just people—what if they're human? Maybe we should just let them come.

But the rest of him immediately dismissed the notion. *You can't risk it. You don't know what they are—maybe that's not even a fleet. Maybe it's a swarm. Or a pod. Maybe you aren't looking at ships at all, maybe you're looking at the monsters themselves.*

There was no time to consider how to handle a head-on confrontation.

Maybe these beings—if they were beings, for all they knew they could be automated sentries. Robots, guarding whatever was out there. That would make sense. How else could they have detected the convoy? The object field was at least two light-years away at its closest, and *Pulse* and *Breath* were so small, and they'd only been here for a few weeks. That wasn't even enough time for physics to *allow* for observation of any kind. There had to be a detection system of some kind—a buoy or a grid they couldn't see.

Maybe these beings haven't seen us yet? he considered, rounding back to his original thought. *Maybe they just happen to be traveling this way? Maybe we're no more interesting to them than any other pebble in their path? Maybe they haven't actually noticed us?*

That could explain their approach. They seemed to be using SD travel—jumping and resurfacing, jumping and resurfacing.

Either this was the typical way they traveled—perhaps they could not sustain SD submersion for more than a few minutes?—or they were giving the convoy a chance to spot them.

Or they weren't appearing right next to the convoy because they were just as wary of the new ships as the humans were of the object field.

If that last scenario were the case, clearly their curiosity had overridden their caution.

All of these possibilities ran through his mind in a blink's time—a checklist of concepts and circumstances, neatly organized and scrolling past his inner-eye. Now, though, was the time to move past the what-ifs.

Because no matter which of them was true—or if none of them were true—the convoy only had one possible reaction: run.

The risk was too great. Dead space was one thing. If it was just a matter of floundering in a sea of stars, that meant they had to deal with humanity against nature and their survival would be the stuff of Defoe novels. But if they had to throw in an external threat—unknown consciousnesses, or automations, or what have you . . .

Entropy was one matter. But something that could outthink or outpurpose or flat out *blow you out of the sky* with its advanced weapons?

They weren't ready to meet anything like that. If the galaxy was a vast sea they were stranded in, they weren't equipped to deal with what lay beneath the surface—sharks, whales, giant squid.

"We need to dive," he said steadily. "Sync the drives and initiate warning lights."

"Where are we going?" Moscovici asked.

"Anywhere but here."

Her face contorted immediately, and he read concern in the lines of her brow.

“Five-minute sprint,” he commanded. “On my mark.”

Five minutes should be enough to get out of the way. If the approaching fleet had other business, then their course would not change. They’d fly right by the convoy’s new position. And if not . . .

We’ll worry about “if not” if we get to that point.

“Four . . . three . . . two . . . one,” Captain Tan said. “Dive.”

The bridge went purple, the light giving everyone’s skin an alien, fuchsia hue.

The minutes passed, agonizingly slow. Tan brought up the images and graph readouts on a monitor above a rear nav station, studying the objects while he took deep breaths.

It was difficult to say how many there were. Ten? Fifteen? Twenty? It didn’t matter, really—anything past *one* put them at a disadvantage. They had no way to defend themselves. Their only option was to run.

The seconds ticked by, and Tan counted every single one of them. He had to remind himself to breathe, to keep focused. Five minutes felt like forever, and as they neared the final moment, he let himself close his eyes. *Everything will be fine.* When the clock struck, he gave the command to resurface. The purple light returned, and moments later the bubble popped.

All they had to do now was orient themselves to—

A mass cry swelled and burst on the bridge. People shot out of their seats.

Their screens were *filled* with ships. Not just aft, but fore. And off either side and top to bottom. So close, it was a wonder that their bursting SD bubble hadn’t caused a problem with the corral.

“Dive again!” Tan ordered immediately. There wasn’t time for a carefully curated list of possibilities to scroll through his mind. He simply reacted. “Dive, dive, dive!”

A rushing roar filled his ears, his vision sparkled on the

edges. The shock had stolen his air, and he listed slightly to the side—but not far enough for Moscovici to notice. He kept himself steady, his posture tight though he was cursing inside.

White, to purple, to white again. They were in an SD bubble once more.

"What the hell was that?" his aide shouted, gruff and booming, German accent thicker than usual.

Tan's mind flitted through ideas, trying to land on the most logical. Wouldn't they have noticed a second fleet? How could they have jumped into the middle of a storm of ships? Thank whichever ancestors were watching over them—his grandfather, his parents, whoever—that they hadn't appeared *inside* a ship. It would have been another disaster.

His heart paused, then thumped heavily—the excess blood punching through his veins. He grabbed at his chest momentarily, before striking his solemn pose once more. He had to maintain his command, his sense of strength. He had to do it for them, everyone on the bridge, everyone in the convoy.

"Five minutes only!" he ordered. Then they'd surface again, figure out from a distance how they could have missed those other ships or whatever they were.

An image of Ming-Na flashed in his mind and he pushed it aside. She would be fine. They would all be fine.

"Three . . . two . . . one . . . surface!"

Instead of shouts, this time the entire bridge gasped. Everything stilled. Their brains couldn't keep up with what reality was throwing at them.

It was like they hadn't gone into an SD at all, like they were stuck in the same location in time and space, forced to hold steady. But they had dived—*they had.*

Tan was positive.

And yet they were once again surrounded. And the ships all maintained the exact same positions as before. It was like they'd all jumped together, as though they were synced. But they *hadn't* jumped together. Tan would have been able to see ships sharing the same bubble.

"Did we move?" he asked. "Are they keeping us in place?"

"Coordinates have shifted. We traveled, but they—they traveled . . . the same?"

This was beyond them. Everyone knew it. Whatever had just happened, there was no explanation. No *human* explanation.

Everyone turned to him, their expressions sick. Some looked like they might faint, others appeared pained. It was all wrong and they were looking to him for guidance.

A strong, weighted beat of pure stillness followed. Tan centered himself.

"Again," he said evenly. "Dive again."

At first no one moved. Brows furrowed, mouths frowned.

"I said *dive again*," he barked, shocking them into action.

One more time. He had to see. He was giving reality one more chance to play by the rules. And if it didn't work . . .

It had to work.

Now the black-light-esque purple glow carried a new connotation. It no longer felt like a benign indicator. It felt like a panic button had been pressed. Code red had been transformed into code purple. Purple for confusion, for a hasty retreat, for a scattered battalion.

I will change that. Purple will be good again, he told himself. *It meant progress, and hope, and it will once more.*

But for now it made his insides coil and draw against his spine. It made him feel small, and helpless, but it did not break the line of his shoulders or shake the firmness of his footing.

They did not wait five minutes this time.

"Now!" he shouted abruptly. "Surface now!"

He'd wanted to see stars—had willed there to be nothing between them and the vastness of the black pseudo-sea. But no. Large, bulky white-and-copper hulls rolled in their vision. They looked like half-dissolved shells on a weathered beach. Some had an opalescence, like the mother-of-pearl sheen on the inner spiral of an invertebrate's home. Some looked rough and tumbled, like dead coral, and had the branches to match. He could note no uniform ship design, only that they all vaguely seemed to belong together. There were themes, nuanced design similarities, but little more.

So, this is it, he thought. *We meet our fate, light-years from home, lost in time. Lost to anyone but these unknown.*

"Again, sir?" asked his second officer.

He could. They could keep trying, for a while at least. Diving and surfacing were the most energy consuming parts of subdimensional travel, though. And while the other convoys had been created with constant SD travel in mind, theirs had not. It was there to get them to and from Earth at the beginning and end of their mission, and for possible ship checkups in between. He'd only used it initially as an emergency tactic.

And look where that got us.

Subdimensions weren't the answer now.

Had they ever been? Was this entire mission a folly?

Now was not the time for existential questions. Now was the time for step two.

If we can't outrun them . . .

"Lieutenant, I want you to hold."

"Aye, sir."

"We are going to wait, see what they want. We won't dive again unless there are signs of hostility, understood? Böhm, get me a security detail, and anyone with experience in ship design or engineering. Anyone who can give me any insight into these crafts. I also want all comms personnel to brainstorm the best way to contact them, all right? What channels, what message. Everyone needs to be focused on this."

"Yessir" echoed throughout the room.

As the hours scrolled by, every little shift or cough on the bridge had him prickling, wondering if any individual crew member's sudden intake of breath or turning from their station was an indication of contact.

But the ships remained silent.

In his ready room, his assembled team of experts scrutinized what little data they had. Tan needed to know exactly how many ships there were, and to identify their functionality if possible. Were these warships or mining drones? Cargo planes, or pleasure cruisers?

Outside, on the other levels, the security teams went door-to-door, reassuring everyone, doing their best to keep the meager population calm. So far, people had mostly taken to cowering in their quarters. He couldn't blame them.

All shuttle traffic had been put on pause—just until Tan was sure they weren't going to be snatched off their flight paths like fireflies on a summer's eve.

By the end of his shift, though, there was still no response and no new revelations. He was loath to leave the bridge, but his first officer entered fresh and determined, ready for her shift. It was time for a break, at the very least. He could go see Ming-Na, explain what was happening.

But then Böhm sauntered up behind him and bent to his ear. "Sir, I received word from the medical bay. Your wife has gone into labor."

Tan blinked slowly, like he couldn't have heard his aide correctly. With everything going on, this couldn't be happening.

"What, *now*?"

Böhm looked at his touch pad, avoiding the Captain's eyes. "Actually, six hours ago. The message begged me not to say anything until you were off duty, she didn't want to interrupt—" he made a sweeping motion with his arm "—*this*."

Tan cursed under his breath in Cantonese. His exterior

mask cracked, bits of it falling away. His eyelid twitched under his brow. His tongue grew heavy and hot.

Oh, So Gwa, *little one, couldn't you have waited to say hello?*

It was a short trip to the med bay, but it felt like centuries. He tapped his foot anxiously in the lift, allowing his nervous energy to finally escape. Böhm side-eyed him, but said nothing. Which was good. Tan needed this brief release, because once he saw Ming-Na he would have to rein himself in again. She needed him to be strong. What she was going through right now took so much strength, so much work, and she did not need the distraction of his frayed nerves.

When the chime dinged and the doors split open, he practically poured himself into the hall beyond, hurrying just short of running.

"I'm here," he declared breathlessly in the medical wing. "I'm here, where is she?"

The medic wore a calm, cool expression, despite what was going on outside. That was good, that meant the doctors were focusing on his wife and not the objects closed around them like a giant bear trap.

"She's in here, Captain, follow me."

The medic took him into a private room that was a somewhat off-putting robin's-egg blue. Inside, Ming-Na was seated in a birthing chair, her pelvis pointed downward so that the baby could drop down into the waiting arms of a supine medic below.

She reached for him as he entered.

"Look at you," he said proudly, taking one of her hands in his and wiping across her brow with the other. Sweat had gathered near her temples and on her upper lip.

"I feel like a car," she said.

He forced a laugh, trying to block out everything except her shining eyes. "What?"

“You know.” She gestured to the wheeled cart the medic would lie on to slide beneath her. “It’s like the doctor’s a mechanic working on my chassis.”

He kissed her forehead, at a loss for words. Normally he might play into her joke, but right now he had no headspace for clever quips.

Böhm quietly crept in behind Tan and seated himself in the corner.

“How are you?” Tan asked her. “How do you feel?”

“Hurts,” she said honestly. “But I’m fine. *Will be,* once it’s over. What was all that diving about? Those lights turn this room eggplant, and I have to tell you it’s not the most comforting color.”

No one had told her?

Irritation bubbled in his esophagus. He wanted to bark at the nearest medic, scold him for keeping his wife in the dark.

But even as his lips parted to tell her the truth, his tongue stumbled.

“I . . . You shouldn’t have to worry about it right now.” The words caught in his throat, and he had to gulp dryly after spitting them out.

“What’s the matter?”

“Nothing. I’m nervous for you, that’s all.”

“*Orlando,*” she said warningly. “What’s happening?”

“There are . . . are ships,” he said softly, frankly. He knew he sounded patronizing, but he wasn’t sure how else to say it. It wouldn’t come out any other way. “They’re very close. We’re trying to hail them. First contact is imminent, I think.”

“Ships?” she said, excitement setting her eyes aglow. “Did Earth receive our distress call? They’re here to help us?”

She looked so hopeful, he didn’t want to kill her sudden enthusiasm. But he had to tell her the truth.

“I don’t think they’re *our* ships. They came from the megastructures.”

"What?" she shrieked. But it was a composed shriek, a *how dare you not say something the moment you came in here* shriek. "Then what are you doing here?"

She wasn't going to ask what kinds of ships, or who they were, she just wanted to know why he was *by her side for the birth of their first child*?

He nearly laughed at the absurdity. "Are you joking? You're in labor—your mother isn't here, *no one you need* is here—how could *I* not be here? Besides, nothing is happening. They're here, but they're . . . quiet. Still."

"I don't care. You're telling me there are—" her voice dropped to a whisper "—aliens—" she said it like some people say *cancer* "—out there and you're spending your time worrying about me. What if they respond while you're gone? You should be the first to speak to them. Who will lead the ship if you don't? You have to—"

She took a sharp breath through her teeth, dark eyes screwing shut as a contraction hit her.

He rubbed small circles over the back of her hand, waiting for her features to soften—to let go of the pain—before responding.

"Give me ten minutes to worry about you. Then I will go back to worrying about the rest of the universe, I promise."

It could have been overwhelming, too much to take in at once. But he found the anticipation of his daughter to be a welcome distraction from outside. This, in front of him, was a human trial. A familiar struggle that he could comprehend. Instead of adding to his stress, being able to focus on his wife was a comfort. He needed this, to be here. He needed the strength of his growing family to fortify him against the unknown he was about to face.

Only seven of his allotted minutes had passed before Böhm piped up from his corner.

"What?" Tan snapped.

Böhm didn't shrink away, just frowned in defense. He understood the gravity of everything happening at once like this, knew how to stay firm.

He's a better man than I am, Tan groused at himself. "I'm sorry. What is it?"

Böhm had a walkie to his ear. The comms system had only been recently reactivated and was unreliable. "The bridge says there's still no answer. But—" he paused, clearly listening for further information "—but there is a small craft. It emerged from one of the larger ships and appears to be on an intercept course with *Pulse*."

"You don't mean a torpedo or a—"

Böhm shook his head. "Bridge thinks it's either a probe or a shuttle."

"Time's up," Ming-Na said affectionately.

"I'm sorry," he said gravely.

"Don't be. Your being the one to make first contact is far more important than this. I know, I know that hurts to hear, but it is. We don't know what it means for us, and you can't leave it up to someone else. You have to meet that craft—probe, shuttle, messenger pigeon, whatever it is. For the ships. For humanity. We will be here when you get back." She searched his face, eyes roaming over every centimeter as though she weren't sure she'd ever see it again.

He sniffed, filling his lungs, holding his breath until it felt like they'd burst. "Thank you," he said through gritted teeth, before diving in to kiss her on the lips. It wasn't the chaste sort of kiss they'd normally share in front of someone, but nor was it lewd. It was intense, possessive. It held sincere-if-hasty promises. He *would* be back. He *would* celebrate their daughter's first day when he got back.

She drew away first, just a breath's distance, to whisper, "Make us proud."

"I will," he promised. With one last peck, he let her go.

As he left the room, he felt like a long thread was tugging at his heart, was caught on its valves. The twine ran through his ribs and past his spine, tethering him to his family. Rather than a leash, though, it felt like a ribbon, comforting and secure.

He made his way to the docking bay's control booth with Böhm by his side. It was a relatively cramped space, boxed in by glass, set high in the bay's stage left.

"I need one volunteer to stay," he told the three crew members on shift. "Then I need everyone else out. Mr. Böhm, see that all personnel within five floors of the bay are evacuated."

"Yessir."

He wasn't going to block this probe or whatever it was from coming aboard. If he refused to open a viable access point, he risked the newcomers tearing into *Pulse* to sate their curiosity. Hopefully they'd see this grant of access as a peace offering.

There was no question the convoy was up against more advanced technology. Either they'd prevented Convoy Twelve from diving into subdimensional space—which seemed unlikely, given the evidence of his own eyes—or they'd somehow been able to anticipate the human's surfacing time and location with psychic-like accuracy.

Truth be told, that also seemed unlikely, given physics itself. But Tan was no idiot, he knew their convoy tech did not reflect any sort of pinnacle of understanding. They were one step in a human technology ladder, one that had likely acquired many rungs in the interim since their accident.

And who knew where this invading tech came from? Were humans of this time more advanced than these new ships, or less?

The bay manager on duty elected to stay. He brought up an image of the area directly outside on his monitor.

Beyond the thick interlocking metal doors, the small craft

hovered. It sat at the bisection of the doors, appeared to be waiting for them to open like a pet waiting to be let in from the cold.

The probe was a perfect sphere in principle shape, but was covered in myriad sensors and wires and protuberances of unknown usage. It was stark white, and seemed to glow.

Please be patient, Tan chanted to himself. He had the comms channels on all evacuation floors open, waiting for security to give him the all clear.

There's going to be bedlam after this. Everyone must have seen by now—must have looked out a window. There's going to be chaos.

He shook his head. He couldn't think about that right now. One step at a time. He had to get over this hill first.

When the floors were empty, and his first officer had reassured him that everything was still a go on the bridge, Tan nodded to the bay manager. "Let it in."

The man's hand drifted to the first button in the depressurizing sequence. "I know it's not my place, sir—"

"I don't have time to hear concerns," Tan said firmly. "This is not a democracy and I'm not going to argue with you. You do your job, or leave and send me someone who will."

"Yessir." His hands flew over the console, and the air withdrew from the shuttle bay.

Tan held his breath as the outer doors unlocked, sending tremors through the walls of the booth. He wasn't sure where to look—his gaze continuously flickered between the monitor and the open staging ground below.

The probe moved seamlessly. Its means of propulsion weren't identifiable, yet it didn't move with the stutter-stop of jet-based directional changes.

Its stark color and glow gave it a phantom quality, as though it couldn't truly interact with the world, just exist within it, like a ghost.

Drifting steadily, as though on a conveyer belt, it took the open doors for the invitation they were.

Tan only hoped he wasn't inviting a wolf into the house.

"Okay, Mrs. Tan?" her ob-gyn asked. She held her patient's hand and rubbed the top of her spine while monitoring the intravenous line that sent an anesthetic to Mrs. Tan's lower half.

"Yes," Ming-Na said, mouth feeling dry. As the drugs worked their way into her system, the nerves below her belly button went numb, but not dark. Now, her body felt heavy. A different sort of heavy than it had these past few weeks. It was a dead weight on her now. Still. There was no sense of a life within, which stole her breath away.

A swift sense of claustrophobia—of being confined to her own body—made her skin crawl. She didn't want to give birth, didn't want the baby out. *She* wanted out—to give up her skin and bones and find new ones.

Relax, relax, relax, she told herself. *Be strong, be strong, be strong.*

She looked at the heart rate monitor, which showed two beats, both rapid, both robust.

There's life in there. It's okay. It'll be okay.

"Shh, shh," her doctor said—like she was soothing some animal. Ming-Na squeezed her hand hard, digging her nails into the doctor's wrist. Her ob-gyn hissed, but did not pull away. Her eyes widened as she caught Ming-Na's glare, registering that she'd caused offense without, apparently, having even the slightest idea as to what she'd done.

A contraction came again—a heavy cramping in her uterus. It was less painful this time, but she still felt like parts of her were being stretched and released like a rubber band. There was a downward punch to it, and she thanked every deity she could think of for birthing chairs. If she'd had to fight nature by lying on her back just to make the doctor comfortable, she was sure she would have murdered someone.

"Your baby's coming quick," the doctor said. "Really wants to get out here and greet the world."

Ming-Na hated the infantile gibberish but would endure it. She would endure this process and she would endure whatever was outside these walls. She, and Orlando, and their daughter would endure.

The glowing white orb drifted into the bay. Now that it lingered next to their own shuttles, Tan got a better feel for its size. It looked like it could pop open and consume one of their crafts like one of those plastic toy eggs, but only barely.

"Close the doors," Tan ordered, his commanding voice now a whisper. "But don't repressurize the bay. If there's anything alive in there, I want them to get the message. We're tolerating their presence, that's it."

The manager still looked like he wanted to protest, but did as he was told.

Hopefully closing the bay was the right thing to do. He didn't know anymore. There was no outline for this—first contact wasn't even close to a mission parameter. The probe had come to them like a gift, and so they'd enclose it in their hands, accept it. But it also reflected the convoy's current position—hemmed in on all sides, surrounded by the unknown. The message would be twofold.

The bay doors weren't quick. As they pressed in on one another, they left the probe plenty of time to dart away should it or its pilot think twice.

The orb seemed to pay its slow capture no mind.

After a few more moments, once the hangar was sealed, the sphere descended to the decking, its touchdown feather light, if indeed it was touching the deck at all.

"Still vacuum in there?" Tan asked.

"As you said," the manager answered.

"Good."

"What do we do now?" Böhm asked.

"We wait."

Wait for what, though? What if it's a bomb and we pocketed it like a shiny pebble? What if it just wanted an easy way past the hull and starts tearing into Pulse's *insides, hacking us open like an autopsy patient? What if we become guinea pigs? Curiosities?*

What if what if what if what if—

What if Ming-Na has complications? What if she starts bleeding, and I'm not there to—

She asked you to be here. *She doesn't want you to wait, she wants you to act.*

"Do these control the bay lights?" Tan asked, pointing at a set of switches.

"Yes, sir."

"Assuming they sent that thing here to learn and not to destroy, we need to give them a sign. We need to communicate."

"Wait!" Böhm shouted, pointing harshly with his walkie. "Look!"

A portion of the sphere glided back, a triangular section, which swooped over the surface and around to the opposite hemisphere, to reveal a darkness within.

After another moment, a long brown appendage tentatively stuck itself out, as though testing the waters.

"Ready? With the contractions, don't fight them. And *breathe.* One, two, three—push!"

Ming-Na did what her body told her, not what the ob-gyn shouted at her from somewhere about her nether regions.

Bearing down, she bunched her face, scrunching her nose, clasping her eyes shut. It felt like the pushing halted in her abs. She knew it continued down, but the anesthetic made it seem distant. The nursing gown stuck to her arms and chest, a thin sheen of sweat making her entire body clammy. She couldn't see between her legs, but she didn't want to. That would make it harder, make it hurt.

The contraction stopped and she gasped. A medic barked at her to breathe evenly, but she gulped air instead. Why was childbearing such a war? Why did the doctors act like they were on one side and the mother was on the other with the baby in the middle? They were all supposed to be on the same team.

A new contraction rolled over the dying flutters of the last. Trying not to bite her tongue, she clenched.

Something dropped in her belly, like her internal organs sliding lower.

"She's crowning," the ob-gyn said excitedly. "A few more, Mrs. Tan, you can do it."

I know I can do it. Women have been doing this since the dawn of time, of course I can do it.

Another push, another slide.

She wondered if she should be hearing tiny baby-bleats by now.

"Keep pushing. Almost there."

So close, she thought, speaking to the baby. *You're teetering on the precipice, you just have to sway forward a little. Just a little.*

She imagined it, could see her daughter as a woman—an amalgamation of many beautiful baby pictures she'd perused while pregnant, but grown—with her toes dangling over the side of a cliff, arms outstretched to embrace the wide sky above and a winding river below.

She realized it was the Xi River—a river she'd loved. Its waters were calm, inviting. Now it was so far away, so real and yet so lost.

Ming-Na shuddered.

Her grown daughter swayed, almost falling. She just needed a push, and she could soar.

"Come on, come on!" encouraged the doctor.

She bore down again, roaring with the effort.

In her mind's eye, the woman looked over her shoulder, smiling at her mother. Ming-Na could see her own hand reaching out—it was old and wrinkled—to settle in the small of her daughter's back.

"Fly!" she cried, then shoved.

The brown, nearly black appendage was swiftly followed by an equally dark body, covered in what looked like a fine sheen of sweat from the way it glittered gently in the bright docking lights. The creature was long and thin, with four limbs of nearly equal length. It stepped sideways out of the capsule, its prominent head roughly as large as its torso.

Its muscles were evident, clearly flexing beneath its skin as it moved—it wore no pressure suit, and yet did not shy away from the vacuum.

The head was covered in a helmet or face mask of some kind. The covering seemed to claw into the creature's head, the flesh buckling around the seam. It created a shining black blankness where Tan assumed sensory organs lay. Once free of its ship, the thing touched down lightly on the deck—too lightly, given its apparent mass and the strength of the bay's gravity. It drifted, like a feather, down onto all fours.

Tan had to swallow his revulsion. It wasn't that the thing had any distinctly disgusting qualities about it, but he found its movements deeply disturbing. It had somewhat familiar proportions. Four limbs, a thin neck, a round head (or, at least, the helmet gave the impression of roundness), and no tail. But it had an extra joint in each of its legs, and all four of its limbs terminated in hands, with clasping fingers meant to grasp substrates instead of merely balancing atop them. The strange way it bent, along with a chameleon-like hesitance to its steps, turned Tan's stomach. The thing was disturbing in a way one finds figures in a horror movie disturbing. There was something familiar to its construction, but unexpected in how the pieces shifted relative to one another. The incongruences between what his instincts told him to expect and what he was looking at sent shivers of repulsion through his insides.

And the creature was not alone. After it came a new shape, one that looked at first like it wouldn't fit through the aperture of the craft. This one was spiny and white—white like its shuttle, with an iridescence that sent small flashes of rainbow glittering through the many stiff hairs covering its bulbous form. It walked bipedally, as far as Tan could tell. But, the means of its locomotion were well obscured by the spines; it could have been sporting any number of limbs at its terminus.

It, too, wore a mask, which looked to grip its small head like a clenching hand. Parts of it wound around the back of its skull, digging into the hairs there in a way that appeared uncomfortable. It followed the other, some small device in hand, which it raised overhead.

"Ask the bridge to run continuous general diagnostics of the bay," Tan ordered his aide. "We need to be sure they're not interfering with the ship's functionality in any way."

"Yessir."

The aliens didn't seem to realize they were being directly observed. They strode around the deck like they were walking on air—only occasionally did they appear to be experiencing the ship's gravity at its full force, which sent another jolt of disturbia through Tan. He had to turn away from them after a few moments, his inner ear revolting at their apparent disconnect from the ship's physics.

"Look, look!" said Böhm after a few minutes. He stared out

the window, jaw slack just like the bay manager's. The two of them didn't seem to share Tan's unease, and were instead fixated on the forms with utter fascination. "Something else is coming out of their pod."

A thick tough-looking claw clamored against the side of the pod's doorway, as though searching for a handle it could not find. Eventually a second claw joined it on the opposite side of the door, and the two leveraged the body out.

At first Tan took it for a hefty, exoskeletoned creature. It had six limbs—all clawed—and walked with all of them, its bisected abdomen slung low in the middle, nearly scraping across the decking. It was the same size as the others, but everything about it moved with a much more mechanical gate, one that still seemed more natural than the other two figures'.

When one set of its limbs ran across a narrow tract in the body, moving out of alignment with the other four, he realized it *was* mechanical. Was it a robot, or was there an organic creature inside?

For a long while, Tan did nothing but watch. The bridge kept pinging Böhm for instructions, at a want for something to do other than monitor the bay's basic functions (which had not changed). They wanted to signal the creatures.

"They don't know we're here yet," Tan said. "We wait. I want to see if they become cognizant of our presence on their own. Meanwhile, we need to look for signs of possible hostility."

It wasn't that he didn't share in the bridge's eagerness to make contact. The aliens were here, there was no hiding from them, so why not push forward? But he reminded himself that patience was prudence. They could learn a lot simply by observing, by keeping themselves out of the equation for as long as possible.

"How are they communicating?" the manager asked.

The three creatures clearly appeared to be conversing with

one another, if the synchronization of their movements was anything to go by. But the bridge insisted there were no radio frequencies in use, no communications they could patch into. If their helmets allowed for verbal or visual communication, that was unclear.

The clawed mechanism wandered over to the bay's inner doors, clearly noting their function.

Tan stiffened. The clamps on the ends of its six legs looked like they could do real damage to the interior walls—slice right through the metal if they wanted.

If it started ripping and those decks were decompressed, they'd need to act quickly to try and detain the creature.

"Put quarantine measures on standby," he directed. "We might need fire doors, understand?" His aide gave him a shaky thumbs-up and executed the order.

The fire doors sported twenty thick centimeters of galvanized steel. Surly that would hold the thing. Surely . . .

The whole ship seemed to hold its collective breath as the mechanical creature raised one claw. But though it tapped at the bay's hall entrance, it did not try to force it open.

They must realize we're worried about decompression and contamination, Tan thought. *Even if they haven't noted what we* are *yet.*

Fifteen more minutes passed, then twenty. The three creatures crawled across the surface of each shuttle, pulling at it, jumping up and down on its roof, performing unknown diagnostics.

Tan's nervous system slowly grew more accustomed to their movements. The fact that their shifting bothered him at all was curious. Glimpsing a new, strange animal had never bothered him before. He'd watched plenty of documentaries on the oddities of the ocean, land, and air. And none of the most alien-looking Earth life had given him the creeps quite like these three—the long thin one in particular.

Just as he felt his heart slow and his breath become steady—as he was becoming acclimated to their presence—they surprised him in a new way.

Once they'd thoroughly explored the bay's deck, they decided to explore its *ceiling*.

They didn't put on jet packs. They didn't climb the walls with suction cups or handholds or spider's web or grappling hooks. They didn't sprout wings.

They *floated*.

Perfectly in control, they moved seamlessly upward, like balloons escaping a child's grasp, until they oriented themselves to the new position with ease, their feet all coming to rest soundly on the hangar's ceiling tiles.

The three humans in the control booth had no words. They didn't gasp, or exclaim, or make any other indication that they were shocked by this new development.

In truth, Tan wasn't sure he *was* shocked. Their movements had seemed strange to him all along. Why shouldn't they be able to defy the pull of gravitons?

And then, the dark-bodied one pulled up short.

It had noticed them.

With a little hop, it left the ceiling and floated once more, flipping over, reorienting itself downward to match the three humans in the booth. As it moved closer, it maintained its elevation, even with the level of the control booth's windows.

"Oh my god," Böhm said, his voice cringing as his whole body recoiled, balling up. He put his feet on the chair's seat, drawing his knees to his chin.

"Stay calm," Tan directed, holding out a steady hand in Böhm's direction, as though the force of his will could keep his aide tethered safely to the seat. *Stay calm*, he said again silently, when he felt his pulse quicken and his knees shake.

Of course, it had to be the one that gave him sickening palpitations. That *had* to be the alien that came closest.

It stopped a few feet away from the glass, long flutes on its back—flutes Tan hadn't noticed until now—fanning out behind it, almost like an air break, except there was no air. It tilted its head curiously, lolling it first in one direction, then the other, then—to Tan's disgust—dropping it over, almost one hundred and eighty degrees from its standard resting position.

On its elbows (elbows—two joints on each limb) were small braces, he noticed. Those and the mostly featureless helmet were the only clear signs of clothing. He couldn't help it as his eyes roamed its form, trying to determine a sex, as though such a thing would be easy to discern—or even meaningful—on a creature not from Earth.

After a moment of head-spinning, it inched forward, clearly curious.

Tan did not draw back, though there was a strange tug at his heart and spine—almost like the invisible tether that bound him to Ming-Na was calling him away. Instead, he pushed right up to the dash, crowding against it, leaning toward the window.

As the creature came forward, the details of its body came into view. The shine he'd mistaken for a layer of wetness resolved into fine round scales. They were button-sized, and domed, most of them deep black with the brown of epidermis barely a pinprick between them. They looked like they'd be smooth to the touch. The musculature was miraculous, so well defined, each long and taut. Despite his earlier unease, he now wished he could see its face. His mind, thankfully, didn't impose any sort of fantasy onto the blankness of the helm—he didn't want any preconceptions coloring his view when they were finally face-to-face.

It continued forward, now only centimeters away. His previous revulsion was completely overridden by fascination.

This is an alien, he said to himself, mind finally catching up with the events unfolding before him. *This is real. They are real.*

And they are here.

He leaned farther still and found it wasn't enough. He wasn't close enough to the glass, he needed to be as near to this being as possible.

He hoisted one foot onto the console and the manager let out an irritated "Hey!" but let his protest go no further.

In contrast, Böhm leapt from his seat, looking to give his captain a boost up.

"Careful!" the manager hissed, flicking switches as Tan's careless foot flipped them on or off.

Lights in the bay flickered, and the alien looked about, taking note.

"They can see," Tan said excitedly. "They can detect the visible spectrum!"

He clawed his way to the top of the dash, until he was perched on the highest dials, one hand braced against the window so that he wouldn't topple over. Still, Böhm kept one hand on his lower back, just in case.

"Flicker the lights again," Tan ordered, after the manager set them right. "Maybe we can communicate that way."

The man complied, flipping the switches at random, just trying to get a reaction out of their guests.

All three seemed fascinated, their heads and arms moving rapidly, taking note.

"*Waa*," Tan said quietly in amazement, his other hand coming up to mirror the first.

He felt like a child again, and for a moment was whisked back to his eight-year-old self. His grandparents had taken him to an aquarium market—the name of which was lost to him now. He'd palmed the glass there, too, adding to the smudges of the children who'd come before, pressing his nose against it, enamored of the dragon fish, and the octopuses with their graceful gliding.

The alien before him was just as graceful in its floating, defying gravity much in the same way the cephalopods defied it in their swimming.

The creature's attention came back to him, its head swinging on its joint in its horror-movie fashion.

Then, the two limbs nearest its head shot forward, banging into the glass at force. Tan reeled backward in surprise, and only Böhm's presence kept him from toppling to the floor and onto his head.

It had pressed the base of its grasping feet to the window, just as he'd had his hands splayed.

The gesture was sudden, but not violent. If anything it was . . . friendly.

With a hearty push from Böhm, Tan found himself settled near the window once more. His hands had gone clammy—almost tacky—where he applied them to the window. Gently, he covered one of its feet with his hand, then the other. It did not shy away.

It was too much. This day, all too much.

Emotion got the better of him. His surprise and fear and revulsion and hope and longing were all mixed together in an overwhelming concoction that fizzed inside his soul like a carbonated drink, threatening to burst out as tears any minute. One more shake of the bottle would do it.

They held their position for long moments, he and the alien. The manager stopped flickering the lights, and Böhm noticeably held his breath.

What do we do now? Tan thought at it. *Where do we go from here?*

As though in answer, it drew back, clutching its foot to its chest before letting its body drift back to its shuttle.

The other two followed it, and as the trio climbed into their pod, Tan let out a shaky breath.

The aliens exited as they'd entered—first the clawed machine, then the spiny white one, and lastly, the dark thin one. It hung out the shuttle's open aperture for a long time, two limbs in, two limbs out, as though contemplating the situation.

Do they feel hope like we do? Tan wondered. *Are they happy? Curious? Do they have any idea what this means to us? Does it mean the same to them?*

Perhaps this was a proverbial walk in the park for them. After all, there were at least two species present, if not a third. Perhaps they met new life forms on a regular basis and had no idea what kind of a world-shattering experience they'd just participated in.

The dark one's head swiveled once more, taking in the bay from corner to corner. Then it folded up its limbs and slid inside, the triangular hatch swooping into place seconds after.

It took a long while for Tan to realize that the pod was patiently waiting to be let back out into space again. But once they reopened the bay doors, the pod glided away, leaving everything as they'd found it, not a shuttle or a human or a panel worse for wear.

Böhm said they should return to the bridge immediately, make up a full report to submit to everyone aboard.

Tan heard him. And that was important, yes. Everyone had the right to know—needed to understand they'd made peaceful first contract. That it was, thus far, a positive in this upside-down of a reality.

But there was another priority that called to him. Someone who needed him. Two someones by now, he was certain.

So he left the hangar's control room and made his way back to med bay. The birthing room was quieter than he thought it would be. The birthing chair had been removed, replaced by a bed for Ming-Na to rest in. Mother and baby were both there, one tucked safely in the arms of the other. Two medics stood in the corner quietly dithering among themselves, and Tan slid in without interference. Böhm waited in the hall.

"We're all still alive," Ming-Na said. Her voice was hoarse, and she coughed on the back end of her sentence. "Everything went well, I assume?"

"Better than I could have hoped for. I'll tell you everything, but first—"

He drew back the edge of the blanket in which his daughter was swaddled. "You did it," he said with pride. The baby's eyes were closed, her breathing steady.

Ming-Na nodded, but there was a sadness behind her smile. "She . . . she hasn't been awake yet," she said slowly.

He shook his head and shrugged, confused. "What does that mean?"

"They, uh, don't know yet," she said. "Her breathing is strong, her heart is good, they said everything—" she gave a mirthless half laugh "—everything is normal. Except that it's usually a bad sign if a baby isn't awake during the birth. You know, it's strange for someone to get shoved through the eye of a needle and not . . . not notice."

Her lip trembled, and he could see the tears coming. Her eyes were shiny, alight with worry. He kissed her quickly, but if anything, that made her tears flow more freely.

"They're going to get an EEG machine in here, just to check," she said when he pulled away.

"She'll be fine," he said confidently. *She has to be. Everything went so right with . . . with them. This has to go right, too.* "Won't you, *little shrimp*?"

Perhaps that would be her milk name. They would not name her properly just yet. It was too soon, and despite the auspiciousness of the day, they would not risk inviting more misfortune.

"I have hope," Ming-Na said, as though trying to convince herself more so than her husband. "Hope for our future."

He kissed both of his girls on the head in turn. "As do I."

Resurgence

CHAPTER SIX

CONVOY SEVEN

ANATOLY: THE POST-MODERN NARCISSUS

EIGHT HUNDRED AND FIFTY-FIVE YEARS SINCE JAMAL THE EIGHTEENTH'S ENGINEERING DISCOVERY

MARCH 13, 1079 RELAUNCH

6666 CE

Vermilion, white, purple, and ultramarine sashes crossed Anatoly Straifer the Thirty-Ninth's torso, draping from his right shoulder down to his left hip. Four sashes for four stations. He smoothed one, pressing its wrinkles down into the black of his formal garb. He unbuttoned the top two buttons on his collar, exposing the gray of a Revealer. Only on a day like this could he openly display the gray in such an audacious manner.

Six inverted triangles, overlapping and splayed like a hand of playing cards, fanned out from the gray collar. Composed of thin, embroidered lines, they could not be seen except from up close. Six triangles for six Reveals. All made by previous genetic iterations, dating back to his Prime Ancestor, Reginald Straifer of Earth. And he hoped to add a seventh before the day was out.

This was a proud day, one the convoy had been aiming for, true and straight like an arrow flung from a bow, for thousands of years. Now the arrow's nesting was in sight.

In less than eighteen hours, the Web would be complete. And he, as head of engineering, would lead them all in celebration.

He took a deep breath, puffing out his chest, holding in the air to steady himself for a brief moment of meditation. Nervous energy wracked his body—excitement threatened to explode from his mouth and ears and fingertips. He had to relax. Rein in the emotions.

The breath seeped out slowly, and he forced his lungs tight against his spine, making sure they were completely empty. He counted to ten, then let himself breathe normally.

He didn't feel any calmer.

"I.C.C., are the Extensions I picked out ready?"

"They are prepped and ready for interfacing on *Slicer*."

"Thank you. I need to imbue them, first. See that maintenance has them in a life-support dock in half an hour."

"Shall I alert Captain Straifer? She has requested to accompany you for most of the day. Since you are a dual embodiment, she thought it would be most appropriate for you to experience the completion of the sphere together."

"Fine." The answer was terser than he'd aimed for.

To be part of a dual embodiment meant that you and another crew member shared a genetic history, but were not direct clones. Anatoly and Joanna were fraternal twins, the biological children of Esperanza Straifer, Revealer of I.C.C.'s Safety.

Anatoly resented being one half of a duo, however. It meant none of his accomplishments ever really belonged to him—they were shared, and not just with his previous iterations.

Ever since Jamal Kaeden the Eighteenth had Revealed the Resonance of Reiteration, the people of the convoy had come to accept that there was a depth to the universe they could not fully understand. And part of that depth was the resonating continuum that let living people connect to their genetic ancestors.

No one knew how it worked, and no one since the Revealer of Resonance had actually seen their ancestors, but everyone, including Anatoly, fully believed that their major decisions were influenced by people from their past.

The prevailing theories of ancestor resonance suggested that each individual left their mark on the Inter Convoy Computer as a subdimensional reverberation that became entangled with the body and mind of the line's current iteration. That their shared genetics gave them access to one another. When Anatoly died, the ships would retain his essence and pass his mark on to the next Anatoly.

Scientists had been trying to identify crew members' individual SD frequencies for centuries, but hadn't been able to isolate them. All they could figure was that it must have to do with living aboard the ships. They saw no reason why Earthlings—even Earth-bound clones—should experience the same internal continuum.

I.C.C., for the most part, did not agree or disagree with the crew's assumptions. It had been studying Jamal the Eighteenth's case for centuries, with little progress. Perhaps it could not isolate the answer because it was too close to the question. Perhaps the frequencies were embedded within the artificial patterns that made up its consciousness. Perhaps that was how it had been able to gain such a vast and mature self-awareness. Earth, when the convoy had left it a thousand years ago, had been unable to create artificial intelligence. Perhaps there had never been a true AI before or after I.C.C.'s inception. Who knew anymore?

Though Anatoly had never seen or spoken to his ancestors, he'd been able to feel the constant presence of the past since he was a boy. The internal pressure of the continuum was unmistakable.

He could feel them now, steeling his nerves and easing his jitters.

"Tell Joanna to meet me on *Slicer*, not here," he said to I.C.C. Her name tasted like stale bread on his tongue.

Entering the hall outside his cabin, he was met immediately by boiling chatter. It rolled up and down the halls like a wave of pure energy. On his way to the shuttle bay he nodded at acquaintances and exchanged pleasantries with friends and coworkers. They all congratulated him, slapped him on the back, shook his hand, gave any little gesture of appreciation they could. Though this was a day that belonged to everyone, he had the honor of placing the capstone. The last portions of the Web would be joined by his ethereal hand.

"Thank you," an old man said, grasping one of Anatoly's hands between both of his. "Thank you. The medical staff postponed all retirements so that we could see this. It will be something we carry with us, always. Thank you."

By the time he boarded a shuttle, Anatoly's emotions overwhelmed him, making it hard to concentrate. He called upon his genetic ancestors, conjuring an image of each past Revealer in his mind, looking to them for assurance and strength: Reginald Straifer the First, Revealer of the Anomaly; Reginald Straifer the Fourth, a Revealer of Its Power; Nika Marov the Eleventh, Revealer of Abandonment; Esperanza Straifer the Only, Revealer of I.C.C.'s Safety; Anatoly Straifer the Ninth, Revealer of Nodular Function; Anatoly Straifer the Twenty-Third, Revealer of New Construction.

Anatoly glanced out the window as the shuttle was swallowed up by the construction ship, *Slicer*. He'd always felt the ship had an ominous quality to it, though he couldn't put a finger on why. Its hull design was significantly different from the other ships, earthy, rock-like. But that wasn't it. He spent most of his waking work hours aboard; it was strange that he should always feel like he was arriving someplace dark and exotic.

The feeling was even more pronounced today, of all days.

When Anatoly stepped out of the shuttle, the sharp scent of metal struck his nose. All of the other ships were permeated with human smells—food, body odor, soaps, oils, fabrics, what-have-you. But on *Slicer*, the inorganic ruled.

A coppery taste immediately settled on the roof of his mouth, as it usually did. It wouldn't leave no matter how many times he tried to gulp it away.

"Here they are, sir," said a maintenance man in a tight spacesuit, helmet tucked under one arm. He gestured to the back of the gigantic bay, where a row of six Extension units stood like robotic soldiers, waiting for the call to duty. "The ones you said respond best."

"Thank you," Anatoly said with a quick smile. He approached the autons, the Extensions, feeling for them with his mind. Only those in the builder departments had implants anymore, strictly for using the life-sized puppets. Most people could control four at once, letting one human worker with Extensions do the normal work of five crewmen. A few of the top experts could control eight or nine at a time. The most ever successfully guided at once was ten.

Anatoly felt most comfortable with six. He turned them on in unison, feeling each connection as a thread of streaming information. These particular puppets were his favorites; they responded a fraction of a second faster to his commands. Anatoly's friends had teased him for professing to feel a lag in other Extensions, but it was true. Just because others couldn't sense the delay didn't mean it wasn't there.

The biological parts of the puppets—the pieces of brain that needed to be continuously grown and replaced—were originally elephant-hybrid. A few centuries ago, though, the crew had swapped the pachyderm cells for full-human because they were more efficient.

The human gray matter had to be grown from clone stock, and whose DNA they'd used was a closely guarded secret.

Anatoly suspected it was a little bit of everyone, and that the reason he connected best with these six puppets was because the cells in their processors were his.

"Everything up to speed?" asked Joanna's voice from behind him. She'd entered through a side door. Apparently she'd been aboard *Slicer* for some time.

"They feel fine," he said, trying to keep his tone upbeat. His autonomic response to her presence was *irritation*. Luckily, today he was able to squash the feeling before it had a chance to root.

Joanna's formal wear was identical to his, down to the gray undershirt displaying the six embroidered points. He'd always been especially peeved that she got to display the marks which his direct clones had earned. Other iterations of Joanna had revealed nothing. Why should she prance around with Anatoly's successes?

But that was unfair. In that case, why should he carry Reginald's marks, or Nika's? Dual embodiment meant they accessed the same resonance. He should be proud to share the connection.

Should being the operative word.

Her uniform did have one difference: a small gold star over her left collarbone, signifying her station as a captain.

"You sure you'll finish on schedule?" she asked.

"Of course. We could have finished a week ago. We waited." He thought that had been obvious. Who'd want to finish something this important without a spectacle? The entire crew would have been in an uproar had the builders quietly placed the capstone on the endeavor. "Is the fleet ready to move?"

"Yes, the captains are standing by for the order. On your mark."

"Thank you. I just need enough time to get the Extensions into place, then we can fall back."

“Of course.” She glanced at the autons. “You won’t be sad if something happens to them? I hear they’re your favorites.”

“I’ll find others. The mission is more important. As long as the convoy is safe, I’ll be all right.”

They could only guess what would happen when the Web was finally complete. They hoped it would automatically turn on and begin storing energy from LQ Pyx. But they weren’t sure. Nothing so quaint as an on/off switch had ever been identified.

Anything could happen, hence the orders to move the ships out of range—orbiting too close could prove dangerous.

Sometimes Anatoly felt like Gregor Mendel, messing about with the cross-pollination of peas without any concept of deoxyribonucleic acid. Similarly, the human engineers built the alien devices with only a rudimentary understanding of their functionality.

Take the SD pockets—the infinity gaps. He knew that they worked, knew they were stable, knew they sucked energy into an SD. But why they did so, and how they did so, was still beyond his understanding. As of now, only a few hours before they were to activate the nodes, they knew energy went into the Web, but they still had no idea how to get it back out.

Maybe it was fitting that *Zetta* had gone off with *Noumenon Ultra*. At least with the split portion of the convoy, it had a use. If it had remained, with its original purpose intact, it would have sat empty, dark and untouched. The innovative battery system, the only one of its kind ever designed, would have been more of a novelty item than anything useful.

Once the sphere was complete, the engineers would go searching for answers to energy retrieval. And all the while, LQ Pyx would make deposits in their node banks, so that when they *could* tap it, there’d be plenty available.

Joanna put a hand on Anatoly’s shoulder—a gesture more

familiar than they'd ever shared. "Good luck today. I know you're just putting on a show for convoy morale, but it's also remarkable. This is it, 'Toly. This is what our entire continuum has been leading up to. Your success isn't just important to all of those in the convoy who have passed, or all of those in the convoy now, or even all of those in our line who propelled us toward this moment. It's important to me, personally, and I feel . . ."

She trailed off for a moment. He couldn't tell if she was searching for words or stifling a geyser of emotion. "I am extremely grateful—and privileged—to share an embodiment with you—the seventh Revealer of our line."

Something finally broke through Anatoly's emotional walls—whether it was the monumental importance of the day, or the openness in her expression, he couldn't say. An overwhelming compulsion to embrace her swept over him, and he gave in. He felt a sense of kinship with his biological sister that he'd never felt before.

When they parted they both smiled and laughed lightly, aware that their embrace was not something they could have achieved on any other day, and might not feel comfortable indulging in ever again. But that was all right.

"Everything's wonderful today," Joanna said dreamily. "Everything." She shook herself—the small shiver wracking her body as she seemed to drift out of a euphoric unrealism back into the now. "I better return to *Mira*. Good luck with the send-off. I'll await your signal." She saluted.

He saluted in return. "I'll see you in the amplifying booth later?"

"Of course."

Anatoly's was the last shuttle for the next twenty-four hours—no one would be allowed to travel between the ships unless an emergency called for it. Almost all normal activity aboard the convoy had ceased. Ninety percent of the crew was now packed onto *Mira*, settled in the arms of friends and family, eagerly awaiting the momentous event.

Once *Mira*'s bay was sealed, a horde packed inside. The large monitors there made for prime viewing of the Web's completion.

The amplifier booth had been constructed within the hangar, off to the leftmost side against the wall. Its sides were clear, so that Anatoly could see the crowd and they could see him. All part of the planned spectacle.

Opposite the booth on a raised platform sat his cycle partner, Jamal Kaeden the Forty-Fifth—he, too, belonged to one of the most important lines, and Anatoly could admit Jamal's had perhaps the most spectacular Reveals of all. The convoy might never have known about the continuum without his ancestor. The silliness of his own self-importance when thinking about Joanna came crashing down, and he almost felt grateful for the dose of humility. He smiled at Jamal, who smiled back. Board members sat all around Jamal on the platform. They looked regal in their high-backed chairs, like kings and queens of old.

Stepping inside the booth, Anatoly connected a few wireless sensors to his temples and settled into the cushy lounge chair. The sensors let I.C.C. connect to his brainwaves and amplify the signal through its system. I.C.C. would route the commands to outer broadcasting units, where they would be reinterpreted back into proper bio-signals and sent to the Extensions working three dozen AUs away.

The Extensions were currently en route to the Web, propelled by a special delivery shell.

When the puppets arrived ten minutes later, Anatoly indicated to I.C.C. that it was time for the captains to reposition the fleet. They sailed away from the star—back, back into the inky black of space.

The monitors in the bay broadcasted various false-color feeds of LQ Pyx and the Web. None of the convoy's cameras could zoom in close enough to make out the tiny workers diligently putting the final touches on the construct. If someone wanted to see that, they needed only turn to the amplifying booth, where Anatoly was acting out the commands given to his Extensions.

Only a few minutes of construction time had passed when Joanna joined him in the booth. "How's it going?"

"Fine. What's happening out there? It's noisy."

"Lots of people are mumbling to themselves—calling on their lines. A group was just breaking out into dance and song on the other side of the bay as I was passing. They're starting to get rowdy."

"What, no drinking games?" He accidentally let a tool slip and had to quickly refocus on the construction.

"Are you kidding? No one wants to risk a hazy memory. They want today to slide as cleanly and clearly into their continuum as possible."

"I don't blame them." Another slip.

"Sorry," she said, realizing she was forcing him to divide his attention. "I'll leave you alone. Just let me know when you're ready for me to announce completion."

The hours slipped by and the party raged on. The excitement built, burgeoning throughout the room, creating its own visible haze and sweet scent. There wasn't a melancholy face or still body to be found. The people formed a mass that jumped and writhed like a non-Newtonian fluid pumped with a heavy bass beat.

It neared a hedonistic frenzy. Whatever felt right in the moment was done. Pure joy exuded from every human being present.

They were ready for their Dyson Sphere to come into being, to reflect the glory of their efforts back to them.

There were so many things they could do with the power from LQ Pyx's Sphere. Their civilization could expand, go on for millennia. They would no longer have to constrain themselves to a hundred thousand souls. Think of how many new Reveals there could be—how many new connections could be formed, how many lines of understanding could be drawn—if they could *grow*. If they no longer had to be confined to their nine-ship environment. They could create other, more permanent structures. This system could become a new home for humanity.

Many people thought maybe it could be more than that—a new refuge for scientists, engineers, and artists. A place those in the Sol system would seek in pilgrimage, to learn the ways of Convoy Seven's devotion and dedication. A place where the resources were plenty, minds were sharp, and creative passions fueled prosperity.

More important to some individuals was what this would signal to their sibling convoy—*Noumenon Ultra*. Hopefully they would receive *Noumenon Infinitum*'s message of triumph and come home, rejoin with the rest of Convoy Seven. They yearned to be one again, sharing in their long-awaited success.

While such hopeful visions of the future flitted between the more cogent crew members, and as the throng's ecstatic vibrations hit a fever pitch, Joanna called out updates. Each of her announcements was met with a hearty cheer.

Meanwhile, Anatoly's brow glistened with sweat. The mental effort of keeping himself in a separate consciousness from the process of building weighed heavier in his limbs than any physical strain. "I'm about to finish," he told Joanna, "And I'm going under. I want to be there—within the Web."

"Do it," she said, laying her fingertips briefly against his wrist. "I'll make the announce—"

He let himself go.

In the next instant the convoy was gone. It sat, invisible to the Extension's eyes, millions of kilometers away. Now all he could hear and feel was the deep resounding quiet of space, and the occasional wisp of solar wind.

The vast globe of nodes and lines fanned out around him, creating mind-bending curves in all directions. His muscles tensed suddenly, as the familiar sensation of being caught in a trap descended. He'd made this mental trip into the Sphere more times than he could count, but the initial sensation of eminent collapse—as if, like a lead fishing net, the Web could suddenly swallow and crush him—never lessened.

It was impossible to become desensitized to the Web's greatness.

Narrowing his focus to one Extension's visual input, he gazed at the others while still guiding their work. One last wire connection and the Web would be whole.

He knew what the Sphere looked like from the convoy's perspective: complete. It had since the party began. Only he'd been able to sense its progress toward final unity.

Please let this work. Please let something happen, he said silently to himself, gazing back, back across the continuum.

He spoke out loud, knowing Joanna would hear his words and repeat them, "I'm about finished. Completing the last circuit and—"

Pure fire—the most pain he'd ever experienced—flashed through him so quickly the signals hardly registered in his brain. The receptors almost couldn't accept the input fast enough.

But he *felt* it.

He lost contact with the Extensions. Their sudden absence kicked him back into his body with the force of a shuttle crash, further adding to his pain. He gasped and thrashed in the chair, confident he was drowning but his lungs hadn't caught on yet.

The rush of sound back into his brain made it seem amplified ten times over. There was shouting and clapping and stomping and whooping.

Everyone was enraptured by the monitors. The only one who noticed Anatoly's distress was Joanna.

She fought with his flailing arms, struggling to keep him still while shouting, "What's wrong. Anatoly? *What is it?*"

The ambient noise from the crowd coalesced into a collective gasp, and slowly Anatoly regained control of himself.

Calm enough for his eyes to focus on the monitors, he was surprised by what he saw:

It appeared as if LQ Pyx was *expanding*. Its light and matter billowed outward with incredible speed, swelling within the net of the Web. In one false-color image, what looked like purple light radiated from each node in streams, locking them together with three times as many beams as the physical tethers that held them.

The burgeoning of the star soon clarified itself. "Oh my god," Joanna whispered, "it's lifting Licpix—siphoning off its external layers."

Each mechanism was forcing LQ Pyx to put forth a massive solar flare, but with a notable inconsistency: the older devices were exerting more pull on the star than the newer ones. But that wasn't what concerned Anatoly. The Web wasn't, as Joanna thought, lifting the star.

It was doing something far worse.

"The Web's doing it too fast," Anatoly gasped, righting himself. "It's ripping the star apart. It should just absorb the output. How can it have the energy to take Licpix apart?"

"I thought the devices were off . . ." Her gaze darted to his.

A pit overwhelmed Anatoly's insides, sucking them in as

quickly as the star was being sucked apart. They'd come to rely on LQ Pyx as their standard of normalcy. To lose their star was as profound a blow as if they were to lose the Web. It was a constant in their universe.

They'd never meant to . . .

What have we done? Anatoly thought, asking all those who had come before.

Their silence was as pure as the vacuum of space.

The people of the convoy stared for hours in stunned silence. The elation of moments previous had morphed into muted denial. No one else wanted to give voice to what Joanna and Anatoly had whispered to each other. Perhaps if they kept watching, their fears would be erased. They'd see that they were wrong—that LQ Pyx wasn't dying.

Long past the start of the sleep cycle, people were still standing and watching. The star's layers pulled back like wisps of smoke, and its brightness dimmed as a candle being slowly carried off into the night. Solar winds whipped the star's atmosphere into a flurry: the nodes extracted both energy and matter.

No matter which electromagnetic input they flipped to, they couldn't figure out what the devices were doing, what force they were exerting. They could identify no magnetic field, no particle acceleration to superheat the outer layers of the star, nothing.

The true nature of the Web was simply beyond their understanding.

All they could do was stand by and watch a core player in their daily lives destroyed, knowing they had killed it.

Anatoly and Joanna remained in the booth, slumped against each other in the reclined seat.

Their only comfort was in understanding that this act should give them enough energy to power their civilization for generations upon generations, that they could leave and explore further, create new missions and new purposes for themselves—presuming, of course, that they could in fact extract the energy from the hungry nodes.

MAY 4, 1079 RELAUNCH

6666 CE

Mixed feelings ran manically across the convoy. Waves of depression washed away waves of hope, and vice versa. The incredible speed at which the devices worked seemed less dire now. No matter what forces were at play, destroying a star took time. LQ Pyx's accelerated life had not yet breached its death throes.

So Anatoly turned his attention to the question of extracting the energy. They weren't destroying a star for nothing. It was a natural resource, not a friend or a god, and they needed to face it as such. There were plenty of stars in the universe, and there was no reason to view this one with emotionality.

We don't dream of Sol. We'll get over LQ Pyx.

Yet, that line of thinking was only a way to fool himself, of course. The convoy losing LQ Pyx was like Earth losing its moon. The changes to daily life would be dramatic. Could they live without it? They would find a way.

Did they *want* to live without it?

That was another question.

No one could face it and not feel a sickening pit in their gut. LQ Pyx was revered and respected, seen as everlasting, even if no one in the convoy had ever matched those words with their sentiments before.

Right now, though, those were notions Anatoly couldn't afford to harbor. There was still work to be done. He couldn't just sit back and mourn.

At the moment, he and a subteam surrounded a harvested

node in *Slicer*'s monstrous belly. This particular node the crew had cherry-picked from the Web centuries ago and replaced with a replica. Like blood-sucking parasites looking for the best place to lay into an animal, they searched tirelessly for an outlet—anything that could be a retrieval point.

Hundreds of years, and they'd still had no success.

"There *has* to be a way to access it," Anatoly stated for the umpteenth time, swinging limply in a sling hung from the scaffolding. He had a hand in among a nest of wires near its top, the other lay at his collar. He was unconsciously touching his new undershirt. Seven points now instead of six. Receiving the garment hadn't been the occasion he'd hoped, what with morale so low. It turned out there were certain things it was no good Revealing. He pulled his hand away. "The project is pointless unless something can be extracted," he said.

Static zinged through his headset. "Maybe the joke's on us," one of the team members replied morosely. "The devices were on the whole time and we didn't know it, gathering enough energy to suck Licpix out of its gravity well. Suppose the buggers who started it are out there, waiting to get the signal that the Web is working, so they can swoop in and steal the finished product out from under our noses."

Anatoly scratched his unshaven chin even as he shook his head, dismissing that idea. Why wait millennia for someone else to build the thing? If the original builders were still out there, wouldn't they have completed the Web themselves? And it didn't answer the question of how the energy was meant to be utilized, accessed.

But something that was just said niggled at him. "'On the whole time . . .'" he mumbled. "You really think it could extract enough energy from one star to tear Licpix apart this fast?"

"Was that a rhetorical question, sir? Because there's only one star here."

But that's what had been bothering Anatoly—something he'd glossed over many times before. The gap had been uneven and damaged before their work had begun. The records said it looked like a section of the Web had been torn away, yet he had never doubted that it was simply incomplete. He'd written the inconsistencies off as natural damage wrought by space junk.

But what if someone had damaged it on purpose? *To stop it from doing exactly what it was doing now?*

His mind was trying to connect the dots, but either his synapses weren't firing fast enough, or he was missing something altogether.

Why had he thought of the frayed edges now? What did that have to do with a lack of obvious output?

Trying to make his thoughts come together, he stared off blankly into the hangar's distance, where a holographic replica of the ancient Nest hovered high above the activity below. *Noumenon Ultra* had taken the real thing long ago.

Why was the Nest left orbiting within the Web? The mystery had long bothered previous generations, but it had never been within his field of study. He thought back to what little he knew about the alien craft.

The crew had perished, and the ship had been left undisturbed. Didn't the crew have companions? A convoy would never leave a ship behind—a human one, at least. But it didn't seem logical, this far from crucial resources, that any beings would abandon such a trove of material. It would be stripped if unusable, anything and everything would be salvaged from the wreck—but the Nest had appeared unabused.

Could a ship that small have traveled solo?

No, no one thought so. It was assumed to be equivalent to one of their shuttles.

An inkling at the back of his mind told him the gap and the Nest had something to do with each other, but he couldn't decide on *what*. Why would a ship come to visit the Web and abandon one of its shuttles? And what was he trying to imply?

That they'd vandalized a portion of the megastructure?

"Sir!" A man approached waving a 'flex-sheet, urgency paling his features. "A message from *Mira*."

Anatoly scanned the page. "Turn on the monitors," he yelled, simultaneously crushing the sheet in his fist. "Now!"

A bank of screens in the nearest wall sizzled to life, each projecting the same feed, but in different false-color spectrums.

Six versions of the Web rotated in unison.

Six versions of the Web appeared to blur.

Six versions of the Web peeled away from LQ Pyx like the rind of an orange.

Anatoly focused on a feed in the middle, and watched as the star shifted into a new life phase.

The Seed—the largest of the nodes, different from all the rest—pushed itself away from the dying star, drawing the Web with it, the lifting completed, the star gouged.

Gravitational waves rippled through the region as a star's worth of mass rearranged itself, shifted. The convoy bobbed, and Anatoly reached for a handhold.

"It *moves*?" someone screeched, echoing aloud the shouting in his own mind.

The Web broke apart, forming into long tentacles that hubbed at the Seed.

Ideas ordered themselves in Anatoly's mind. They'd all been taken for fools. The Web wasn't unfinished when they found it—it had been decommissioned.

Because it moves.

The Seed edged away slowly. Its pulsing varied, softly making course corrections while propelling it into dead space at a thirty-degree angle to where the convoy sat. Its speed was that of a starfish over rough terrain—at this distance, it seemed barely a crawl. Yet it felt like the stalking slink of a great beast. A calculated lumbering, like a carnivore sneaking up on its prey.

All was still in the belly of *Slicer*, the people once again shocked into a frozen hush.

Eventually Anatoly turned to the messenger. "I need to get over to *Mira*. I need to see the captain. Kaeden, will you—?" He signaled for his cycle partner to accompany him.

The trip by shuttle was brief but agonizing for Anatoly. Every moment he spent stagnant in the shuttle, the Seed pulled their energy farther away.

Joanna, notified of his arrival, met them at the docking bay. "In my ready room," she indicated, pivoting with rigidity, hands clasped direly before her, leading them onward.

Margarita Pavon, Donald Matheson, and Joanna's first mate, Michael Nwosu, were already there when they arrived. It was a small gathering of board members—whomever Joanna had been able to summon on such short notice.

Captain Straifer took her seat at the head of the table. "We need a plan of action," she said immediately. "And we need to know what's happening and why it's happening."

"It's delivering a payload, the energy," Nwosu said confidently.

"How do we stop it?" asked Matheson.

"I don't know that we can," Anatoly said.

"I don't think that we *need* to," said Kaeden.

"What?" Anatoly asked, surprised.

"We can follow it, harvest devices as we go. We can take enough of them away to make this endeavor worth our while before it reaches . . . well, wherever it's going."

"And what if the recipients don't like being shortchanged and come after us?" asked Pavon.

"We did the work," said Kaeden. "Sucks for them."

Anatoly, though, couldn't help feel what they were implying didn't make sense. "What if . . ."

"Anatoly?" Joanna asked. He looked up at his sister, his eyes haunted. It wasn't all clicking just yet, but the train of thought about the Nest and the gap . . . there was something about all this that still didn't sit right.

"I don't think it's heading back to the home world, to whoever designed it," he finally said.

That gave the room pause. "Where then," Joanna entreated, "do you think it's going?"

He briefly outlined his shaky train of thought, laying out the dots, hoping the others would help him make the connections. "If . . . if . . . Okay, what do we know? The Nataré broke into the Seed, and it fried their ship, right? Killed the crew, maybe even vaporized them. We thought they were just trying to investigate its inner workings, but what if they weren't? What if the frayed edges of the gap—what we'd long thought to be caused by collisions with space debris—what if that damage was *consciously* wrought?"

"You think the Nataré came here and *destroyed* parts of the Web? Tried to harm the Seed?" Joanna asked.

He shrugged. "Maybe. What if they originally came to build, just like we did. And when they turned it back on, they learned the truth."

"What truth is that?"

"I don't know, but why would they try to decommission it? Presuming they spent at least as many hours, as many resources, as we have, why then would they try to undo their work?"

"Because it's not a Dyson Sphere," Matheson said, arms crossed firmly over his chest. His gaze was fixed on a shiny fleck of gold in the green tabletop. "It's not something useful, it's something dangerous."

Anatoly gulped dryly and palmed at his mouth. "There are two things we know about the Web for certain. It's mobile, and it can kill stars."

"My god," Joanna said, standing, turning away from the group for a moment. "Did we . . . Did we reactivate an ancient weapon?"

Was it all for nothing?

Worse than nothing—for the destruction of LQ Pyx's system, and the next? And the next. On and on until . . . What?

"It's a star-killer. A system-destroyer. Maybe." Joanna pinched the bridge of her nose, eyes shut in exasperation. "But why—why would someone build something like that?"

No one had a good answer.

Everything they'd ever believed had been turned on its head.

Anatoly felt like he was rotten inside. Little bits of him were crumbling into black-and-green putridity. He'd been the man at the top: the head engineer who would see to the Web's unity. The Revealer who would show the convoy the supreme power of ancient technology. The convoy member who would give all the lives in his continuum a renewed purpose. He was supposed to close chapters and open new ones: glorious, wondrous chapters in humanity's history.

But now? Now he was the man who had unleashed the monster.

He wasn't Prometheus stealing fire from the gods. He wasn't even hapless Pandora, sticking her nose where it didn't belong. No, he was some caricature of Narcissus, who'd been so enamored with his own glory that he let truths float down the river of time and over the falls of inevitability. He was Icarus, flying too close—perhaps literally—to a sun. The obviousness of the Web's malign existence glared at him from the bottom of those falls, swallowing the hopes and dreams of his life.

"The Revealer of Its Power knew," he mumbled. He realized he was staring at his lap while the rest of the group stared at him. "Reginald Straifer the Fourth *knew.*" Yes, I.C.C. said he'd died of an aneurysm, that it had made him hallucinate. But these days, no one was sure it could trust such an old recollection. They understood things now, about the continuum, that they hadn't before. Could Reginald have truly been visited by the consciousness of the Seed? Could he have known all those years ago that they were acting in service of a monster?

"It's a weapon," Anatoly said vehemently. "It's a brilliant construction. It destroys and gathers energy for the next kill at the same time."

"And you think someone put it out of commission before? The crew of the Nest?"

"Yes," he said firmly.

"Do you think *we* can do it?"

He shook his head *yes,* then *no.* "I don't know. It turned on when we completed it, which would suggest it can be decommissioned with a few slices. But there were AUs of Web missing when we found it."

"I'm still not convinced it's a weapon," Joanna said. "Just because it doesn't behave as we anticipated doesn't mean its malevolent. I want to know what it's trajectory is before we jump to any conclusions. I.C.C., get me an astronomer. Whoever's fastest at calculating interstellar destinations. You've been monitoring the Web, yes?"

"Yes."

"Good. I want to know where this thing is pointed. That might give us a clue as to its mission—what its target might be, its . . . intent."

"Of course. And, if I may interject?" said I.C.C.

"Please," said Joanna, making a gesture that said *you have the floor.*

“When the sphere activated, I detected extremely high bursts of uniform radiation. So uniform, I find it suspicious.”

“You think it sent out a signal? Was it alerting someone?”

“Perhaps. But the bursts were not aimed at a single point. I detected sixteen separate trajectories.”

The board members let a pause build. Eventually, Joanna said, “Is that all?”

“Yes. I’m sorry, but I do not have enough information to formulate any hypotheses for you. I have alerted Dr. Ka’uhane to your need, though, and she is currently on her way.”

“Thank you,” Joanna said tersely.

Twenty minutes later, a disheveled Dr. Ka’uhane stumbled into the room, several ‘flex-sheets pressed to her chest. “I did most of my work on the shuttle ride over,” she said immediately.

The ‘flex-sheets fluttered as she shuffled between them. “Ah, here.” She squeezed in between the captain and first officer, smacking a sheet against the table. “At this trajectory, its nearest possible target is this system.” She jabbed at the data. “There isn’t so much as a wandering rock between here and there. But I don’t think that’s really its destination.”

“Why not?” asked Joanna.

“Because, at its current speed, it would take twelve thousand years for the Web to get there.”

“I hardly think that rules it out,” Joanna said, crossing her arms. “How many trillions of man-hours went into building the thing in the first place? Twelve thousand years is nothing.”

Anatoly explained the weapon theory to Ka’uhane. “Is there any reason you can infer—or, heck, take a wild stab at—for it to target that system?”

The astronomer shook her head. “No. I mean, it’s the closest system to LQ Pyxidis, but that’s it. No planets that we’ve been able to detect, either. It’s just the next star over.”

“So, it’s just random? What’s the point of killing the closest star?” Joanna sighed. “A weapon would have more intent.”

"It could be strategic, we don't know yet," said Anatoly, sliding the 'flex-sheet closer for a better look. "Or, maybe it's MAD."

"The Web is angry?" Joanna asked skeptically.

"No," Anatoly shook his head. "I mean, what if it's a true doomsday device? One created so that it would never be used because its activation would lead to Mutually Assured Destruction. I mean, as far as we can tell, the Web was designed to be perpetual. To exist forever. I think it might even have the capacity to make its own minor repairs. I found evidence of internal damage on one of the devices we harvested for replication. It had been fixed, and I assumed it had been fixed by previous builders, but now . . . I don't know anymore. If it is a doomsday machine, then maybe eating everything in its path *is the point*."

"That's so *senseless*," said Nwosu.

"We can't expect all interchanges between civilizations to be jovial," said Anatoly diplomatically. "Look at what happened when the convoy went back. Those were our own people, but the cultures were so far removed they couldn't help but clash. Just imagine two alien cultures meeting for the first time—why should we assume everything would be all pinks and blues? I think it's easy to see how one civilization could want to wipe out another. If you perceived someone as an ultimate threat to your way of life, you'd want to get rid of them. What's better, then? A prolonged war, or one swift genocidal swoop?"

"Not *so* swift," someone mumbled.

"But it should have stopped," Pavon protested. "Any conflict it was built for has to be over. No one would really make a doomsday device that would go on forever. *No one*."

This felt so wrong. They'd devoted themselves to the Web for a thousand years. A thousand years of hope, gone because they'd failed to see the truth before activation. *Silly children—pressing buttons and throwing levers when we don't know what they do.*

Anatoly took a deep breath. "You're right, it's too extreme, too—" A morbid idea struck him. "Maybe it hasn't destroyed the enemy yet."

The room had been fairly quiet before, their conversation subdued, but now a deafening silence swallowed everything up and refused to spit it back out again.

Eventually, Joanna pried her voice free. "But we haven't found any other civilizations, there's no one within range except—No. Why? Not—"

"Earth?" Anatoly said.

Dr. Ka'uhane held up a finger. "But it's not angled the right way, its trajectory—"

"Might only suggest that the gun isn't loaded yet," said Anatoly, standing. "The Web isn't from here. It didn't start at LQ Pyx. Those beings who commanded the *Nest* followed it here and stopped it before it ate our star."

Something clicked for him. "Do you remember the stories about the dark planemo? Where we stopped and our convoy split? There was evidence of a staging ground, that they were building something. And their maps showed a gravity well worthy of a star—a star that *wasn't there* when we arrived. What if that's where the Web originated, or even just where the Nataré found it? Maybe that's where they began working on it, and it *ate that star, too.*"

Maybe that's how they knew, why they came here and tore through its tentacles.

He thought about the convoy splitting, about the reasons *Infinitum* and *Ultra* had gone their separate ways. One had wanted to build, and one had wanted to study. But the two paths weren't at odds. If only *Infinitum* had listened to the

Ultra crew—if only they'd truly understood the importance of the Nest and the Nataré—maybe they would have realized that to build was folly.

The already-deep pit of despair in Anatoly's belly grew deeper still.

"Back up, what do you mean 'the gun isn't loaded yet'? Joanna waved her hands in front of her chest. "You don't think the *star-killing* part is the weapon?"

"Maybe it needs the energy to load the proverbial gun."

"And then what? A *death ray* comes shooting out of the Seed?"

Anatoly shrugged.

"Hold on," said Nwosu. "Why would the Nataré care? I mean, if it's coming after Earth? And I'm still not sure why we think it's Earth at all? We were barely blips on the biological radar when this thing was built—less than blips, not even ghosts. There's no way of knowing, and no reason to think, that anyone even knew there was life in the vicinity. It would have been dead space, silent around here."

"Silent? Like it is now?" Matheson said.

"Well, sure. But, I mean, there'd be no reason to see Earth as a threat, presuming some advanced civilization even had the means to spot it."

Anatoly snapped his fingers. "What was that theory? An old theory. It was about a superadvanced civilization plotting out—"

"Ultra Civilizations?" suggested Dr. Ka'uhane.

"The concept of an Ultra Civilization was introduced in 2067 by Doctor Tia Dacascos," I.C.C. offered.

"Right." Anatoly's hands trembled as though he was sick with the shakes, but he wasn't sure if it was fear or excitement—the thoughts evolving in his mind evoked both. "A civilization so vast and advanced that it has calculated its needs for survival until the end of the universe. Every decision they make depends upon those calculations. What if the Web's purpose is to take out potential competition? If their calculations indicated that the only way for them to live until the end was to destroy fledgling life-forms, they would do it. They would eradicate all other life to preserve their own. So the theory states, anyway."

He heard the words coming out of his own mouth, but could only think of them as an abstraction, as the intellectual dithering they were supposed to be. An Ultra Civilization couldn't exist, not really. Could it? Aliens that might be so hell-bent on preserving themselves until the end of time that they would kill all other life-forms at the drop of a hat?

If the Web really was of such making, could the convoy have divined that years ago?

Why, oh, *why* hadn't the convoy studied more before it began building? Why was it more important to finish than to understand? Why hadn't anyone seriously considered the thing as a potential danger?

Did any of that really matter now? What's done was done. What they were *going* to do, though . . .

"We have to stop it," he declared, finding new, sudden strength—strength that came from Nika Marov, his biological grandmother. He was familiar with the sensations that came with tapping into her portion of the continuum. This was the side of himself that refused to give up when situations seemed dire. The part that was afraid to fail, but at the same time refused to. "It doesn't matter what its purpose is or who built it. We know it's dangerous. It ate *our* star. LQ Pyx. Until we know more, we can't let it continue."

"I'm detecting a change," I.C.C. broke in at decibels far above the norm—the equivalent to a human's panicked scream.

The room's main monitor flickered on. Within the frame the Web—now more like a living cephalopod than an artificial sphere—floated.

The Seed's new arms flexed, drawn toward it with dramatic curves, then uncurled and shot straight. The Web propelled itself away with new speed, like a squid blasting through the inky depths and out of sight. It left exhaust trails in the immediate vicinity, curls of haze expelled by each individual device, save the Seed. Though they could no longer see it, they could tell its trajectory had remained the same.

Nothing the artifact did now could shock them—not anymore. So instead of adopting a new stony silence, the room erupted into action.

"I.C.C., order the emergency landing of all shuttles, now," Joanna demanded. "Dr. Ka'uhane, I want you to study that recording and calculate its speed. I'll get you whatever personnel you need. We've got to drop into SD travel ASAP and *follow the damn* thing. Everybody go, now—make sure all areas and crew members are secured."

The force of her orders struck Anatoly like they never had before. She'd been placed in command for a reason, and this was it.

She *did* deserve to wear the marks of a Revealer. Perhaps more than he did. He'd spent his entire life using the thrust of their line to create a monster. She would use it to put down the creature and save stars—and perhaps countless fledgling life forms with them.

The others vacated the room, leaving the two of them alone. She grabbed for his hand before he could exit.

"You know this isn't your—"

"My fault? Oh, but it is. I failed to reach beyond myself, to understand that I don't understand. I can't think of a more damning action. What's that old saying? A little knowledge is a dangerous thing. I knew just enough to resurrect the monster, and now my punishment is a lifetime watching you try to undo my work. I'm sorry, Joanna. My arrogance forced this mess on you. On everyone."

“We’re all to blame.” She touched her collar, where the points lay. “But blame isn’t what we need to focus on, now or ever. what matters is that we’ll make it right. Horrible things happen in the pursuit of knowledge, but we only fail if we don’t seek to correct them. We’ll catch it,” she assured him.

“If only we didn’t have to,” he said, giving her hand a squeeze. And when he said *we* he didn’t mean the convoy, he meant her and him. Why had he spent all the good times avoiding her, and only now in a time of crisis come to understand what she meant in his life? They were family, and no amount of pride should have ever gotten in the way of that.

“But we do,” she said firmly. “The responsibility is ours. And we *will* succeed.” She let his hand go, gave him a strong, reassuring smile that held determination and respect, but no mirth.

And now we cross the cold expanse in pursuit of the life which we should not have given, he thought. All these millennia later, Dr. Frankenstein still hadn’t learned that the secrets of the universe were not his to control.

CHAPTER SEVEN

CONVOY TWELVE

JUSTICE AND CARMEN: SASQUATCH, CINDERELLA, AND THE ENIGMATIC KALI

ONE YEAR SINCE FIRST CONTACT

FOUR HUNDRED AND TWENTY-TWO DAYS SINCE THE ACCIDENT

It's been a year since everything went down. First contact. I've never been big on questioning the universe, wondering about grand schemes and gods and whatnot. But life's been . . . surreal this past year. Horrifying and wondrous. Almost magical, mystical. And what is magic but science unexplained? What is the "great beyond" other than a magnificent construct designed by an intricate consciousness and its desire to go on and on forever?

Justice reread the paragraph half a dozen times. The words didn't feel like hers, even though they stuck out in her bold flourishes with loops on the *T*'s and everything.

She dropped the pen to the page, rocking absently in the old-fashioned wooden rocking chair. There were five of them set around the medical bay's receiving room. Only one other was occupied, by Mrs. Tan. Enfolded in her arms was her tiny sleeping daughter.

Justice glanced at the diary entry once more. These weren't

her words. She was direct, crass, grounded. Whoever'd penned these remarks was some kind of pseudo-philosopher, trying to put a spin on their reality. Make it pretty, poetic. Make it *mean* something.

But it didn't. That wasn't how science worked. There was cause and effect but no narrative niceties.

There's no rhyme or reason to being flung thousands of years into the future, right into a nest of aliens. There just isn't.

Coincidence was built into the system. Physics needed chance encounters—chemistry did, too. Without chance encounters there would be no life.

She looked to where Mrs. Tan sat, her baby wrapped in a yellow blanket and now hefted onto her mother's shoulder. The captain's wife appeared uncomfortable in the rocking chair, but held on to her daughter like the unconscious child was a stuffed animal.

Mrs. Tan caught her looking and said, "It's her birthday today."

"I know," Justice said warmly, softly. There was something about the waiting room that made her pitch her voice low and quiet. "Happy birthday."

Mrs. Tan smiled in acknowledgment, then turned her face into her daughter's warmth and closed her eyes.

Baby Tan was like their own little celebrity, both a spot of joy and utter tragedy. She was a healthy baby, physically. All her fingers and toes, strong heart, steady lungs. She was growing slowly, though, the doctors said. But that didn't trouble them so much as her mind, where there was nothing. No consciousness. Her brainstem worked as it should, but the rest not so much. There was no sign of damage, her brain was fully developed and intact, but she just wasn't *there*. It wasn't like a coma, and she wasn't vegetative. It was . . . *different*. The medics couldn't explain it, had marked it off as a cruel accident, just like the one that had gotten them tossed through time.

“Are you waiting for someone?” Mrs. Tan asked.

“My friend, McKayla Johnson,” Justice said, her tongue tying itself in a proverbial knot right after.

It was no secret—at least, not in Justice’s circles—that McKayla wanted to have a baby. McKayla herself was fond of telling everyone within hearing distance that she and Samir were trying to get pregnant. Usually her proclamation was met with one of two reactions: joy or confusion. But Justice suspected it would only hurt Mrs. Tan to hear.

Justice herself had been in Camp Confusion: why on Earth would McKayla—or anyone—want to have a baby *now? Here?* But then she’d realized that people historically had conceived babies in all kinds of uncertain nows and heres.

When McKayla and Samir had settled on expanding their family, their whole demeanor had changed. They no longer seemed downtrodden victims of circumstance. They were making a happy decision, a hopeful decision, and it wasn’t Justice’s place to be anything but supportive.

After all, the convoy had a steady supply of food now. It wasn’t like they were rationing bites. One more mouth to feed wasn’t going to put a strain on their supplies like it would have nine months ago.

Utilizing her molecule chain builder and a sugar-protein bath, Justice had initially been able to clone potatoes and yucca from mess hall scraps. While she’d never gotten the resulting yucca to seed, and the adult plants were smaller and less hardy than they should be, the potatoes had produced viable tubers, and both plants had held everyone over until the aliens had stepped in and given them a boost.

Of course, even though they were no longer on Famine’s doorstep that didn’t mean the crew was healthy.

Justice’s own body felt bony, angular—a far cry from the roundness she found comforting. With her big frame, she was starting to look like the old her in the mirror, the one from years ago. It was disconcerting. She'd done so much work just to feel normal, it disturbed her to see it slipping away.

But at least her hormone supplements were on lock. She could replicate those forever, easily, as long as they convinced the aliens to help them keep supply stocks high.

That was a whole 'nother ball of wax she didn't want to think about right now. The aliens were why Yolanda's office was booked solid this week. Anniversaries of life-changing events tend to send people reeling.

Instead of a psychiatrist, McKayla had wanted to visit the doctors for a physical. She and Samir had been trying for six months with no results, and McKayla was getting anxious.

It was no surprise to Justice, though. Everyone had been under so much stress, she would have been shocked if anyone's body was in well enough condition to support zygote implantation, let alone fetal development.

Hell, even back on Earth, most fertility doctors weren't concerned about infertility until someone had been trying for a year—and that was under normal circumstances.

Still, she'd come to support her friend, and to take advantage of the waiting room. She knew it would be quiet. She could think here, center herself. Focus on the science, on the emerging puzzle whose pieces were just now begging to resolve into firm shapes.

Because though McKayla's inability to conceive thus far wasn't strange . . .

There weren't any flies aboard.

Those two thoughts might seem totally unconnected to anyone else, but throw in the fact that none of the cloned yucca had produced viable seeds, and Justice saw the beginnings of a pattern.

Flies were one of those things humans couldn't get away

from. No matter how well you tried to regulate what went on a ship of *Pulse*'s size, you'd inevitably end up with insects. Mostly flies, definitely mites, sometimes beetles. Ants once in a while. If everything and everyone didn't go through the strictest of decontamination processes, you'd get bugs . . . and sometimes even then.

Convoy Twelve regularly received visitors and shipments prior to their accident, and while basic precautions had been taken not to spread illness aboard, there'd been no reason to bleach and scrub and sanitize.

Hell, open one hatch Earth-side for thirty seconds in the middle of a clear day, and *bam*, flies. It didn't take much.

But now, Justice couldn't remember the last time she'd seen a fly. Had they all died off?

With the yucca, she'd thought perhaps she'd failed at manual pollination. That maybe the reason the few seeds she'd gotten hadn't sprouted was because she didn't make a very good moth substitute.

But what if it wasn't just Dr. Kapoor and Baby Tan who'd been affected by the accident? What if there was more to it?

She realized her wrist was turning, and she looked down. She'd drawn loops upon loops on the page below her last paragraph, her mind turning over and her hand absently echoing.

Maybe she was wrong. Maybe the flies and the yucca and McKayla were all unrelated. But what if they weren't? Either way, Justice was determined to find out.

When she'd signed up for this job, she never imagined that her expertise could be so critical. She was a genetic engineer, sure, but her role in the experiments was purely as a technician. Dr. Kapoor put together the outlines for the pods, decided what types of organic compounds or molecule chains she wanted included, and Justice simply built them.

But now, the entire crew depended on her to feed them. They didn't know it yet, but they might also depend on her for perpetuation.

If, indeed, perpetuation was ultimately a goal.

That would depend on what they could learn from the aliens, if they could communicate their plight properly, get the creatures to listen, to help them find their way home.

I don't want to think about the Lùhng, she said to herself, poising her pen once more over the diary.

That was what the captain had decided to name the aliens: *Lùhng*. Dragons. He thought the name auspicious. Many Eastern dragons were good, bringing luck and fair seasons.

He hadn't been thinking about Western dragons, who were almost entirely malevolent across the board. They tormented villagers, breathed fire, and devoured virgins.

The aliens weren't a puzzle to Justice. They were a plight. Things would be simple without them, in a way. They would need to focus on survival, on finding a way back to familiar space. That's it. But now they had to contend with the will of something else. And she was so far removed from that question, from communication with the creatures, that to consider all the possibilities threw her thoughts into chaos.

Her heart rate had jumped and her blood pressure increased, just letting her mind drift to them for a moment. It was better to shut them out of her considerations completely.

Just think about McKayla, she told herself, breathing steadily in through her nose. It smelled so clean in the receiving room—a soft, powdery sort of clean. Maybe even buttery. Like a newborn's skin, even though there weren't any newly borns in the room.

Once more, she looked to Mrs. Tan, who'd settled more comfortably into her chair and was now rocking her daughter, muttering sweet nothings against the one-year-old's black hair.

Her mumbles became hums, sweet notes, then words. She was singing, a Chinese lullaby Justice had never heard.

"Yut gwong gwong ziu dei tong
Haa zai nei gwaai gwaai fan lok cong
Teng ciu aa maa yiu gon caap yeong lo . . ."

After a few moments, in which Justice had been transfixed, Mrs. Tan caught her eye and said in English, "Bright Moonlight, Shining on the Ground. I sing it with the hope that my little shrimpling will grow up fast. She sleeps now, but . . . But we would all like to meet her."

Justice drew in a shaky breath. She felt incredibly privileged. Mrs. Tan was usually very private, and yet she'd shared this with her. "Your—your voice is beautiful," she stuttered, hers coming out in a harsh croak.

"I hope she likes it," Mrs. Tan said sadly, kissing the top of her little girl's head.

Her makeshift lab on *Pulse* was cramped. It used to be a bathroom, and it was the only area of appropriate volume that they could manage to turn into a proper clean room for molecule construction. The single-person quarters beyond had been transformed into the gowning room and fiber checkpoint. A white adhesive strip outside the door replaced the ratty welcome mat the previous occupant—who was either killed during the accident or left behind in the twenty-second century (either way, they were dead)—had thrown in front of it.

She stepped on the adhesive, sure to rock back and forth to make sure the bottom of her shoes were freed of loose debris. The door automatically opened at her behest, and a blast of air washed over her, blowing bits of hair and dust away into the hall. Inside, she put any loose items from her pockets into a locker—today she slipped her diary and pen into the small space—then pushed through the newly inserted wall of draped plastic (like the tongues in a car wash) to where the white clean suits and pale blue booties awaited. She'd been suiting up and stripping down her entire career, and it took no time making sure her clothes and shoes were sufficiently covered.

Drawing the string of the hood tight around her face, knotting it beneath her chin, she placed a pair of goggles on her nose and slipped in the second and third interior doors to her UV-protected lab.

The tiled walls and floors were still disconcerting, and she wondered if the grout would have been an approved clean room material under different circumstances. It hadn't been a problem thus far, but still . . . it irked her.

Her centrifuge and electron microscope took up the area where the sink used to be. The shower stall was now an incubation tank, where the molecules were tested for strength via subatomic particle bombardment. The toilet had undergone the largest transformation, now a fixed desk bearing her chain builder.

She'd just about settled into her routine of checking on the previous day's work (to make sure none of the new DNA strands she'd put together from scratch had fallen apart or tried to self-replicate overnight), when the comm unit outside in the gowning room cackled to life.

"Justice Jax? Bridge calling for Justice Jax."

She stilled, unsure if she'd heard correctly over the constant hum of the clean room's air unit. No one on the bridge had ever called her before. There wasn't any reason they should.

"Bridge calling for Justice Jax."

Scratching the back of her ear absently—the confines of the hood always made her hair bunch up oddly against her skin—she exited the clean room. She approached the comm unit like one might approach a wound-up jack-in-the-box.

Carefully, she depressed the answer key. "Uh, yeah?"

"Doctor Justice Jax?"

"That'd be me."

"Captain Tan requests your presence on the bridge."

Her eyebrows did a skeptical dance. "Can I ask why?"

"That's currently classified, but you will be fully briefed as soon as you arrive."

"Er—"

"Now, Jax."

"Yeah, okay, I'm on my way."

She reversed the process she had just gone through and made her way to the principal's office.

Not only had she never been ordered to the bridge, she'd never so much as been invited onto it.

It was smaller than she thought it would be. And somehow, not as shiny. She'd pictured it as an amalgamation of a plethora of bridges she'd seen in sci-fi flicks, but it looked more like the bridge of a boat. Orderly, utilitarian, with a wide range of screens acting as windows to the outside world.

Captain Tan's aide met her just outside, where the doors were flanked by security guards, then led her in.

She might not have had occasion to be on the bridge before, but she'd met with the captain several times in the situation room, both before and after the convoy's cosmic positioning had been verified.

"Jax," he acknowledged, nodding firmly when she entered. The aide bid her stand beside Dr. Kabir Ratha, a medic, and Carmen Sotomayor, the navigator in charge of the positioning team.

She gave them each a brief hello, signing it in American Sign Language for Carmen. She knew Ratha as well—had spoken with him on several occasions. Everyone aboard knew everyone—that was just how it was when your world was reduced to seven hundred people.

But, what she had in common with these two, under the circumstances, she couldn't say. Their new jobs had nothing to do with one another. Why had Tan summoned them?

"Three hours ago," Tan began, facing Carmen squarely and annunciating so she could read his lips, "we noticed a change in one of the *Lùhng* ships."

The primary display screen changed from pure black to a close-up of one of the remaining alien craft. Most of the alien ships left within a few days of their first encounter. What remained, the crew assumed, were those who had been assigned to babysit their new discoveries. Over the past three hundred and sixty-five days, the six remaining alien craft had been slowly guiding the two human ships back in the direction they'd come; they were a small fleet lumbering toward the field of massive constructs.

Now, on the display screen, one of the ships sat with an airlock open. A gaping maw, lit up with a pale yellow glow.

Justice's eyes went wide. "Is that for us?" They'd tried on several occasions, especially early on, to mirror the aliens' first-contact method. They'd taken shuttles up to presumed doorways and waited to be let inside. But nothing had happened.

And few *Lùhng* pods had followed the first. There had been only six direct human-to-alien interactions since they'd met. Each time, a different set of dragons had boarded *Pulse*. Each time, they'd stayed for less than an hour, observing the humans who'd come to watch, scanning with strange devices, but never probing, never taking invasive samples—at least as far as anyone could tell.

So this was new. Unprecedented.

Justice reiterated her question in ASL, for Carmen's benefit.

"Perhaps. Nothing has come out," Tan said. "At this point, we're taking it as an invitation."

"But . . . today?" Justice asked. This was . . . this was so *strange*.

“What about today?” Dr. Ratha asked.

“It’s the anniversary of our first contact, three hundred and sixty-five days out.”

“Why is that weird?” Dr. Ratha asked again.

“Because it’s an Earth-based anniversary,” she said. “It means something to us, but it should be arbitrary to *them*.”

“We’ve considered that,” Tan said. “We’re taking it as confirmation that they have been able to understand at least some of the information we’ve tried to communicate to them. We sent them details of our solar system, identified which planet was ours. The orbital mechanics were all included. Mathematically speaking, if they could understand the visual models, then they could logically conclude that this chunk of time might be significant to us.”

Justice thought that a stretch, but wasn’t about to argue. “So you think it shows their willingness to communicate? To try to understand us?”

“Yes. We should look at it as a good sign, like when they sent us the proteins and sugars.” He looked pointedly at Justice.

Early on, along with information regarding their origins, Tan had also sent a plea for aid. Within a few days, the *Lùhng* sent them a care package. Simple molecules, raw necessities, which Justice had been able to reconfigure into supplements for the crew.

The assumption wasn’t that they’d understood Tan’s message, but rather that they’d simply scanned their ship and deduced the convoy’s plight.

Not that anyone complained. The resupply was a good sign—a friendly gesture. But the fact that the shipment had only contained left-handed molecules was significant. Human bodies can only utilize “left-handed” proteins—the same molecule, only right-handed, passes uselessly through the body. The *Lùhng* could have sent both left-and right-handed, leaving the humans to sort out which ones were consumable and which ones would need to be broken down and reconfigured. But they'd taken the time to figure out which type human biology was based on—either through scans or analysis of a random hair strand or skin cell.

Since they'd shown such care, it served to reason that they'd be interested in further, more in-depth interaction. But up until now, that didn't seem to be the case.

The convoy didn't know how to reconcile the *Lùhng*'s effort in some arenas with their seeming lack of interest in others. Communication was slight. They had sent many messages to the *Lùhng*, but as far as they could tell, the *Lùhng* hadn't sent anything back. When aboard, the aliens had only responded to physical gestures, and so Tan had sent them a visual library of ASL signs, hoping to bridge the gap with a preexisting language.

It wasn't perfect, of course. Though the alien limbs could potentially mimic the hand signs, the facial expressions would not translate, nor anything that required finger spelling. Still, Tan considered it their best bet.

Thus far, however, the *Lùhng* had made no indication that they'd received the broadcast, let alone attempted to decode the language.

Of all of the scenarios humans had imagined for their relationships with alien intelligences, Justice couldn't ever remember one of *mild disinterest* being suggested.

If any of that bothered Carmen, the navigator didn't let it show. "What does the bay contain?" she asked, signing emphatically as she spoke. Carmen seemed much more prepared for this meeting than Justice, as though she'd been waiting for just such a call from Tan.

So, what am I here for? Justice wondered. *Does he want me to analyze whatever a probe brings back, or . . . ?*

"The bay appears empty," the captain said. "I'm setting up an away team, and I'd like the three of you to lead it. Sotomayor, you'll take point."

Justice fought with her face, trying to keep her expression neutral, sure she was failing. An away mission? He wanted her to go *aboard* the alien ship?

"We'll take five hours to set up a plan—nothing too complex, we're taking baby steps," Tan continued, either refusing to acknowledge Justice's clear anxiety, or simply failing to notice. "I know it seems hasty, but we have no idea how long the hatch will be open. If, when we've finalized everything, we still have an opening, you go in.

"I'm picking you three because you are fluent in ASL, and have scientific expertise that could help us understand their origins." Since the aliens had responded to a few signs, a good portion of the crew had made an effort to learn. Most people had at least a small ASL vocabulary these days.

Justice guessed the three of them had been deemed the most proficient.

"You'll be accompanied by a security detail of four," Tan continued. "Sotomayor will be our primary communications point. Though they have an ASL lexicon, it's doubtful you'll be able to hold a conversation should you encounter them, but still, baby steps. Jax, you and Doctor Ratha will gather samples for analysis. We've given them enough info about us—it's time we get a little in return. I expect the trip to be short and professional. No wonder tours, okay? I want you to set a peaceful precedent so they'll invite us aboard again. If we're lucky, they'll try to start an actual dialogue.

"With that in mind, the guards will stay aboard the shuttle as long as you don't leave the initial area, got it? Do not wander farther into the ship. This is a get in, look around, get out trip."

This is a terrible idea, Justice thought, locking her knees after she noticed they were trembling. She'd seen *way* too many monster movies, and she knew exactly how this kind of shit went down. And if there was one sci-fi horror flick rule to follow, it was this:

Never be on the first away team.

Ever.

Because that's how you turn into a redshirt, and she wanted to be in all the sequels. "With all due respect, sir," she said, her voice hoarse. She swallowed dryly. "I'm not sure I have the temperament for this mission."

He pursed his lips, unimpressed. "Oh?"

A little voice in the back of her mind told her not to question this. *Just do it. Suck it up and take the order. You were a soldier, for god's sake. You know how this works.*

But she was not a soldier here. This was supposed to be a civilian posting.

So, she pressed her case.

"I'm good with people. I get people," she said, as Tan let the silence stand. "And I'll head into a combat zone any day of the week. But I've never been much for animals."

Carmen raised an eyebrow.

"I know, I know they're not animals," Justice said quickly. How could she explain? She thought of Stone's father's farm, then. About the homecoming celebration she'd ruined. They'd both been honorably discharged from the air force, and Stone had invited her to come along with him to Puerto Rico. Stone's dad had introduced Justice to his horses. Beautiful things, six of them in all. She couldn't tell you the breed if her life depended on it, but they were pretty, deep-brown creatures with flowing black manes.

But there was this one, real skittish. And Papa Perez had laid out the ground rules for interacting with that horse right up front. Gave her all the pointers on how *not* to spook it. But of course she'd spooked it. She'd scared the *shit* out of that poor creature.

It was still a sore spot between her and Stone—that damn horse . . .

But she had the same worry now.

What if I spook the dragons?

"What I mean is, I've never been in negotiations. I don't know what the proper diplomatic etiquette is for dealing with a hostile I *can* communicate with. Whose thought processes are *human*. When it comes to something whose understanding of my motives is limited or nonexistent, and vice versa, I've never been . . . I worry my nerves will get the best of me."

"You'll be fine," Tan said confidently. He punctuated it with a frown and a firm nod, as if that settled everything.

But what if I'm not? she thought. Already, her throat felt tight and her clothes too restrictive.

[Don't worry,] Carmen signed, [Dr. Ratha can bring some tranquilizers and shoot you up if you cause a problem.]

Justice touched her chin. [Thanks,] she signed sarcastically.

"All right," Tan said. "Time to meet with the security staff and go over our plan."

In a few minutes, they were standing with the security guys. She was surprised to see Steve Weaver, Stone's prison guard, as well as Mac Savea among the security detail. Steve gave her a rough grunt in acknowledgment but said nothing more.

Tan called them to order before laying out their approach, and the conditions for success. Basically, if they landed the shuttle on the foreign ship's decking, they were to consider their mission accomplished. Everything else was just gravy.

"Everyone will meet in the shuttle bay in four hours," Tan said at last. "As long as everything is tight and ready to go—and the hatch is still open—you will make us proud."

Justice didn't scream out loud, but nothing could put a cork in the voice inside her head. Only it wasn't her usual internal chatter. It was that horse. The panicked cries of that damned old mare would not leave her. Except now it was coming from the mouth of a dragon.

A dragon with teeth and claws and fire . . .

Give her a baby any day. Crying wasn't a problem—*human* crying she could handle. The little things could coo and poop and upchuck all day and she'd never bat an eye. Her nephew—

Nope. Best not to think about that, either.

That kid was gone. Hell, that horse was gone.

In a way, that made this easier. *All you've got is today, so suck it up,* she said to herself, marching into the suit room at the appointed time. She secured her helmet to the suit's inner guide ring, taking a deep breath, trying not to feel the sudden claustrophobia inherent in sticking one's head in a fish bowl.

The EVA supervisor double-checked the team's work, then sent them on their way to the designated shuttle.

With a confidence Justice herself could not muster, Tan gave them all firm handshakes and wished them well. She tried not to "ha!" at his encouragement—after all, it was unquestionably sincere.

The flight over was short. Too short. She looked out the nearest portal, marveling at the clearness of the universe. Like looking down through an ice-chilled pond. The stars were little tadpoles, the nebulae algae patches. You couldn't get this kind of impression staring out of your private quarters on *Pulse*—the curvature of the ship got in the way. This sense of distance, of being unsupported over a vast chasm, was new. She was sure some people would get a stab of vertigo, reeling back away from all that emptiness. But not her. She could stare into the depths forever.

In fact, if she could freeze time and stay like this, permanently suspended in space, instead of having to venture even an inch into that alien bay, that would be A-OK with her.

Not that it was *all* comforting. The six alien ships still surrounded the convoy, each wondrous, each terrifying.

The yellow light of the open hatch on their target vessel eased into bright white as they approached. It was difficult to tell where the light came from—it seemed as though the walls and the decking were themselves alight, rather than illuminated.

The ships dwarfed the convoy craft. If they were animals, they could have eaten *Pulse* whole, swallowing it down easily. Their contours were dramatic, shell-like, and their opalescence made them appear more threatening than beautiful.

As the little shuttle slipped inside, the outer doors of the hatch immediately began to close. They hadn't officially touched down before they were fully swallowed by what appeared to be a simple supplies bay.

Justice was most surprised by what she *didn't* see.

There were no goo pits or slimy membrane walls. No slithering wires or plantlike connections. Nothing moved—the walls didn't heave in and out as though with breath, and nothing peeled itself from the bay's corners like so much living wallpaper.

She was equal parts relieved and disappointed.

The only two unusual qualities were the light—which, since it came from all directions, ensured nothing cast a shadow—and the lack of uniformity. The convoy ships had a lot of ninety-degree angles, internally speaking. Sharp, harsh corners that gave well-defined boundaries and evenly quantified use of space. Here, everything flowed. There was no clear delineation between the floor and the walls. Seams did not exist.

"All right, all ashore who's going ashore," said the pilot. He sounded as nervous as Justice felt.

His words ran across the inside of Justice's helmet as well, a ghostly water-blue.

Carmen took the lead, approaching the door first. *Unlike* Justice, she looked ready. Not just ready—eager. She'd come here to make a mark, get some answers.

I guess I'm eager, too—to vomit. But whatever. To each their own.

Surprisingly, Justice wasn't the most uncomfortable. That award went to Dr. Ratha, who was currently the personification of "sweating buckets." Behind his faceplate, his chin dripped every few seconds, as did the end of his nose and the lobes of his ears. He blinked rapidly and shook his head, trying to keep the stuff from his eyes and failing. His comb-over now looked like it was painted to his scalp.

"Hey, you okay?" she asked, tapping him on the knee. He had yet to unbuckle from his seat, and everyone else was already standing. Though the guards weren't to leave the shuttle, they were stretching, prepping—just in case.

Ratha licked his sweat-shined upper lip. "I—I uh—"

People. I can do people. She crouched in front of him. "Look at me, huh?" She'd done the same sort of mothering during her enlisted days. If one of her squad members went into panic mode, she was there. She'd danced this dance before.

Eh, maybe Tan wasn't so off the mark, ordering me along.

Ratha's eyes wandered up to hers before darting away like a scared rabbit. "Look at me," she said again, nodding encouragingly when he complied. "There we go. Listen—we only have room for one screwup on this away mission and I called dibs."

There was a microsecond of a smile, but then he shook his head emphatically. "Not going to go out there. They . . . we don't know anything about them. Tan sent us over like we're . . . what? Canaries?"

"Wow, coal mining reference. Oldie but a goodie. And dead wrong. He sent us because he trusts us. Look, we touched down. Like he said, mission accomplished. We'll dart out the door here and wave for the cameras, and then dart right back in, okay? Really, you don't have to go out there for more than five seconds."

"Do not feed me shit, Jus-J-Jus . . . J. J."

"Not my name, but I'll let it slide because you're melting like the Wicked Witch of the West. Dehydration makes the mouth do funny things."

"Give me his gear and I'll do it," said Mac. Mac, like a big gross ground beef patty. *Meathead for sure.* He hadn't done much to help Stone out in his time of need, and Justice wasn't ready to give him any slack.

She didn't have anything against the security personnel in general, but Mac and Steve had a long way to go to earn her trust. She glared at him.

"You are supposed to stay here," Carmen said and signed, cutting off Justice's more acidic retort. Carmen then turned to address her directly. [It's okay, Justice. He doesn't have to come.]

[I can get him out there. I can,] she signed back, then turned to the doctor once more "Ratha, I know you. You are going to kick yourself for the rest of your life if you don't put two feet on that alien floor, am I right? Two boots—one, two. That's it."

He took a deep, raggedy breath through his nose. "Yeah. I can do that. Two boots."

Justice helped him up, then jostled the security guards out of the way. She was bigger than nearly all of them, but, more importantly, she knew how to stare down a thug until he put his tail between his legs.

Shit, and these are the guys who are supposed to protect us?

The pilot let them out, and Carmen went first. Justice maneuvered Dr. Ratha in front of her and followed him down the two rungs to the decking.

When Carmen hit the floor, both of her arms shot out to help her keep her balance. "Careful," she said. "Not stable."

Dr. Ratha kept one hand on the shuttle, locking his gloved fingers around the door seal and swinging himself down to the surface. Justice slid one boot out, as though she were testing ice over a pond, and found that it wasn't low friction that had given Carmen the jolt, but a squish to the material. It depressed as she put her weight on it, like thick memory foam.

If this was a supplies bay, as she suspected, this was an innovative approach to preventing the items from shifting. She glanced at the shuttle's landing struts, and, sure enough, they'd sunk into the material.

The texture wasn't sticky, though; it didn't grab her boot, simply cradled it. Once she got the hang of planting her foot and letting a beat pass before taking another step, she found it wasn't too difficult to get around. It was a bit like walking on sand—strenuous, but workable.

It was difficult to gauge the gravity in the ship—what with the added bulk of her suit and the unexpected challenge of the surface. But it clearly had artificial gravity, which meant she should be able to figure out the quantity of captured gravitons and their spin.

Yanking one of her meters from its Velcro fastening at her chest, she began performing the requisite scans. Carmen approached a far wall, clearly preoccupied with finding how the aliens entered and exited the bay from within. Ratha stuck to the shuttle's hide like a barnacle on an old carrier ship.

"Okay," Justice said, glancing at the meter's reading, talking to herself out loud. Carmen turned in her direction—the scrolling dialogue in her helmet letting her know Justice was speaking. "Gravitational strength is . . . nine-point-eight meters per second squared. That's Earth standard." It was also convoy standard, so nothing to get too worked up about. Most likely, the aliens had made it comfortable for them.

After all, the humans couldn't fly like the aliens could. How they managed *that*, no one had been able to guess yet.

"Still no atmospherics," Dr. Ratha added, one shaking hand raised with equipment beeping away. "They're keeping us in vacuum, just like we did with them."

Justice unleashed her sampling brush and went to work sweeping at the soft decking. If there were any little bits of dirt or skin or otherwise, she was going to find them.

"Any follicles yet?" Carmen asked after a time.

Justice dipped the base of the brush into a receiving tube on her hip, capping the vial and changing out the brush head. The little red and green lights, which indicated excess particle presence in the vials, were all still red. "I got nothing," Justice said. "There aren't any seams for anything to catch in." She did another cursory glance around the space, searching for a lip or vent to take her brush to. But everything was smooth. "Maybe this space is always in vacuum?" she suggested. "I see no way in or out besides the hatch—for air or otherwise. Maybe they don't actually come in here personally."

[Keep looking,] Carmen signed.

"How are we doing?" the pilot asked over the comms channel.

Carmen turned to his window and signed that they were still busy, for everyone on the shuttle to sit tight.

Justice guided her brush over the outside of the shuttle, thinking that perhaps some static discharge from their craft might have attracted a few stray particles. She outlined Dr. Ratha where he stood, like she was outlining a murder victim in chalk.

"Very funny," he groused at her.

"Well someone's got to liven up this amazingly uneventful mi—"

The brightness of the bay intensified. A *snap-flash*. Brilliant, blinding white engulfed everything. Everyone cried out, and Justice ducked away from Dr. Ratha, pulling into herself, throwing her hands in front of her helmet's visor, which did nothing. The light streamed in past her fingers, past the UV protective layering of the glass, past her eyelids even.

It was so bright she could see it with her eyes closed.

She took a stumbling step back and her boot heel caught on the side of the shuttle's stepladder. She tumbled, spinning herself so she could put her hands down. But instead of a firm smack of suit-to-ground, falling to the alien deck was like falling into a marshmallow.

The light went on, and on. She crouched on the deck, faceplate pressing into the soft floor, hands over the back of her head, knees pulled into her chest.

Everyone shouted and cussed, but no one was really saying anything. It was pure distress, all chatter and no substance. Not even a coherent cry for help.

Their pilot slammed on the emergency call button that bypassed the shuttle hangar and went straight to the bridge. "We can't . . . Too bright. There's so much—they're *blinding* us!"

And with that cry, the light winked out. It could have gone back to its previous luminosity, or it could have gone off altogether, leaving them in utter darkness. But Justice couldn't tell. Her vision was completely wiped out. It wasn't a blackness—it was more like a giant sunspot in her eye. Like she'd stared directly into a star for a full five minutes and now there was nothing but a bright pink smear and static grayness beyond.

Oh my god, oh my god, oh my god. Why did they do that? Oh my god oh my god oh . . .

"Carmen?" Justice called. "Carmen, do you copy? Are your gloves working? Carmen?"

"Yes," Carmen said over the audio—not answering her questions, simply giving an affirmative that she was present and could feel that Justice was talking.

Thank heaven for small blessings, Justice thought. Carmen

had specialized gloves with an emergency backup communication indicator. They were meant for blind crew members in case audio went out—but Carmen had insisted on a pair for herself.

Right now, Carmen had Justice's name in braille rolling over her fingertips.

"My pressure indicator is beeping," said Ratha, voice a high panic. "External. They're pressurizing the bay."

"Yes," Carmen said again. Once more, only an indicator, not an answer.

Justice did her best to crawl in Carmen's direction, having only a general idea of where she was when everything had whited out. Someone flopped to the ground beside her—not Dr. Ratha—probably one of the security guards. They must have stumbled out.

"This is bullshit," somebody grumbled. "This is all . . . Get back in here! The three of you need to get back into the shuttle right this second! This is bullshit."

Whump.

Justice didn't hear it so much as feel it. There was, simply put, a strange, deep *whump* that blasted into her core. It immediately made her feel woozy, and she stopped crawling.

Whump. Whump. Whump.

Was it a deep bass? Was it just a sound? So low she couldn't hear it, but could feel it in her organs, reverberating through her suit?

"What the fuck is that?" shouted Mac.

The sounds of someone puking in their suit followed.

Then everyone began shouting again, all of them barking orders.

"I don't know—I don't know!"

"Get back inside!"

"*Pulse?* Captain Tan? Captain, anybody, come in."

"I am here," Carmen said. "What's happening? I'm here."

"Stay put!"

"No, get inside!"

"Captain? *Pulse*, come in."

Whump. Whump. Whump.

More puking.

Justice's head throbbed. As the deep whumps came on faster, each cresting through her only a moment before the next, her ears began to ring. She clutched at her middle, at her head, and thought *This is a really complicated way to kill us*, before she blacked out.

Justice was beyond surprised when she woke up. She hadn't fought dying, like she always assumed she would when she found herself facing the void. Maybe her body had instinctually known it wasn't dying, though her mind had insisted it was.

Either way, she was conscious now. And half of her wished she wasn't. Her skull felt like it was split open along the sutures, and she swore she could feel her *brain* throbbing. A quick, panicked thought before she opened her eyes had her wondering if her skull *was* cracked open—there was no end to the alien dissection fantasies she could conjure.

None of this made sense. If they had wanted to hurt the convoy, they'd had a year to do it. So why now? What had changed?

Her hand went to her face and hit plastic. She was still in her suit. Her vision was still slightly blurred, but now her eyes felt burned instead of blinded—like they'd been open to the wind for too long.

Blinking tears out of her eyes, she sat up. Rolling her neck, she looked at the ceiling, expecting to see the white of the supplies bay.

Boy was she wrong.

She looked straight up—or down—into the faceplate of an alien sitting at some kind of desk-like structure. It, too, had its neck craned back, as though her rustling had drawn its attention.

Why the hell am I on the ceiling? Maybe I did die. I died and I'm having an out of body experience before I disappear forever.

Out of her peripheral she detected movement. She shrank away from it, scrambling back. She elbowed someone in the stomach, and over her comms she heard a distinct "oof."

Everyone was there—all of them. Carmen, the pilot, Dr. Ratha, and all of the security team, were laid out to her left and right on some kind of platform, equally as squishy as the bay's flooring.

Like meat in a market . . .

Stop that!

The movement in her periphery was another alien, standing near the platform, gathering all of the human's instruments, scanners, and loose accessories into a clear bowl.

Since first contact, the same *Lùhng* had never come aboard the convoy twice. Their preparation for this trip had included a flash card test, wherein Tan had shown them multiple pictures of the aliens they had on record, just in case they were to encounter one of their visitors. But these two hadn't been in the stack.

She tried to focus on them, to blot out the bizarreness of the room—in which every wall was covered with equipment, so much so that it was obvious that *wall* was the wrong term. Every centimeter of the room was a floor, bowing out and up and over. It was mind-bendingly disorienting.

She made a point of focusing on the *Lùhng* so as not to think of the mobius floor. The alien nearest her was the type with spines. Its hair was thick, straight, and very dark—almost black, but with hints of browns and tans. It reminded her a little of porcupine quills, with the ends tapering into somewhat lighter shades than the rest. And it was big—thirteen feet tall if it was an inch. Around its neck it wore some kind of chain from which an incredibly thin, hand-sized black rectangle dangled.

So far the humans had identified five "classes" of aliens. It was difficult to discern individual species because some appeared to have cross-traits of others. It was also difficult to pinpoint the social and biological configuration of *Lùhng* society. They hadn't seen enough alien-to-alien interactions to distinguish any sort of hierarchy. Genders weren't readily apparent—and Justice knew just how misleading physical traits could be in that department. Some aliens wore mechanical suits, some thin clothes, others seemed to be completely naked save a few accessories like helmets or braces.

Unlike the other hairy ones they'd made note of, this one's arms weren't covered in the same follicles. Instead, these looked strange, holding the bowl, like they didn't actually belong to the creature—or like the hair was a suit.

She imagined what a man wearing a full bear skin would look like, with his arms independent of the bear's arms. It was like that—thin, pale, nearly translucent arms threaded their way out from beneath the spines, so narrow compared to the rest of its bulk, and placed so far beneath what she thought were shoulders, that they looked like spider's legs with sharp, grasping fingers needling away from its wrists.

Again, its anatomy was unique. It had attributes of those that had come before, but had to be a completely separate species.

I cannot wait to map their genetic tree, she thought, holding on to the notion because it was a comfort. *Genetics, yes. Let's think about biology. Taxonomy. Concrete things. Things that don't have too many downs and too many dimensions and no doors—oh, god, why don't they have any doors?*

She shut her eyes and breathed through her nose. *Stop. Look at the other one. What's unique about the other one?*

With a harsh swallow, she glanced up again, and suppressed a reeling sense of vertigo. Beside her, Dr. Ratha and Mac both started to stand up.

The creature was about three meters above her. *Okay, that one's got four limbs. Four limbs, is it weird that most of them have four limbs?*

Most aliens in science fiction had never been alien enough to her mind. They always recalled terrestrial things—lizard people, fish people. She thought of *Star Trek* with its barely-altered-cranium people.

These weren't people-like, for certain. But there were familiar patterns. Which felt so wrong.

Was that just how life was? Certain structures were just statistically more likely than others? Four limbs were stable. Four limbs were hardy. Was a four-limbed creature that much more likely to evolve a big brain and grasping hands and survive long enough as a species to make it into space?

Okay, four limbs. And it's got the bead-like scales. And it looks big—as big as this one. Another twelve-footer.

Its middle was a bit obscured, but there was something unusual about it. There were colors there she didn't remember seeing anywhere in the flash cards. Pinks and purples and blues.

She noted that—presuming the sasquatch's hair wasn't a bear suit—neither of them appeared to be wearing clothes, except for the faceplates and the rectangular necklaces. They had yet to see any of the aliens without the masks on. If that was their one protection against contamination, it was likely here to stay.

Contamination—the word sparked something in her. Was that what the bright light had been, maybe? Were they preparing to bring the humans aboard by flash-frying the exterior of their craft and suits to ensure all exterior microbes had been eliminated?

The bigfoot-looking alien—*Sasquatch. I'm naming you Sasquatch, buddy*—pulled its flying/floating trick and sailed over to where the other alien sat, doing a barrel roll midflight to orient itself to the new floor.

The second alien pushed itself away from the desk, presumably to receive the bowl of goodies, and that's when Justice got a good shot of its abdomen.

Son of a—

Her stomach roiled. The alien's abdominal cavity was completely transparent. Enough so that every organ was visible. The purples and pinks and blues were muscle and blood.

The glimpse was quick—too quick to gather any specifics about what their internal structure really looked like. But it was significant that the colors were familiar. Their blood had to have a similar iron content to terrestrial-evolved blood. Perhaps their biological bases were the same—perhaps there was only one reliable set of chemicals that animal life could use to evolve a complex circulatory system.

That would be an amazing discovery—a fact of biochemistry that could not be proven without interaction with extraterrestrial life.

The see-through one sat back down, and Justice strained for another glimpse of its belly, to no avail. *And you I dub Cinderella,* she thought to herself, fighting off her growing anxiety with levity. *Because you kind of remind me of a glass frog. And, well, glass frog, glass slipper—it makes sense to me, it doesn't have to make sense to anyone else. I need designations for you, regardless.*

Sasquatch and Cinderella. She wondered casually if anyone else had come up with their own private names for any of the other dragons.

"No. Stop. Stop it!"

Justice whirled to her left. Sasquatch had come back and was pawing at one of the security guard's helmets.

The guard—*Steve, of course, it had to be Steve*—had upchucked in his helmet. Perhaps it was trying to be helpful?

It. She hated calling them "its," especially now that she'd named them. *Okay, your pronouns are* they, them, *and* theirs *for now,* she decided.

She reached for her atmosphere gauge, to try and figure out if the air was breathable and the room appropriately pressurized, but of course it was gone.

And of course, even if the aliens could understand what Steve was saying, they couldn't hear him in his suit.

Carmen, who'd only awoken moments previous, quickly slid to Steve's side. [No,] she signed. [No. Dangerous. No.]

Now they'd see if sending the ASL lexicon had been a futile measure or not. Justice knew Carmen had signed to a few of the other visitors, that these might have been words she'd used before. But that didn't mean the *Lùhng* had made any attempt to learn, and the humans had never truly been given a chance to teach.

Meathead—okay, Mac. Maybe she'd been too hasty in assigning him the nickname—joined her in franticly signing [No.]

Steve struggled with Sasquatch, pushing their spider-hands away. He tried to crab-walk backward, but the *Lùhng* caught him by the ankle. Those arms might have looked frail, but they held him fast.

Justice joined in the signing. [No. Dangerous. No.]

Mac hooked his arms under Steve's pits and yanked. Steve cried out as strain was put on his ankle and knee, but he slipped free. Quick as a wink, he scrabbled off the platform, away from Sasquatch, tumbling to the floor.

Carmen moved in front of the alien, still repeating her gestures, trying to keep its focus on her. [No. Dangerous. No.]

As though exasperated with her interference, they held up the rectangle dangling at their throat.

The blackness left the shape, and Justice realized it was a screen. Up popped a fragment from the ASL lexicon Tan had sent, followed quickly by a second. A brunette woman in a purple T-shirt first signed [yes] then [safe.] The two signs looped over and over again.

Carmen froze. Justice knew the aliens had only ever mimicked before. They'd never shown any indication of understanding, let alone *replied*.

Having stunned her, Sasquatch gave chase to Steve, rounding the smoothed edges of the platform, following the security guard with long strides, though Justice could not see their feet or legs.

Without thinking, Justice jumped down herself. Even if the atmosphere was suitable for humans, there was still the possibility of contamination. Before, she might have doubted that their biologies could interact. But the mounting evidence in this room alone suggested they might share enough similarities to contaminate each other with their microflora.

"Stop!" she yelled at Sasquatch, for her own benefit more than theirs. She wound herself up, getting ready to do something incredibly stupid.

Steve ran up the wall, never once losing his footing. The room was like a bubble—mostly round, with all surfaces equal in gravity. Justice kept her head down in her pursuit, sure that a glance upward or to the side would throw her off balance.

Steve dodged under a structure to his right, giving Sasquatch the slip. The alien tried to dodge with him, but their reflexes were marginally slower than a human's due to their size. Sasquatch skidded to a halt before changing direction.

And that's when Justice pounced.

She barreled into the spiny fur, gloved hands outstretched, clasping, looking for purchase. Not to pull, not to drag down, but simply to anchor. She needed them to understand, to accept the humans' rejection. Sasquatch wanted to lay hands on them, so her only recourse seemed to be a similar level of physicality. But she didn't want to be a threat. She didn't mean to injure or alarm.

She just needed Sasquatch to leave Steve alone.

Unfortunately, the alien did not take kindly to being manhandled. Those fine little arms possessed major tensile strength. Even as she attempted to keep her hold on the side quills, Sasquatch ripped her away, tossing her aside like a pest. But she was not deterred. As soon as they turned their back, she tried again, reaching out.

Justice grunted under her breath, struggling to keep hold. The hairs were smooth, and her gloves wanted to slide away.

Sasquatch's faceplate snapped in its companion's direction. It paused, and the two seemed to be conversing.

Justice held on, hoping—

Whump.

Not again. Son of a bitch, can't they see—

Whump. Whump. Whump.

This time, the bass felt like rough kisses over a bruise. They stung, gave her insides an aching throb. She wasn't sure how many times her organs could tolerate the abuse before bursting.

Once more, she lost consciousness.

When she woke again, she tried not to scream. She tried not to breathe, tried to keep every soft orifice closed.

She was back on the platform, supine as before, laid out like sardines next to her away team.

But this time, she had no helmet. She had no pressure suit. There was nothing between her and the alien air except her thin temperature-regulating unitard.

Clamping her eyes closed, throwing a hand over her nose and mouth, she held irrationally still, willing her systems to slow, to dwindle. It was no use, of course—even if she had such control over her respiratory and nervous systems, she'd already been exposed. As she'd slept, she'd sucked it in. Right now, it was being circulated through her body, pumped into every nook and cranny by her ignorant heart.

Damn them, she thought, tears prickling in the corners of her eyes—brought on both by her ridiculous insistence she hold her breath, and by the extreme sense of violation.

Eventually she had to gasp. There was nothing for it. One did not prevent death-by-microbe via suffocation.

When she did, she sobbed. She couldn't help it. She took in another shuddering breath and felt her lips pull wide and taut over her teeth while she moaned in distress. Her interlaced fingers moved from her lips and nose to her eyes. She had to hide from this, somehow. She no longer had the protection of her pressure suit, so her own bare hands would have to do.

As she shifted, she felt a deep-muscle pain in her left forearm. It felt like an old impact wound—like someone had punched her hard. Between quivering breaths, she glanced at it, to see if she could identify the injury.

A soft tangerine light blinked back at her from beneath her skin.

Her first instinct was to claw it out, not to question what it was. She took her right thumb to it, trying to force it out through the small pinprick that must have been its entry point—like she was trying to push out a sliver. But the light wouldn't budge. Her skin crawled with a rhythmic, *get it out, get it out, get it out.* It was like noticing a worm—something foreign and wriggling and dirty.

On the next inhale, her memory provided her with a helpful frame of reference. She thought of Stone's family farm, of the plastic tags stuck through cow ears like jewelry.

We've been tagged. They tagged us. Like . . . like animals.

We've been approaching this all wrong. They don't want to learn from us. They don't want to communicate with us. We're not just some hillbillies from the universe's back end to them.

No, we're freaking animals.

No one fought as the aliens cleaned them up. It wasn't a bath like Justice ever would have thought of a bath, but obviously it was meant to make the unhygienic little apes more pleasing to their *not a loose follicle to be found* hosts.

Cinderella, who'd put on some sort of shift for the event, much to Justice's chagrin (she'd *wanted* to see their insides, to put on her scientific cap—it kept her grounded), lifted Justice's arm by the wrist and ran a device that emitted an electric blue light over her armpit.

God, are they going to put us in a zoo? Keep us in a lab?

Dr. Ratha had been crying uncontrollably for the past fifteen minutes, and both Sasquatch and Cinderella had taken a stab at stopping the tears. They'd even gone so far as to pull up ASL gifs on their screens of [why?] and [wrong?], and Carmen had very forcibly explained *exactly* what was wrong with the medic. She'd probably gotten a tad too complicated with her signs, but her ferocity had bolstered Justice.

We'll get through this. Captain Tan will figure out how to get us out.

For now, Carmen had ordered them all not to fight—an argument she'd had to make to Mac and Steve more than once before it sank in. As long as they didn't try to do anything else invasive, the aliens were allowed to touch.

Justice suspected this was a tactic to keep the team calm more than anything. If everyone felt like they'd made a decision, like all of this probing was their choice, than maybe it wouldn't seem so awful.

When Sasquatch and Cinderella approached them all with strange, jelly-like orbs attached to long tubing, while the nameless ASL woman signed [face,] Justice asked, [does this count as invasive?]

Carmen looked uncertain. The aliens held them out, several of the jiggling, toilet-bowl-cleaner-blue spheres balanced in the spread of their palms while the gif signed [face] over and over.

So far they weren't trying to force these objects onto the humans, so that was a sign of some sort. Wasn't it? She tried not to think about the thing in her arm.

[Do it,] Carmen instructed with a heavy sigh.

They each held out their hands, and the aliens distributed the globes. Justice cringed as she brought it up to her nose. *This is a bad idea.* Holding her breath and screwing her eyes shut, she pushed it onto her face like she was pieing herself. It even felt a little like smashing into the filling of a banana cream.

She knew something awful was coming. When she felt the tubes probe at her mouth, nose, and eyes, she yelped involuntarily. That was enough to give the plumbing access. They shot into every orifice—pried her eyelids open and snaked around her cheekbones and into her ears. She screamed into the jelly and saw the others squirming out of her peripheral vision, but couldn't hear them.

Thick goo filled her nostrils and esophagus—oozed in her ears and coated her eyes. She fought her gag reflex, tried not to breathe, but took a gulp into her lungs nevertheless.

Tearing at the globe did nothing—chunks of it fell away in her grasp, squishing between her fingers, exuding through them like warm butter, but the overall invasiveness remained intact . . .

Until the tubes retreated suddenly, and a large hand slid under her chin, holding it steady though she tried to struggle. A rough cloth swept over her cheeks and nose and lips, wiping away the excess blue goo.

“You stupid sons of—” she started to shout at them, but tripped over herself when her voice didn’t sound like her voice. It was muffled, as though through water.

And she could still breathe, still see, still hear. But her sight was clouded blue, like she’d been given cobalt glasses.

She felt sick, disoriented. The sly masochists hadn’t tried to force those things on them because they didn’t want to start a panic. They knew if they tried to perform whatever the hell that procedure was one at a time, they’d have to use their knockout whumps again.

Maybe I should find it comforting that they're allowing us to be awake for all this. They could perform whatever tests they wanted if we were out.

Yeah, maybe I should, but I don’t.

Cinderella came back with a second set of blue globes. [End,] their screens signed.

[No,] Ratha signed and said. [I will not. No. No. No.]

“Okay, surely *this* counts as invasive, right?” Mac shouted, his voice three octaves higher than it had been a half hour ago, even with the blue-goo interference.

[No,] Carmen signed to the aliens.

[Clean before visit,] Sasquatch explained with their screen. [No end, no visit.]

Justice had earlier guessed that this was all one long decontamination session, and this seemed like confirmation of her theory, but it was still not a process performed among equals. The aliens hadn’t bothered to explain *before* they put hands on the humans. They hadn’t bothered to ask for permission in most tasks. Hell, Cinderella hadn’t even trusted Justice *to lift her own arms* so that she could be cleaned with the blue light.

They were treating them like infants at best, mindless animals at worst.

[No clean, stay. Clean, visit.]

Carmen turned to her team, mouth pursed, brow heavy. [You can each choose,] she signed. [No one has to do this. But if they're going to take us into the rest of the ship, I'm not turning that down. If you choose not to, we'll get separated.] She turned to the aliens. [If some of us refuse, what happens?]

[No clean, stay,] Sasquatch's screen signed again.

Hopefully that meant they'd remain in this room until the others returned.

[Yes, for me,] Carmen said.

[No,] Ratha signed immediately.

They went down the line. Only Justice and Mac also agreed to the second spheres.

She gave Mac a smirk when he agreed. "What?" he asked. "It's my job to protect you. I'm not going to send you out there without security."

Like it makes a difference, said Justice's dark inner voice.

Reaching *into* the platform—pulling up part of the cushiony substance like it was clay—Cinderella built low, temporary walls around each of them.

They have a concept of privacy, Justice noted. *Funny how I couldn't tell before,* she thought bitterly.

Once the three of them finally had all of their holes plugged—*God, who knew inter-intelligence relations could be so humiliating?*—the walls *weren't* pushed back into the whole of the platform like she expected, oh, no.

Instead, Cinderella drew them up higher *and folded them over the humans.*

Justice was a shouter, she'd come to accept that about herself. Whenever she was startled or mad, she yelped. Now was no frigging exception. Cinderella folded her into the platform like a filling in a human pie, and then shoved down—pushing her in, in, down, into the foam. It wasn't sticky, but she moved through it like it was honey or marshmallow cream.

Here, there was no air. She couldn't breathe. The spongy

material enveloped her face, contouring to its shapes and protuberances. She opened her mouth and it tried to fill the space.

Her heart jumped into her throat, her lungs burned as she tried to gasp.

They're not going to kill you. They've gone through too much trouble to kill you.

Maybe they don't know this will kill us, she snapped at herself. *People kill animals by accident all the time.*

So she kicked and reached, trying to swim, to move the material past her. There had to be an out, this had to lead somewhere. But the material wouldn't shift for her. Her momentum sprang solely from Cinderella pushing on her spine.

But then her hand burst free. She could feel it—open air. She stretched for it, trying to hold on to the thin atmosphere like the lifeline it was. If only she could pull herself to safety this way, if only—if only—

She sprang from the foam and flopped on the other side, like a beached fish. She couldn't have been in the platform—the wall, whatever—for more than thirty seconds, but her anxiety had made it feel like a lifetime. She wanted to hit things, to cry, to tear all of Sasquatch's spines out one by one.

What gave them the right to treat them this way? Why wouldn't they explain things first? Why did they have to push them around? Why couldn't—

She looked up as a mechanical thing stopped before her. It had eight legs and three claws, and out of the top—spinning around like a light in a lighthouse—was a head. A head without a helmet. No faceplate, no mask. Just a head, organic and terrifying.

It was engulfed almost entirely by two silvery compound eyes, set opposite from each other, one in the back and one in the front. At least, she thought the side with the wide, thin mouth beneath the bulbous eye was probably the front. But was it a mouth? When it opened, it made no sound and had no teeth.

It peered at her curiously, the whirling of its neck halting for half a moment to give one eye a constant view. It bent its mechanical knees, coming closer to her level. The various bits of its suit made sounds—like metal hinges, and there was a gurgle of liquid—but the creature itself stayed silent.

What did it look like on the inside? Did it have that many limbs, or was it also four-legged?

She had to turn away from its face, unable to hold its surreal gaze.

It jumped back when Carmen and Mac pushed through the floor beside her. Cinderella and Sasquatch weren't far behind.

She was surprised to see both of them. They trusted the other humans alone in the deCON room?

Then again, perhaps a "babysitter" was on their way for Dr. Ratha and the rest.

Other *Lùhng* began to gather around. Justice realized they were in a hallway—a tube that went on and on in a straight line for as far as she could see. As with the bubble room, all surfaces were "down."

Carmen huddled close to Justice, and she threw an arm around her. A quick glance to her right saw Mac quivering in his proverbial boots, so—with an internal shrug—Justice roped him in as well. Without the rest of his security team, all his pretenses seemed to fall away. Whatever performative hypermasculinity he'd been clinging to was suddenly replaced with a heady dose of real-world vulnerability. He clung to her shoulder, happy to share in the solidarity.

Cinderella indicated that the humans should get to their feet. As though they were a mirror of the six-legged monstrosity before them, they wobbled upright, never losing contact with one another.

Sasquatch waved their colleagues—crewmates, shipmates, Justice wasn't sure what to call them—away from the visitors. The mechanical crab appeared to take issue, gesturing at the humans emphatically, its clawed arms and head all whirling around and around. Sasquatch maneuvered itself in front of Justice in a manner that could only be read as protective.

How were the two aliens communicating? Not with their mouths, or with any other sounds as far as she could tell. No one else wore screens, so that wasn't a standard method, either. The hall was eerily quiet. Not a single creature apart from Mac—who was whimpering, seemingly unconsciously—made a purposeful noise. No clicks, no thumps, no wild gurgling calls or whistles. There was only the gentle swish of fabric from those dressed, the soft rattling of quills, and the scuffling of feet. The mechanical suits whirred, and there was the occasional grind of metal, but nothing like the beeps or sirens of Justice's own pressure suit. Beneath it all was a faraway thrum, most likely the sound of the spaceship's bowels going about their business. But that was all.

The silence made Justice want to fill it. It felt suffocating, oppressive—like the foam doorway. She wanted to punch through it, tear a hole in the atmosphere with a deliberate sound wave of some kind. But she suppressed the impulse, knowing she was already so deep that to disrupt whatever was going on here could be counterproductive. Instead, she tried to focus her thoughts on questions and potential answers rather than simply reacting.

Which brought her back to how these beings were talking with each other. If not sound, then perhaps they communicated visually? But there had been no formal gestures exchanged between Cinderella and Sasquatch, and none exchanged now. Nothing akin to ASL, or any other movement-related language. There was no color shifting, as with some nautili. She observed no bioluminescence or artificial light exchange.

Could they rely on chemical communication? Smell?

She breathed deeply, trying to gauge the air for herself, but to no avail. The blue jelly compound blocked out everything and had no noticeable scent itself. Clearly the stuff was meant to keep foreign chemicals and microbes out, just as it was meant to keep theirs in. Maybe it only let necessities, like oxygen, through.

Speaking of oxygen, the majority of the aliens in the hall were without the customary faceplates, but they seemed unperturbed by the makeup and pressure of the atmosphere, which had to have been customized especially for the visitors. Perhaps that wasn't strange, though—those who'd come aboard the convoy had been equally unbothered by vacuum. It all added up to something curious, yet Justice couldn't connect the pieces yet.

Cinderella started to herd the humans away as Sasquatch continued to run interference, but another alien stopped them, embroiling Cinderella in what looked like an entirely new argument. Others stopped to watch the humans pass, leaning into one another, but seemingly saying nothing. One's clothing caught Justice by surprise, in that it resembled a burqa. She could see nothing but the creature's two eyes. And though the body beneath was bulky and monster-like, the eyes were soulful.

She shivered.

When Cinderella stooped abruptly to pick Carmen up by the waist, Justice and Mac both shouted.

[Put her down!] Justice demanded, but Cinderella completely ignored her. Instead, Carmen was thrust bodily back through the wall they'd just exited, and was covered over by the foam in half a blink.

Justice backed away from Cinderella, dragging Mac with her. "No!" she shouted, entirely unsure if Cinderella even had ears to hear her.

The denial was important. She knew saying no would, in practical terms, get her nothing. But it was essential for her own sense of personhood, of agency. She refused to go along with whatever their captors (for they *were* captors) wanted simply because it was going to happen either way. Her wants and choices would not be erased.

"No!" she spat again, in unison with Mac.

They backed away quickly, but as soon as she felt a sharp pricking along her spine, she froze.

Sasquatch's quills bore into her back as it pressed forward, grabbing both humans in its spindly hands and thrusting them back into the invisible aperture.

And even as it bothered her, Justice's scientific mind wouldn't shut off. She was reasonably sure now that these foamy entrances served as their own airlocks, likely automatically protecting every room and hallway from sudden depressurization. But surely it had to be unpleasant for the *Lùhng*, too, mining their way through a stack of pillows every time they wanted to get from one space to the next.

From the hall, to the wall, to the platform they popped onto, the directional changes had Justice's insides doing acrobatics. Her inner ear was revolting, and she knew if gravity changed on her one more time in the next sixty seconds, she was going to hurl.

Let's see the little blue plug deal with that, she thought, crouching on her hands and knees. Then a sudden thought brought her up short. *I'd probably just drown in my own vomit . . .*

The rest of their away team looked puzzled, several asked what was wrong.

[We don't know,] Carmen said and signed.

Cinderella and Sasquatch returned.

[What went wrong?] Carmen asked. [Did we do something wrong?]

[Inappropriate,] Cinderella's screen said.

[What was inappropriate? What did we do?]

Whump.

Not again!

Whump.

Son of a—

Justice wanted to scream at the top of her lungs.

You alien bastards!

Then, darkness.

"Ow! Son of a—" Steve looked like he wanted to punch Dr. Ratha right in the face.

"As you can see, all attempts at extraction have failed," the medic said, holding Steve's wrist so that the blinking light in his forearm was displayed to all those gathered round in the situation room.

Steve had volunteered to be the example, to put on a little show-and-tell for Captain Tan and the department leaders.

Convoy Twelve had nothing like the official boards or government systems of the other convoys. Captain Tan was unquestionably in charge, followed by Captain Baglanova of *Breath* and so on down the ships' command line. But Tan had chosen to include a few others not directly involved in the away mission for this debriefing. In addition to the captains, their first officers, and their aides, were Dr. Vanhi Kapoor and Dr. Gabriel Dogolea.

The rest of the crew, though they knew how the away mission had begun and how it had ended, were currently in the dark as to the specifics. And no one liked it.

The entire convoy was restless. They weren't sure what to think, how to act, how to feel.

Justice was, internally, livid. Her thoughts were a haze of colors, of *how dare they*, and spikes of fear.

The aliens had worked the humans back into their space suits, then deposited them back on their shuttle. They'd awoken several minutes later to shouts over their intercoms.

The away mission was supposed to be some kind of grand scientific endeavor, but it only proved what they already knew: they were at the mercy of the *Lùhng*—these dragons Tan had wanted so desperately to believe in. He wanted them to be saviors, helpers. He wanted to have a relationship with them, to be equals.

But there were no equals among animals. There was only predator and prey.

She'd already given her account to the table, explained how trapped she'd felt.

"I was able to dissolve the blue matter they applied to our orifices," Ratha went on. "And at some point they covered us in a thin film made of clear quantumfibers, which they may have applied via that spray—" he turned to Justice "—Remember? Anyway, the film tore away easily after I discovered it, so I believe it was meant to be temporary. I think it prevented us from dropping any skin cells or follicles that might have contaminated their craft, which may explain why they haven't left any similar biological traces during their visits to the convoy.

"All that is to say, everything else they forced upon us has been removable, but, every time we've tried to physically excise one of the *Lùhng*'s—well, tags, for lack of a better word—it has burrowed deeper. I fear for the musculature, and even the bone, should we continue to try and cut it out."

"What other options do we have?" Captain Tan asked, posture stiff, shoulders taut.

"I did try to short it out in Savea's case. But a direct application of current did nothing to the tracker. Unfortunately, Savea's forearm didn't fare nearly as well."

He gestured to where Mac sat. The security guard waved his bandaged arm, smiling a smile that was more masochist than mirth. Steve frowned in commiseration.

"The objects themselves don't seem to be causing any issues. There's no clotting around them, no white blood cell increase, no inflammation. All of our bodies appear to have accepted the object with more ease than a splinter." Ratha's gloved hand went over his own small patch of lit skin. "If it wasn't for the damn blinking keeping me up at night, I'm not sure I'd mind it in the long run."

"Speak for yourself," Steve spat. "I don't like the idea of any one of those motherf—" he took a deep breath. "I don't like the idea of them cataloging my routine. No one except me and my doc need to be concerned with how many trips I take to the john in a day."

"Thank you, Weaver," Captain Baglanova said. "You may step down."

Steve complied with a grumble.

"So, did this quantumfiber film prevent you from picking up any biological traces of the aliens? No hairs stuck to your skin, or . . . ?" Dr. Dogolea asked.

"Nothing," Justice said. "And there were no viable samples left in our shuttle or on our suits. Could be we came away clean because they were worried about contaminating us, could be they don't want us to have their genetic information. Which I get. That information can be used against them, just as it can be used against us. I would prefer they didn't have a human genetic profile, but I'm pretty sure we're way past that."

"If they were going to do something hostile with our information, wouldn't they have done it by now?" Dr. Kapoor asked.

"They seemed pretty damn hostile to me," Steve said.

"We don't know what their intent was. This is likely a misunderstanding," Captain Tan said pragmatically.

"We've got these *things* in our arms," Steve said, yanking his sleeve up once more, letting the blinking light wink its evil eye at the captain. "Let's see how hostile you think they are after they shove something inside *you*."

"Weaver, watch your tone," Tan snapped.

Steve retracted his arm, abashed.

"He's not off base," Captain Baglanova said.

Justice wasn't sure whose side she came down on. She'd felt like an animal, out of control, at the whims of something bigger, stronger, and clearly more intelligent. There was no question their interactions aboard the alien ship had been disrespectful and dismissive from a human perspective. But, as a scientist, she knew not to jump to conclusions.

"What we need is to establish a dialogue," Tan said. "Sotomayor and I will compose a diplomatic message to be sent immediately. They need to know they offended us, but we need to give them the opportunity to explain. This situation is fragile, and what I need from all of you now is a commitment to convoy morale. No one is to relate their experience aboard the craft in a negative light, understood? The safety and well-being of the crew has to come first."

After Tan contacted the *Lùhng,* the response was surprisingly immediate. Carmen was at her nav station, and the captain gestured for her to follow him into his ready room.

"They've sent us a visual message. I need you to be the direct point of exchange."

"Of course," she said, moving in front of the paper-thin screen that occupied the wall opposite his desk.

When it came on, she wasn't surprised to see the woman in the purple T-shirt. The gifs were cobbled together haphazardly, with little thought applied to pauses in between. She scrutinized the message, let it loop multiple times.

"The signs they've chosen are somewhat confusing. Could

be they don't yet have the ASL vocabulary to fully explain," Carmen noted. "The apology is clear, but their explanation is difficult to interpret. When they told us something was inappropriate, they didn't mean us. They meant their own behavior. Someone, in the midst of our mistreatment, had worked out that something was wrong. I believe the explanation—or, justification, as it were—indicates they communicate telepathically, and that the lines between one being and another are highly blurred at any given moment. Full autonomy seems to be a foreign concept."

"That doesn't explain why they failed to seek your consent," Tan said.

"It might if they are a true hive mind," she said. "If an individual body is not seen as an individual being, their capacity to give a simple yes or no might be limited. However, they clearly understood our 'no's when signed, and proceeded regardless. I believe they did not seek our consent because they did not fully trust in our capacity to give it."

Tan's eyebrows rose in surprise. "How so?"

"Dr. Jax was apt in her description of our treatment as animals. Though I would be a little more charitable and say we were treated more like children. Adults make decisions against the wills of children all the time. They don't want to bathe, we make them anyway. They don't want to eat vegetables, we make them anyway. I believe the *Lùhng* thought our protests unreasonable and disregarded our 'no's' because they feel we are unable to make grown-up decisions." This was something she'd come up against more than once in her adult life, even. Ableists who had no concept of her experience as a deaf person sometimes made assumptions that directly infringed on her autonomy and did not respect her capacity as an adult.

"If we were animals," she continued, "we would be back in our pens and they wouldn't worry about explaining themselves. But children, whose autonomy is often disregarded, need comforting and guidance. Which is why they feel the need to apologize."

"So, they see us as infant space farers?"

"Yes, exactly. But there's more here than an apology. They'd like to make amends. They want us to come back, to visit them again."

Tan was silent for a moment. Carmen realized he'd thought she could compose an easy response, just an acknowledgment. But this required a carefully weighed decision. "Please contact Captain Baglanova, and the rest of your away team. We need to discuss our approach."

APPROXIMATELY ONE MONTH LATER

FOUR HUNDRED AND FIFTY-EIGHT DAYS SINCE THE ACCIDENT

"I can't believe we're doing this again," said Steve, holding tight to the bar above his head as the shuttle set down once more on the cushiony surface of the *Lùhng* bay.

Carmen scowled at the readout in her helmet. She wanted to admonish him, but for the sake of unity, took a deep breath and kept quiet. Steve was stressed—they all were. Different people handled it differently, and that was okay. As long as he did his job—and she was confident he would—he was entitled to a little bit of griping.

"You didn't have to come," Justice said to him, double-checking the seal between her helmet and her EVA suit.

The readout in Carmen's helmet added, "*I* didn't have to come," and she realized Justice had probably said it so quietly, no one else had noticed.

"Yeah, I did," Steve countered. "*I've* already got a tag, I know what's coming. I wasn't going to make some other poor schmuck go through it." His gaze fell to Dr. Fitzwilliam, a physician from Trinidad who'd taken Dr. Ratha's place on the team.

“I’ll be fine,” she assured the group.

“We’ll all be fine,” Carmen said.

But would they?

The negotiations for this visit had been long and arduous, both between the humans and the *Lùhng*, and between the humans themselves.

Captain Tan and Captain Baglanova had argued about the next course of action—Tan wanted to return to the alien ships, but Baglanova thought it too risky. The away team had been equally divided, with Steve, Dr. Ratha, and most of the security team falling on Baglanova’s side. Mac Savea, Justice, and Carmen had been the only ones in favor of returning themselves. Justice made her misgivings clear, but felt it was her duty to see the operation through. Captain Tan had, in the end, made an executive decision: if the *Lùhng* agreed to all of their demands, the away team would visit once more.

The *Lùhng*, for their part, had explained all of their actions, had repeated those explanations until the humans counted themselves satisfied, and then once more. And the captain’s long list of caveats and conditions was met with little resistance.

When a human said no, a *Lùhng* was to stop immediately.

When a human asked a question, a *Lùhng* was to answer.

The humans were not to be separated under any circumstances.

Autonomy was to be respected.

The humans would be allowed to keep their clothes and communication devices at all times.

The aliens had agreed to all of the demands, but that didn’t mean that Carmen felt completely secure. Their presence was their only bargaining chip: agree and we visit, disagree and we don’t. What was to stop the *Lùhng* from doing whatever they felt like once the humans were sealed inside, separated from their convoy?

Would they respect the arrangement, or would they do whatever they wanted?

Carmen knew that answer lay in their motivation, something that was still entirely unclear. They'd helped the humans, but only minimally. They'd studied the humans, but mostly from afar. Had they been testing them, trying to discern their level of intelligence before developing more in-depth relations?

Or were they keeping them at a distance because they were more of an unexpected burden than a curiosity?

A dog had wandered into her yard once, back on Earth, when she'd lived in the Spanish countryside. It had been mangy, and so thin she could see its ribs. But it lunged at her when she'd tried to pet it. She hadn't wanted to alert the pound, and hadn't wanted it to wander off and die, so she'd put out food for it, and stayed inside, and kept a careful eye on its comings and goings.

It had lived near her house for five years. She kept water out for it, called to it in Spanish sometimes from a window. But it was never her pet, not really.

Perhaps the dog was to her what Convoy Twelve was to the *Lùhng*.

The pilot released the locks on the shuttle door, and the team stepped out once more. Carmen was immediately taken back to that first visit. Her insides recoiled, pressing against her spine at the memory of that bright light and the pelvis-rattling *whump*.

As long as everything went to plan, this time there would be no sudden blackouts, no manhandling, no strip search.

When the whole team was settled, they stood together in a group, watching the walls, waiting.

Everyone had been given the opportunity to back out, but only Dr. Ratha had taken the offer. Carmen was impressed. The violation she'd felt after that first visit had nearly knocked her out of *Lùhng* relations altogether. She'd only interpreted their messages because she had to—because at least she was dealing with gifs instead of their eerie faces.

Slowly, she'd eased into the idea of coming again, for much the same reasons as Steve and Justice's: *she* knew what she was getting into. She'd lived through it before, dealt with it—come to terms, as it were. It was something she felt she needed to do, both for the convoy and for herself.

And, if she was being honest, the fact that ASL was their primary form of communication gave her a thrill. It was *her* first language that bridged the gap between their species. *She* wanted to be the ASL ambassador, rather than a hearing person.

"There!" Mac said, gesturing at a far wall, the readout in her helmet drawing Carmen out of her thoughts.

A long, dark, thin arm jutted straight through the material, and appeared to beckon them.

Unsteady on the squishy surface, they toddled toward it and waited. The fine digits grasped and ungrasped, as though looking for a handhold.

"I think they're going to pull us through," Carmen said.

"Oh, great, yeah, this is much clearer communication-wise than last time," Steve said sarcastically.

Carmen ignored him. "I'll go first. There shouldn't be any problem with our comms channels, but if you lose me, abort mission immediately, got it?"

Everyone agreed.

Here goes, she thought, slipping her gloved hand into the outstretched one. It immediately drew her forward, into the wall.

Unconsciously, she held her breath, and slipped back into an alien world.

Getting through the strange material was much more difficult with the suits on. It compressed oddly, pinching Carmen's sides, squeezing her chest uncomfortably. The substance tugged at her boots and gloves, threatening to tear them away.

More hands were required to pull her out. Alien paws littered the faceplate of her helmet, all tugging, twisting, doing their best to bring her through intact.

This must be why they stripped us, she realized. And why most of them appeared to live naked. Their airtight apertures seemed to work best on objects that were firm or tight. The more malleable the substance, the more difficult it was to move through the material.

She emerged into the decontamination room they'd been in before, and she wondered briefly about the other walls in the bay—was each a hidden door that led to a different room?

The *Lùhng* Justice had referred to as Cinderella greeted her, as did three others she'd never met before. Soon the rest of the away team followed, and the dance began.

Dr. Fitzwilliam was the only one asked to remove a part of her EVA suit. They needed to give her an implant—which the aliens had insisted was used to combat radiation poisoning. The RADs on parts of the *Lùhng* ship were so high, the humans' suits could not protect them.

Though many of the team were skeptical of the explanation, they'd long ago accepted it. Dr. Fitzwilliam took the injection without complaint.

Their suits were scrubbed just as thoroughly as the humans themselves had been the first time, and were sprayed with the quantumfiber coating, then, with much pushing and shoving and pulling from the other side, the away team—all of them this time—were welcomed once more into the ship proper.

Those who'd never made it into the hall before looked around with wide-eyed wonder at the flow of aliens around them, traipsing by on the curved walls, floor, and ceiling.

Cinderella pointed at the screen dangling from their neck. [This way. Guide, this way.] the gif signed.

With anticipation roiling in her chest, Carmen followed, and the others fell in line—Mac and Steve flanked her, and the rest of the security team brought up the rear. The one thing the aliens had insisted on was no weapons. The humans had obliged. If things got dicey, the security team would have to rely on their hand-to-hand training, and, well, with the *Lùhng* holding that *whump* device over their heads . . .

In a way, the security team was just for show. She tried not to think about it too much.

The aliens scuttling, hovering, and winding through the hall gave them a wide berth, parting like the red sea around them. Even though their faces were difficult to read—many moved in unrecognizable ways or were hidden behind visors—Carmen knew jittery caution when she saw it. Their quick sidesteps, long stares, and carefully maintained distance clearly meant the *Lùhng* were just as wary of the humans as the humans were of them.

Carmen took in the white walls, the subtle vibrations, and the constant gravity inversions with interest, searching for any extra clues as to the best way to communicate their questions and needs. They knew nothing about *Lùhng* culture, or biology, and she'd been tasked with deciphering what she could.

The others seemed distracted, off task. They chatted about how eerie the silence was, and Carmen appreciated that it was one less thing she had to worry about. The shift in their usual experience seemed to steal their focus, while it sharpened hers.

She attempted to ask questions while they walked, but Cinderella gave the same answer every time. [Not qualified. Wait for guide.]

Eventually, the *Lùhng* stopped in front of a bare patch of wall like any other and pointed. [Guide inside, can answer.]

"All right, everybody in," Carmen directed.

With the help of additional *Lùhng,* one by one they were shoved through the aperture, their suits hugging and pressing uncomfortably, but they all made it to the other side. Cinderella did not follow.

Carmen was unsure what she'd been expecting—a throne room, maybe. She'd thought they might get to have a classic "take me to your leader" moment on a bridge or in a grand ballroom-type arena. But instead they seemed to be in the guts of the ship.

These walls weren't smooth or white. The light was dim, and the thermometer on her suit said it was 4.44 degrees Celsius. The space was large, but strung through with thick gray tubes and long wires. What looked like bundles of cloth dangled from the ceiling every few meters, and steam swirled around them. Condensation dewed on every surface, and the walls themselves heaved in and out.

"This feel right to you?" Mac asked. "Where's this 'guide' we were supposed to be getting?"

Everyone turned expectantly toward the aperture. Perhaps their guide would be clamoring through at any moment.

All was still.

Carmen's heart rate ticked up a notch. Maybe the *Lùhng* weren't going to stick to the deal after all.

She turned back around, looking for clues in the room. She noticed something sticking out from one of the bundles, something she was sure hadn't been there before.

It was angular, and long. The surface was pearlescent white, striped through with bits of shining black. The entire parcel gave a shuddering twist and Carmen gasped.

The bundles were alive.

"Everyone," she said slowly, calmly. "I need you to hold your positions, but look up there."

The bundle shuddered, bits of fabric twisted away, revealing more skin. The parcel rolled and writhed, squirming as though filled with snakes.

"I knew it," Steve muttered. "We're fucking *dog treats* is what we are. Shoved us in here to feed us to their pets."

"Maybe we should go," Mac said.

"Assuming we can," Steve snapped. "Can you lock that wall stuff you think?"

"Everyone hold," Carmen repeated, signing the direction as well.

Tubing snapped away from the moving bundle, spewing a dense fog over the mass and down onto the floor. More of the cloth pulled away, and one long limb slipped free, dangling limply toward the ground, which the spindly fingers barely brushed. Then another arm lifted, at a sickening angle to the first, wrist heavy and slack.

Then there were more—more arms, more than Carmen wanted there to be, all haphazardly reaching forth, each either drooping as though lifeless and vestigial, or shaking as though with palsy.

"We need to go!" Steve insisted, grabbing her arm, tugging her toward the aperture.

"It's just another *Lùhng*," she countered, though her heart was in her throat.

What if I'm wrong?

We don't know what their motives are. For all we know they could be looking for cattle, a new source of cheap meat—

"It's my job to protect you, and we should—"

"She says stay, we stay until the threat's been proven," Mac said, pulling Steve's hand off Carmen.

Though both Dr. Jax and Fitzwilliam had looked away, Carmen forced herself to meet the creature head on. She didn't *want* to see what was beneath those many layers. Didn't want to know how those spider limbs all came together, or what sort of grotesque phantasm they belonged to. But she would stand there and face it.

Look at it. Just look. It's better if you see.

It's the sort of thing one tells oneself at night. When it's cold, and dim, and you're alone but know you're not alone. When there's a breath hanging over your shoulder, outside your front door, when you're struggling to get your keys out. And it could just be the wind, or it could be a person. Or if you're young enough, it could be a monster. If you're old enough, it could be both.

But Carmen didn't have to let her imagination run wild. The tension she felt, the presence, wasn't her mind playing tricks on her. There really was a monster, just there, right in front of her. Looking or not looking wouldn't make it go away.

But it might give them a fighting chance.

Eventually the creature tumbled to the floor, a mass of fabric and legs going every which way. The floor shifted slightly as the new weight settled onto it. More tubing and wires disengaged, snaking back up into the ceiling.

Slowly, the creature stood, unfolding itself.

The arms were an alternating black-and-white—the black looked hard, like a beetle's carapace, and the white looked clammy, weak, nearly translucent, like Carmen could pull the muscle away from the bones as easy as putty.

From this angle, ports where the hissing wires had been embedded in its skull were clearly visible.

It was more humanoid than Carmen had expected, and reminded her a bit of the Hindu goddess Kali—graceful, many limbed, and terrifying. When it reached its full height, it stood perfectly still for a moment, arms outstretched, each of its eight hands poised differently.

The bundle of fabric now formed a long robe around the

alien, hiding its bottom half entirely. Had it feet? Hooves? A tail? Carmen couldn't tell.

Its face was almost birdlike, with a crest down the center, and two sets of eyes—their pupils large and round—on either side.

Carmen signed at it immediately. [Are you our guide?]

[Yes. Friend. Here to help.] It signed these things itself, without the aid of a gif-projecting screen, the top limbs moving deftly.

She let out a sigh of relief. Finally, progress. [Will you tell us about your species? About all the species on board?]

She'd expected a curt yes, but all four sets of Kali's limbs began moving wildly, gesticulating firmly. It took Carmen a shocked moment to realize what she was seeing—each set of hands was signing something different, holding a conversation all its own.

[One at a time,] she pleaded. [Our language is only meant for two arms—answer one at a time.]

[Perhaps better if show,] Kali signed slowly.

[Yes. Thank you.]

[All aboard same species,] Kali explained. [Look different because modified.]

Justice couldn't believe her eyes. All of the aliens were the same creature?

Kali strolled slowly through the hall, answering everyone's questions—Carmen's sanctioned ones as well as many others—though not all answers seemed complete. Perhaps it was as Carmen suggested; their vocabulary wasn't up to snuff yet.

They stopped other *Lùhng* as they passed, and Kali used them as illustrations. See-through bodies were easier to attend to medically. The scales many sported would be shed and reapplied—rather than regrown on the body—and were used as a sort of solar-cell suit, absorbing excess radiation while turning it into energy for the wearer. Many hands—like Kali's—coupled with the ability to split one's attention meant many tasks could be completed simultaneously.

[Almost all modifications based on home planet nature,] Kali explained.

[For what reason were you all modified?] Justice asked.

The set of limbs that were speaking with her gestured grandly before replying, while another set pointed down the hall to direct Carmen's attention, and yet another said something curt to Mac. [Work in space,] they signed.

[Work on . . .] She wasn't sure how to sign *megastructure*, and finger spelling would get them nowhere. [Big objects out there?]

[Work in space,] Kali repeated.

Close enough, she thought. What she really wanted to ask about was SD travel. The *Lùhng* used it, clearly, so she wondered if they'd ever encountered anything like Vanhi's jumping. But she had no idea how to effectively phrase such a question. She tried anyway.

[Has space travel ever made one of you ill? Have you modified for travel illness?] She knew it was confusing the moment she signed it.

Kali blinked at her a moment, then said. [Modification help prevent many illness. Work in space.]

Maybe she needed to take a different approach. If she had a more fundamental scientific understanding of the *Lùhng* and their modifications, maybe it would help point her in the right direction. [May I take biological samples of *Lùhng*?]

[No,] Kali signed simply.

Oh, now *you understand no*, she scoffed internally. [Why?]

[Human medical methods invasive.]

[A shed scale or dropped spine would be fine,] she signed. Maybe they didn't understand where human science lay on the invasiveness scale? Perhaps Kali thought they'd need to draw fluids. [Or you could provide samples. I don't need to take them.]

[No.]

[Why?]

Kali considered for a moment. [Your motives unclear.]

[Scientific curiosity,] she signed.

[No,] they signed again, then turned away from her. Apparently, her question and answer session was done.

She couldn't say that their denial was entirely unreasonable. It seemed to coincide with her earlier assumptions. Genetic information was a powerful tool, and their interspecies level of trust just wasn't there yet.

No matter. You couldn't go two feet on the convoy without finding a bit of human genetic information. She didn't see why here should be all that different. Now that she wasn't in panic mode, finding loose samples should be a breeze.

For the rest of the visit, she picked up whatever scraps she could find. Maybe all she had was lint, but maybe it contained traces of *Lùhng*. She'd find out when she got back to her lab.

. . . Or not.

When the first suit's power started to get low, the visit was deemed over. On their way back through the decontamination room, their exteriors were thoroughly cleaned once more, pockets, sample bags, and all. Any little bits Justice had collected were summarily swept away.

Carmen was ecstatic, and grinned from ear to ear when they reboarded their shuttle. She'd asked Kali to try to contact Earth on their behalf, and the *Lùhng* had agreed.

Even though Justice had come away empty-handed, the

visit had been amazing. Unlike the first away mission, this one felt like a true success. Perhaps Convoy Twelve and the *Lùhng* were on their way to an equal footing after all.

Every few months, the *Lùhng* allowed a visit. Carmen started to enjoy them immensely, and though communications were still rough and translations were difficult, she'd come to think of Kali as a friend.

And yet . . .

There were still times when she questioned the *Lùhng*'s forthrightness. Kali had taken Carmen to their equivalent of a bridge, had shown her how messages were sent, though at the time had only used it to contact another *Lùhng* ship. It seemed Kali thought the basic demonstration would appease her, get her to stop asking certain questions. But it only served to raise her suspicions.

"Every time I ask about communications with Earth, Kali signs the same thing, and I get the feeling they're brushing me off," she confessed to Justice.

The two women currently occupied the stationary bikes constructed for Steve's pet project: a gymnasium. Their original rec center had been on *Life*, and until the convoy had stabilized, there hadn't been time or resources to devote to a facsimile. Who needs to lift weights when you're lifting kilos of parts day in and day out? Who worries about getting their reps in when they're preoccupied with starving to death?

But now that Justice's little farm had proven sustainable—with asexually reproducing plants taking up the majority of the slack, while other plants needed constant recloning—their relationship with the *Lùhng* was in an upswing, and their ship repairs looked like they'd hold, there was room again for other things. Namely: stress relief. Of which everyone on board was in desperate need.

Carmen found her stress had risen, rather than lessened,

since that second, promising visit to the *Lùhng* ship. Sure, she wasn't in a constant state of high anxiety, like in the weeks right after their accident. This nervousness was different, but equally as insidious.

She couldn't help but feel as though the *Lùhng* were purposefully steering her away from asking the important questions, from getting to the big picture.

[What, exactly, does Kali say?] Justice prompted.

They'd been cycling hard for a quarter of an hour, and both women had worked up a sweat. Carmen wiped her brow. It was good to feel her muscles burn, her body pushing itself hard without the immediate threat of danger behind it.

"Every time I ask if they've sent a message to Earth, Kali says yes. But then I ask about the content of the message, and they act like they don't understand. I ask about how their communication system functions, and they say they don't understand. I ask if they've ever contacted Earth before, and they say, 'yes, when you asked, we contact.' I ask about how long it might take to get a reply, and they say 'a long time.' I press Kali about a specific timeline and they repeat, 'a long time.'"

[And you don't believe it's a translation issue? We've only been steadily communicating for six months, it's amazing we can say as much as we do to each other, isn't it?]

Carmen shrugged, leaning farther over the bike's handles, pedaling faster. "It is, and it isn't. Something doesn't add up."

She'd been happy when they'd agreed to contact Earth on behalf of the convoy. Their communications technology had to be light-years ahead of the human's, which meant the likelihood of actually reaching the far-flung planet was far higher with the *Lùhng* backing them. But the agreement, and the subsequent assurances that they had already sent their message seemed . . . too easy.

"If this was their first time sending a message to Earth, their first interaction with a new planet, surely it would take careful planning and long-term thought," she explained. "*Yes, hello, we've found two of your ships, would you come and get them please?* isn't exactly a prime example of a first-contact message. And what would it invite? From the *Lùhng* perspective, alerting a new species to your existence in such a casual way isn't the most intelligent move."

And if there was one thing the *Lùhng* seemed to be, it was cautious.

Which meant one of two things in Carmen's mind: "Either this message was not the first they'd sent to Earth, which means they've encountered humans before. *Or*, they haven't actually sent a message at all, and have no intention of sending one."

Both options were chilling in their own way.

Justice put her hands on her waist for a moment, still pedaling, but considering. [If they've met humans before, that would explain why they were able to learn ASL so quickly.]

"Yes, it's possible they could already have an understanding of human concepts and thought processes, which would make learning the language easier. But if they've met humans before . . . why haven't they said so? And by the same token, if they have no intention of contacting Earth, why lie?"

Both of them turned introspective for a moment, turning over all the little red flags in their heads.

"Hello!" Steve said, sliding in front of them, interrupting the tension only briefly before it snapped back into place again. "You two all right over here?"

Steve was quite proud of his new gym, as he should be. The guy could be a bit . . . how had Justice put it? . . . boneheaded at times, but he was doing his best to push through, just like they all were. He'd wanted to give the crew a place to take the edge off, and he'd done well.

There were bench presses and other weights; he'd commissioned the bikes, an elliptical, and a stair-stepper (Carmen knew several of the engineers who worked on them, and they'd been grateful for the opportunity to take their minds off the larger questions for a time, to ease into the simple and the basic). But his most popular addition had been the punching bags: five heavy bags dangled on thick chains, two speed bags were mounted in one corner, and three freestanding bags were routinely moved around what had once been a support lab for the EOL.

Carmen took a swig out of her water bottle, while Justice signed and said, [We're fine].

"You sure?" he pressed. The knowing look on his face indicated he'd been eavesdropping, and he leaned in conspiratorially.

Though Carmen was fairly adept at reading lips, she smiled when Justice started interpreting Steve. [I'm in here whenever I'm off duty, and lots of people have been asking questions like yours, you know? Captain Tan wants to play like everything is smooth sailing from here, but the crew knows different. Like you said, things don't add up—and you'd know better than anyone.]

"So what do we *do* about it?" she asked. "The more I question Kali, the more they're going to give me the runaround."

Steve shrugged. [Don't know there's much we can do. Not without . . .] He trailed off for a moment. [Doesn't matter. *I* don't have an answer for you, but I do know a great way to let off some steam.]

He pointed toward the bank of heavy bags. One was twirling on its chains, and as the far side rotated into view, Carmen noticed that someone had drawn on it. The punching bag now sported a bug-eyed, fang-mouthed creature. A *Lùhng* face for an eager fist.

She raised her eyebrows. "Captain Tan isn't going to like that."

[Who cares? We're on *Breath*, and Captain Baglanova already saw it, didn't say a word. People are upset, wound tight.

They need something to point their anxiety at, and right now it's the *Lùhng*. I don't see anything wrong with that. *They* are our number one threat right now. They control everything we do, there's no question. If you want to go punch a dragon in the mouth, it's better to do it here than crack on an away mission, right?]

"I guess . . ." she said, unable to put a finger on why the caricature made her queasy. It was one thing to be angry with them, to question their sincerity and their motives. It was quite another to visit violence on an effigy.

[Go ahead,] Steve prompted. [Take a swing at it.]

Toweling off her face and neck, she slipped from the bike and wandered over. The white paint had been sloppily applied to the gray skin of the bag, but there was no mistaking the sketch for anything other than a *Lùhng*. She stopped its swinging, holding it still, peering into the glaring eyes.

Nauseated, she pivoted and left the gym.

SIX HUNDRED AND FOUR DAYS SINCE THE ACCIDENT

Justice, like Carmen, might not have approved of Steve's "stress relief" methods, but their conversation had been turning over and over in her mind in the days since.

The humans and the *Lùhng* couldn't keep orbiting each other like this, of that she was certain. Something had to change, to give. Steve was absolutely correct in his assessment of the power dynamic: the aliens had all the control, the humans had none. If the convoy crew simply sat back and allowed things to progress as they were, would anything change? Would they ever get more than the scraps the *Lùhng* were willing to feed them?

She could feel the crew's tension rising as she walked through the ships. It wasn't the chaotic tension of the accident, or the bereaved depression that had followed. It was more . . . angry. It *burned*, like matchstick points—small, but painful. It was evident in every sudden glare and snap answer. People walked with it licking around their bodies like eager little flames. It wouldn't take much to see the wisps of it turn into a blaze, consuming the crew like a wildfire.

Something had to give. They had to tip the scales of power away from the *Lùhng*, just a little bit, in order to put the fire out. Because if the anger grew, if it became a conflagration, there would be no dampening it, not smothering the heat before it ate through the command structure like kindling, and left Tan and Baglanova without an eager ear or a willing hand to put their orders into action.

But she had no more of a plan than Carmen or Steve.

Here she was, staring at a ticking time bomb, knowing it could go off any moment, and she had no idea how to defuse it.

On their next away mission, she felt distracted. There had to be something she could do, besides watch and wait.

But what?

The away team had chosen not to wear their EVA suits—it made moving between apertures easier, and the length of their visit wouldn't be dictated by battery life or oxygen consumption. There were only three of them this time: Mac, Justice, and Carmen. They'd found Kali to be more open when their audience was small.

Today the *Lùhng* guided the humans to an aperture they'd never used before, and indicated they should enter first. Carmen pushed through immediately, but Justice, still distracted, hesitated.

Mac seemed to mistake her pause for fear. "Together?" he asked, holding out his hand.

Her first instinct was to scoff, but she bit it back. There was genuine openness in the offer, and marveling at herself, she said, "Yeah, all right."

The suffocating sensation went by more quickly this time. Familiarity bred only slightly less panic, and having Mac by her side offered more of a comfort than was logical. Why was it that not having to face something alone—to investigate a scary sound, or feel around in the dark, or undergo a monotonous task—always made it more bearable?

The sudden directional change on the other side sent them both tumbling. What was up in the hall was down in this new space. Justice lost her grip on Mac.

The gravity was less here, and though everything lay in utter darkness, she could sense a vastness. Too vast. The air moved in uneven breezes, like the wind on a mountain top. And it was cold. The hairs on her arms prickled, and she groped for Mac, who had to be nearby. When she could not find him immediately, she attempted to crawl. The floor had an even springier quality to it than previous ones, more like a trampoline.

If she pushed too hard, she worried she might thrust herself off into oblivion.

The fact that she couldn't see anything should have had her fearing for her own safety—anything could be hiding in the dark—but it was Carmen she thought of first. Without light, without their gear, there was no way to contact her.

"Mac?" she whispered, as though trying not to alert whatever was waiting in the shadows.

"Over here," he said.

She stood on jellied knees, took baby steps toward his voice with her arms outstretched, afraid she might bump into something. "I don't know where Carmen is," he added.

Something clammy touched her shoulder and she jumped. If it hadn't gripped her, she might have flown off the ground and into the void. "It's me," Mac whispered directly into her ear, a desperate hitch in his voice.

"Help me find Carmen," she said, pulling him down to his

knees. She began pounding her fist against the "floor" in a blatant SOS, hoping the kinetic ripples might alert Carmen to their position.

After a brief pause, there was an answering "fine" in Morse code. The ripples were faint—she wasn't as close as Justice would have liked, and she wondered why Carmen hadn't simply called out.

"I don't like this," Mac whispered.

"Oh, no?" Justice asked sarcastically.

"Shut up."

"You shut up."

Two bright spotlights flickered on from only centimeters above their heads, throwing their faces into sharp relief, highlighting how close they were to one another—noses nearly touching. Justice yanked her head back, but kept hold of him.

Elsewhere, two other spotlights appeared. One above Carmen, who was thankfully only meters away.

The other revealed Kali behind them, floating above the floor, perfectly content with the shift in gravity. [Come, and behold,] they signed, floating off into the distance.

The four spotlights traveled with them, keeping each figure in a halo of illumination, but all else in darkness. They traveled deep into the inky cavern, and Justice got turned around. Which way had they come in? There was no way she'd be able to find her way out again on her own.

Eventually, Kali paused. [Behold,] they signed again, each set of limbs echoing the first.

Then they raised their arms upward.

Another lone light flickered into existence—a pinhole in the dark. Through the opening, something pushed, forcing its way into the room like an egg being laid.

Maybe that's exactly what it is: an egg.

The emerging object had a distinctly ovoid shape, and its "shell" was thick-looking, yet translucent. Like Cinderella's torso. A hazy amniotic fluid, light blue through the cobalt eye coating, swirled inside.

Was this some kind of birthing room? Was the big queen alien crouched above them like a colossal ant, slowly excreting her encased babies?

When the globe released from the "ceiling" it drifted gently downward, and was soon followed by another and another, each a different size. The spheres began to rain down like balloons dropping at a New Year's Eve bash—their journey from the eyelet a gentle drift instead of a dramatic fall.

As they floated closer, the fluid inside shifted from hazy to clear, and seemed to be providing its own light. The first bubble—for that's what they most closely resembled—didn't encompasses a yolk or an alien fetus. Inside was a metallic contraption, roughly toaster-sized, piped through with tubes that were likely red, but looked purple through the film. It was boxy in shape, and appeared to have hinges and latches.

What on Earth—?

The next held an equilateral triangle made of wax or resin. At first, the structure appeared featureless, but as it bobbed close to Justice—never falling fully to the floor, but drifting on undetectable gusts—it swiveled to give her a good look at one flat side. Figures were etched into it—likely writing, accompanied by a few geometric symbols. A secondary light source flashed from within the triangle's sides, revealing etchings on the back side of the resin, as well as within the resin, adding a whole new dimension to the surface inscriptions. Two-dimensional lettering made three dimensional.

And they kept on coming. Items of all sizes and all kinds floated about the room. Soap bubbles protecting unknowable wonders.

There were hundreds now, each its own spot of brightness in the vastness. The more bubbles the ceiling produced, the larger the room seemed to grow. Justice had yet to identify a single border.

When one bubble bumped into her spine unexpectedly, she whirled with a shout. Mac snickered at her until he saw what lay within.

"Ew—what the heck?"

The bubbles weren't eggs, but there was something most definitely alive in this one. Or—scratch that—it had most definitely once been alive. Now it was preserved—the fluid in this sphere was slightly sallower in color. It could have been a plant, what with the multitude of fronds fanning up and out of the torso, but it seemed to have joints and a bone structure. Little bits of it had congealed and flaked away, parts of it looked sickly and bloated, just like a pickled two-headed fish in an old-timey science exhibit.

[What are all these?] Carmen asked.

There was something familiar about the setup. It was unscientific, scattered. None of the objects seemed to relate to one another. They were just things. Curiosities. Keepsakes? And the darkness, the spotlights—it was all very showy. Unnecessary, yet it set the mood. There was an artistry to it, like . . .

[Artifacts,] Kali answered, wandering off, poking at the bubbles, tossing them into the air like a child with a balloon.

[It's a museum,] Justice said.

[We're not additions, are we?] Mac asked, clearly a joke.

[You don't show the fossils the Smithsonian before you wire them together, right?]

[Guess you never saw a zookeeper give a chimpanzee a tour of the zoo?] Mac countered.

Kali circled back, their arms filled with specimens. [Enjoy?] they asked. [Interesting?]

[Yes, very interesting,] Carmen replied quickly.

[This us,] Kali said, showing them what looked like a petri

dish with a bit of brown substance in it. [This sample of successful permanent modifiers.]

Justice eyed the baseball-sized orb covetously. She could imagine Kali was waving it under her nose on purpose—a scrap of alien genetics she could look at, but not touch.

Kali held up another orb, then another. [This rock of home planet.] It was a smooth white pebble, river-tumbled and speckled through with crystals. [This word of Progentor.] This one contained what looked like a scrap of parchment, with a mechanical diagram drawn in ink.

Noting a basketball-sized bubble floating by, Kali snatched it from the air with two of their right hands, cradling it delicately. Inside was a small segmented piece of machinery, made of something coppery and something with the matte finish of lead. [For navigation,] they signed. [Very old.]

Justice saw an opening. [Has navigation ever made you sick? Travel—has travel modified you?] She was positive now that her yucca was incapable of reproducing on its own, and that their fly population was extinct. And poor McKayla and Samir were still childless. Several of Justice's other friends had volunteered for infertility testing, and so far she'd found weaknesses in all of their sex cells that could prevent zygote formation.

She needed to know if this was a common SD side effect, or something unique to their circumstances.

[Our travel accident changed some crew,] Carmen signed, and Justice knew she was specifically referring to Vanhi. [Some of our people are sick. Need your assistance. Do you have a doctor or scientist who would visit our ill ones?]

[No. Contamination possible,] Kali signed.

Justice let out a frustrated sigh. [Not that kind of sick. Genetic sick. DNA sick—] Every finger-spelled letter was useless, but she did it anyway. [Will you come examine?]

[Sick people in immediate danger?]

She wanted to lie. Badly. But indicating yes might raise Kali's hackles, might make them more fearful of cross-contamination. [No,] she signed.

Kali backed away from the humans, suddenly warier. [Must return you to decontamination.]

[Not contagious,] Justice said again, [Illness cannot harm you.]

[We are not sick,] Carmen tried, but it was no use. Kali was spooked.

Great, well done, Justice berated herself. *Now they think we're plague rats, and we'll never get them back over to the convoy.*

Hell, if they couldn't convince Kali everything was fine, would the *Lùhng* refuse to let them board again?

[This way,] Kali demanded, and the humans obediently followed.

All except one.

[We—] Carmen began to protest, then shrieked in surprise. Her eyes were wide; she'd caught sight of something.

Her shout was so shrill and sudden in the near silence that Justice froze. Kali and Mac were just as startled. The *Lùhng*'s top hands went to small round orifices on the side of their head—they must have been ears, though Justice had often wondered if they were nostrils.

Carmen turned to her crewmates, gesturing emphatically, then signing [table] with a force.

Justice was sure her signing vocabulary was failing her. [Table?]

Kali bent over, Mac twirled in confusion, and Justice signed that she didn't understand. Clearly unwilling to wait for her crewmates to catch on, Carmen took off, sprinting into the blackness, indicating they should hold their positions.

"Wait—Carmen!" Mac shouted ineffectually.

She continued to point while she ran, bouncing over the

floor as though she could not contain whatever was driving her. She made exclamations as she went, and it was difficult for Justice to tell if these sounds were happy, sad, terrified, or all three at once.

Soon, Carmen was jumping. There was a huge bubble she was trying to reach, one that could have easily fit the three humans lying head to feet. Despite the fraction of Earth's gravity in the room, she couldn't launch herself high enough.

A chair-sized bubble floated close to her, and she took a chance. She threw herself on top of it without knowing if the display case would come crashing down under her weight. But it stayed aloft.

With a strange, guttural squawk, Kali raised their hands and went after her.

"Hey!" Mac shouted, reaching for the ghost of his shock baton, at the same time chasing down their host.

Beside Justice, the small bubble containing the petri dish bobbed. It would be easy to conceal inside her unitard if she had the guts to grab it. It shimmered slightly, like its surface was winking at her.

Swiftly, she snatched the orb from the air. Its surface was cool, smooth, like glass. Quickly, she secreted it away, shoving it down the front of her unitard to settle between her legs, figuring that to be less noticeable than a third boob. Just as quickly, she straightened the garment again, and allowed herself a small smile at the personal irony. *Never thought I'd be stuffing instead of tucking.*

Kali was still making their strange noises, while Mac yanked at the hem of their robes like a small child. Carmen had now bounced from bubble to bubble high enough to lay her hands on the giant display.

Inside, Justice could now make out what had gotten her so excited.

It *was* a table. Just a table. Long, but relatively featureless.

They'd seen table-esque structures in the quarantine room, so that in and of itself was not so shocking.

Anyone else might not have seen anything special about the table. Anyone on any other mission from any other time. Unless you were familiar with *this* table, there would be nothing to call out, to make a fuss over.

But Carmen knew this table. As did Justice, and anyone else who had ever spent time in Tan's situation room.

It was a solid-stone long table. Sculpted by a master artisan. There were only twelve of them made, one each for the twelve "home" ships of the Planet United convoys.

This one was so dark green as to be nearly black, with flecks of something highly reflective dotted across it—very similar to theirs. A few of them had been white with different-colored mineral veins running through them.

Unlike the one in the situation room, this one had been snapped in half, and a leg broken clean away. The three main chunks hovered more or less in their proper relation to one another, implying the full table rather than making it.

How in all of creation had the aliens come by *that*?

Did this mean . . . did it . . . ?

What does this mean?

Putting that aside—the question just too large to tackle at the moment—she now understood why Carmen had rushed to get a better look.

Each table had been etched with its corresponding convoy number on one of the legs. They needed to know which convoy this belonged to.

With the stolen bobble tucked firmly, if uncomfortably, between her legs, she rushed to help Mac, to keep Kali from getting to Carmen for as long as possible.

But there was no time to be had.

Four, then five, then a sixth small spotlight came on to their left, highlighting the entrance of a half-dozen more aliens.

Each was decked out—not in the robotic suits, but in something more closely resembling riot gear.

One dashed for Mac, pulling him off Kali as he kicked and screamed. Three more sprinted after Carmen, and another wrapped Kali in their arms, as though shielding them from a rabid animal attack. And one, of course, came at Justice.

She tried to run, though she knew there was no point.

She swatted at the spotlight above her head. If she could put out the light, it might buy her a few more minutes to . . . to what? The lamp darted away like an annoyed horsefly, but would not leave her side. It was an accusation all on its own, screaming, *Here she is. Take her. Take her!*

The illuminated globes swirled in every direction, some now distant dots in the vast space. It was like running at night in a field of fireflies and birthday balloons. Under different circumstances, it would have been magical.

But now her heart thumped like hooves in her chest, and her thighs rubbed against the stolen artifact, and her arms pumped like a combustion engine's pistons as she ran, trying to propel her forward to a safety that did not exist.

And then she felt it. That dreaded *whump.*

Shit.

There was no hiding from the deep vibrations. No outrunning it.

This time it'll liquefy my brain and that'll be it.

She tripped over her own feet and fell to her knees, hands outstretched to catch her.

Shit, shit, shit. They'd messed up. What if all it took was this simple infraction? Maybe the humans were just too much trouble and weren't worth the effort . . .

Whump.

Was this it? Had she been born in a trailer park in Iowa, only to die on an alien spacecraft thousands of light-years from Earth? Like this was some morbid, futuristic *Comedy of Errors*, and she was some sort of object lesson in cosmic extremes?

Don't panic, she told herself. *Don't panic!* she insisted, her head buzzing, guts screaming, and lungs stuttering.

She squeezed her legs, felt the globe roll against them. Once again, she had the distinct impression that the cases were really eggs—full of potential, full of life.

We're going to make it. We're going to make it and I'm going to keep this, damn it!

She crawled off into the dark, tried to ignore the figures coming for her, the claws lifting her off the ground, hoisting her into the air.

Whump.

No matter how hard she willed the static to leave her vision, it continued to invade. The darkness was coming for her. She could not stop it.

Justice wasn't just surprised when she woke up, she was ecstatic. She felt like utter crap—not just crap, like the stomped-on, caked-on, mixed-with-hay crap in the cracks of a horse stall. But any level above death was a distinct improvement on her expectations.

In the millisecond that seemed to pass between unconsciousness and wakefulness, she'd been transported somewhere much more cramped than the museum, though it was still pitch black. And there were bodies all around her. Warm bodies. Groaning bodies. And there were windows, through which she could see stars, and ships, and—

And a shuttle. One of *their* shuttles.

Yellow emergency lights flickered on along the floorboards. They were back in their own shuttle—everyone, the entire away team. It seemed they had been stacked inside like kindling, their spacesuits shoved in after in one giant heap. Then, apparently, they'd been thrust out the airlock.

Even the pilot was in the main bay with them. He moaned, scratching the back of his head as he extricated himself from beneath Steve.

Justice's arm tingled as she pulled it out from under Carmen's shoulder. Directly on top of her was Mac, drooling on her collar like a baby.

She shifted, her legs tingling as she kicked free. There was a distinct heaviness between her legs—which she found both confusing and alarming for half an instant before she realized, somehow, she'd gotten away with her heist.

The monkeys threw a temper tantrum so they stunned us and tossed us back in our cage.

It was like they hadn't known what to do, so they simply shoved the humans away.

Would they even notice that one small case was missing? Would they care?

Outside, a second shuttle was preparing to intercept. The door opened—someone in a spacesuit leaned out, extending the emergency umbilical.

Carmen sat up suddenly, just as startled to find herself elsewhere as Justice.

Getting her hands free, Justice quickly signed, [Did you see? Did you see the table's convoy number?]

Carmen nodded, her face grim. Flexing the sleep tingles from her hands, she paused, then signed simply: [Seven.]

Captain Tan was *not* happy.

He had the meager away team lined up in his ready room. They all stood at firm attention, faces stoic. Twinkle stood beside him, translating as he berated them.

"What happened?" he demanded. "The *Lùhng* ships have widened their net, like they're expecting an attack. No one is answering my hails, and they set my away team adrift. I'd like to believe this is some bizarre behavior on their behalf, but I expect someone disobeyed my direct orders."

"Captain, if I may," Justice said. "We were shown artifacts in a *Lùhng* museum, and the contents were disturbing. They had human artifacts, sir. Well, one at least. And I think it's fair to assume, now, that they have in fact encountered our species before."

Carmen recalled the visit's events for him, laying out exactly what she'd seen and why she'd acted so rashly. "I'm sorry, Captain. My conduct was unbecoming, but I feared Kali would lead us away from the table if I asked about it directly. I'm surer now that we're being contained, given the brush-off."

"I was able to retrieve this," Justice said, holding up the orb. "It's not proof of *Lùhng*-human relations, but Kali did tell us it contains *Lùhng* genetic material. When we started asking medical questions, Kali became agitated, and was hypersensitive to the possibility of contamination. If they think our biologies can interact in such a way, maybe their modifications can work for us as well. This might hold the key to addressing Dr. Kapoor's condition . . . and any other genetic problems we might encounter." She'd only recently suggested to the captain that the entire crew could be infertile. They still needed to do more research to be sure, but she didn't doubt the information would be made public soon.

Tan eyed the orb, expression still as stern as before. "As soon as we're through with the debriefing, you should begin analysis. Whatever you need, let me know."

"Thank you."

"But this table—I don't want to jump to conclusions. You're sure it's from Convoy Seven?"

"Yes," Carmen insisted.

"Let's first assume, then," Tan said, "that the *Lùhng* have not encountered humans before us. Is there another way they might have acquired the table?"

"It's been a hundred thousand years," Mac said.

"Exactly."

"It might have been salvaged," said Mac. "Buddies of mine used to go treasure hunting—there was a shipwreck off Fagamalo they liked especially. They came home with all kinds of trinkets. Put them out in their sheds or on the mantel. Lots of it was rusted-over junk. Table could be like that."

"Yes, but where did they salvage it from, then?" Justice asked. "Did they get it directly from a Convoy Seven ship, or from a garbage heap—natural or otherwise? In a shoal of space trash, like a galactic version of a Pacific garbage patch?" Was that possible? Could gravitational waves create similar convergence zones in space? "If they salvaged it from the convoy itself, doesn't that mean they would have recognized *Pulse*, since it's the same basic design as Convoy Seven's habitat ship—*Mira*? Which means, even if they haven't met *live* humans before, they still hid that recognition on purpose."

"That assumes the *Lùhng* aboard their fleet now are the same ones who found the table," Tan said. "We have no way of pinpointing when they acquired it."

"Which means they might not even know it's a human artifact," Carmen said, nodding to herself. "Which would explain their reaction to *our* reaction, wouldn't it? They might have no idea what set us off. Might have seen my running around as entirely irrational."

"We're being very generous in our assumptions here," Justice said. "What if it's a trophy, acquired in battle? If they've met humans before, it would explain a lot—they're lack of interest in studying us, for one. Why poke the frog if you already know how all of its innards work? They learned our language remarkably quickly, they had no qualms contacting our home planet—or so they say."

"I see no reason to jump to hostile conclusions," Tan said.

"And I see no reason to stick our heads in the sand and ignore the possibility," she countered. "If they've met humans, why wouldn't they say so, unless those interactions went poorly?"

"If previous interactions with humans were negative, why wouldn't they just let us go? Or kill us outright?" Tan asked.

"I don't know. We're a science convoy, with no weaponry to speak of. Maybe they're the same. If you find a rabid animal in your backyard, are you just going to let it go?"

"I'd call an exterminator," Mac said.

"Exactly," Justice said.

"Exactly," Tan echoed. "You don't feed it. You don't *keep it alive*." Tan took a deep breath. "We're getting ourselves worked up. Over a table. Truth of the matter is, all we know is that they have it."

"And that they won't let us go," Justice mumbled. "Hopefully it's not because they blew our home planet out of the sky, leaving nothing but a table."

Tan abruptly moved into her space, pointing sternly. "I never want to hear that again. I will not tolerate rumors that Earth is gone. We have enough harsh realities aboard without suggesting that we are the last of our kind and that our . . . *hosts* mean to eliminate us. Do I make myself clear?"

"Yessir," she said somberly.

"Good. Now—" he tossed the orb at her "—you have an egg to crack."

It didn't take her long to cut open the orb. The substance was tough, but nothing a bit of circular saw action couldn't handle.

The orb's content was clearly organic. It faded from greenish to black and was well preserved. She thought it might be a portion of a hand, or paw, whatever. Treating the sample with care, she cut several pieces away and deposited them in various solutions for dissolving. "We'll figure you out yet," she promised, loading each test tube into her centrifuge.

Sitting back, waiting for the machine to do its work, she tried to keep her mind as far away from doomsday scenarios as possible. But it was a struggle.

What if the reason Kali had so quickly agreed to contact Earth was because they couldn't? Maybe Earth was gone. Maybe humanity was gone.

And if everyone aboard Convoy Twelve proved to be infertile . . .

But, dear god, how—how could all of humanity be gone? Why was her brain leaping to complete annihilation? What would it take to completely destroy a multiplanet, star-faring species? A slow decay into nothingness was one thing. But an extinction-level event across multiple heavenly bodies would take a perfectly timed gamma ray burst . . .

. . . or a very advanced weapon.

What, exactly, were they building out there?

When she got her results, she checked them again. And again. And once more. She would have given her right arm for a qualified professional who could do an independent study, but she wasn't getting that kind of outside verification anytime soon.

I can't . . . how?

She had to go straight to Captain Tan.

Heart pounding, breaths coming quick and deep, she ran all the way to the bridge as soon as she'd compiled her evidence.

Tan stood just within the door, wide-eyed and flabbergasted when she burst in. Everyone behind him shifted at their stations.

"Can I see you in your ready room?" she demanded, holding up crumpled holoflex-sheets. "We have to talk. This—this changes everything."

With a curt nod he led the way, keeping silent until he was sure the door was secure behind them.

"They're human," she blurted, giddy with the revelation. "They. Are. Human."

"You mean the organic sample in the ball wasn't alien? It was just another human artifact?"

Justice slapped the sheets down on his desk. She felt high, elated, and scared. The situation suddenly seemed clearer and completely clouded all at once. "No," she said excitedly. Her face hurt from smiling. *Knowing* felt so freeing, she couldn't contain herself. "My samples weren't contaminated, and I'm sure this comes from the *Lùhng*. The material is base-human. But not *totally* human, you get me? The chromosomes were wild, okay, and even though I found twenty-three pairs in what I'm sure are somatic cells, the chromatids in the autosomes are shaped superfunky, so I was pretty surprised when I unraveled them and they were so *familiar*. They've been spliced all to hell, and there's a triple helix instead of a double, which I think explains all the variations—they've got to have some way of activating only certain traits, though I think this one—"

Tan put a hand on her shoulder. "Slow down. Breathe."

She gulped and realized her fingers had gone all tingly. And she was talking with her hands like she never had before, waving them wildly. "I'm sorry," she said, "I just can't believe . . . It's so weird."

"You're telling me those aliens, out there, that we've been in communication with for nearly two *years*, are actually human?" He said it slowly, as though once she heard it for herself she would recant everything she'd just said.

Instead, she stood taller, looked him straight in the eye and said, "Yep."

"No," he said with a shrug of denial and a flick of the hand.

"Yes. How they started down this path, or when, I can't say.

I can't imagine what would drive them to modify themselves so dramatically."

"I can't accept this," he said with a baffled sigh. "We can't prove whose—what's—DNA is in that sample. If they were . . . were . . . *post*-human, why wouldn't they tell us? *They would tell us.*"

"Do you think they have the capacity to tell us in a way we would have understood? Would have accepted? Shit, I'm giving you hard evidence right now and you're looking at me like I'm peddling crystals."

He glared and she demurred.

"Like I'm peddling crystals, *sir*," she added. "What I can't figure is why they'd trap us. They had to know we'd react negatively to being hemmed in. I mean, we ran and everything."

Tan palmed at his mouth before saying gruffly, "If you found a group of human ancestors from a hundred thousand years before our time, would *you* let them wander off?"

"No. I'd probably try to keep them safe until I could track down someone who knew what to do with them."

They shared a wide-eyed look.

"Do you think," Justice started, "that means someone's coming?"

CHAPTER EIGHT

CONVOY SEVEN

MICHAEL: WE'RE ALL MAD HERE

THIRTY-FOUR YEARS SINCE THE WEB BEGAN TO MOVE

JUNE 15, 1113 RELAUNCH

6992 CE

We didn't want to be right. We wanted to be wrong. Needed *to be wrong.*

He'd thought, *Maybe.*

Maybe they'd been too hasty in their assumptions, too panicked after watching the Web behave in ways they'd never dreamed—

But it's there on my monitor now, clear as glass, evident as the single Revealer patch on my uniform.

Captain Michael Nwosu glanced over at his cycle partner and first officer. Joanna Straifer's gaze was narrowed, her jawline stiff, head bowed like a ram's, ready to run straight at the problem.

They'd risen from SD travel only moments previous, and already the truth of their fears was manifest.

The long lines of the Web's tentacles retracted as they watched, its nodes having performed their vile act once more. Stellar murder was not something anyone wished to see, and

Nwosu had seen it twice. Here was the killer gulping down the last of its victim, as it had done before.

But before he could so much as give an order, the tentacles coiled up—as they had when he was young—and the megastructure, in all its cephalopod-like grotesqueness, jetted off, leaving only swirling exhaust trails in its wake.

Did it travel by means of subdimensional access? If so, it didn't form a type of SD bubble he recognized.

Truth was, they didn't have enough information to really grasp anything about the Web. They'd arrived too late, and now all they knew for sure was they had a killer on their hands.

The entire bridge was quiet. Not a stunned silence, but a mournful one. They'd known the Web was dangerous; not a single soul aboard had had any doubt.

"I want samples of those trails taken ASAP," he said gravely, as though ordering an autopsy on his own family member. "And I need its new trajectory, *now.* We can't waste a minute mo—"

"Sir!" cried his lieutenant at the navigation console. "I.C.C. is detecting an SD bubble bursting less than three astronomical units aft of the convoy."

"Show me." *By the iterations, what now?*

All of the convoy's past assumptions—their fears—came flooding into the forefront of his mind.

It couldn't be the original builders, could it? Many people had speculated on whether or not they still existed—were a damn *Ultra Civilization.*

Could they have come here to stop the humans from taking action against the Web? Had they finally deigned to show their ugly faces now that their exterminator was under threat?

What threat? We don't even know what to do with the thing if we catch it.

But how would an Ultra Civilization know they were there?

Was this some kind of latent trap, held secretly in an SD until some unwitting, space-faring race wandered into the system?

The image on the forward monitors shifted, as did Joanna. Her stance remained tight, but she raised her head, lifted her chin, as though daring a new confrontation to emerge.

As space shimmered, the skin of the bubble pulling back and eventually tearing, a new excitement took Nwosu. It *was* an SD bubble popping. Disintegrating into normal space to reveal . . .

Ships. Three in all, emerging—rising from the darkness. Two of them like rough and tumble asteroids, one bulky and spined like a beetle.

He knew those ships, everyone did.

Elation battled with fear and sadness in his chest, and he clutched at his breastbone. "How did they find us so soon?"

He'd asked his ancestors every night to carry these ships across the galaxy safely. To see that, one day, they arrived outside his airlocks. He wanted, desperately, for an iteration of his line to oversee the reunion.

Joanna lost her hard edge, she seemed more baffled than he was, more shocked to see the spacecraft. "It's the Nataré group," she gasped. "*It's Noumenon Ultra.*"

They'd left a beacon in the center of what was once LQ Pyx's gravity well, hoping that, one day, Convoy Seven-Point-Five would find it and understand what happened. Many, including *Mira*'s previous captain, had feared this new development would mean they'd never see their sister convoy again. After all, they could leave the coordinates of the first system in their sights, but what about the system after that? And the system after that?

Of course, the prayer had been that there would be no later systems to run to, no Stellar Murderer to hunt.

They'd been so wrong on that account.

"But we left the beacon only moments before we dove," Nwosu said. "The only way they could have found us so quickly was if . . ."

"If they were already on the way back to us when we activated the Web," Joanna said.

"Even then, they . . . their arrival was so close, nearly on top of us. They couldn't have been traveling in the same SD. They had to be using a *new* one."

The captain and first officer shared a wide-eyed look.

"Signal them," Nwosu directed.

"Already on it, sir," said the communications officer. "Utilizing ship-to-ship frequencies in use when the convoy split."

"Good, good."

"They're responding," the officer said, his excitement barely contained. "Would you like it on a private channel, with a headset, or—?"

"No need. Put it on speaker."

"This is *Mira,* Captain Nwosu on duty," the officer announced to their counterpart across the distance.

"*Noumenon Infinitum*, this is *Noumenon Ultra*," came a crackly voice on the other end.

The swell of realization—that this was really happening, their brethren had really returned—crested through the bridge and burst in an outpouring of cheers. Their contact's next words were swallowed in a tidal wave of hoots and hollers.

"Settle!" Joanna commanded. "Settle down!"

"This is Captain Nwosu," he announced. "Who am I speaking with?"

"*Noumenon Ultra.*"

"But who specifically? Which captain or crew member?"

"All of us."

Nwosu furrowed his brow, brought one hand up to brush a pensive finger at the corner of his chapped lips.

The voice sounded strange. Like they had a bad connection. *Noumenon Infinitum* had long ago upgraded its communications systems—mostly to ensure a better connection to the autons working on the Web, but the effects had trickled down throughout the entire convoy. Was it simply that the old channels were more prone to static and breakage? Was the distance between the ships, with no communications buoy to boost the signal, creating a weakened connection?

"But who am I addressing, directly? Who are you?"

"*Noumenon Ultra.*"

Captain Nwosu gave Joanna a sideways glance, asking silently, *Does this seem strange to you?*

She answered with the slightest of shrugs.

"Well, *Noumenon Ultra,* we'd like to extend an invitation for some of your crew members to come aboard. I'm happy to accommodate up to a dozen at this time, to make sure that our decontamination processes aren't stretched too thin." Convoy Seven had spent a thousand years working on the Web. Convoy Seven-Point-Five, having spent much of that time traveling in SD from point to point on the Nataré map, would have experienced far fewer incidents, but all the same: a hundred years alone was plenty for viral and bacterial evolution to diverge.

"One body shall come aboard."

"If that is your wish." It was fair for them to be cautious. The beacon had to have been a shock, the message disturbing. Though the two convoys had truly only been out of communication for a short amount of time, Nwosu could appreciate their hesitancy.

Still, one seemed an odd choice.

"We will be ready in an hour. Please send over the individual's specs as soon as you've designated a visitor. We want to have the proper dosage amounts prepared for—"

"The body will have no exposed biological materials."

"Fine, fine. Do you still have the capacity to dock with *Hippocrates*?"

"Our shuttles are in order."

"Then that is where we will receive your envoy."

It was strange how suddenly an entire crew's mood could shift. The flow of today's emotional story was nearly the opposite of what it had been the day they'd turned on the Web. This morning had begun bleak, but now there was a fervent chatter, excitement, hope.

The deCON specialists on *Hippocrates* worked with an urgency Nwosu had never seen. There were smiles—work was a happy occasion again. No one's work had been a thing of joy for a long while now.

He and Joanna waited nervously outside of the designated umbilical airlock. The head specialist and her team attached a portable hazmat cleaning shower to the airlock's exterior door, ready to douse the crew member as soon as they emerged.

Wearing a pressure suit was a good call, Nwosu decided. It made the deCON process shorter, meant their reunion could happen sooner.

Joanna scrolled through a list of clone lines on her tablet—Seven-Point-Five's manifest—staring at the same thousand names over and over, barely reading them as they flicked by on her tablet. A deep furrow dug between her brows, and her eyes were so fixed on the screen, Nwosu hoped she wasn't putting too much strain on them.

It could be anyone, he told her silently. *The answer isn't going to leap off that list.*

A far-off *thump* and a strangled hiss marked the arrival of the shuttle. Nwosu thumbed at his mouth. He knew he played with his lips too much when he was nervous, but it was a habit he'd never been able to throw, no matter how many times a Joanna—both his mentor and his apprentice—called him on it.

A shape moved in the small bay beyond. Through the plastic and the layers of portholes, he could only make out something dark-colored headed their way.

Carefully, he smoothed down his uniform and pressed open his collar, unveiling his single Revealer stitching. His line had earned it by delivering the convoy safely back to the Web, by steering the fleet straight and true.

He used to wonder if he should remove the triangle, after the Web abandoned them. Once, he'd taken a seam ripper to it, unraveled one edge. But he'd immediately regretted it. He did his best to repair the patch on his own, too ashamed to bring it to the supplies division on *Bottomless II*. He called to his ancestors, looked deep inside himself, down his line, and begged for forgiveness.

The concept of Revealing and Revelation, which had been a cornerstone of their society these many centuries, was on shaky ground. How could there be destiny—cosmic divinity—in the mission, knowing what they knew about the Web? Surly it had all been folly, some said. Surely it was simply hubris.

But Nwosu felt his faith bolstered by this reunion. He was acutely aware that, after today, his line would likely receive a second mark.

He faltered for a moment, the concept sinking in.

He would likely be named a Revealer. Maybe twice over, should the concept be reinvigorated *and* the original convoy reunited.

It was unlikely the *Noumenon Ultra* crew had encountered the truth of Revealing on their own. He was excited to introduce them to the divine concept.

"Captain?" Joanna asked. "Are you all right?"

He realized he was breathing harshly through his mouth. This event suddenly felt less *joyous* and more *momentous*. It was a crux in his line—a crux he could have never predicted. "I'm fine," he said, voice shaking. He smoothed his uniform once more. "Fine."

There was *pressure* now. It had been there from the moment they made contact—both convoys needed this to go smoothly, wanted what was best. But now . . . now it felt different.

"Can you ask for the astronomers to send me an update on the Web's possible next location at the top of the hour?"

"They might not have anything of use ye . . . Yes, sir." If Joanna was anything, it was loyal. Dedicated. She hardly ever wavered, ever questioned. At times, it seemed like she had more discipline in her little finger than the rest of the convoy possessed as a whole.

As far as Nwosu was concerned, her line was the best choice for fleet command anyone had ever made.

One airlock repressurized; the initial scans had been made. I.C.C. would analyze the visitor and determine what kind of measures were needed in the next airlock. But the visitor moved through the second stage with such speed, Nwosu frowned.

"I.C.C.?"

"Yes, Captain."

"I didn't see any chemical discharge. Is deCON functioning properly?"

"Yes, Captain."

"But there was no surface blast, no UV bleach."

"That is because the surface is already free of dust and particles."

The next door slid aside. Their visitor was almost to the shower.

"The suit's already been cleaned?"

"There is no suit, Captain. The individual boarding *Hippocrates* is—"

The final door slid back. Nwosu and I.C.C. named it together.

"An auton."

The auton was much like the ones they'd used in construction of the Web, but possessed unique modifications. Most autons were simple puppets. Human-shaped tools. They had sleek, hard bodies and blank, faceless, featureless, interestless skulls protecting the meaty partial-brains that functioned as the onboard computer.

But *this* auton had a face. Purely digital, like an avatar of old. It was gray, and somewhat cartoonish, with eyes that were too big and a mouth that was too simple, an inert nose, and eyebrows that seemed to have a total of three settings.

"Hello," it said in the same static-filled tones Nwosu noted earlier. This was why the voice had sounded strange: it wasn't emanating from a person. The realization sent a small shiver up his spine. Autons were puppets, not ambassadors. Why would someone have used an auton to answer their hails?

When the auton spoke, the mouth moved, and though it appeared to shape itself around the sounds, there was no depth, no tongue. It was . . . off-putting.

They'd scrubbed its surface in the shower, just to be sure, though I.C.C. insisted the auton was clean.

Now it gleamed, its armor-like exterior smooth, scratch-free. Their own autons bore scars from all kinds of construction accidents. If those were weathered soldiers, this was a pampered tool of privilege.

It stood before them like its cousins, stiff, waiting for orders. When not speaking, its face was neutral, still.

"Hello," Nwosu answered. "Might I know the name of your operator?"

"I represent everyone, and so should be considered no one."

"Once you are assured that our convoy is safe, will crew come aboard?"

"No. Everyone is sleeping. I make a dream of this for them." It opened its arms wide, as though encompassing all it could see. "I make a dream of you."

"I see," he said, though he did not. "I.C.C., I'm not speaking to an AI, am I?"

"The auton calling itself 'No One' does not appear to have any greater capacity for independent thought than those we possess. I believe it is still a proxy for an individual."

Joanna typed something on her tablet, and Nwosu glanced over her shoulder. "What are you writing?"

"I have to log the visitor," she said frankly.

"'Noah'? You're calling it Noah?"

"I'm *not* calling it No One. If Odysseus taught us anything, it's that that's a bad idea."

"I agree," said I.C.C.

"Are you amenable to the title 'Noah'?" Nwosu asked.

"Yes, we are. Why did you not heed our warning?"

The captain was taken aback. "What warning?"

"Before *Noumenon Ultra* deviated from its path, causing the two Enigma Machines to lose contact, we warned *Noumenon Infinitum* to cease construction. Why did you not listen? It is the reason we abandoned our mission to aid in aborting yours."

A sick sense of vertigo swelled inside Nwosu. He'd felt such a swamp of illness before—it was a kind of undoable regret. The squeezing, nauseating, maddening sense that you've done something wrong that can never be fixed, that will change your life for the worse forever.

It was like tar in his belly—gumming up his insides and weighing on his bones.

"We received no such warning," he said softly, his tongue tasting mealy in his mouth. Did they know? No, no. If *Nou-*

menon Ultra knew the Web was sinister, if they could have stopped this . . .

"What did you try to warn us about?"

"The grand war between the Nataré."

Nwosu knew there would be questions, knew his fellow convoy leaders deserved to hear the entire story as much as he did. So he called an emergency meeting of the board, and was unsurprised when I.C.C. announced that half the members were already standing outside the situation room, waiting for his summons.

The assigned security team had difficulty steering the auton—Noah—through *Mira*'s throngs. So many people had stopped to stare, had come pouring out of their places of work, out of their quarters just to *see*. Mostly, the halls were filled with boisterous chatter, but a few people wept. They seemed to take this reunion as Nwosu did—as an auspicious sign. Whether the two crews had been steered toward one another by the vibrations of their lines, or by sad chance, it didn't matter. It still *meant* something, even if it only meant something in the moment.

Once in a while, a hand shot out of the crowd to graze the auton's chassis—most often out of reverence, but a few children mimicked their parents in play.

By the time the party reached the situation room, Noah's once-spotless exterior now bore handprint upon handprint, like the subtlest dabs of war paint.

The board itself was not without its awed members. Nwosu nodded to Vega Hansen and Min-Seo Park, who he knew had a special stake in this reunion. They nodded back. The rest of the board parted to make way for the auton, marveling at its familiarity and strangeness.

Everyone piled inside after, but no one took up their usual seats at the long table. They watched as the auton skirted the marble, dragging the very tip of its robotic fingers across the surface, as though it could feel the cool slickness of the slab.

When Nwosu urged them to sit, the board did so hesitantly. There was no place for the visitor, but it didn't seem to mind.

Noah didn't take long to reiterate what it had already told the captain.

"We found evidence of a great interstellar war between factions of Nataré." Noah's expression was appropriately, if cartoonishly, grave. "We still have an incomplete picture of the social climate that led to the conflict. But we have clues.

"At our third stop, we discovered a second megastructure. It is very unlike the Web. Instead of a sphere, it is more of a diamond, with nearly solid sides. Many blast marks decorated its body." The auton drew its hands over its chest, as though in illustration. "There was damage. Holes. We sent autons into the holes. They never returned. We called this structure 'the Void,' sibling of 'the Web.'"

Noah's speech patterns were so bizarre, it was difficult to accept that a human had to be controlling it. Could language have really changed that much in the years they were separated? Did he sound strange to Noah's user?

They expected their societies to diverge, but it felt like *Ultra* had changed much more quickly than could have been reasonably expected.

"There also, a second Nest. But mostly obliterated. Then we found an outpost. War outpost. With documents of destruction and chaos." Noah covered its head, crouched down, as though ducking a bombardment. "We still do not know if war began because of the structures, or if the structures were simply utilized during the war.

"We found two more megastructures. Broken, still. By the Nataré, we think. But we are also certain the Nataré built, as you did.

“We found no definitive evidence of Nataré extinction. Or even, a definitive end to the war. Though, much destruction. Much, much destruction . . .”

Noah turned its back on the board, grew silent. Nwosu was about to prompt it, to make sure it hadn’t gone into sleep mode, when it whirled. “Nataré may be diminished, but still alive. If so, we don’t know what they do. Do they still build? Do they decommission instead? We don’t know.

“When we knew the Web should not be completed without better understanding of these questions, of Nataré history, we abandoned our mission. We sent you a warning. We ran to your aid. But our worst nightmare, very worst, is now real, for you did not receive our warning. We never made it to map’s end, our ultimate goal . . .” It sounded pained, sad. The inherent failure was a great personal disappointment to Noah’s operator, clearly.

“What was at map’s end?” Nwosu asked.

“Many megastructures, we think. A field. Perhaps the key to understanding why . . . why do the structures exist?”

Nwosu kept their theory about an Ultra Civilization to himself. Just for now, until he understood Seven-Point-Five better. So far, they were a strange people. Not at all as he’d expected. This pain, this distancing-through-proxy, this collectivism—it all intertwined like a mass of slippery eels inside Nwosu’s mind, urging him toward caution.

“But, we are with you,” Noah said emphatically, voice building, full and taut and terrible. “We will fight the Web to end the Web alongside you. We shall hunt the others if the Nataré are still building.”

It banged its metal fist on the side of the table with inhuman force. The entire board jumped, those closest to Noah reeling back.

Nwosu leapt to his feet, as did Joanna, who was closer to

the robot. Instinctually, she reached out as though the auton were human, grasping its shoulder. It stilled, looked at its hands as though surprised by what it had done.

A long crack zigzagged like a plasma bolt away from the auton's hand. It raised its arms stiffly, palms open. "We shall hunt," the auton repeated darkly. It stood straight again, little flecks of green marble falling away from its fist. "To show our dedication, we bring gifts."

Nwosu wanted to shout *Look what you've done!* but restrained himself, as any good diplomat would. He felt his hands shaking, legs quivering. He kept his breath high in his chest, trying to inconspicuously steady himself.

For the first time, he doubted the operator behind the controls. There was a barely restrained anger behind those automated eyes. Could whoever it was be lying to them? Not about the Nataré or the Web's siblings, but about the other crew?

They're sleeping could easily be a deranged person's euphemism for far worse.

"What gifts?" he asked cautiously.

Noah's grit-covered hand went to its chest plate. With a few carefully placed taps, the front opened, revealing a compartment. Inside, tiny servo motors whirred. And, settled in the divot, was a cloth package, wound up with twine like something out of the seventeenth century.

To Nwosu's relief, it bore no stains. Red or otherwise.

"These I must present to you," Noah said, striding around the table, package outstretched. It left its compartment open, autonomic functions visibly chugging away.

The "you" it was referring to seemed to be a pair. It settled itself between Vega and Min-Seo, neither of whom leaned away, instead sitting up confidently in their chairs.

Noah held out the package expectantly, until Min-Seo took it. But the auton kept its palms outstretched, as though waiting for an exchange.

Vega reached into her jumpsuit pocket. But before she could extract what was inside, she rose to her feet, peering directly into Noah's digital face. "Caznal?" she asked. "Are you a clone of Caznal?"

"I am No One," Noah reiterated.

"Our exchange was to be with either a clone of Caznal or a clone of Diego Santibar," she said stiffly. "That is the right of our lines."

It was a shared heritage that had kept the Hansen and Park lines closely bonded for centuries, as was no secret.

"We are Caznal, we are Diego, we are all, and I am No One," said the auton.

Nwosu tried to signal the women, to indicate they shouldn't upset Noah's operator. At this point, he was unconvinced of the individual's emotional stability.

But when Vega said no more and pulled her empty hand from her pocket, Noah simply dropped its arms. "The bodies you speak of are aboard *Shambhala*," it said.

Nwosu shivered. "Then we shall go aboard *Shambhala*," he announced. "If, that is, *Noumenon Ultra* will have us."

"We shall have you," Noah said evenly.

Captain Nwosu did not disclose his fears to his first officer. He worried Joanna might try to bar him from boarding *Shambhala* if he did, which would have been a right and reasonable move on any other away mission. He was sure the only reason she was letting him go uncommented upon now was because—technically—there was no away mission. *Shambhala* was still Convoy Seven, still part of his fleet as far as Earth's paperwork was concerned.

Not that Earth's opinion mattered, but it gave him precedence.

With him were Hansen, Park, three members of the medical staff, and a security detail.

Before their shuttle launched—with Noah accompanying the team—I.C.C. sent a probe to ping the three ships.

"I cannot yet reconnect with *Shambhala*, *Hvmnd*, or *Zetta*," the AI told the captain on his pressure suit's private channel. "But the probe was able to interface with the ships' baser systems. There are nine hundred and thirty-two active signatures aboard that could possibly be human. I do not think No One's operator has murdered the rest of the crew."

Nwosu cringed. *He* hadn't used that word, but I.C.C. only used euphemisms sparingly. It wouldn't see the reason to gloss over the captain's worries. "Thank you."

The ride over was brief, even if it was the longest single shuttle ride the captain had ever taken. When they docked, deCON procedures were much the same as Noah had endured, since the team wore pressure suits. The only difference was the cleanings were administered by autons—run by the same operator as Noah, as far as anyone could tell.

"Why is it so dark?" Min-Seo asked.

In *Shambhala*'s docking bay, there had only been a single spotlight. Now that they were past the airlock and into the ship proper, everyone had to turn on their suit's exterior lights. They halted to check their instruments and get a readout of the darkened causeways beyond, the halo of light they'd created offering little confidence or comfort.

"Noah, couldn't you turn on the lights?" Min-Seo prompted.

"They no longer function."

Glances swapped between all members of the away team.

"Why is it so quiet?" Vega ventured—tone indicating she hoped for an answer from their host, but didn't expect one.

There was no echo of chatter beyond. No rustle of activity. Little more than the whirs and whines of the ship itself.

"We do not snore," Noah said—a joke, which eased no one.

"Temp's low," Nwosu noted. "Barely ten C."

“It aids the sleep,” Noah replied. “Come. You wished to see dreamer Caznal and dreamer Diego.”

It walked on ahead, with no regard as to the circumference of the light. Nwosu had to jog ahead so as not to lose the auton.

Their footfalls were easy to distinguish on their external mics, which sent a chill up the captain’s spine. There had to be more activity, with so many signatures . . . He knew that on *Hvmnd* back in the day, those acting as servers had caretakers. Where were the caretakers?

“Why is the entire crew asleep?”

“They dream,” Noah said pragmatically. “It is collective. Giving all access to all.”

“Is it like the mind-to-mind they did on Earth?” Min-Seo asked.

“Better. Deeper. More creative. More intimate. You should experience our stories, fairy tales. You should hear our music. Besides scientific endeavors, we have contributed thousands of artistic works to the world.”

“I look forward to viewing these works,” Nwosu said, glancing up and down the hall’s walls, looking for signs of struggle, of undo decay.

Noah’s head spun, doing a one-eighty to face the captain over its shoulder, while its body barreled on straight ahead. Nwosu—to his credit—scarcely jumped. “The works can only be experienced in the dream,” Noah said wistfully.

Nwosu averted his eyes, trying to blot out the robot’s eerie contortion from his mind’s eye. “Of course.” The way the operator spoke made him wonder if he was currently cut off from the collective. Though he was creating an experience for them, was he perhaps separate?

A cacophony of sharp *creeaaaak*s struck everyone’s microphones, halting them all midstep. The clatter was immediately followed by a plethora of thumps that had everyone ducking close to the walls and covering their heads, as though parts of the ceiling might collapse on them.

"What the *hell* was that?" Vega demanded.

"The shift," Noah said from far ahead. He never broke stride. "The sleepers move for their bodies' health."

The image that conjured for Nwosu—of people rolling or flopping in their beds—was unsettling, but it was good to hear Noah speak of health.

When the hall opened into a large space, the captain checked his map and realized they'd entered what used to be "dessert row."

Nearby should be stairs leading up into what was once a grand ballroom. Then, farther ahead, retrofitted crew quarters and food processing.

Initially, the space seemed empty. Everyone's night vision was shot, the lights on their suits becoming a hindrance more than a few feet out, so when Nwosu stumbled upon two people sitting at an ancient-style café table, hand in hand as though on a date, he reeled away.

At first he thought maybe they were mannequins, they held so still. Then, with how pallid their skin was—one man's a pale white, the other's a washed-out brown—he thought, *Corpses.*

But as he ventured closer, he could see them breathing. Could see the tubes threading away from them like puppet strings, and the thin bare-bones exoskeletons holding them in place.

Other members of the away team gasped as they came upon their own sleepers. Each poised in a storytelling tableau, as though going about their lives one frame at a time.

Standing next to the two men was a woman. Her eyelids were shut, eyes flickering wildly behind them, her lips quirked upward in a smile. Nwosu ventured closer, observing as much about the three as he could, taking measurements and notes aplenty.

The creaking began again a few moments later, and Nwosu barely had time to duck as the sleepers *moved*. The two men let their hands drop, one taking the woman's instead as she bent toward him, the other rising to his feet.

"What are they doing?" Nwosu asked, turning, trying to find Noah with his high beams. He spotted the rest of his crew easily, but no one's light fell on the auton.

"Noah? Noah, where are you?"

"Come," called the auton from the top of the grand staircase. "I cannot give you your second gift until the first exchange is complete."

The captain backed away from the trio slowly, looking for any indications that they were in pain, that they'd become puppets against their will. But there was nothing. Only the occasional flicker of a happy expression.

Taking the stairs two at a time, Nwosu was careful to avoid the grouping of children—*children!*—huddled around an open book as though marveling at its pages. The paper book was, in fact, blank. He stopped by their side for only a moment, looking up at the ceiling to note where their wires and tubes were attached to mechanisms running along tracks in the ceiling.

They were like little figurines in an antique cuckoo clock, spinning out their mechanized lives at the striking of designated minutes.

"Why are they like this?" he demanded, taking the top step to stand level with the auton. Its operator didn't seem to understand the question. "Why are they all asleep, why are they positioned like dolls in a child's playhouse?"

"They are living their lives—many times over," Noah said. "To be a dreamer is to live more fully, more efficiently. One can command automations to explore distant worlds while learning to play a classical instrument and making love to a partner. We used to experience events one at a time, like you—like I am confined to at the moment—but realized long ago that we could never do all we wanted, all we *needed*, that way.

"The dream may be less concrete than your experience, but it is no less reality. No less living."

"But why the puppet show?"

"Muscle memory is important. Human contact is important. The dream still consists of what exists in the waking world."

"I don't like this," said Donald Matheson, head of the security team, jogging up the steps with the rest of the away team.

"Contact the convoy, make sure these ships are maintaining their same distance," Nwosu said. "I don't think they mean us harm, but . . ."

Matheson nodded. "*But*," he agreed.

The captain's notes indicated the ballroom had been transformed into a classroom before the split. But, somewhere along the way, the Nataré team had changed it back. There were elaborate sconces, and dormant chandeliers in its high ceilings. The wide open floor was littered with dancers—all perfectly still, perfectly poised, though none of the groupings seemed to be dancing the same dance.

Nwosu could identify a couple mid waltz, and another near the end of a tango. Three women appeared engaged in a story told through Odissi, while others took part in tribal dances from around Earth and throughout its history.

Noah wove its way expertly through the still crowd, coming to rest on the outskirts of a circle. Here, six people held hands, their heads all leaning to one side, their left feet all raised in a kick across their right shins.

"Dreamer Caznal and dreamer Diego Santibar," Noah indicated.

The two clones did not move.

"Wake them," Nwosu said.

Noah's operator laughed. "They do not wake. They have never been awake."

But, just then, the creaking began—sooner, it seemed, then the last interval. But not everyone moved. Only Caznal and Diego.

Their eyes were still closed, their bodies visibly at the whim of the exoskeletons. They let their circle partner's hands go—the other dancers made no indication they noticed their physical absence, never wavering in their own stances—and turned toward the group. They stood with their hands overlapped and outstretched, Diego's under Caznal's.

"They do see you," Noah said, addressing Min-Seo and Vega. "I have made the dream clear. They are happy."

Min-Seo took Vega's gloved hand and nodded. They both seemed to realize this was the closest they would get.

Nwosu understood their disappointment. Tears glistened in both of their eyes—more obvious in the harsh glare of the suit lights than was normal—but they were not tears of joy. They didn't know how to process this new culture they'd found, didn't know how to reconcile it with their expectations.

The captain felt similarly, but he knew he couldn't be feeling it as starkly. These two had had the weight of anticipation tangled in their clone lines for iterations upon iterations. To expect one thing and have reality provide quite another was destabilizing. Confusing.

Like finding out the Web was a weapon . . .

But, we need to appreciate them for what they are, who they are, Nwosu told himself diplomatically. *As long as this way of life is truly their choice, then we cannot call our expectations* right *and their existence* wrong.

Vega split the Velcro on one of her pockets, drawing forth three tiny resin cubes. Within were small sculptures, one of

Hvmnd, one of *Shambhala*, and one of *Zetta*. She placed them in the open palms, then made as if to step back.

At the last moment, she surged forward, throwing her arms around the stiff forms.

The embrace was awkward, both the exoskeletons and the pressure suit's helmet impeded the gesture.

The joints on Diego's skeleton, as well as the mechanisms above, made their telltale squeak as he moved once more, reaching a hand out and turning his head toward Min-Seo.

Hesitantly, she stepped forward. When she was within reach, everything shifted. Both exoskeletons moved their bodies' arms wide, then enfolded the two women.

The group hug was strange, unlike any show of affection Nwosu had ever experienced. And yet, Vega and Min-Seo dropped their heads to the dreamer's shoulders, squeezing back as the sleeping clone's cheeks pressed against the swell of their helmets. A tear leaked out of the corner of Caznal's eye, dropping to Vega's visor, creating a single rivulet down its curve.

Maybe this will work after all. We are different, but maybe we are not so different.

"Human contact is important," Noah said happily.

Their second gift was housed in a lab on the top deck of the ship. Though the sweet moment between the *Infinitum* and *Ultra* crews had taken some of the eeriness out of the dark, bizarre environment, Nwosu didn't let his guard drop. Just in case. The two convoys still had a lot to learn about one another.

There were many more dreamer clusters along the way, and the captain tried not to let them bother him. Besides their pallidness—likely from lack of exposure to even an artificial sun—they all appeared healthy. There was no stench of unwashed bodies, no visible sores or emaciated forms.

“Where are the caretakers?” he asked eventually, remembering his question from earlier. Someone had to tend to the physical needs of the sleeping, to the maintenance and control of the ships.

“Autons perform that function now,” Noah explained.

“Run by whom? Someone else has to be awake, besides your operator.”

“There is only ever one awake,” Noah countered. “And they are not awake long.”

The lab was a clean room. But instead of a lower particle count, it seemed to be designed to maintain a high-density fog. They stopped outside, peering in through the windows while Noah explained.

“We have a specimen from our last stop. We keep it in a constantly resanitized state, since we are unsure if we could corrupt it, or it us. Since you are all suited, you all may enter.”

“Wait—a *biological* specimen?” Nwosu asked.

“Yes.” Noah said. “Come.”

The fog swirled around their boots as they entered the gowning room. It had seeped out of the main lab, and chased their heels like a puppy at play. Long flaps separated the fogged space from the gowning room, and they slid through them with hands outstretched. Everyone had to dim their suit lights, as the beams bounced off the fog, creating a harsh whiteout.

As it had before, the auton strode ahead while the humans cautiously inched their way inside. “Here,” it called from somewhere near the center of the room.

A large shape, oblong and ovoid, slowly resolved next to Noah as Nwosu approached. The silhouette reminded the captain of a dinosaur egg, and the comparison made his breath catch.

For, sure enough, inside the translucent outer shell was a shape. Clearly a creature, curled and coiled over itself. The skin—or hair, it was difficult to tell—looked like moss in both color and texture, though he wasn't sure if that was from decay or not. The thing was clearly flattened, like it had purposely been dehydrated.

It's mummified, he realized.

There were bones, and at least six limbs if the bumps and protuberances were telling the story he thought they were. But the creature was bent and folded in such a way that it was impossible to tell what the exact structure might be. He couldn't even identify a head, if indeed it had one.

"Is that . . . is that a Nataré?" Min-Seo gasped.

"We believe so," Noah said. "We found it traveling in a sharp, elliptical orbit around the star at our last location. We suspect, given our research, that it was originally meant to be on a decaying path—that it was meant to fall into the sun long ago. We believe this is their common burial practice. But a miscalculation must have been made in this case. Instead of falling into the star, it was set to pass through the system once every sixty-two years, like a comet."

"Can I touch it?" Vega asked.

"Of course. The shell itself is not delicate. In fact, it took us many years to penetrate the ovoid."

Vega knocked on it. It barely made sound, as though it were exceedingly dense.

"We hoped to discover the biological mechanism by which they manipulated gravitons, but, alas. We could not identify the specific related sequence in its genes. Now, we give it to you. Perhaps you can unlock its secrets."

"This is amazing," Nwosu said. "Thank you. Your mission—" He stopped himself. He nearly said, *Your mission was a success.*

But that wasn't right. It wasn't a failure, for certain. But with the Web out there, killing, both of their missions felt like folly.

"And now," Noah said eagerly, "we fight?"

Nwosu nodded, his voice catching in his throat. "Y-yes. Now we must figure out how to combat the Web. Together."

A week later, the astronomers were confident enough for navi-gation to lay in a new course. But they were not yet ready to begin their pursuit anew.

"You located us very quickly," Nwosu said to Noah, who'd come to deliver additional findings, notes, to *Infinitum* on *Holwarda*.

"We have learned new tricks."

"From the Nataré?"

"Their remaining records, yes."

The mummy currently being scanned and sampled before them—the long ovoid caged deep within an MRI—was the only biological trace of the creatures they'd found. And yet *Ultra* would not go so far as to assume them extinct.

"We were able to discern which SDs they used for travel," Noah continued. "Can access several."

Nwosu didn't hide his surprise. "That's—that's amazing." There hadn't been a new travel SD discovered since before the Planet United Missions commenced.

He vaguely remembered that there had been a convoy devoted to SD study. The littlest one. But there'd been an accident, it was destroyed . . .

Had they finally, all these centuries later, accomplished what those poor souls had set out to achieve?

"Yes. Amazing," Noah agreed. "One of them is much quicker than Convoy Seven's preferred. Of their machines that we collected, three can be powered by *Zetta*. One detects ripples created by SD penetration. Gravitons create gravitational waves. So, too, SD bubbles create space-time wakes as they 'brush' its surface. We followed your wake. Caught you easily."

"Can the rest of the ships use this new SD?"

The auton smiled its caricature of a smile. "Yes. Programming is a simple matter. The dreamers will calculate."

Finally. The twelve ships would dive, together, sharing the same SD bubble. They would be one convoy again.

A technician wearing a medical mask waved Nwosu and Noah over to a monitor. The display resolved to show a three-dimensional map of the mummy. As the captain watched, the technician cut away digital layer after digital layer, revealing the alien to them bit by bit.

There was no part that could be classified as a skull. The creature was headless, and it seemed there might be sense organs up and down its limbs, which, when properly positioned, looked like they might jut outward, like the arms of a starfish.

"Initial reports from chemistry confirm it's carbon based," said Lindum Shelby, a geneticist who'd been put in charge of discerning the Nataré's fundamental building blocks.

"You should find it has deoxyribonucleic acid as well," said Noah.

Much of what they were doing today was verification of *Ultra*'s research.

"The samples we found were not stored in a simple double helix, however," Noah continued. "Supercoils happen regularly inside human cells, making them look like loops or even solid bars. But in the single instance of an uncorrupted molecule we found, the Nataré DNA was a tetrahedron."

"The shape of a molecule often affects activation and transcription," Lindum said. "In fact, many supercoils are wound so tightly that some of their base-pair bridges *snap apart* while they're being stored in a cell, without any long-term detriment to the molecule. This mechanism, we believe, also helps keep certain traits from being expressed at different times.

"A shape like a tetrahedron might allow for different base-pairs to be 'unhooked' at the same time. But not for storage purposes—a tetrahedron wouldn't be nearly as compact as other available shapes. Could be this is how specific traits are *activated*, rather than deactivated, and could in part explain why *Ultra* was unable to pinpoint a genetic sequence related to graviton manipulation, even after decades of life-form modeling. If you only had one fully intact molecule, and after mapping didn't include the exact placement of the breaks in your models, you could be missing a mountain of information."

"This observation is sound," Noah said. "Perhaps you will find more viable molecules and be able to apply your theory."

"Just imagine what we could do with this," Lindum said to Nwosu. "If their DNA is at all similar to terrestrial DNA in expression, then we could clone our own Nataré. Or engineer something entirely new, using alien and Earth-origin—"

Nwosu laughed and slapped Lindum on the back. "Don't get ahead of yourself. We have bigger things to worry about than splicing genes."

"This could be useful," Lindum pointed out. "That's all I'm saying. Think what we could accomplish if we could *fly*."

Once the SD drives had been properly reprogrammed and retrofitted to allow access to this new Nataré travel SD, Nwosu wasted no time returning to the chase. He knew they had to change the way their convoy functioned. No longer were they scientists and explorers, builders and dreamers. Now they were warriors, and they had to start behaving as such.

We must become what we were first created to avoid, he realized. All those years ago, the Planet United missions had been built to bond all nations together, to push everyone away from Mutually Assured Destruction and toward Mutually Assured Cooperation. Earth built science convoys to avoid building military ones.

The change would require greater discipline, and he knew Joanna was the one to enact the shift.

And they'd need new tools, to develop new weapons and strategies. But, most importantly, they needed to learn from the Nataré's mistakes.

Noumenon Ultra still had a fractured understanding of the war that had decimated the aliens. But they'd been able to piece together a picture related to the Web.

The Nest crew had likely been comprised of survivors. They were not the original designers of the Web, but hapless builders, just like the humans. They had worked on the Web at the planemo where Convoy Seven had separated, and that was where they'd activated it.

Their war seemed to have begun because of other megastructures in the galaxy—megastructures which clearly predated the Nataré. *Someone* had originally designed and begun all of these massive machines, and yet whoever it was didn't appear to be around to claim them. The Nataré had stumbled upon them, just as the humans had, and conflict had ensued over whether to decommission the constructs or continue to build them. Different factions had reached different conclusions about the megastructures' purpose—some saw them as controllable war machines, others as useful tools (as the humans had), and yet others saw them for what they were: as destructive and uncaring as any force of nature.

When the Web was activated, it spurred the decommission faction into action. Others tried to stop them.

Whether the Web and other devices had destroyed their civilization, or if the Nataré had done that to themselves, was a mystery. Had the megastructures been utilized as weapons during the conflict? Or were they simply the catalysts for conflict? The record was incomplete.

Either way, the structures were a proven danger. There could be no arguments against stopping them.

But *Noumenon Infinitum* wasn't the only group that needed to learn from the past, to buckle down and change in the face of their adversary.

Noumenon Ultra would also need to evolve. At least some of the dreamers would have to wake, to focus on lucidly controlling an army of autons if nothing more.

Their two missions had to mesh once more. To learn from each other, to dive headlong into darkness together.

It had been six months, eleven hours, and thirteen minutes since the two convoys had merged.

And today, Captain Michael Nwosu would receive his second Revealer mark.

He'd invited a special guest to attend the ceremony: Noah's operator.

He traveled from *Mira* to *Shambhala* to retrieve the individual himself. Waiting with their shuttle in the dim spotlight, Nwosu held his breath as the bay entrance opened and the operator was unveiled.

In truth, he half expected the individual to send Noah again. Perhaps it would be too much, revealing themselves.

But no, the man who approached was flesh and blood. He walked with the aid of an exoskeleton, his coppery skin flush under fine brown curls, the exertion of remaining awake evident in the constant droop of his eyelids.

The man stopped three feet from Nwosu and saluted. "Doctor Ivan Baraka. Permission to come aboard, Captain?"

"Of course, *Noumenon Ultra*," he said with a smile, extending a dark hand to shake Dr. Baraka's. "You are all welcome here."

CHAPTER NINE

CONVOY TWELVE

STEVE: INTO THE SUFFERING CITY

SIX HUNDRED AND SEVENTEEN DAYS SINCE THE ACCIDENT

"Mother*fuckers*!" Steve yelled as soon as he was alone, secure in his quarters. "Goddamned sons of dogs! What in the ever-loving, shit bag—" He railed on and on, yelling at nothing and everything at once.

Those freaks weren't *aliens*—they'd let the convoy believe that, though, which was as good as lying. They'd hemmed in Twelve, pushed them around, prodded and implanted and not even had the decency to tell the fucking truth about who they were.

But they weren't *human* either, no. He didn't care what Dr. Jax said. They might be based on the same stupid molecules, but they'd *changed*. They'd thrown away the bits that made humans *humans*, as far as he could tell. If they'd thought human bodies so inferior, so unacceptable, then why wouldn't they think the same of all the rest? All the feelings and morality that made a regular person a person.

Tearing at his hair, breathing through flared nostrils like an angry bull, Steve turned around in his entryway, looking for something to throw or punch. His eyes landed on the doorjamb.

Above all, he wished he could slam his door. That used to be one little thing he could control. Mad at the boss? Slam a door. Want to punch some jerk's face in? Slam a door. About to chuck a defective appliance out a fourth story window?

Slam.

A.

Door.

But no, up here everything was automated—the doors slid politely aside and then back again.

He could go to his gym, wail on a heavy bag. Maybe the one with the *Lùhng* likeness . . .

They should all *have Post-Fucking-Human faces.*

He let out another frustrated growl.

Why would the *Lùhng* hide this shit? Why not greet them with open arms and a polite, *Oh, hi fellow people of Earth*? Why all the manipulative bull crap?

And now they weren't even answering Tan. He and Sotomayor were composing new messages every day, confronting them with the facts, and the *Lùhng wouldn't even reply.*

If the last away team's outburst had spooked them, *good.* They deserved to feel some of the terror they'd thrust upon *him* that first outing. With them pushing, prodding, implanting, stripping—knocking them all unconscious, for fuck's sake.

The smell of vomit returned to him, as it did every time he thought about the indignities of that mission. He ran to his kitchenette, bent over the sink and retched dryly.

Dr. Jax was on his side before all this. But now she thought the fact that they were base-human made things better. He didn't see how.

He guzzled a few ounces of water, changed into his offduty workout gear, and grabbed an extra pat of chalk.

Every single punching bag was getting a *Lùhng*, and when he'd punched all their faces into smears of white powder, he'd draw them on again.

When he arrived on *Breath* and made his way up to the gym from the shuttle bay, the place was already packed. A line curled out the door. Frustration furrowed brows and clenched fists.

Acting as proprietor rather than patron, he pushed his way past the queue, and realized the line was for the original *Lùhng* bag. Nothing was a state secret aboard the convoy, and the *Lùhng* news was no different. Someone had already taken the liberty of adding another face to a speed bag, this one in red lacquer, and a line was forming there as well. A smudge on the left side of its evil smile indicated they hadn't even let the paint dry before taking a swing.

They all need faces. Every last one.

With a grim smile, he went to work breaking up the chalk he'd brought, coating his fingers in the dust before spreading it on the artificial hide of the next nearest bag.

He hadn't drawn the first face, nor the second. But he'd draw them again and again until he and his crewmates stopped wanting to punch them—if that meant never, so be it.

The resentment in his chest only grew with each grainy line. He felt like the indignation had no end, would never ebb.

The steady *thwap-thwap-thwap* of punches landing nearby was more poignant than usual. It matched the outraged *thump-thump-thump* of his heavy heartbeat.

A light chatter eked its way into Steve's ears as he drew, bits of conversation, grumbled exclamations of outrage.

". . . I mean, Captain said they've got human DNA in them, and they didn't tell us. What else are they lying about?"

“. . . damn dragons.”

“. . . I bet *they* did something that brought us here. Accident my ass.”

“. . . you know those implants, the ones that are supposedly for radiation-protection-something-or-other?”

Steve paused his drawing to glance at the orange light in his arm. He was already on the third bag and his first two effigies were currently being put to good use.

The voice he’d heard continued. “You ever see a sci-fi movie where they put some kind of little explosive or cyanide cap in a person? Bet that’s what they really do. They’re little pet trackers, but if we get out of line—*bam*!”

Steve cringed, and his grip on the chalk pat tightened, crumbling it in his palm.

“Why did they give us a bunch of raw materials instead of food?” Dalisay Ocampo, who worked on Dr. Jax’s farm, mused nearby. “If they were human, they’d know what constitutes real food, and a pile of sugar doesn’t count. Were they testing us? ‘Let’s see if the apes can figure out what to do with this? And if they die in the process, oh, well’?”

He almost turned to reply with Dr. Jax’s assumption—that maybe it had something to do with the way they synthesized their own food. It was on the tip of his tongue before he realized how *alien* the explanation was.

And then—mortified—he realized he’d been about to *defend* them, and he swallowed his words completely.

He ducked his head and tried to close his ears, but the theories kept raining down around him.

“. . . I think they’re experimenting on us. We’re like rats in a little maze, scurrying after their proffered cheese. Maybe we’d be home by now if it wasn’t for them. Maybe a future-Earth rescue team already came, but the *Lùhng* kept us.”

“. . . for all we know, there’s a war going on between the

real humans and the post-humans, and we're political prisoners and we don't even know it."

"Maybe that's what those megastructures are—war machines."

"Or maybe the war is over and all of the *real* humans are *dead*."

Steve started to get lightheaded, and he realized he was breathing too quickly, hyperventilating. Finishing the last stroke on his fifth drawing, he dropped his chalk and stumbled over to a bench. He sat down heavily, bending over to dip his head between his knees.

It's just speculation. All of it, he told himself in an attempt to calm down.

But why shouldn't they think the *Lùhng* were malevolent?

He smelled vomit again, and then he was back on the *Lùhng* ship, puking into his helmet. But then another memory forced its way between his teeth, another time he'd been pushed around and no one did anything . . .

The specifics were foggy—because of the concussion. It was sixth grade and that asshole, Trevor, had punched him so hard his ears rang, he threw up, and he passed out. The worst part was the guy walking his dog who'd just stared. Grown man had watched some kid knock another unconscious and hadn't done a goddamned thing.

He'd vowed never to be that guy. If something was wrong, he had to do something to stop it.

He felt like he'd failed on that promise during his first away mission. That was why the vomit smell was coming back to him so hard now—it was a reminder of his gutlessness. He should have been the one to stand up to the *Lùhng* then. He'd told himself he was staying behind with the others to protect them, but truth was he hadn't accompanied Jax, Savea, and Sotomayor because he was afraid.

You were afraid then, but that doesn't make you a coward. Not if you resolve to do better. Not if you make amends.

And this can't stand. This omission was it for him, the last straw. He couldn't think of a single positive reason why the *Lùhng* might keep their lineage hidden.

If someone was coming for them, like Dr. Jax surmised, it wasn't going to end well for the convoy, he was sure. They had to do something before they ended up slaves, or lap dogs, or Soylent Green.

We can't stay here. But they couldn't run, either. And they had no way to fight.

Or did they . . .

Steve stood outside the service entrance to *Breath*'s shuttle maintenance hangar, staring through the narrow slit of a window in the door, his breath fogging the glass.

Inside were the remaining experiment pods. Each sat in the angular mandibles of a hydraulic lift. They looked like scrumptious pink fruit in the clawed palm of a monster—something out of an altered fairy tale, like those Steve's mother had read to him when he was young.

He liked fairy tales, truth be told. There were heroes, and there were villains, and no one fudged on the matters of morality.

When dragons appeared, you fought them. It didn't matter if they were there to eat virgins, burn down houses, or hoard gold.

Dragons were for slaying.

But swords wouldn't work against their dragons. Neither would shock batons. With that *whump* device of theirs, all melee weapons were off the table.

They could machine the parts they needed for guns, probably. And he figured it might not be a bad idea to put that into motion. But you had to be close enough to see a dragon to shoot it.

What they really needed was a way to cripple the *Lùhng* ships themselves, from afar. Trap the bastards in their caves, so that when the convoy tried to run again, no dragon would follow.

Explosives would do the trick. A nice remote-detonated blast would be very satisfying.

But he had something even better in mind.

Steve tapped a jaunty rhythm against the window, pleased with himself for realizing a well-placed SD bubble could be as devastating as any bomb.

It's why we're in this hellish nightmare to begin with, after all.

And it would be so easy—launch a pod, dive it into a known travel SD, and program it to reemerge wherever you wanted it to—say in the middle of a *Lùhng* engine room? Or the bridge?

Or Kali's horror show of a bedroom?

There'd be no way to stop it.

The calculations wouldn't even be all that complicated—the *Lùhng* ships maintained steady distances, their drift was uniform, and their speed constant. He was pretty sure even *he* could do the math.

Careful coordination would be the tricky part. They'd have to launch all the pods without arousing any suspicion, and the minute they were sure the local *Lùhng* were distracted, they'd have to dive—the *Lùhng* near the megastructure field could arrive in no time to provide backup, and the humans would need to be long gone by then.

Once they left, he was sure they could make it on their own. They had plenty of water, Dr. Jax's farm was thriving, and all of their convoy repairs were holding.

We can do this, he realized. *We don't have to just give in, sit back, and wait for whatever they're going to do with us.*

With a spring in his step, he made his way back to his quarters on *Pulse*, pulled out some extra holoflex-sheets, and began to formalize his plan.

Under different circumstances, Steve would have presented his ideas to the lead security officer, and let him decide if it was worth presenting to command. But he didn't want to waste time jumping through any more hoops than he had to. Luckily, he was able to leverage his position as a member of one of the *Lùhng* away teams to wrangle an immediate meeting with the captains in Tan's ready room.

His presentation was brief, but detailed. Tan occupied his desk, while Baglanova stood at ease.

Aksel Baglanova had made his earthly home in Saint Petersburg, Russia, and had run ships in the Baltic long before running them in space. He was a taut, angular man, with a shock of straight sandy hair that he always kept slicked back with what looked like industrial-strength hair gel.

Both captains were calm, precise men. Both were stern and discerning.

Neither spoke until he was finished, but Steve could tell by the hardening expression on Tan's face that he did not like what he heard.

Steve tried not to feel deflated.

"You're proposing a preemptive strike," Tan said flatly.

"Yes. But the goal isn't to kill *Lùhng,* or even destroy their property, just to disorient them. Keep them busy with their own problems while we get away."

"Not destroy their property?" Tan asked incredulously. "And yet *Lùhng* casualties *are* likely."

Yes, and who cares? Steve grumbled internally.

"Yes, it's dramatic. But I think this is an excellent idea," Captain Baglanova said suddenly. "It risks minimal equipment and personnel, and has a high chance of success."

“I don’t agree with that assessment in the slightest,” Tan countered. His eye twitched ever so slightly. It was clear he was doing his best to maintain his stoicism, but beneath, something was boiling. “We would be destroying the majority, if not all, of our experiment pods, limiting Kapoor and Dogolea’s investigation into our accident. And if something goes awry, we’re risking *the entire* convoy. Say the pods fail to hit their mark, or the extra *Lùhng* ships arrive sooner than expected and are able to give chase—what would they do when they caught us? Our standing with them is razor thin as is.”

“But we haven’t *earned* such handling,” Baglanova pointed out. “That’s part of the point. They pull us in, push us away, won’t let us leave. Won’t let us do anything else, really. They have no reason to fear us, but they keep treating us as though—”

“So, you propose we *give* them a reason?” Tan asked. “Our goal right now should be de-escalation, not some hairbrained attempt at escape that can only be managed by committing an *act of war* against a more advanced civilization.”

“What is the point of staying, Tan?” Baglanova asked. “They haven’t shared anything valuable with us since our initial plea for basic necessities. They’ve even stopped responding to our messages. I know you believe they can help us with our medical crises and our displacement, but they’ve given us no reason to trust that they will.”

“Diplomacy, these types of relationships—”

“Take trust, patience, I know,” Baglanova interrupted. “And if the *Lùhng* had handled things differently, I might believe as you do. But there is no proof they’re acting in good faith. Just because we know they’re post-human doesn’t mean they relate to us on a human level. Doctor Jax compared their position to us finding human ancestors, correct? Just how human would we treat a group of Neanderthals, do you think?”

“We have more of a fighting chance here—where we have access to resources and information—than out there, *alone*,” Tan said firmly, ignoring the other captain’s flippant comparison.

“We don’t know that,” said Baglanova.

“Yes, *we do*. End of discussion. We are not going to attack our allies based on fearmongering. I’ve heard the speculation, the rumors. We are a scientific convoy, and we do not bend to conspiracy theory and hearsay.” Tan pointed roughly at Steve. “There will be no preemptive strikes on my watch, understood?”

“Then ask to leave,” Baglanova said lightly, crossing his arms and leaning back against the wall. Steve was sure he was trying to pull off “casual suggestion” and “firm challenge” simultaneously. “If they’re so benevolent, communicate our concerns and tell them we wish to leave. We have their coordinates—if we want to return, we can.”

Captain Tan was silent for a long moment, calculating. Finally, he said, “That would put undue strain on our relationship.”

“Our sitting here is putting undue strain on our relationship with our *crew*,” Baglanova countered. “This *waiting game*, it feels like giving up—”

“Our crew is reasonable. And they can be made to understand that patience *is* an active measure. We don’t truly know how volatile the post-humans are, as you keep saying. And you are absolutely right, they hold an incredible amount of physical sway over us—”

“Which is why Weaver’s plan is a sound choice. If we remove ourselves from the threat, we can regroup and reassess the post-humans from a distance. We can write our own terms of engagement. We don’t have to give in to their whims or their demands.”

Tan stood abruptly. “Thus far, *we* are the only ones making demands. We are the ones that showed up out of nowhere. We are the ones that required resources and—"

Steve grew bold. "But that doesn't give them the right to treat our crew members as they have." When the captains didn't immediately order him into silence, he continued. "Respect is important. Dignity is important. If they're willing to disregard our autonomy under such benign circumstances, doesn't that point to a larger threat? A contempt for our independence that could mean more than this bizarre version of house arrest we're under? Why should we believe they wouldn't outright imprison us? Or trade us? Or kill us just because we've become too much to deal with? The longer we stay here without communications or concessions, the easier it is to believe that our well-being is not a top priority for them. And why should it be? As you said, Captain, we're an unexpected burden."

Tan ground his teeth, seethed through them. "We have no evidence they mean us any harm."

"So why shouldn't we back away?" Steve asked. "We ran to begin with because we weren't sure what their intent was. Truth is, we still don't know."

Tan looked between the two men, face taut. "You rail against the *Lùhng's lack* of humanity, but want to engage in the most fundamentally abhorrent aspects of ours. A first strike is never an option, do you understand me?"

"Yessir," Steve said.

Tan glared at Baglanova, until he, too, said, "Yes . . . *sir*."

"I will ask them to move off to a symbolic distance—whatever would satisfy you," Tan conceded.

Steve opened his mouth to protest. There was no *symbolic* distance far enough. The point was to ensure they were out of the *Lùhng*'s reach.

He'd only uttered a single syllable before Baglanova held up a hand and interrupted with, "What if they refuse?"

"Then we will reassess at that time."

Both captains stared at one another, their bodies rigid lines, each an exclamation point on his own statement.

Tension filled the air with an invisible prickling, like crackling static, and Steve wondered which man would blink first. No one was getting what they wanted, but the tide was turning—something was changing, their understandings of one another rearranging.

"Are we adjourned?" Captain Baglanova asked tersely.

"Aye," Tan replied, tuning on his heel, leaving abruptly. The tension wafted out after him, like a cloud of irritated flies.

Over the next few days, Steve attended to his duties quietly, waiting for news. He had no reason to doubt Tan would send the message, but he wondered how long the captain would wait for a reply before admitting diplomacy had failed.

The worst part was, whatever pull he'd thought he had with Tan, being a member of the away team, seemed to have evaporated. The captain wouldn't grace him with more than a curt nod in public.

He felt unfairly cut off. So what if he'd proposed something Tan thought unsavory? Why should that earn him a cold shoulder?

Nearly a week after his proposal, he appealed to Sotomayor for information. But all she'd say was that Tan had given her a direct order not to discuss the situation.

He pressed others around the gym, hoping the casual setting would relax some lips. Dr. Dogolea on the stair-stepper said he was out of the loop. Esmée Jensen, grunting through her bicep curls, said she didn't even know what he was talking about. Guy de Roux, who worked on *Breath*'s bridge and was currently doing push-ups near the mirrors, said he hadn't heard anything. "But Captain Baglanova is anxious about it," he said. "If you find anything, you be sure to let me know."

He was so hard up for a scrap of new info, that when Mendez Perez sauntered into the gym and hoisted himself onto the pull-up bar, he nonchalantly headed over to the former ADCO's side.

They'd never really gotten over Stone's time in the brig. They weren't friends, that was for certain, but it wasn't like they were sworn enemies. And he had no idea where Stone came down on the post-human revelation: was he pro-or anti-dragon?

"Hey," he said, trying to act casual.

"Hey," Stone said, mid chin-up.

"Tan have any luck persuading the *Lùhng* to chat again?"

Stone gritted his teeth as he eased himself down before hoisting himself up once more. His dog tags and Dr. Kapoor's sundial hung inertly against his chest. "No idea."

"Kind of fucked up they didn't tell us, right? About the genetic hybrid thing."

Stone side-eyed him. "I guess."

Steve scoffed internally. *You guess?* "Do you think the captain is handling this right?"

That seemed to give Stone genuine pause. He let go of the bar, dropping deftly to the floor, having done a whole six reps. "You'd handle it differently?"

"You don't think he rolls with the punches a little too easily? Shouldn't he stick up for us more? Demand respect on our behalf?"

"How's he supposed to do that?"

Over Stone's shoulder, Steve caught sight of the doorway. "Speak of the devil," he muttered, brushing by Stone (whose huffy response he ignored).

In walked Captain Tan, flanked by Mac Savea and Kurt Böhm. It was the first time Tan had made his way to the gym since before its opening.

"What can I do for you, Captain?" Steve asked.

Tan wrinkled his nose instead of answering. Steve noticed

how pungent the space had gotten. Too many sweaty bodies in one place. He'd do an extra wash of everything when he closed down today.

"I'm sure Lieutenant Way would be happy to vacate the stationary bike if you'd like a go, or I'd be happy to spot you on weights. Anything you want to try." Maybe if he put on a friendly face, the captain would see that he'd meant no offense. He wanted to protect the convoy just as much as the command team.

"That's not why we're here," the captain said firmly, his gaze pinpointing something on the other side of the gym. "I was informed there's been a conduct violation. I'm here to vet the report myself."

Steve was genuinely confused. Everyone who'd used the gym had done so with the utmost respect for both the equipment and their crewmates. There hadn't been any fights, any harassment. No destruction, or improper usage of any apparatus. "Conduct violation?"

Tan, whose expression remained stern, pointed a firm finger. "That. The vandalism."

He was pointing at the punching bags. "You mean the faces?" They all had permanent likenesses now. "I wouldn't call that vandalism."

"You authorized it, then?"

"Yes. And Captain Baglanova said it was fine—"

"Captain Baglanova and I disagree on many things," Tan said curtly. "Planet United Consortium regulations prohibit the defacement or mutilation of communal property. In addition, the depictions are vulgar. In my opinion, they have the potential to erode convoy morale and deteriorate future interactions with our hosts. I want those bags scrubbed and those caricatures gone by 1900 hours."

With that he turned and left, Mac and Kurt following after. The gym-goers were left in stunned silence, and Steve stood frozen to the spot, astounded by the captain's overreach of authority.

Stone surprised Steve, coming up on him from behind to give him a patronizing pat on the shoulder, "Point me toward the soap," he said, aiming for the towel rack.

He was followed close behind by Sotomayor. Steve remembered how she'd turned up her nose at the original *Lùhng* bag with a holier-than-thou attitude.

Oh, yeah, Steve thought sarcastically, *I wonder who the snitch was.*

As he grabbed a few more towels, stomping off to the supplies closet to prepare a wash bucket, he silently seethed.

Here he was again, getting sucker punched by the big kid with an authority figure just standing by, idle and inept. Only this time the big kid was a horde of post-human monsters, and it wasn't just *Steve*'s brain taking a bashing. The whole convoy was getting screwed.

He slammed the full wash bucket on the deck beneath the speed bag with the red face, and water sloshed over the edges to soak the thin carpet. He didn't care.

The first wet swipe across the crimson graffiti left a smeared red streak right through the grinning face, pulling the grotesque lips wide. It was almost like it was laughing at him. *See, you can never escape,* it giggled. He scrubbed at it all the harder, the soap turning pink and foamy, his pale knuckles staining red.

No. *No!* He wasn't going to give up that easily. Getting the hell out of here mattered now more than ever, because Captain Tan was clearly long gone. He'd given up, given in, and Steve . . .

Steve no longer recognized his authority.

And that . . . that was fine.

It was for the greater good. This needed to be done, and if Tan was too enamored of the *Lùhng*—or too brainwashed or too weak, whatever—it wouldn't stop Steve from doing the right thing.

And he was certain Baglanova would have his back.

He wouldn't meet Captain Baglanova in his ready room or on *Breath*'s bridge. Instead, Steve asked to meet in his own quarters. Hopefully it would look more informal that way. Just two guys having a chat.

Hopefully it wouldn't look like what it was: a mutinous proposition.

"Tan is too far gone," he said, once he'd made his guest a hot drink and they'd both settled into bucket seats at the table. The lights were dim, but not dark, and the room was warm. He wanted the captain to be as comfortable as possible. "I think he's putting the chance to cure his daughter ahead of the crew. Besides being knocked out, she's not aging right. And he knows, logically, that we're not safe here. But the doctors are out of ideas, so he's taking a leap. He thinks her last shot is *Lùhng* aid. But you and I know his chances of getting it are slim to none."

Baglanova said nothing, simply sipped his tea.

Steve took a deep breath. This was it—the convoy's chance at salvation. Either he'd read Baglanova correctly, or he was about to up and move house . . . to a nice brig cell. "When a leader can't be counted on to make unselfish decisions, when he puts his own personal gain above everyone else's safety, he's not fit to lead."

"His control might be faltering," Baglanova said, "but not everyone's lost faith."

Steve understood the cryptic segue: the captain wasn't ready to commit one way or the other. But it also meant this topic wasn't verboten. "Those directly under him are, as far as I can tell, very loyal," he admitted.

"My staff is the same. Very loyal. *To me.*"

“Good. That’s good.”

“I think you’d find it difficult to get either command crew to refuse a direct order from their captain.”

Steve smirked. “Then it’s lucky we have the advantage.”

Baglanova’s mug paused before it reached his lips. “How so?”

“I’m not suggesting we remove Tan from command. Not right away. In fact, I think we need him exactly where he is. But *Breath* contains everything required to execute my plan effectively. *You* have the pods. *You* have the farm. If you initiate our . . . diversion—” he was very careful not to say *attack*, that wasn’t what it was “—and announce your intent to leave, Tan will have no choice but to commence a synchronized dive. If he hesitates and we leave without him, he might not find us if he follows. Which means a food crisis aboard *Pulse*. If instead he stays, the *Lùhng* will surely take, if not destroy, his ship. He won’t have time to dither—he knows the possible outcomes. He *will* order the dive.”

“But if he doesn’t?”

“We go anyway,” Steve said confidently. “We save who we can.”

“That’s all well and good, but what about after?” Baglanova asked. “When we’re out of the *Lùhng*’s grasp. Tan will still have to . . . step down. He’ll have shock batons, we’ll have shock batons. It’s not exactly a sure thing.”

“I might be able to get us an advantage there, too.”

Baglanova raised an eyebrow in question.

“I have a man who can make us a few handguns. Pin action, revolver types. Nothing fancy, but easy to conceal.”

“Good. Just how many personnel have you spoken to?”

“Not as many as we need, but I have an easy way to track down our allies.”

They would need supporters on *Pulse*’s bridge, no question. The transition from Tan’s command to Baglanova’s would need to be as clean and efficient as possible.

Luckily, Steve had a ready-made litmus test. He would sit in the gym, watch, and wait.

Inevitably, someone would chalk a *Lùhng* outline—he'd already seen people do it. It might be a small thing, but it was a direct defiance of Captain Tan. Minor disobediences were symptomatic of shifting loyalties.

SIX HUNDRED AND SIXTY-TWO DAYS SINCE THE ACCIDENT

Tan had just started his shift on the bridge. The bitter taste of breakfast was still fresh on his tongue, and the image of his little shrimpling's face was warm in his mind. He was ready to try again—to put out another plea to the *Lùhng*.

We need your cooperation. Please, just answer us.

He gazed out the false windows, sighing internally. He had the screens set to shallow focus, visible spectrum only. The *Lùhng* ships still held their positions, their white-and-orange pearlescent hides pristine. Above, below, all around—*Pulse* and *Breath* were hemmed in on all sides. No windows blinked, no hatches opened, no shuttles floated between the post-human vessels.

They were as inert, silent, and oppressive as ever.

Creased, overused holoflex-sheets were handed to him, and he scanned the previous night's report. No change.

He wasn't sure how long he could do this. How many days—weeks, months—should he call out to beings so unwilling to hear?

Without warning, the convoy-wide emergency system came on. The bridge lighting shifted, and everyone's heads snapped to and fro in confusion.

"This is Captain Baglanova," came the familiar voice over the emergency channel.

Tan immediately sprang to answer. "Report."

"I am enacting the Weaver Protocol," Baglanova said.

It took Tan a moment to understand. *There is no "Weaver" protocol, what could he possibly . . .*

Steve. Steve Weaver.

The man with the plan.

"Stand down, Captain," he barked immediately. Then, to his crew, "Bring up *Breath*, now! I need to see it."

Confusion hardened many faces, but no one questioned him.

"Stand down," he repeated over the comm, "or you will be immediately detained and sanctioned, stripped of command."

What was Baglanova thinking? He knew this would put everyone's lives at stake, he knew it! If they damaged *Lùhng* ships, if they *killed* any of the post-humans . . . What was to stop them from pursuing the convoy for all eternity? Why shouldn't they seek revenge? This was reckless, stupid, murderous, *and* cowardly all at once.

"Pods, launch on my mark," Baglanova said. "T minus sixty seconds, Orlando. You aren't going to get the dragons to hear you by then. I'm sending you SD route projections. Initiate the dive sequence and we can all get out of here safely. But be careful, dive before I set these pods off and you *know* we'll be caught again."

Tan had to think fast. What could he do? How could he stop this?

Baglanova had experiment pods to throw, but what did *he* have? He'd never get a shuttle launched in time to intercept the pods before they dove. He had to keep any of the devices from getting into open space—

The other captain was right; he couldn't just force a synchronized dive, they'd run and the *Lùhng* would follow, and as soon as they surfaced Baglanova would just try to scuttle them again . . .

He had to interrupt his focus, stop the countdown, distract him. But how—?

What could he do in sixty seconds that would guarantee the safety of his crew, really?

Tan knew the answer deep in his being, though he fought the suffocating notion with every ounce of willpower he had.

There was nothing—*nothing*—he could do.

Anticipation made Steve's fingers tingle. He itched to jump the gun, to bulldoze his way past these pesky seconds, waiting for the first few pods to launch. The dance that was to come flashed its way before his imagination: the pods going dark, shrouded in their bubbles. The anxiety-filled minutes that would follow before they'd pop back into existence, shredding through machinery, through that gross marshmallow putty they called doors, through bodies even, slicing them open, slicking their pristine decks with blood . . .

He shivered.

And then the convoy would plunge under, and be gone. The dragons would be left far behind, nothing but a bad memory.

It would be perfect. Everything was perfect.

Before him, Captain Baglanova stood tall, expression calm. He wore his dress uniform, as though this were a celebration. He was the picture of efficiency, of immaculate style and high attention to detail. "Pods ready?"

"Yessir," came the reply. "T minus three, two, one . . . launch."

Through the display screens, Steve watched the little dots scatter, set free of the maintenance hangar like little BBs from a child's toy gun. They weren't dangerous yet. That prep came next.

"Tan," Baglanova said, arms held behind his back as he paced, thoughtful, back and forth behind his crew's stations. "Are you set to comply with my orders?"

Orlando Tan wasn't the kind of man to shoot expletives across the bow of his opponent's ear. He was a frank, curt man. "Aksel," he said, ignoring the question, "this is the moment you stay your hand or damn us all."

Baglanova shook his head, a condescending smile on his lips. "All stations set?"

"Aye, Captain."

Breath's command crew had emotionless faces. Some of them had anticipated this moment, knew that a coup was happening. Others simply followed orders as they always had, unsure what had led them here, but confident in their captain's judgment.

Steve nodded to Guy de Roux, who gave a grave nod of the head back. Willis Stalker, from navigation, kept a firm eye on the security camera feed, watching the hall outside the bridge, making sure no one was approaching who shouldn't be. Secreted away in the man's jumpsuit was one of the few guns. They'd tooled seven in all for use in the mutiny. Three were on *Breath*, four on *Pulse*.

Steve hoped Stalker wouldn't have to pull it.

Turning back to the screens projecting the pods' progress, Steve noticed something odd. In the distance, one of the *Lùhng* ships was rotating, inverting. A bright point of green light burst into being on its port side—aimed directly at the convoy. Maybe it was nothing, but the timing . . .

"Uh, Captain?"

Baglanova held up a hand for silence. "Let's give those dragons something to worry about. Activate pod SD drives."

As Steve watched—as Baglanova spoke—the green spot blossomed, furling outward, sparking and sizzling, a shimmering wave of force twirling from its center. The color was sickly, sharp, and fluorescent, with edges of deep emerald shifting into sludge-dark, near black.

It was a weapon, no question.

Steve grabbed for Baglanova's arm. "Captain!"

He wasn't sure what he expected Baglanova to do, but he needed him to do *something*. The wave rippled through space as it rushed toward them, distorting their view of stars and ships alike. There was no way to evade it, no chance of emergency maneuvering.

In the next instant it would tear through them, doing god knows what to craft and crew alike.

Half a heartbeat of dead air followed as Steve held his breath.

"Brace!" the captain called. "Brace for impact!"

Sharp exclamations of dread rang out across the room.

At a loss for what else to do, Steve covered his head. But he could not look away.

Breath wasn't the only ship in the wave's path. "Aksel, *what have you done*?" Captain Tan shouted. Then the line cut out—empty static filled the air.

The pods tremored as the force flowed across them, bobbed like flotsam adrift on the sea. Envelopes of green enshrouded them, shrunk around them, as though the pods were soaking the wave in.

Milliseconds later, it hit *Breath*, tossing the ship aft-ward. The impact was jarring, sent crewmen to the floor. Steve's bones vibrated at a painfully high frequency, and his whole body hurt. He was sure his marrow was stiffening, shattering. How else could an ache lodge itself so deep?

The bridge lights flickered, but came back on in an instant. Despite the ship's yawing through space, it held together.

The pain slowly ebbed out of Steve's limbs.

"Report!" Baglanova shouted, having never lost his focus or his footing. He grabbed the back of his helmsman's chair, knuckles white, nails digging in.

“Life support systems green.”

“Communications systems green.”

“Computer systems green.”

“Graviton cyclers look fine, Captain. I don’t know what—”

“If everything’s green, then launch those pods!”

“. . . Pod drives not responding.”

No! It wasn’t possible!

Steve wracked his brain. How could the dragons have anticipated this? How could they possibly know what was coming? How . . .

“I want them back on line *right now*,” Baglanova yelled. “I need a damage report ASAP!”

Steve raked his fingers over his cheeks, wiped them across his eyes.

How could we have been so naive?

The *Lùhng* had a way to calculate SD surfacing, to predict it. Of course they were able to figure out the humans were up to no good. They were too advanced, just too—

But what do we do now?

He watched as the captain floundered, looking for a solution, trying to get the pods to respond, to do their job.

But the entire plan had hinged on the element of surprise. The *Lùhng* wouldn’t let them succeed now, not a chance. But they couldn’t abort now, either. Everything had been set in motion, they’d already undermined Tan, there was no going back.

“They’re moving off!” someone shouted.

It was true. Miracle of miracles, Steve had been wrong. The *Lùhng* were backing down, as though throwing their hands up. The coral widened, giving the humans room to breathe. Room to *flee*.

“Look, look look look,” Steve said, pointing for Baglanova. “It worked. We spooked them. They stopped the pods, but now’s our chance. We have to go. We have to move!”

The captain's face had gone ashen, and a sheen of clammy sweat graced his brow. Whatever the wave was, it had shaken him, rocked his foundations just like it had rocked the ship. But he was a captain through and through—not one to freeze in the middle of the action. "T-Tan," he said over the ship-to-ship. "Are you prepared to synchronize a dive?"

"I have people down over here! Injuries—and they're your fault. You failed, Aksel. It's done."

"No!" Baglanova shouted, the color rapidly returning to his face. "Initiate the dive or we're diving without you. Right now!"

Tan did not reply. On screen, *Pulse* was still.

"We can still be heroes," Steve said to the captain. "We can still save everyone on *Breath—*"

"Be quiet!" Baglanova snapped.

Steve slunk over to the door, clutched his trembling hands together, but he didn't shut up. "We have to go," he insisted, heart pounding, still not sure Baglanova could be spurred into action now that the first half of the plan had gone awry. "Either the *Lùhng* are letting us go, or they're pulling back because they're about to initiate a strike. You evacuate your own troops before you carpet bomb a region. *Do you hear me,* Captain?"

Maybe they'll blast Tan out of the sky, and we can dive in the interim. Maybe they won't even realize we're gone.

Clearly Baglanova had never imagined they'd actually need to leave *Pulse* behind. He thought it would work, that they wouldn't need a contingency.

"Captain?" Steve prodded.

"I'm thinking!" He took a deep, rattling breath, then turned to the boatswain's mate. "Initiate ship dive."

"Aye, sir."

The lights shifted purple . . . then winked back to white. Nothing happened.

"Why aren't we diving?" Baglanova demanded.

"SD drive is not responding."

The wave had scuttled them, too.

Damn it. *Damn it!*

The convoy-wide emergency alert system blared overhead. "*Breath*, this is Captain Tan. Aksel Baglanova has been officially removed from command. I need him apprehended immediately."

Baglanova pulled at his hair, dragging his neatly styled strands into a lunatic's fringe. He dove for the ship-to-ship. "Commence phase two of the Weaver Protocol."

A moment of total stillness followed.

Both captains had essentially given the same—but contradictory—order, demanding the other's arrest.

Baglanova eyed his crew, daring them to step out of line, to act on Tan's command.

Steve met his stare firmly. They could still get ahead here, still take control. But as Baglanova's eyes left him, Steve looked around himself, trying to gauge reactions, take the temperature of the room.

And he didn't like what he saw.

Resolves were cracking—even those crew members Steve would have counted on to back Baglanova to the grave revealed reluctance in the tight lines of their faces. Once-confident postures were stooped. The solid expressions of trust had melted into indecisiveness.

Because they now all saw what Tan saw.

Not one thing Baglanova had promised would happen *had* happened. If one pod had hit its mark, just one, perhaps this part would be easier. Perhaps the dogs wouldn't look so keen to turn on their master. But they hadn't—

A single security officer, Chen Kexin, unholstered her shock baton. Its stinging sizzle was like a starter's pistol.

The entire bridge moved en masse. Several people scrambled for cover, ducking behind whatever they could. Others dove forward, slamming themselves toward Baglanova in an attempt to end things quickly. Half a dozen moved to protect their captain, however, to stand for him at all costs, and a melee broke out.

More shock batons buzzed to life, shouts rippled through the air. Bodies pitched and writhed, punches landed, clubs swung.

Stalker drew his gun and waded into the fray, pushing Steve aside.

There was movement on the monitor he'd just abandoned. The outside hall was packed with people, most struggling to get to the bridge. Steve looked closely, trying to discern if his plants had the upper hand, or if they were the ones getting dragged away. He pinpointed Mac Savea in the crowd—the bastard had Dalisay Ocampo down on her knees, was securing her hands behind her back.

Bang!

Steve jumped.

A gun had gone off. Stalker's gun.

The shot glanced off the wall near Steve's head. A second caught the display screen, punching a hole straight through, killing the security feed from the hall.

Diving away, to the floor, Steve crawled past stamping feet and struggling forms.

The smell of gunpowder was foreign, disconcerting. It had no place on a spaceship. All at once it dawned on Steve that guns were a *very* bad idea in a place where a tiny hole could kill them all.

What did we do?

What we had to, he thought with conviction.

Steve looked for the captain's shoes. They'd been shiny

black this morning. Well polished. When he found them now, they were scuffed—one leather toe had been cut into, snagged on a sharp edge.

The captain himself was stumbling backward, pushing off a lieutenant commander, dodging a fist as he went.

With a heavy grunt, Steve pushed himself upright, grabbed for the lieutenant commander's collar and yanked him away.

Bodies thrashed together nearby, knocking into Steve before he could grab Baglanova to shield him.

The bridge door began to open, then swiftly shut again. Those doors were supposed to be on lockdown—Steve had people in place to see to it. But Savea's team was attempting to force them open, which meant that Steve's people were overwhelmed.

Soon Savea's team would be inside.

This chaos had to end, this panic had to stop. Baglanova needed to take control again. He was the authority here, why was no one respecting that? How had they abandoned him so quickly?

And for what? To honor Tan's cowardice? To stand by as victors these next few minutes, until the *Lùhng* killed them all?

He punched his way back to the captain. "Don't worry, sir, I'll get you—"

Bang!

The gun had gone off again.

Baglanova swayed. Steve jerked back in surprise.

The left side of the captain's head turned red, his sandy hair stained crimson. The color splattered, oozed.

Swiveling, Stone looked for the pistol.

Stalker no longer had it. No one was pointing it.

Everyone near the captain stumbled backward. Steve pitched forward instead, catching Baglanova as he began to fall.

"Captain?" he implored. "Captain, can you hear me?"

Baglanova's head lolled to the side. His eyes were open—wide with shock. But it was an empty shock.

Aksel Baglanova was dead.

Stunned, Steve dropped him. The body slumped, its splattered head bouncing grotesquely when it hit the floor.

The crowd froze.

The smell of vomit overwhelmed Steve, filling his nostrils with a vengeance.

No. No no no!

The bridge was silent. Savea's detail still banged on the door outside.

For an instant, Steve thought that was it, that everything was over.

But it was the startled calm before the true frenzy. Before everyone began fighting each other, trying to delineate friend from foe.

The gun. The gun. Who in the hell has the gun?

He felt dazed, lost. His ears rang, and yet he heard nothing. People were screaming, and Steve was locked in his own mind with one thought.

Who has the motherfucking gun?

He searched hands, the decking. Scanned the tops of the command stations and kicked at nooks and crannies between equipment.

A fist caught him in the side of the head. A glancing blow, so he didn't care. He just kept searching.

Is the same thing happening on Pulse? he wondered.

Did that ship still have its captain? Or had the mutiny succeeded, only to find Tan's replacement dead? Was Tan dead, too?

Were they all adrift without a leader?

The thought scared him, but he didn't feel good and truly lost until Savea finally succeeded in forcing the door. Using a shock baton, he propped it open. A battalion's worth of security personnel streamed inside, their shock batons at the ready. Savea ordered everyone to stop fighting, to kneel down and put their hands behind their heads.

Most people complied.

As the crew followed orders, descending to their knees, Guy de Roux was one of the few left standing.

He had the gun now.

It swiveled in Savea's direction, ready to blast through his body, tear into his chest, pierce his lungs or burst his heart.

Steve had a choice. Savea was so close, he could dive for him, knock him out of the way.

Or he could do as he was told. Stay on the ground, hands behind his head.

He didn't move.

He wasn't sure when he'd come to hate Mac so much. Why he was content to let Guy kill him. Perhaps it had started back on the *Lùhng* ship. Perhaps it had been just now, when he realized Savea would always be Tan's stooge.

Guy pulled the trigger—

—just as Kexin grabbed for the firearm. She took the shot straight through the hand. Everyone gasped, and Kexin clubbed Guy with her shock baton.

The bullet never reached Savea.

"Stupid bastard!" Kexin shouted, her palm streaming blood, dripping buckets onto the floor.

The universe wouldn't even give Steve that one little satisfaction. It had taken Baglanova, but wouldn't take Mac, too.

"Aksel?"

The room went quiet. It was Captain Tan.

"Aksel, I'm still here. I expect to speak with you shortly. Let us pray the *Lùhng* don't kill us before then."

Steve leaned forward, pressing his cheek to the thin carpet.

Now he understood why that man hadn't stepped in all those years ago.

Why stick your neck out in a world that doesn't care? Why try anything when it can get you and everyone you know murdered by future freaks millions of miles from home?

Why step up for people who might hate you for it?

Now he'd have to live—no matter if the *Lùhng* made the time he had left long or short—with everyone's contempt. He kept his head down, averting his eyes as he was dragged off to the brig.

CHAPTER TEN

CONVOY SEVEN

JOANNA: ALL THAT MADDENS AND TORMENTS

ONE HUNDRED AND TWENTY-FOUR

YEARS SINCE THE CONVOY REUNION

FEBRUARY 11, 1237 RELAUNCH

8172 CE

No matter what we do, we never arrive in time.

Fleet Admiral Joanna Straifer the Forty-Ninth stood statuesque on *Mira*'s bridge, staring out the main viewing screen. A thin haze pooled and swirled before the ships: all that was left of the Web's last meal.

Seven, her mind screamed. *It's eaten seven stars since LQ Pyx. If we keep doing things the same old way, it'll eat through the galaxy before it's caught.*

At that moment, she'd had enough.

I'm done following my great-grandparents' methodology.

"Shall we drop back into SD and reinitiate pursuit?" asked the nav specialist, already keying in the commands.

"No." She held out a hand to stop him, and he responded with an expression of confusion. "We stay put. Wait for my orders. Before we chase that thing another meter I'm calling a cabinet meeting." She pivoted on her heel and stomped off the bridge, arms clasped tightly behind her back. Her knuckles were white against her wrist. She knew if she let go of herself she'd lash out at the nearest object—be it inanimate or not.

Captain Nakamura and First Officer Hansen's gazes followed her out the door. Joanna's line was no longer captain of *Mira*. Captain Nwosu, Revealer of Rejoining, had shuffled the crew. They weren't builders any more. They'd become warriors, soldiers—antibodies of the galaxy, out to destroy an infection. And so everyone needed new purposes, new positions. Their political and command systems had undergone a complete overhaul in the first few years following Convoy Seven becoming whole again.

He'd known they needed a lone leader like they never had before—someone who could give executive orders. An Admiral.

And he'd dubbed Joanna's line the most qualified. Joanna Straifer the Forty-Ninth was the sixth to occupy the position. She had no cycle partner—for the first time in convoy history, no other clone line shared the power or the burden.

It's just me. Me before, me now, and me after.

Her heavy footfalls propelled her down the hall, toward the shuttle bay. "I.C.C., alert the cabinet members and tell them to meet me—except Nakamura, tell her to hold—on *Eden*. They're too comfortable in that damn war room."

***Eden*'s temperate quarter was as warm and welcoming as the** last time she'd visited, which had not been long ago. She never let more than a few weeks pass without a stint aboard. It was where she felt safest and strongest. The brightest spot in her bleak life.

It had provided her with comfort and a means of escape on the day of her first command failure. A day not long after she'd been appointed to her station, when she'd lost the Killer for the first time. Her father had been so angry that day he'd punched the frame that held her mother's picture. "I knew it!" he'd screamed at her. "What a waste of command training!" He'd screamed as she cowered by the front door, screamed as she'd bolted from the cabin, screamed as she'd run down the hall.

She'd finally found solace and silence on *Eden*. It was a place for calmness and clarity.

And now it would be the site of a coup. A coup against failed strategy.

The cabinet members arrived in trickles instead of a wave. They all walked into the artificial sunlight with their arms up, shielding their eyes. She almost made them sit in the grass—so soft and pliable—but instead gave them leave to stand. When the last one arrived, she began.

"We're here because we needed new surroundings in order to generate a new strategy. This process of running after the Star Killer, only to arrive too late, has got to stop. It doesn't matter how many or what kind of weapons we build on *Slicer*. If we can't get close enough to the sucker to use them, what's the point?"

She turned to the chief mechanical engineer, Ivan. "Are you positive we can't get any more speed out of the fleet?"

"Yes, ma'am," he said. "Not without risking meltdown. Especially not the older ships."

"We are working on something that can attack from a light-year away," said Anatoly, Chief of Weapons Engineering.

"The last time the convoy was within a light-year of the thing, none of us had been born yet," she said.

"I've had more and more of my people request time in the dream state these past couple of years," he said. "They're putting in double hours—double *lifetimes*—that way. We can do it."

Lots of the *Infinitum* crew had begun adopting *Ultra*'s ways. When your work could be the key to averting interstellar destruction, you take every advantage you can get, even if it means sacrificing your consciousness.

Joanna shook her head. "Look." She chopped her hands through the air in small, concise movements, punctuating her words. "This is what I'm thinking. We're not waiting around to see what path it takes next. None of this follow-the-leader crap anymore. I want to cut it off at the quick. Put me one step ahead. I want projections of where it will go *after* its next target. And I want to get there first."

"But how are we supposed to know that?" Dr. Ka'uhane, the chief astronomer asked.

"It always attacks a main sequence star, right? So far, all of K to M typing. The stars are small enough for the Web to get its arms around, and have medium to low energy outputs. We know where it's going now, so let's figure out where it's going next, after that. I want possibilities calculated. Because I want us to finally kill the damn thing. To finish what got dumped on us. We're not going to dump it on our children, got it?"

They all nodded.

Through gritted teeth she said, "Make it happen."

As the group broke apart, Joanna felt like she was about to break herself. She was tired. Exhausted. She'd been exhausted since the day she was born. She'd been told—everyone had been told—of the convoy's glory days, when hope reigned. When their purpose had been to discover and to build. She wondered what it would be like, to live in such a time, when every day was full of bright potential.

Instead, she lived in a world where every second weighed on the crew members, each leaden with dread. There was no happiness in this pursuit of the Killer, no pleasure to their purpose. How could there be when every waking minute drew you closer to the realization that the Killer could not be stopped, that it would continue forever, destroying all that lay before it?

She refused to accept that their lives were forfeit to the past. They *would* accomplish this task, and they would accomplish it with her at the helm.

Joanna the Forty-Fourth may have been declared the first fleet admiral, but this Joanna would declare herself *the last.*

In a few hours, the astronomy division turned in their findings.

After the Killer's current mark, there were seven candidate stars. According to I.C.C., most of them had under a 7 percent chance of being the Web's meal-after-next, and only one—An M class star they dubbed *Ishmael*—had anything approaching positive odds: a 58 percent chance.

It will have to be enough, she thought.

Back on the bridge, she gave the orders. "Captain Nakamura, tell your crew to head for these coordinates. Come malfunction or malediction, we'll beat this monster to its victim."

She knew the calculations could be wrong, knew a different star entirely could turn out to be the target. But she was an all-or-nothing kind of person. They'd send a probe to trail the Killer, to keep them apprised of its movements via SD communications. She was confident in her decision, and they would not lose track of the Web.

AUGUST 4, 1254 RELAUNCH

8319 CE

Years went by as the convoy staked out the star. They'd spent a decade and a half racing toward a guess, then two years lying in wait.

Joanna had squashed doubt at every turn. She espoused her confidence in this new approach every chance she got—not just for *their* sake, but for hers as well.

You have to get this right, said a stern male voice inside her head. *You have to do it, there's no one else. All this chasing is driving you mad. You can't let anyone else fall to this thing's dark need.*

I will, she told the voice. *I can do it.*

You won't have to be angry anymore, added a childlike version of herself.

Her confidence bordered on arrogance. She wouldn't let the faintest scrap of chance into her consideration—chance that things might not happen as she willed them to.

On a mid monsoon day, she was summoned from the refreshing humidity aboard *Eden*'s tropical quarter into the ever-constant conditions of *Holwarda*. She didn't even bother to dry off before answering the beckon. There, Dr. Ka'uhane revealed her team's latest findings. Her office was papered in long-range snapshots of the Seed and the Web. Many of the 'flex-sheets on her desk bore ring stains from where she'd placed her tiny espresso cup, but the scent that lingered in the air wasn't coffee. The room smelled of ink and alcohol; instead of typing up the data, she'd drawn on the 'flex-sheets with permanent markers. Joanna wasn't even aware the fleet manufactured such things.

"I get them printed special," she explained, a proud lilt to her voice. She seemed blissfully unaware that she'd ruined reams of reusable sheets. In the next instant her tone turned grim, "But this—this is what I wanted to show you."

"No," Joanna whispered. She pushed the dripping strands of her graying hair away from her face to get a better look at the sheet.

"The Killer has consumed another star and its orbiting planets, and as predicted, has moved on. However, it hasn't turned toward Ishmael."

"How could we be wrong? We were sure. All this time, wasted."

Joanna glared out the window toward the nearby star. She'd

intended only a glance, but the light held her gaze. It was bright, yet left her cold. They'd spent two years orbiting this star, proposing to save the shining orb, though they'd been unable to save the others.

But it had never been a target. They were investigators trying to keep ahead of a serial killer whose logic was dimensions away from their own.

She'd just said they'd been sure, but the truth was, that was a farce. *She'd* been sure. She'd needed this, counted on it.

So you lost a goddamned coin flip, railed her father's voice, *so what? Aren't you used to losing, to failing?*

At the edge of her hearing, Dr. Ka'uhane was trying to explain why precedents didn't matter. But she could barely parse the words. Joanna was too busy balking at the time wasted. The convoy had spent *seventeen years* aiming for a star that would go untouched by the Web.

Joanna knew the deep lines of her face made her look aged well beyond her actual years. Every crease felt hot now, though the sensation was overshadowed by the tough tug of an intense frown that barely hid her gritted teeth. Grasping at whatever she could, she said, "You told us this was the most likely target. Where has it gone, then? Toward our number two choice? Our number three?"

The willowy woman appeared at a loss for a moment, as though unsure how to explain. Her tongue seemed to rush ahead of her thoughts as she said, "It's not something we could have predicted. It's changed trajectory, and there are no stars within its typical range of pursuit. We had no reason to think it wouldn't continue on as usual. But it's not following its pattern. There was no reason to suspect it wouldn't go—"

"Can we cut it off?" But Joanna waved the astronomer silent before she could answer.

Would the nightmare never end?

She asked another question instead. "What's in its line of sight?"

Ka'uhane let a beat pass before answering. Then, "It's aimed directly at Earth's system."

The admiral's skin pricked, the muscles underneath going cold. The air suddenly smelled rancid in her nostrils. "Tell me that's a sick joke."

Ka'uhane turned up her palms, half imploring, half shrugging.

If Sol was indeed the Killer's target, the megastructure would take the better part of a century to reach the system. Joanna would issue a warning, but it would do little good if Earth couldn't receive the message. They hadn't been in contact with the planet in what felt like an eon, and SD communications—the only signals fast enough to get there before the Web—were outmoded planet-side. If Earth wasn't looking for an SD packet, sending one would be about as effective as screaming into the vacuum of space.

No—they couldn't count on Earth to do anything. Either they finally caught up to the Killer, or their planet would be no more.

You better redeem yourself, little girl, said her father's voice. *Don't be like those failures before you.*

Maybe I already am, she thought bitterly.

AUGUST 15, 1254

If they changed course immediately, they could intercept it within a decade. At least their mistake had given them the opportunity to head it off instead of continuously trailing after it.

Small victories.

She sat in her office. Pictures of each of *Mira*'s captains hung on the walls, judging her. It was not eerie to find previous versions of herself staring back, nor was it strange to see only eight different profiles in the myriads of portraits. Some of their expressions seemed full of pity, others appeared to share her guilt. They'd each made decisions that had led to this moment, for better or worse.

She often played a thought game with herself. She tried to imagine what it was like for the first travelers—she didn't simply think about them, she tried to embody them. She tapped the continuum and reached back as far as she could, trying to touch the first members. How had they felt, blasting away to discover what made that far-off star twinkle as it did? They must have been encouraged by their prospects, but slightly sad, knowing that their world would change while they were gone, knowing that it would not belong to them once they left.

But they couldn't have anticipated this. They couldn't have imagined that by leaving home they could destroy it.

And what about Reggie Straifer of Earth? The ultimate Revealer of all—though also the most ignorant of all. *Noumenon* he'd named it. *Ha!* Insubstantial, untouchable things can't kill you. The truth of a thing couldn't kill you. Death itself might be a thing impossible to hold in your hand, but *causes* of death were measurable. She'd seen the recordings—his plea of a speech to those voting for the Planet United Missions. He'd been so passionate, so enthralled with the mystery. Hope and wonder had oozed from his every pore in an ethereal cloud. She wished she could suck it into her bones, use it as a steeling agent.

What a wonderful thing *not knowing* was. It built an artificial world where mythical things like *hope* could live.

She wanted to find his original mindset and claim it for herself. The only thing she'd ever felt while in pursuit was sadness and urgency. This was no great quest, nothing to be romanticized. Correcting a dire mistake was no heroic feat.

Trying to appease an angry man's ghost wasn't exactly a courageous endeavor, either.

Damn ignorant idiots. She didn't think her attitude toward former phases of the convoy was unjustly bleak. The current crew felt far more pressure than the Explorers or the Builders ever had. She and her Chasers had every right to question the actions of those who came before, and she would hear no argument to the contrary.

Joanna strolled up to one of the portraits and stared down the individual's likeness. "How different would my life be if they had listened to you?" She asked Reginald Straifer IV, the only one to prophesize this Armageddon. History said he'd been ill, *Revealing* said he was a saint . . .

Joanna thought him a harbinger of doom.

She looked internally, hoping the members of her continuum could drown out the frenzy of her thoughts and let her genetic instincts shine through. "We can intercept it before it reaches another target. But can we stop it? Will destroying a tentacle kill it?"

She pulled a chair from the desk and sat facing the portrait. With her elbows on her knees, she clasped her hands as if she were praying. Her eyes remained locked with Reginald's. "The devices were on when you found them. It wasn't dead then, just dormant. Is that what the Nest—the alien ship—was after? Does the Seed need to be destroyed for the Web to die forever?"

Her gut told her yes. The universe would never be rid of the Killer unless they put its hub out of commission.

They had years to figure out how to do that—it was their sole mission now.

Soon we won't be Chasers. Soon we'll be Destroyers.

MARCH 11, 1263 RELAUNCH

8406 CE

They had been wrong, *again*.

Joanna could hardly stand it, not knowing what the Web

would do next. How could she fight it if it behaved inconsistently? At least the previous iterations of her line had been able to count on its hunger for star matter.

And that was truly what it appeared to be: hunger. It consumed stars. Ate them. Sometimes she thought it behaved far more like a creature than a weapon.

On its presumed way to Earth, though, the Web traveled into a small nebula. A rather insignificant swath of dust and gas—so much so that they'd thought its proximity to the Web's path coincidental.

No one on board so much as speculated that the nebula—which they could find no earthly designation for—was the Web's intended destination.

Yet, when it reached the nebula, it immersed itself in the cloud, settling in. It did not globe its limbs, or take another shape. Instead it just sat there, biding its time . . . as if waiting for the convoy to catch up.

And now they finally had.

Today the convoy would come within range. The ships would be close enough to deploy their long-distance weapon. Despite Anatoly's original promise, it wasn't effective up to a light-year. They'd only been able to reach a fraction of the distance, seven billion kilometers, but that would have to do.

Joanna went over the newly collected data in her ready room. The most recent snapshots revealed that the Web's intrusion into the cloud had triggered a sort of condensation effect. Molecules coalesced along the length of its arms and the Seed's body, drawn in by its sizable gravitational pull. Considering the Web's new behavioral changes, Joanna had to examine the inkling that rested at the back of her mind—the one suggesting the Web might be more creature than automaton. Since it appeared to be making choices, rather than simply following a set of directives, the artifact could be possessed of its own intelligence. Not unlike I.C.C.

“What do you think?” she asked the AI. “Does it know what it’s doing?”

“A fair question,” it said after a barely noticeable pause. “And though I don’t have any definitive proof, I do not think so.”

“Why not?” she asked, scribbling commands onto a ‘flex-sheet with a stylus. She still wasn’t sure which approach was best. Should they try to cripple the Web first, or concentrate all of their fire power on the Seed? If it was intelligent, as she suspected, it might be able to evade their attack.

“Because I have made repeated attempts to contact it.”

“You *have*?” She looked up from the sheets and subconsciously put a fingertip in her mouth to chew the cuticle. “Who put in the request?”

“No one. I performed the task via my own initiative, certain someone would inquire in the future. I did not want to wait. If you’d asked me to begin now, I would not have enough time to compile sufficient data to make a sound judgment as to its sentience before you wish to act.”

“And you think it isn’t because it didn’t respond?”

“And because it doesn’t seem to be ignoring our pursuit so much as it seems *unaware* of our pursuit. It does not notice, let alone understand.”

“*Understand*,” she mumbled, noticing her finger in her mouth and whipping it away. “What I wouldn’t give for a distilled drop of True Understanding.”

“There are hints of uncertainty in your vocalizations.”

“Hints? Is that all?” she said sarcastically. *Now that the time has come, I must not falter. I must not second-guess myself. I must finish the job my ancestors could not. I must not—*

“Are you questioning its function?” asked I.C.C.

“As what?”

“A weapon.”

“No.”

“Your words say one thing, your inflection another.”

"It's just that . . ." She let out a large sigh and slumped against her ready room's rear wall. The paint smelled musty. She thought that if her life had a smell it would be similar—aged, with a hint of mold. Her life and the room needed a good scrubbing. Better yet, a good gutting. "It hasn't hurt anything. Nothing living. It's simply used matter—like we do. We mine for repairs, break things up and break things down into things we can use. We're not considered 'killers,' are we? So, why do we call it the Killer? I mean, what has it actually *killed*?"

"But there has been nothing in the vicinity *to* kill—nothing except Earth. Does the fact that it has yet to complete its task make it any less dangerous?"

"But *is* that its task? That's still just our speculation. And that's all we've been doing for the past two thousand years. Speculating. But let's ask another question: Why hasn't it made for Earth yet, for real? As a weapon, it's extremely inefficient. If it was meant to destroy a fledgling intelligence, why take so much time? Why give that intelligence the chance to develop? To grow? To perhaps reach a technological tipping point where they could save themselves—which is exactly where we're at."

She shivered and contemplated asking I.C.C. to raise the room's temperature. But there was nothing wrong with the climate controls—the chill came from inside. And it was not the cold of letting a killer escape. It was the type of internal frigidity that earned a pause, required thoughtfulness.

"Perhaps its original builders did not expect its parade through systems to halt," I.C.C. suggested. "There might have been no accounting for the Nest's crew."

"I suppose that should be proof enough for me—someone else thought it a danger. But the Nataré assumed as we did, both before and after construction. But here's the thing . . ." She picked herself off the wall and began to pace. The carpet beneath her feet was worn, with a treaded path clearly visible across the weave. Joannas prior had walked the same stretch of floor. Had they contemplated the same things? Not daring to enter them into the record for fear they would appear cowardly or lazy? Or had they always trusted their mission, at the same time knowing they were never in a position to truly do anything about it anyway?

"You trailed off," I.C.C. said.

"Right . . . I'm just wondering. Why rely on other civilizations to build your weapon for you? How could you count on them?"

"The fact that we completed it should be proof enough of their plan's effectiveness."

Joanna stopped. She'd never heard I.C.C. use "we" in that context before. "You remember—" she said "—what it was like during the building days, the discovery days."

"I remember . . . everything," it said softly. "Back. Long back, when I was young. Even when I was more my parts than the sum of my parts . . ."

That seemed to mean so much to Joanna, and yet so little. She had spent innumerable hours reaching for the beginning of her genetic line, trying to grasp their lives and their feelings through the ether of time and space. And here was a contemporary of them all. The only convoy member who *was* the convoy. The only consciousness aboard who had lived through everything.

"You *are* greater than the sum of your parts, aren't you? You're the sum of us all, I.C.C. What do *you* think we should do when we come within range?"

"I don't think we should leave the universe in worse shape than we found it."

"What does that mean?"

"I don't think our legacy should be nine disappeared systems *and* a hunk of immobile metal."

It was being cryptic. She hated when it was cryptic. It always did that when it had an opinion, but wanted you to reach its conclusion on your own. "The alternative legacy is the destruction of Earth."

"Not necessarily."

"So you don't think it's a genocide machine, then?"

It didn't answer. Whether because it thought its opinion didn't matter to her, or because it wanted her to take the silence as its own answer, she wasn't sure.

So what if the Web *might not* be a weapon? They couldn't risk the chance that it was.

Right?

It was a shame to think I.C.C.'s life would add up to be as meaningless as hers. Scientific missions shouldn't have zero sums. No one builds things just to knock them down again. But what was *Noumenon Infinitum* but the anti-*Noumenon*? The two missions annihilated one another. Canceled each other out as explosively as matter and antimatter.

I.C.C.'s experience of the hope and wonder made the pain of failure all the more pointed, she was sure.

The AI had spent millennia waiting to see the end of this human endeavor. She shouldn't be surprised that it was hesitant to shoot the artifact out of dead space. It didn't want everything to end how it began: shrouded in mystery, daunting and unknowable.

But I.C.C. did not make choices rooted in sentimentality—or did it? Now she wasn't sure. It definitely did not act off assumptions. It acted based on what it knew, not what it didn't know.

It knew it didn't understand the Web. And that . . . worried it?

"I want to wait," she blurted. "I want to see if it gives up its secrets."

"But what if it slithers off again?"

"Then we'll keep chasing."

“You might miss your one chance to stop it.”

She gulped past a knot in her throat. “I know.”

How dare *you?* asked her father’s ghost.

She wished she had an answer that would satisfy him.

THIRTY-EIGHT YEARS PREVIOUS

The normal buzzing and whirs of the ship faded out, and all Joanna could hear were her father’s insults. It was like the sound version of tunnel vision. Everything else in the family cabin slipped away.

“We’re not genetically suited for this mission, okay?” she yelled at him, hiding her eyes behind shaking fingers. “All I was ever meant to be was an overseer. I’m supposed to keep construction on track, not lead a military campaign. No one meant for me to head a charge after some apocalyptic enemy.”

“Our system has made us *weak*,” he spat back. “You think people back on Earth are only expected to perform if they’re *genetically suited*? No. None of us were picked for this, but who gives a crap? Things have to get done, whether we’re the best ones to do them or not. We’re the only ones here, damn it.” The hard, twisted ridges of his face slumped. The wrinkled skin looked like it was about to melt off his ragged face.

“If there’s one thing your bitch of an ancestor did right, it was to take control. *She* knew it took initiative, decisiveness. She knew that if the damn board hadn’t sat around philosophizing they could have cut the Web down before it got anywhere. You might not have been picked for this by some nerdy gaggle from Earth, but you damn well were by *her*. She accepted executive powers, she formed the cabinet, bore the title of fleet admiral like the badge it was. And look what the rest of your line have done with her foresight. Now you shit on her memory. I’m sure she’s extricated herself from your continuum.”

He grabbed her wrists, forcing her hands to her sides. "*This* is why your mother died, because none of *you* have ever been able to take responsibility. She believed in your line. I tried to convince her we shouldn't accept one of you to raise, but she insisted. It was an honor to raise a fleet admiral, she said."

Tears rolled down Joanna's cheeks, hot as the oil from an overworked motor. "But, she thought I—"

"She thought you'd never have to be one. She thought the beast would be exterminated in our lifetime. She believed it so fully she couldn't go on once she realized she'd been living in a fantasy land. And it's your line's fault for not making it happen. It should have happened generations ago, when the damn thing came to life." He threw her hands away from him, as though they burned his palms. "She killed herself today because of *you*."

Joanna tried to suppress the memory, but the more she tried to banish it, the more it engraved itself on her mind. The relationship between her and her father had always been tenuous, but when her mother committed suicide it shattered. Any love they might have shared died with her.

Joanna hadn't even been appointed admiral yet when he'd poured his boiling rage on her head. They'd missed the Web once again, and the entire fleet had watched it lumber off into the night for the sixth time.

Joanna's mother had been positive their horrid endeavor was about to end. When it proved a continued battle, she denied it for days. She pretended the quest was over. She even threw a party that no one came to.

When reality hit, she just couldn't bear it.

Joanna knew it wasn't her fault. Knew in her marrow. But it was her father's wrath that made her wonder if her *mother* had known. Joanna was just an apprentice, in charge of nothing but her continuing education. But had her mother realized?

Or was the only reason her father blamed her because her mother had lost hold of reality long ago?

She'd never asked her father, and now he was gone. Retired ages ago. She was older now than he'd been when he lost his wife.

If she failed to stop the Web, wouldn't she be proving him right? A weak line would take the easy way out, waffle on the decision, let inaction call the shots.

But in this situation, waiting *was* the hard decision. If she was wrong, she could damn every last human being.

A buzz at her ready room door roused her from introspection. "Come in."

Mira's Captain Nakamura emerged from the other side. "We're within range. Standing by for tactical orders."

"Hold weapons," she said simply. "Continue to approach, half-speed with caution."

"Hold weapons?"

"That's what I said." Joanna rose and ushered the captain out onto the bridge. "We watch and we wait."

"For what?" She was flabbergasted.

"A reason to believe this hasn't all been in vain."

Whatever they were expecting, it wasn't a dance.

When it began to move again, Joanna nearly panicked. *Oh my god, I was wrong, I was wrong, we have to stop it* now. She opened her mouth, on the verge of calling everyone to battle, when the Web took a graceful twist to the left.

The artifact swirled in a circle, kicking up the nebula, whipping it into a dense froth. The tentacles swayed and spun with rhythmic fluidity, while the Seed swooped in circles, like the weighted end of a pendulum, around the gasses, pulling them and pushing them. The motion was mysteriously stirring.

Mesmerized, Joanna waited along with the rest of her spellbound crew.

She listened to her gut. There was no reason to think the movements weren't threatening, but she sensed the convoy was safe.

She let the Web do as it pleased.

Other officers and cabinet members hailed her over the comms, pleading for her to take action.

"What are you waiting for?" they cried.

Joanna couldn't say. But whatever it was balanced on the precipice of her mind, hovering over a deep, dark chasm. She felt like a heretic sailor journeying to the edge of the world in ancient times, before mankind knew the Earth was round. *Here there be monsters,* her crew seemed to shout.

She'd been screamed at, she'd been cursed, now she was being bargained with and denounced at the same time. But she intended to see, to understand what truly lay at the fringe of understanding. If it was as terrible as modern legend said, she'd let the mob tear her to pieces—a fate her father would have approved of.

But that won't be enough, a tickle of doubt hissed at the back of her brain. It sounded like her father. *If the world really is flat, it won't just be your ship that goes over the side. Are you sure you're not letting your desire for hope get in the way? Are you sure you're not trying to subvert the truth—that life is pointless and dire, and that all anyone will ever find at the end of a great struggle is tragedy?*

No, she shoved doubt aside. *I refuse to live in that universe.*

Then prepare to damn us all.

So she did.

Joanna let the Web continue its dance for months. The protests, pleas, and late-night poundings on her door finally let up, subsiding only because nothing new had happened. She hadn't even called a cabinet meeting in that time, purely because she wanted tempers to dissipate and panic to subside.

In a different situation, she might have feared a mutiny.

But no one wanted her responsibility. If they were going to fail, they were content to blame her. That was why no one had attempted a genetic reevaluation back when the first and second (and so on) admirals had failed, and why no one else had ever offered to step into the position.

The cabinet members were mellow when she finally gathered them all together. They'd exhausted their adrenaline reserves and couldn't bring themselves anywhere near a frenzy.

"Can we at least send shuttles?" asked the exasperated captain of the *Slicer.* "Sitting here, doing nothing, it's . . ."

"Cowardly," said Anatoly helpfully.

"I think interference can only cause problems," Joanna said.

"I didn't say we should interfere, just observe. Do . . . something. It would appease the rest of the crew. Otherwise, Anatoly is correct, it makes us look afraid."

"We *are* afraid."

"Sure, but being afraid and appearing afraid are two different things. One causes chaos."

She scratched her chin. "We can send a probe."

"And have it short out like all the others? Nothing's ever been able to probe the Seed. Even our long-range scans have told us little. Fluid vats for course corrections, that's all they've found. No, we need to send a team."

"It's too dangerous. I don't want to risk anyone."

They all looked at her as though she'd just said she was betrothed to I.C.C.

"You're risking *everyone* by not *firing,*" said Anatoly, his protest tripping out over his tongue.

"The convoy has devoted century after century to that thing, and we want to blow it out of existence," she said without elaboration.

"This is ridiculous," declared the captain of *Aesop.* "I demand a vote—on a manned observation mission. If you won't let us fire—an apt course of action for a *military* mission—then let us return to our original functions as scientists and engineers. We can't just sit here."

She didn't like the idea. What if I.C.C. was wrong and it wasn't just an oblivious machine acting automatically? But she couldn't think of a solid argument that would convince them not to go. "Fine. Make your scientific selections for the crew, and we'll launch a shuttle tomorrow."

That appeased them . . . but they never got the chance to see the appointment through.

The Web stopped its swirling and behaved in an all-too-familiar fashion, globing around its newly gathered ball of gas and dust.

More panic, more cries of *kill the monster* immediately boiled through the comms.

She only went so far as to order the weapons on standby. She still refused to shoot.

You're weak. It's your fault. It's your fault she died, and now you'll kill everyone else, too.

Shut up, she mentally screamed, locking the dark voice away, bracing her mental walls with that firm feeling she harbored—that feeling that told her the entire history of the convoy was *not* a tragedy.

Standing on the bridge, she held her breath, staring at the image of the Sphere that filled the screen. It was so beautiful, wrapped around the purples and blues and pinks that whirled within.

It didn't need to gather such a thin soup to feed on—there were plenty of stars available—so what was it doing?

Suddenly another shift. A brilliant flash of light—so strong she had to shield her eyes. "I.C.C., reduce input, shift resolution," she demanded. "I can't tell what's happening."

The brightness decreased, the contrast increased.

"What in the name of—?"

The consumer of worlds, that great demon artifact which sucked up every scrap in its path, was now *spewing.*

Utilizing unknown forces, the Seed catapulted energy at the nebula fragment. Giant streams of matter shot toward the center of the Sphere, hot and sizzling in a plasma state.

"By the continuum, what's happening?" asked Nakamura.

What is this? Joanna's mind screamed. *Something not destructive,* she tried to reassure herself.

Only minutes passed before the Seed broke free of its legs. It tumbled away into space as the Web fused behind it, leaving no gap and shrinking the size of the Sphere.

"What should we do?" asked Captain Nakamura. "Follow the Seed?"

Joanna took a deep breath. *I will not be Ahab,* she told herself. "No. Watch."

"You're insane," said a lieutenant, leaving his station to face her. "We've got our chance again. Shoot it, shoot it *now.* Give the order, damn it!"

"Back to your position," she ordered calmly.

"To do what? Standby forever? Act!"

"Lieutenant," snapped the captain. "The admiral gave you an order."

Seething, his hands clenching and unclenching at his sides, the man did not move. "I don't recognize her authority."

Joanna did not waver. If the bridge crew thought her order to hold was made by a feeble will, they'd soon change their minds. "Matheson," she said to her chief of security. "Hand me your sidearm."

Without hesitation, he snapped open its sheath and pulled forth his deep-shock bar, a ranged weapon based on the shock batons. At its highest setting it could fry a person's cerebral cortex in under .28 seconds. He placed the weapon firmly in her outstretched hand.

In the next instant it sat level with the lieutenant's eyes.

“You will report to the brig and wait for court martial. Or, you can refuse. In which case I’ll shoot, and Matheson can drag you away by the heels.”

A split second’s worth of defiance remained in the man’s eyes. For Joanna, it was a split second too long. She aimed the head of the deep-shock bar between his eyes and pulled the trigger.

The lieutenant jolted as every muscle in his body contracted. Then he slumped to the floor, unconscious.

Thanking Matheson with a nod, she returned his weapon. “Take him to a doctor. Give him a cozy bed and something warm to drink when he wakes up. Then put him in the brig.”

Matheson did as he was told, ever the stoic soldier. He threw the lieutenant over his shoulder and stalked away.

All eyes were on Joanna. The crew was stunned. No captain had ever shot an officer before. But she wasn’t a captain, she was a fleet admiral. “Look,” she said, gesturing lightly at the forward screen. Reluctantly, heads turned.

The Seed was making no attempt to flee. It hadn’t abandoned its legs, just separated from them. Acting independently of its parts, and keeping its concave face toward the Sphere, it circled the Web. Slowly at first, but with every passing second it increased its speed. It twirled faster and faster, keeping just under the speed of light, skewing their view.

What was happening within the Web’s reach became a mystery. Nothing could be seen past the Seed’s incredible display.

But somehow, Joanna knew it was something wondrous.

The Seed’s hyperactive dash went on for months. Who knew what might happen if they shot now? All they could do was continue to observe the Seed’s mesmerizing behavior.

When the Seed slowed once again, Joanna was in her quarters, caught firmly in a deep sleep. I.C.C. roused her, its volume levels nearly double the norm. "You have to see," it said in the face of her drowsy eyelash batting. It turned on her monitor without asking.

Joanna's eyes snapped shut against the screen's glare. Coaxing them open, she forced her vision to focus through the grog of exhaustion.

The Seed sat completely still again, and hovered on the edge of the camera's vision. The Web was gone, cannibalized by whatever processes the Seed had exerted.

What appeared to be a brown dwarf lay in its place.

Tripping over her sheets, she stumbled toward the bright image. Her palms pawed at the screen, as though she could make tactile sense of what she was seeing. "Why eat so many?" she asked, rubbing at her eyes, then at her sleep-numbed cheeks. "Just to create a dim substitute?"

"This footage is from twenty minutes ago," I.C.C. said. "I don't have enough information to form a hypothesis. We must continue to observe."

Over the next weeks, the Seed began to circle again, expelling its liquids and even more gathered matter. Joanna watched, transfixed as the hours went by, her eyes glued to various feeds every waking moment. The Seed moved at near the speed of light around the dwarf, maintaining a distant orbit, making four rings of muddy liquid that instantly froze.

When its stores seemed exhausted, the Seed stopped its expulsion, and with its gravity set the rings spinning.

"I don't understand," she breathed one day. "Why don't I understand? It destroyed so many systems . . . for this? Is it a failed experiment? A weak attempt at replication? What good . . . ?" she trailed off, biting her lip.

She knew her dark eyes must be wide and startled—like those of a concerned child. That's exactly what she felt like: a child who could not comprehend a grownup's actions.

"It pains me to admit that I don't know what it's doing," she confessed to I.C.C. "It burns my insides like a gut-shot from a deep-shock bar. I could keep speculating, but there's been far too much of that on this . . . *trip*." She spat out the last word as though it had left black rot on her tongue. "We shouldn't have interfered in the first place if we didn't understand. That is a fatal flaw in human nature. Our curiosity is too strong, and our noses tend to find themselves in places they don't belong."

"Yes," said I.C.C. in a distinctly solemn tone.

Joanna let her forehead fall against the monitor in her quarters. Its cool, smooth quality soothed the pounding in her head. "All I know is this . . . It's creating instead of destroying. I have to take that at face value." *I don't know how else to take it.*

She recalled, then, a good moment she'd had with her father. When he'd taught her about planetary creation. It didn't justify his years of abuse, but . . . it helped stay her hand now.

At least the wretched man's memory was good for something.

Except, the next morning, the Seed went back to destroying.

It crashed through one ring, then another, hurling sections this way and that. The icy pieces threatened to leave orbit, but were drawn back by the well of the brown dwarf. The falling portions collided with other remainders of the rings, fracturing them into smaller and smaller scraps as the Seed continued its carefully calculated march of devastation.

Everything seemed to happen so fast. Cataclysmic cosmic events that usually took eons were happing in a relative blink.

Months later, the ring fragments were directed to coalesce by beams of energy from the Seed. The beams left behind four globes—three rocky planets and one gas giant, all encircling the brown dwarf in broad, distant orbits—each with its own large moon. Joanna thought the moons very curious.

After completing the planets, the Seed continued to circumnavigate its children, spraying each with more liquid. Water and nitrogen and methane fell to the surfaces. Oceans splayed out over the planets.

"I want us to be ready, for when it's finished," Joanna told the cabinet, once again aboard *Eden*, this time in the tropical quarter. The first flowers of the season were blooming, unfurling their petals among clusters of small new leaves on rope-like vines and stems. The air smelled of nectar, and the false-sun's rays felt unseasonably warm. The squawking of a toucan echoed in the distance. "I want to know the exact composition of those planets, their orbits, and their rotations. In the meantime, anyone have postulations as to why the Seed is building a modest brown dwarf star system?"

Anatoly, his typically smug features flat, said, "Doctor Ka'uhane—" he waved his hand briefly in the astronomer's direction "—thinks the central object isn't a brown dwarf—just a gas giant. In which case the *planets—the smaller gas giant included*—have to be called *moons*."

She crossed her arms. "Your point being?" She widened her stance in a display of rigid self-assurance, but the effect was spoiled by her knocking over the metal briefcase she'd brought with her. She let the case lie in the ferns.

"We're looking at this too simplistically," Anatoly said. "Just like the way we approached the Web. As we saw a sphere and attributed familiar scientific hypothesis to it, we now see what appear to be common cosmic objects and are attributing typical behaviors to them. But what if they don't adhere to Newtonian physics? Or what if they aren't as inanimate as they seem?

"What I'm suggesting," he said, raising his voice in spite of the cabinet's blank stares, "is that the Seed might be creating another machine. One whose function and processes we can't disrupt this time."

"We have the power to destroy the Seed. You think we can't destroy those planets as well?" Joanna asked.

"That's not what I meant."

"I understand what you meant. If it's a machine it's most likely one we can't stick our wriggling little fingers into. No cogs to place, no wires to bond. You're saying the Web's creators had us and other unsuspecting civilizations work on a machine that we *can* understand in order for it to manufacture a machine we cannot. Interesting idea, I'll give you. But what's the point, I ask, if we can just blow it all to smithereens anyway?"

"Perhaps it's disguised as it is so that we'll hesitate." The accusation in his tone was palpable; it stuck to the roof of Joanna's mouth like a wad of peanut butter.

"Or perhaps your alarmist behavior is just what it's after," said Captain Nakamura. The cabinet turned toward her with eyebrows raised. "Doctor Ka'uhane, what would happen to Earth should a supernova or the like occur at this proximity?"

Dr. Ka'uhane wrung her hands, and her lips opened and closed like a fish's. She hated being put on the spot, and everyone knew it. "Well, it, uh, should the blast be angled just so, that is, well—"

"Spit it out," demanded *Aesop*'s captain.

"The resulting wave of gamma radiation could rain down on the planet and terminally irradiate much of its life. It might even blow away atmosphere and meddle with their magnetic field," she finished with an audible gulp.

"There's not enough mass there to create a supernova," said Anatoly, understandably skeptical.

"Oh, no?" said Joanna. Popping open the metal briefcase, she extracted several sets of 'flex-sheets and passed them around. "It's eaten eight main sequence stars that we know of. Who knows how many it might have lifted before the Nest got to it? Ten solar masses are plenty enough to create a type II supernova."

Dr. Ka'uhane eagerly nodded her agreement.

"What are these?" asked Anatoly, squinting at the images cycling across one of his 'flex-sheets.

"Images taken an hour ago—of the Seed. I know it's hard to make out—we're too far out to resolve the picture properly—but I'd like to draw your attention to these three dots." She pointed just off the concave side of the Seed.

"They look like errors. A problem with the camera?" asked the captain of *Morgan*.

"I.C.C. would not have reported errors," Joanna said out of the side of her mouth. "These are objects, each roughly the size of a major Earth city, expelled from cavities within the Seed. I.C.C. tells me one fell to each rocky planet, and all were lost to its sensors because they sank in the oceans.

"What Nakamura seems to be suggesting, and correct me if I'm wrong, is that the Seed or its new planets could be waiting for us to strike. Say we assault the planets and trigger those objects—the addition of our weapon's energy could send a carefully balanced matter-containment system over the edge, triggering a nova-like event."

"Or those objects could be for something else entirely," said Dr. Ka'uhane with a smile. The pep in her voice made the others look at her as though she'd just proposed they run naked through the corridors: a mix of reprimand, disgust, and skeptical amusement. She was normally reticent, quiet. Perhaps Joanna wasn't the only one holding on to a ray of hope.

"Yes," Joanna said warmly. That's what she'd prefer to think. "So, we need to organize probe missions. We've got to find those objects and determine their function."

"Not probes, people," insisted Dr. Johar, her chief of science.

"I won't order anyone to the surface."

“Then ask for volunteers,” he said. “The science division has been dying for a chance like this. Let them go.”

Though her gut told her good things were happening out there, she still didn’t feel prepared to let her crew risk coming into close proximity with the Seed or anything it might create. Johar’s use of *dying* struck her as particularly problematic. But she saw on the faces of those around her that giving in on this one point would raise their morale. If she wouldn’t let them kill it, she had to let them study it. Investigation was in their genes.

After all, she’d approved an away mission before. Now she’d let them complete it.

“All right,” she conceded. “Volunteers only. And I want to brief them personally. They have to know my concerns. Know that if I can convince them to stay, I will. And I don’t want anyone to set foot in the oceans. They can go to the surface, but they are not to personally come within a kilometer of those objects. Remote study only.”

“Fine.”

Joanna stood, tense, on the bridge. She never sat on duty anymore—hyperattuned to every bump and vibration the ship made, her bones couldn’t bear to stay parked.

Though the away shuttles had disappeared from view hours ago, she continued to stare at their vanishing point, anxious for a visual sign that the teams were all right. They’d cut communication with the convoy as a precaution. They had no idea what might set off the Seed, which hung like a chrysalis only a few AUs away from the outermost planet, so they were taking no chances. Only once the teams gathered their first findings would they risk contact.

The trajectories of the objects had been easily plotted, so the team shouldn’t have any issues locating them. She suspected there might be problems analyzing them, though. In all the centuries the convoy had spent in close proximity to the Seed, no one had ever detected such objects within. She could chalk it up to sensor failure; the Seed had never appreciated getting prodded and scanned.

It didn't make it easier to accept, though. The Seed had hidden these things—what else could it hide?

When a team finally called in—from the planet they were currently calling P3—she instructed the feed to broadcast live throughout the convoy. Nothing they could find could send the crew into a panic the way her initial inaction had. For better or worse, she wanted everyone to experience the discovery at the same time.

And *there*—she caught it. A twinkle of hope. The entire force of her continuum was focused on what was happening millions of kilometers away.

She straightened her rumpled uniform—the fabric soft with overwear—and took a deep breath. "All right, go ahead."

The audio report was accompanied by images of the surface and the data scans.

With the brown dwarf distant and cold, and the skies consisting of bare wisps of atmosphere, the surface lay in twilight. Muted, muddy reds and grays covered the land, punctuated by the occasional bright orange hot spot of volcanic activity. Joanna could almost smell the sulfuric acid from her command post.

"The object here on the third planet," began the appointed reporter, "is a compartmentalized capsule, filled with three kinds of mixtures. We've speculated that the greater amounts of fluids stored in the Seed previously masked its existence.

"Each concoction in the capsule has a different ratio and combination of materials. There are three assortments. The first contains ammonia, methane, hydrogen, water, and a few other trace elements. The second set contains three different sugars, bases, and phosphates."

Was she imagining things, or did that second set sound familiar? Could it mean . . . ? Her cheeks burned, tender and tingly with possibility. A swell of emotion rose in her chest—one that she could not say was connected to any named feeling she'd ever had before.

"The final set," continued the narrator, his own voice cracking with emotion, "contains *premade* RNA, tRNA, and simple amino acids. There are also smaller, empty compartments located in the capsules, leading us to believe that the soups were only recently mixed. And the capsules are abuzz with electricity, clearly there to help facilitate reactions."

We've all been so, so wrong.

It is not a Dyson Sphere.

It is not a Star Killer.

It is a God Machine.

As if reading her mind, the audio chimed in, "The Seed appears to be making a system that can support life."

A glimmer of logic broke through the pure wave of emotion wracking Joanna's mind. *Life, life!* most of her screamed, while a small fraction of her being prodded her pattern recognition centers.

It's too cold, her logic said. *Life can't arise around a frigid half star.*

"Get out of there!" she screamed suddenly, realization breaking through. "The Seed's not done. Get the hell back to the fleet, now!" She turned on the communications officer. "Tell all of the teams to come back, and to leave any equipment they might have set up. It's not worth the risk. If they don't abandon the mission this instant, they could all die. The system needs a better sun."

Though they had no visuals, the crew could sense the mad dash as the away teams broke communications to adhere to her orders. Silent minutes passed. There wasn't a living being on board not holding its breath. Everyone from the engineers to the security division, to the cows on *Eden* and the house cats in their cabins. Even I.C.C. seemed to still.

Get out of there, Joanna chanted. It could happen at any moment: the Seed's final act. The only thing left for it to do.

The brown dwarf needed more mass. And there was only one logical way to get it, now that thc Seed had emptied itself.

Get free. Get free of the orbits.

As if knowing it was being thought about, the Seed shifted, rotating ninety degrees to aim one pointed end at the heart of the brown dwarf.

"Away team one," she said after ordering a comms channel open, "are you secure? Away teams two and three, report."

Like a lumbering animal charging a mortal enemy, the Seed thrust forward. Its movements were languid-looking, considering the distances involved. The Seed would not reach its final destination for hours, or even days, but the ensuing gravitational ripples made the area dangerous, would give the returning shuttles trouble. Could cause them to crash back to the planets' surfaces.

Everyone on the bridge leaned forward, waiting, listening.

"What's it doing?" someone asked of the Seed.

"Finishing the job," Joanna said.

She still had no visual of her people.

"Are you secure?" she repeated. "Are you out of orbit?"

She held her breath.

"We're all okay," came the ecstatic reply.

She clutched at her chest in relief.

A collective cheer rang out across the bridge. 'Flex-sheets flew into the air. Some officers clapped their approval. Others jumped to their feet.

"Yes," Joanna said to herself. "We're all okay."

Joanna stared at the Seed as she never had before, filled both with dread and admiration, but not disgust. Their great enemy was about to perform a sacrifice—to cast itself in the brown dwarf to provide the would-be sun with enough mass to begin its fusion. The convoy's long history with the Seed was coming to an end. Soon no trace of the alien artifact, no record of the trillions of hours of construction or the great struggle of their pursuit, would remain.

The brown dwarf ate the megastructure with glee, burgeoning. Bit by long bit, the Seed disappeared, gone forever, consumed in a swirling soup of dark gasses and bright fires. The star expanded, and the four planets fell into tighter orbits—the three rocky planets descending into what had to be the habitable zone. Each fogged as the greenhouse effect took hold and created thick atmospheres. The gas giant's orbit changed as well, but it remained far afield of the other planets, sweeping the vicinity, like a protective sibling, gobbling up extra debris to prevent it from raining down on its rocky neighbors.

This gas giant would do for this system what Jupiter did for Sol's.

The moons made sense now. Bigger moons played an important role in orbit stability and reduced planet wobble—she knew that much about planetology. Large moons even helped regulate climate.

Stability, safety . . . both important factors, when concerned with a planet's suitability for life.

At least two civilizations had been disrupted to bring this system into existence. She'd risked her command, her crew, her mental well-being to see the Web's legacy through to the end. She couldn't wait to see what these planets had in store for the convoy, for Earth—for the *galaxy*.

The crew of Convoy Seven were happier than they'd been in years, excited for the exploration and study to come. Joanna herself was awed, overwhelmed. The sense of wonder would not leave her, and she basked in the feeling.

And, finally, she could put her father's ghost to rest. She'd been able to accomplish what no other Joanna had even dreamed of. She hadn't succeeded where others had failed—instead, she'd sought her own path.

She'd been raised a warrior, but it was the heart of an explorer that beat in her chest, and its desires had saved them all.

CHAPTER ELEVEN

CONVOY TWELVE

VANHI: THE UNIVERSE IS NO WILDERNESS

SEVEN HUNDRED AND THIRTY-ONE DAYS SINCE THE ACCIDENT

Vanhi felt like a ping-pong ball.

Back and forth, back and forth. One minute she was in the EOL talking to Gabriel, or eating lunch, or walking through the hall. The next she was by Stone's side. She'd get a few uninterrupted weeks—sometimes months—and then she'd disappear again, winking out of existence only to appear in Stone's presence what felt like moments later. Only it wasn't moments. It wasn't even minutes or hours or days.

The length of her absence was getting longer with every jump.

Seconds ago—she could have sworn, only seconds—the convoy-wide emergency alert had sounded.

What had happened before then? *Think, Vanhi, think.* Her short-term memory recall was always stunted right after a jump, which only heightened her sense of disorientation.

She'd been working on an experiment pod. Right. Checking the AI's threshold for SD propagation containment, when Dalisay Ocampo had come in with a sizzling shock baton and ushered her out of the shuttle maintenance hangar. Vanhi had demanded an explanation, told her Captain Tan would hear of this, and Dalisay had *laughed*. Not *at* Vanhi, per se. It wasn't a cruel laugh, it was self-satisfied. Almost relieved in its effervescence.

Mutiny! Vanhi remembered. Captain Baglanova had taken control—or had he only tried?

Now, in the blink of an eye, all was quiet once again. But her heart was still hammering at her insides, her adrenaline still surged. She was ready for a fight, a struggle, but the room around her lay calm.

She was no longer on *Breath*. This was *Pulse* for sure—she'd recognize those blue-and-red walls anywhere.

Stone's quarters were slowly getting brighter. The dimmer was automatically bringing up the lights to mimic sunrise. He was still in bed, covers half on, half off, with one naked leg dangling over the side of the mattress. His chest rose and fell steadily.

She quickly leaned over him. Not to rouse him, but to get a better look out the window.

The *Lùhng* ships seemed farther away than she remembered. But they were still there.

Stone made an endearing whimper, like a puppy, before snorting awake.

Willing her heart to slow and her breath to steady, she kissed him on the forehead.

When she started to pull away he stopped her, wiped the sleep from his eyes, and said, "Thank god. I was so worried. When they couldn't find you, I'd hoped you'd jumped."

"Shh. It's okay, I'm here. What happened?"

He sat up and put his arms around her. He smelled warm and spicy. "Yeah, everything's okay now. Well, not okay, but it's not worse, at least. Let me start the non-Joe, and I'll tell you everything."

Non-Joe was what they called the strange brew of hot

water, caffeine pills, and artificial kahlua flavoring that served as convoy coffee. Not many people prepared it on the regular, but Stone liked to be shocked awake.

Throwing off the covers, perfectly comfortable in nothing but his tags and birthday suit—*So different from that time in the shower,* Vanhi thought fondly—he scratched at his bare backside and dragged his feet all the way into the kitchenette. While he worked, he detailed the mutiny for her, as well as he understood the events.

"The conspirators on *Pulse* gave up almost as soon as the order was given. Baglanova . . . he didn't make it."

"He's *dead*?"

Stone nodded.

She let that sink in for a moment, then asked, "And where are the rest of the perpetrators now?"

"En el Oso Blanco de Convoy Doce."

She shook her head, confused.

"The brig, Vanhi. They're in the brig. Where else would they be?"

"Dead, too," she said flatly.

"Well, some are. Went down in the fight. But Tan doesn't believe in the death penalty, especially now that . . ." he trailed off. "You sure you don't want a cup?"

She wrinkled her nose. "No. Wait, actually, let me change that to 'Hell, no.'"

He shrugged, grabbing his full mug and strolling back over to the bed to sit beside her. He very modestly pulled a blanket across his legs.

"You've been gone for about—" He wriggled his fingers in the air, as though he didn't know exactly how long it had been off the top of his head. "Six weeks and three days. Give or take. Right, Broki?"

"Right, Stone."

Vanhi smiled. "Broki?"

"Yeah. C's my little buddy." He smiled into his mug. "Don't make fun of me—you make it call you 'sir.'" He stood up rigidly and saluted, the gesture made all the more ridiculous by his nakedness. "Yes, sir, Vanhi, sir."

She playfully stuck her tongue out at him.

"Anyway, since then we've only heard from the *Lùhng* once." He took a swig of his non-Joe and grimaced.

"And?"

"And they pretty much put us in our place. Now that our SD drives are all but lifeless pieces of junk, we're stuck, no question. They informed us Earth itself told them not to interfere with us, save when essential, because of—and this is a direct quote—the 'volatile nature of Homo sapiens.' Well, we went and proved them right, didn't we? Good ol' volatile humans, ready to lash out violently because we're uncomfortable."

"So they no longer consider themselves Homo sapiens?"

"No. They didn't give us a new designation, but Justice has taken to calling them *Homo draconem*."

"Their message also suggests that . . . that there *aren't* any Homo sapiens anymore."

"That is the assumption we're working with, yes. But I guess we'll learn more when the Progentor arrives."

Vanhi didn't know how to feel about any of this. She thought that such a severe revelation—the extinction of her entire species—might manifest as a gut punch or nausea, or delirium. But it felt abstract—too unreal to *be* real. Like suggesting that the sun had been replaced with star anise or that SD drives were fueled by tacos: ridiculous.

Tan doesn't believe in the death penalty, especially now . . . now that we're the only Homo sapiens left alive.

"Justice's theory—" she said, "about the crew, our infertility, has she come to a firm conclusion yet?"

"Everyone who's hit puberty has to submit for mandatory

testing now, so she can be sure. I went in last week." He rubbed at his face. "I can make your appointment, if you'd like."

Her old guilt reared its head.

Whatever had happened to the rest of humanity—whether it had all evolved into something new, or had died out—she couldn't take the blame for that, no. But she had undoubtedly condemned the crew to a reality without people. They were the last of their kind, members of a soon-to-be extinct species found roaming in the wilderness, starving and homeless.

No wonder the *Lùhng* had stuck to them like ticks. No wonder the post-humans had seemed distant, estranged.

She and many others had thought their separatism a sign of disrespect or disinterest, when really the *Lùhng* had shown great restraint. If Earth had ordered them not to interfere, they hadn't listened, not really. They'd probably had to justify every interaction as being essential to Convoy Twelve survival, even when, truthfully, it had been to sate their own curiosity.

"What's . . . what's a Pro-gentor?" she asked suddenly, almost absently. She was trying to assimilate too much new information at once.

"We're not sure. Carmen says Kali finger spelled it, so who knows if that's even really what they were trying to say. I think maybe it's a ship, carrying government officials or something. Justice thinks . . ." He went quiet.

"What? What does she think?"

"She's just worried," he said quietly. "I don't think she really believes it. We were speculating . . ."

"Tell me."

He sighed. "Maybe it's a weapon. Something more effective than their 'whump.' Not to kill us, but maybe to *control* us." He waved the idea away, as though he didn't want to deal with it. "Whatever it is, the *Lùhng* have sworn off interacting with us until it gets here."

She shook her head and looked out the window again. His

words were starting to burrow in. She fisted the blankets, and after a moment realized she was shaking.

"Hey," Stone said, putting a soothing hand on her arm. It was warm from the non-Joe. "I know it's a lot."

"Yeah," she said, the acknowledgment bursting out of her. "No kidding."

"I'm just glad you're back safe."

She leaned into him in a half hug and tried not to let her thoughts become words. *If I hadn't caved to Kaufman, none of this would have happened. None of us would ever have dreamed of a future without humans, let alone needed to live in one.*

It wasn't fair to herself—but it for damn sure wasn't fair that they were stuck here, either.

She gripped Stone a little tighter.

Another two jumps and it was December already. Sometimes she got to stick around for months, sometimes only a few weeks. Time flies when you're not ruled by it.

She reappeared in Stone's quarters once again. Their quarters, really. She rarely went to hers anymore. The room was pitch black, and Stone was softly snoring away in bed. Vanhi threw off her work uniform, found a night shirt, and tucked herself in behind him.

"Hmm?" he asked vaguely, shifting aside for her, so that she pressed against his back with an arm slung over him. Stone automatically entwined his fingers with hers.

"Just me," she reassured him, nosing at his neck.

"Thought you might miss New Year's," he said, voice sleep heavy.

Had it really been that long? Almost three months.

"Why do you keep waiting for me?" she asked.

He was clearly too groggy to understand. "Why wouldn't I wait for you?"

Three months is a long time to . . . to hope to see someone

again. She could easily imagine what it would feel like, not to see Stone every day, but thinking she might. *Now is he coming back? Oh, someone's behind me, is it him?* The excitement, the anxiety, the constant state of readiness—it had to hurt. Had to be difficult to live with every day.

"I missed you," he said.

She held him tighter. "I missed you, too." She'd only seen him a half an hour ago, but she suddenly realized how very long ago that half an hour had been. She missed him desperately now, in this very instant, as though to make up for all that time she hadn't experienced.

"What do you miss most about winter? Back on Earth?" he asked, oblivious to her sudden, relentless need for him. "I miss coquito. It's like eggnog, but better. Would never drink non-Joe again if I could have one more sip of coquito. What about you?"

She shook off her swell of emotion, trying to keep her voice steady so as not to worry him. "My little sister begging for a Christmas tree," she said. "Papa hated it. You know how some kids go around bugging their parents for a puppy? It was like that, but for a Christmas tree. She liked the lights—the Christmas lights—just like Diwali lights. Papa would go out of his way to make Diwali extra special for us, and I think it was in an effort to keep Swara from asking about a Christmas tree once winter hit. But, when you're young, and most of your friends' family traditions are different than yours, it's difficult to understand why you shouldn't have a pretty tree like they do. Every year Papa said no, but every year he caved.

"If Swara'd had her way, there would have been a festival of lights every month. She put up strings and strings of them in our bedroom, the little twinkling ones. I always loved them, too, but I made her do all the begging by herself. I miss the lights. And I miss . . ." Her voice caught in her throat.

Now she missed Swara, too. And her parents, and Parth,

and everyone—her cousins in Pakistan, her little nephew, Ryan.

She snuggled in deeper and tried not to cry.

Stone rolled over to face her. "I'm sorry," he said, rubbing a thumb under her eye. "I didn't mean to."

"I know," she said, trying to sound chipper. But there was a hole in her chest now, and it felt so deep, she wasn't sure it could ever be filled.

"I'm sorry," he said again, and kissed her.

Vanhi sank into the kiss, letting it take the sadness, letting Stone breathe calmness and love into that deep, dark feeling.

She got to stay for New Year's. She made some progress with the pods—not in discerning what had caused their original accident, but in deciphering how the *Lùhng* had disabled them. The strange green blossoming waves the *Lùhng* had generated had apparently precipitated micro black holes—or something similar: more stable and destructive, yet equally short-lived—within some of the key components. The weapon had indeed been designed to target SD drives specifically.

But she wasn't sure how such precision targeting was achieved, nor if they would be able to find all of the damaged points, seeing as how each black hole equivalent had evaporated nanoseconds after it was formed, punching perfect little holes directly inside parts that looked otherwise undamaged.

She was anticipating a long drawn-out discussion with Gabriel about the findings when she jumped.

When she came back, she came back grumpy. Facing a blank wall, putting both hands on it to steady herself, she let herself gripe. "Son of a . . ." She was so sick, so utterly sick of—

Someone cleared their throat behind her.

It didn't sound like Stone.

With a deep breath she straightened, turned—and realized she was in the situation room on *Pulse*. Every seat at the long table was occupied. Justice stood in front of a wall screen, clearly in the middle of a presentation.

All eyes were on Vanhi, and she tried not to feel embarrassed, but that was easier thought than lived.

Stone, thankfully, was in attendance. "Here, take my seat," he insisted.

Trying to make herself as small as possible, she sheepishly slunk over to him, plopping herself down in the chair.

"Do you need anything?" he whispered in her ear. "Water?"

"Water, yes, please." She feigned an itch on her forehead and ducked her head, hiding her face. As Stone moved to the refreshment cart, she apologized and bade Dr. Jax continue.

"It's all right, we can take a short break if you—"

"Thank you, I'm fine."

Justice nodded, then cleared her throat. "In summary, I've concluded my analysis of the *Homo draconem* sample. That doesn't mean I've come anywhere close to mapping the genome of the entire *Lùhng* family—this sample is very old, has likely been made obsolete by their current modifications, and there could be dozens, or hundreds, or, if every individual is uniquely modified, infinite branches on the *Homo draconem* family tree.

"The good news is, this isn't simply an academic exercise. I believe my studies provide a firm foundation for addressing our unusual ailments. For instance, as I'm sure many of you know by now, eight people thus far have attempted to get pregnant, and all have been unable."

Vanhi had spoken with several of the individuals who'd attempted to conceive. They'd each thought they would be the one, that it couldn't really be a convoy-wide problem. It was almost as though they thought that if they could have a healthy child, their world wouldn't be so upside-down.

In a way, she knew how they felt. A little semblance of normalcy could go a long way.

"The entire crew, all except for the children under thirteen, have been subject to fertility testing," Justice continued. "And the results are conclusive. All of our sex cells are unviable. The cell walls are weak—the spermatozoa and ovum annihilate instead of merge. And even when the medical staff attempted to lab-grow embryos for implantation, zygote cleavage did not occur and no blastomeres were formed.

"We don't have the capacity to clone the same way our fellow convoys did. But I fear, even if we did, we would not be able to produce a viable fetus. I believe there's an unidentified problem in our genetic code itself, and until we can pinpoint the problem *and* solve it, we, as a species, cannot procreate."

Everyone shifted uncomfortably. They'd suspected as much, but that didn't make the confirmation any easier to stomach.

"Now that we are fairly confident Homo sapiens such as ourselves are obsolete anyway," Justice went on, "if not outright extinct, we need to decide what's important to us. It seems obvious, basic even, that we should want to preserve our species. But humans *haven't* died out. Our legacy lives on. Why shouldn't we understand ourselves as just another rung on the ladder of evolution, and accept that time has passed us by?

"Well, practically speaking, this presents a dilemma. If the *Lùhng* never interact with us again, we're facing a reality where we all grow old and die aboard a facility that is not designed to care for geriatric patients. There will be no caretakers, no other workers. And someone will inevitably be the last human, alone, left to run the ships *by themself.*

"So, ultimately, we need to decide how to proceed. Presuming the Progentor isn't what we suspect—" Vanhi noticed a small hitch in Justice's voice when she said "Progentor" "—and the *Lùhng* have no plans to deal with us, no place to take us, then we will live aboard Convoy Twelve for the rest of our lives.

If we have no viable children, both our species' survival and our own personal survival are at risk.

"I, for one, don't think that's our path. Further, I believe I can use my understanding of *Lùhng* DNA to help us. If there's any chance I can convince the *Lùhng* to share their modification techniques, we might not be so in the weeds. But, even if I can't—if, as I said, they've totally abandoned us—then I believe the sample we have is enough to set us on the path to developing gene therapies and other modifications that might be able to correct the genetic defect.

"Isn't that counterintuitive?" asked Glen Harrisburg from the *Breath* command crew.

"What do you mean?" Justice asked, crossing her arms, jutting out her jaw, clearly perturbed by the interruption.

"If the idea is to preserve Homo sapiens," Glen continued, "doesn't modifying our DNA make us something else? Aren't we just another version of *Homo draconem*, then? We need to survive, yes, but *purity* is important. Isn't that how the other convoys were designed? With an emphasis on genetic preservation? We don't want to become the *Lùhng* and lose the very thing we're trying to save. I feel we should stay away from modifications at all costs; they are clearly a blight on the human virtues we're striving to preserve."

Justice made a surprised expression, but quickly squashed it. Nodding to herself and pursing her lips, she leaned on the table to look Glen in the eye, and said pointedly, "First, I'd like to point out that the consortium's view on genetics was *never* widely accepted by the majority of geneticists. You might not have been taught about the scientific uproar their decision caused, but I was. The consortium claimed they chose clones to preserve talents—and yes, I'm sure to some degree it did that. But they disregarded the very well-known part environment plays in a person's life. We are *totally* our genes, and we are *totally* our experiences. The two are unquestionably intertwined. I believe they ultimately decided to go with clones to solve a very concrete staffing problem. Above all, they either couldn't find the volunteers or didn't want to lose the people they already had. So, they compromised. Whatever the case, their emphasis on genetic consistency has never been ours, and there's no reason to adopt it now."

Glen raised a finger, on the verge of interrupting again. She cut him off and continued. "Secondly, human beings have been modifying themselves since time immemorial. Every piercing, swath of body art, and slather of makeup is a modification. Eyeglasses, hearing aids, artificial limbs, all modifications." She gestured up and down his torso. "Clothes—a classic.

"The thing is, any given modification is neither innately positive or negative. Tattoos you choose for yourself—like Mac's *Pe'a*—are good, while tattoos thrust upon you—like in a concentration camp—are bad. It's the situation, not the tattoo in and of itself, which makes the difference."

She took a deep breath, centering herself. "As a trans woman, I have modifications that help me fight my body dysmorphia. I am alive today because I was able to change my outer appearance to fit who I am. Other trans women choose to take their modifications even further, others choose to make fewer changes than I have. There's no one right way to live as a trans person—or cis, or nonbinary, or intersex person, etc.—because *there is no 'right way'* to be human. Individuals are unique and require different modifications—or no modifications—based on their specific wants and needs.

"If humans can modify themselves and their surroundings to keep on living once they've been born, to make their lives better, why shouldn't our entire species be modified if it's the difference between life and death? And it *is*, believe me. The line we want to draw between ourselves and the *Lùhng—us* and *them*—is artificial. There's nothing wrong with thinking our current forms have value and deserve to be preserved, but the idea that it's original model or scrap the whole line, that it's purity or nothing—which has been a racist dog whistle for centuries, *just saying*—is all, frankly, fundamentalist *bullshit*."

"Yes, but . . ." Glen stuttered. "There is a point where you're not preserving a species any more, you've changed it so much that it's not the same genus. Not even in the same ballpark. If we're going to get all high and mighty about saving our race, doesn't it still have to be *our* race?"

"This is not a scientific argument you're making," she said. "Life isn't *actually* divided into the neat taxonomies we try to shove it into—never has been, never will be. All life is a continuum—evolution is a continuum—and evolution guarantees change. It is the ultimate mechanism of preservation; the ability to be modified. There is no biodiversity without it. There are no Homo sapiens—no *Homo draconem*, no *Homo habilis*, or *Australopithecus*, on and on."

She stood straight and crossed her arms in a dare. "Do you see what I'm getting at? Am I getting through? *You* don't exist without modification. None of us do."

"All right," Tan said. "Doctor Jax, you've made your point. You are absolutely right, we need to adapt to survive. But what concerns me, here, is that we have none of the usual medical safeguards, and no way to apply them. How will you test your 'modifications,' be they gene therapy, medications, new prebuilt DNA chains, or otherwise?"

"If I decide to build some humans from scratch, we can discuss the ethical ramifications of failure then. For now, I'm not prepared to go that far. Most testing will have to be done purely through digital modeling. From there, I'll need volunteers. "

"Oh, great," said Glen. "I always wanted to be a guinea pig."

"Vol-un-t—"

"I'll do it," Vanhi said, cutting off Justice's sarcastic reply.

Everyone turned sharply.

"Especially if these modifications include one to keep me here, in the greater dimensions. I have no problem taking part in whatever human trials you need me to."

It was the easiest decision she'd ever made. She already felt like her life was one big experiment-gone-wrong. And she'd roped all of these people into it. If it helped the crew, that was more important than any possible harm she might suffer.

Stone squeezed her shoulder, handing her a glass of water.

"Thank you for trusting me," Justice said. "But I'll need others. This is going to take a long time, I want to make that clear. There are no magical cures or overnight fixes. And there's no guarantee, no matter how many resources we pour into this, that it'll solve anything."

"We'll make it happen," Vanhi countered. "I know we can."

ONE THOUSAND ONE HUNDRED AND ELEVEN

DAYS SINCE THE ACCIDENT

. . . OR APPROXIMATELY THREE YEARS

More jumps, more missing time, more hours with Stone and days in the lab. Everything was happening so quickly and so slowly all at once. The mood aboard the convoy shifted instantaneously to Vanhi, though in actuality morale went through dips and curves over long periods.

It had been over a year, and still no Progentor. Justice wasn't anywhere near developing something she could test on Vanhi, and the SD investigation department was chugging along under Gabriel's direction just fine.

In fact, Gabriel was certain they'd found the source of the accident, the very reason pod thirty-three had malfunctioned in the first place, tipping over the first domino that sent all the rest toppling.

It was a single line of misexecuted code. Essentially, one

if/then command had been misinterpreted by the mini-drive computer as having a secondary "then" action that the programmers hadn't intended. It was amazing the command had been executed correctly in the thirty-two launches preceding.

Which meant it was no one's fault, really. One defective command had caused cascading failures.

It was a simple mistake.

With devastating consequences.

Just like my mistakes, Vanhi thought.

And now that Gabriel had the investigation well in hand without her, she wasn't really sure where she fit in anymore.

When she opened her eyes after the next jump, her vision was blurred—the aftereffects were always slightly different; it felt like being squeezed in and out of your skin through completely different pores. The only thing she knew for sure was that she was surrounded by lights.

They weren't the delicate lights of a Christmas tree, nor the glaring fluorescents of a clean room, or the harsh pinpoints of lasers. They were everything else—all kinds. Flashlight bulbs, microscope bulbs, night-lights, overhead lamps, faux candles, and emergency exit stripping. Everything glowed.

"What in . . . ?"

As the scene came into focus, she realized she was in the mess hall, but it glittered like a diamond, reflective surfaces and facets everywhere. The walls were lined with lights and bits of shiny things. Most of the tables were empty, save for sets of clustered lights.

Alone, in the center, reading a book at his usual dining spot and wearing sunglasses (of all things), was Stone.

"Look at that, Broki, you win," he said, lifting the sundial from where it dangled. "Four months and ten hours."

"Pay up," chirped C.

"Gladly." He extricated himself from the table and held out his hand for Vanhi.

“What’s this?” she asked, at a loss for an assumption of her own.

“Everyone helped, the whole convoy,” he said. “Every light they could spare. I wanted to give you something you missed.”

She quickly tried to calculate what month it was. “It’s not time for Diwali. Or Christmas.”

“No,” he admitted. “But it’s high time for something happy.”

She took his offered hand, but quickly let it go again. Something came away in her palm.

It was a plain steel band.

Her heart fluttered and her breath caught in her chest.

“And what’s this?” she asked, cheeky.

“Well, I made a bet with C about when you’d come back this time. I promised I’d ask you to marry me if it won.”

She closed the ring in her hand and propped her fist on her hip. “You’re asking me to marry you because you lost a bet with my PA?”

He shrugged noncommittally. “Them’s the rules.”

“And if you’d won? Would C be asking for my hand instead?”

“Sir, he’s being facetious,” said C. “We made no assumptions about your return. Stone has occupied the mess, alone, for eight evenings in a row. The bet is simply a playful pretext for—”

She grabbed the sundial, yanking Stone forward by the chain. “Thank you, C.” She laughed against Stone’s lips. “I get it.”

She kissed him with fervor, savoring everything about the moment. Her entire being was warm and relaxed, from her head to her toes. It all tingled in a good way, and Stone was strong against her, but pliant in her arms.

It was all so perfect.

She broke the kiss.

Too perfect.

"Is that a yes?" he asked, grin wide.

"I—Not yet. There's something I need to tell you."

She didn't want to. She'd intended to take her guilt to the grave. But *she* was the reason they were here. She was the reason so many people had been separated from their loved ones—wives, husbands, lovers. Why should she get a happy ending with Stone when her mistakes had robbed so many others of theirs?

His smile immediately faded, and she didn't know how to reassure him. "I love you," she said firmly, not wanting him to doubt that for a moment. "But I haven't been honest about . . . about . . ."

Memories filled her throat, choked off her words.

It had been too long and was still too soon.

She led him over to a bench seat. He put his arm around her, but didn't say anything.

She clutched the ring tighter, took a deep breath, and began. "I only became Convoy Twelve's mission head because Doctor Kaufman, my advisor, destroyed Doctor Campbell's career. On purpose. He lied . . . And I knew." She paused, swallowing harshly, willing herself to go on. Stone was quiet.

"I *knew*," she continued, "and I didn't say anything. I thought I was protecting all of the convoys—I thought that if more corruption was revealed that the whole consortium might go up in flames—" *Did I really think that? Or was I just protecting myself?* "Or . . ." The words caught in her throat. "Maybe I was just a coward. Either way, my complacency is why we're here. It's why Tan's daughter never got to wake up. It's why we'll never see Earth again. It's why everyone was separated from their families and have been forced to live in these stupid ships for the rest of their lives. Everything that's happened is on *me*."

The truth made her throat ache and her voice vibrate. She wasn't crying, but her head hurt with the potential for tears.

And she couldn't look at Stone. His grip on her shoulder had gotten tighter and tighter as she spoke, but she couldn't tell if he was clutching at her protectively, or in anger.

"I should have told you—I should have told everyone. I know the truth doesn't fix anything, I know it makes it so much worse. But I can't let you . . . *ask me this* . . . without knowing."

"Did you ask him to do it?" Stone asked, voice deep and inscrutable.

"No. No, I didn't. I would never do something like that." She cut off his next question. "And yes, he did threaten me—my career, my parents' home. But that doesn't matter. What I did . . . *I* did. And I can never make up for it."

"What do you want me to say? To absolve you of blame? To forgive you?"

She bucked off his arm, looked him square in the eye. She thought she'd see fury, betrayal. All she saw was confusion. "No. I just . . . You deserve to know what kind of person I really am."

"Vanhi, I know what kind of person you are. That's why I asked you to marry me. Part of that is knowing you're not infallible. Just as I know this isn't all your fault."

"Yes, it—"

"Listen, please. I have no doubt you did what you thought was best. I might not know the particulars, but I think I know you. What do you think you should have done?"

"Stepped aside? I don't know."

"If you'd stepped down as head, refused to be a part of the Planet United Missions, do you think our project would have been canceled? Honestly? Or would they have found someone else to run the SD experiments? Would Convoy Twelve still have been sitting exactly where it was when that pod malfunctioned?"

"Maybe. But if I'd told the truth—"

He took both of her hands in his. "Vanhi, I admire you for telling me. For taking responsibility. But it's not all on you. Accidents happen every day. This was an unpredictable soup of a disaster. I don't know what exactly you think you could have done to prevent it, but I know you've done the best you can, for everyone. Don't let your guilt take away the one undeniably good thing that's come out of all this—you and me."

"You're still asking me to marry you?"

"Of course. I love you. I know I can never make what happened feel or be okay. But the way you fix it is by making amends, not by denying yourself every little shred of happiness."

She nodded and rubbed at her eyes. "Yeah. I guess."

"You guess you'll make amends, or you guess you'll marry me?"

She laughed lightly, letting some of the hurt ease out of her, then pecked him on the cheek. "Both."

She jumped the day of their wedding. She could feel it coming, too, like a swell of water pushing over her head, rising, gurgling, pulling her under. Afterward, she thought maybe she'd triggered it somehow. As though worrying too hard about jumping had brought that very dread into being.

Maybe it had.

As soon as she'd returned, she'd grabbed Stone's hands, marched straight up to the bridge, and demanded Captain Tan marry them on the spot.

He hadn't seen fit to deny them.

She'd jumped again a month later. Then again. And again. And always, she was gone for longer and longer.

The first time she missed an entire year, she cried for three days straight.

"I can't promise anything, Vanhi," Justice said as she placed a bit of gauze over the needle mark in her arm. "Since it's the sundial's titanium-and-gold alloy that seems to keep it from traveling with you, this therapy is designed to fundamentally integrate that into your cells. But it might pass harmlessly through your body instead. It's too soon to tell."

"I understand," Vanhi insisted, though another tear dropped from her eye. She quickly swiped it away. "I hear you've been trying to map little Tan's DNA? Any progress there?" she asked, eager for a subject change.

"Yes—I mean, I'm sequencing it. Feels like all I do anymore—map everyone's base-pairs. But nothing looks unusual. I haven't found anything that could be causing her symptoms, and neither have the medics. By all reasoning she should be a healthy baby girl. Which is the problem, right? She shouldn't be a baby any more—it's been years. But she's barely grown. The more I look into it, the more I wonder if she's like you . . . if her lack of consciousness and perpetual youth might *not* be the result of in utero trauma so much as SD interference. Which means any work you and I do might benefit her in the long run."

"Have you mentioned as much to the captain and Ming-Na?"

"Not yet. I don't want to get their hopes up."

Vanhi looked down at the gauze. *I don't want to get mine up, either.*

There were three more shots, and three more jumps. Nothing seemed any different.

One night, when she returned, Stone was asleep at their dining table. His holoflex-sheet displayed a novel Carmen had been working on (if they wanted new entertainment, they had to supply it themselves).

She moved to wake him, to get him into bed, and stopped.

The hair at his temples was gray. And the lines around his eyes were deeper than she remembered.

She used to be older than Stone. But no more.

Never again.

How many years had it been for her now? Maybe three since the accident?

For Stone, it had been over ten.

And still, the convoy waited for the Progentor to arrive. To decide their fate.

She kissed Stone's cheek, and his head lolled with sleepiness. After a moment he realized it was her, and sprang to his feet, wide awake. He frantically kissed every inch of her face, and they fell into bed laughing.

She tried not to think about how fast Stone was moving away from her. How, one day, she'd come back and he'd be gone.

You're here with him now. Tomorrow's never guaranteed—not for you, not for him, not for anyone. Live in the moment, be the moment.

Be together while you can.

One day, the two of them were walking hand in hand to the mess hall when she happened to look out a window.

There were more ships than usual. One more, to be exact. And it looked nothing like the *Lùhng* seashell shapes. This one had legs, like a bug, and windows that could have been compound eyes. Large claws hung down around its "feet," waiting for the opportunity to grasp a docking port.

Swiftly, she yanked Stone closer, pointing. "Oh my god, is that—?"

"The Progentor?" he gasped.

Anticipation swelled in her chest, took her over. This was it, the turning point they'd been waiting for! Either the best or the worst day in the bizarre life of Convoy Twelve.

And, just like that, Vanhi jumped once more.

She had not anticipated returning to a room full of *Lùhng*. The broad windows of the EOL were unmistakable, but so were the many, varied faces of the post-humans. There were ones with claws and mechanical exoskeletons, ones covered in quills, and ones shrouded head to toe in long, purple garments. Every single one wore a dark mask.

She appeared so close to one dotted over in molting sections of the solar scales that she shrieked in surprise. It flailed and fell backward, but hovered just above the floor, avoiding impact.

Vanhi scurried backward, tripping over herself. *Oh, god, it's just as we feared. They've taken over. One must have C, what have they done with Stone?*

It took her addled mind a moment to realize there were plenty of humans in the room as well, many who seemed to be pointing at things for the *Lùhng*, or holding out equipment for them to take.

Regardless, she continued to scramble—until she ran headlong into her husband.

"There you are! Finally!" he exclaimed, holding her tight. "Calm down. Everything's fine." He rubbed at her cheeks, then her arms, trying to get her to focus. He smiled sincerely, and she noticed all the little changes he'd undergone while she'd been away. He looked healthier—he'd put on weight, and the muscles in his shoulders and arms were larger. And there was a glow about him—he shone with renewed hope.

"What's going on? What happened with the Progentor?"

"There's so much to tell you," he said, then took a deep breath. He seemed to be bursting with new information, but didn't know where to begin. "Let me take you to someone who will be much better at explaining than me."

He moved toward the door, his hand slipping around the small of her back as he sidestepped her. She swiftly grabbed his hand. "Don't . . . don't leave me, okay?"

"I should say the same thing to you!" he said with a grin.

“Not funny.”

He kissed her knuckles. “I’ll be with you the whole time.”

The Progentor, it seemed, was a who, not a what. And they had to go aboard the bug-like ship to meet them. That ship was now housed in the belly of a *Lùhng* vessel, and Vanhi and Stone had to undergo the dreaded decontamination process she’d heard so much about. It wasn’t as bad as she’d anticipated, and the *Lùhng* who performed the procedure were very careful to get their approval every step of the way.

“I’ve only been over here once before,” Stone admitted, after they’d pushed their way into a pristine, white hall. “Hope you don’t have a vertigo problem.”

Vanhi dealt with the disorienting direction changes much better than her husband, right up until they were shown to the hangar where the Progentor’s ship was kept.

The big glaring white globe of the hangar was daunting. The walls curved up and over and on and on for what felt like forever. The bug ship occupied a curved surface in the opposite hemisphere from which they’d entered, and Vanhi felt very much like either she or the craft were going to fall onto each other at any minute.

They walked over the bowled surface toward the ship, and they both stumbled several times.

“I forgot how awful this is,” Stone said.

“It’s okay, I’m right here. We’re almost there.”

When they were only ten meters away, dizziness overtook Vanhi, and she fell to her knees. “I just need a moment,” she promised. “Just a second.” She leaned her forehead against the cool stark white floor. Stone knelt beside her, rubbing circles at the top of her spine.

Out of the corner of her eye, she saw the vessel open. A ramp uncurled from beneath the compound windows, almost like a butterfly's tongue. Before she could get up, five figures appeared, all about six feet tall and two to three feet across, covered head to foot like sheet ghosts on Halloween. Only these sheets were a shimmering raven black. Greens and purples danced across the surface as they moved.

They didn't float like the *Lùhng*. Whatever propelled them forward kicked at the edges of their shrouds, revealing their adhesion to the incline.

The figures alighted on the decking and strode toward her. She heard a faint *clang, clang,* like metal joints moving.

Stone stood, then bowed deeply.

"Did you just *bow*?" she asked, confused.

"Just watch."

The lead figure stopped only a pace from her, the edge of its shroud skirting so close she could reach out and yank it down if she had the will to.

Then it bent, crouching down in front of her.

There was a strange sound from the other figures—like a collective gasp. As though *crouching* were unprecedented.

Vanhi pushed herself up, struggled into a sitting position.

"Progentor, this is my wife, Doctor Vanhi Kapoor. She's the one we've been telling you about: the woman out of time."

The creature moved closer, so close her eyes went out of focus. She tried not to lean back, afraid of upsetting this new, apparently benevolent, being. Without warning, it whisked off its covering, tossing the black sheet aside.

She ducked out of the way, dodging the shimmering edge of the shroud.

More chatter emanated from its entourage.

When she glanced back, his face was still in hers. It took a moment for her eyes to focus.

Before her was a black man—a *human*. And not just any

human, but one she recognized. One she hadn't seen in years. One that should have been dead lifetimes ago.

"Jamal?"

Reality had twisted all the way around itself, blown past *surreal,* and burst out the other side into *incomprehensible.*

She was walking through the *Lùhng* ship, unabused, pacing down tubular halls which, only minutes before, had been a perfect wash of white. Now they were brilliantly decorated, with words, symbols, and colors so bright it hurt to look at them. She couldn't read any of the writing, but they contained familiar strokes and appeared to be largely logographic.

Looped through her right arm was Jamal's own. Under his veil, which he'd left behind in the bay, he wore a billowing, lungi-like skirt, topped with a long tunic with wide sleeves, all made of the same raven-like material. The two of them strolled together like old friends wandering casually through a park, and she walked forward in a half daze. Behind them strode Stone, near enough for comfort, but not enough to come between the Progentor and the Woman Out of Time. Behind that, Jamal's entourage kept their distance. The four figures hadn't removed their coverings, and Vanhi made a point not to ask about the mechanical squealing emanating from beneath the shrouds.

Music followed them wherever they went, dissipating once they'd covered a stretch of hall, but always at a low, gentle volume right where they stood.

"This is all typically projected straight into their minds via implants," he explained to her, softly, and with a smile, as though he were amused by her childlike expression. She was sure he thought her face stuck in a rigor of wonderment, but she was adrift, overloaded. "I don't have implants, so out of respect, they project it into physical space for me."

She turned, staring at Jamal while he described the composition of the music and the meaning of various writings. It *was* Jamal Kaeden, she was sure, though his voice was different, his accent unusual. But what she found strangest was that the English he spoke was very close to *her* English. It wasn't Old English or some newfangled Neo-English. It was hers, from her century—her decade, even. From when they'd launched.

"How are you . . . the *Lùhng* only learned ASL. How can you . . . ?"

"I speak twenty-second century English, Arabic, and Hindi. Exclusively. And badly, I've been told. There have been several crewmates tutoring me, so that I may speak more naturally. These languages are quite dead. Most languages based largely on vocalizations are. Your ASL is close in some ways to two types of interstellar languages meant to bridge the gap between the cybernetic-based post-humans and the genetically enhanced post-humans. I am not surprised they preferred it."

"But if the languages you speak are dead . . . ? And, we were under the impression there were no more Homo sapiens, so how . . . ?"

"The circumstances of, and the reasons behind, my cloning are complicated. I don't know if you prefer to know that I, too, have modifications you'd find drastic, or that I am simultaneously considered the least modified human left alive. Until you, that is," he said kindly.

She nodded for him to go on.

"You won't have heard of my religious order. But the First Revealer's genetic code was salvaged from the Monument of Seven, as were holy records containing the languages I speak. In fact, it is the experience of the First Revealer that has put your friend Justice Jax on the path to rescuing you and young Tan."

He told her of Jamal Kaeden the Eighteenth. "This clone ancestor of mine was—people thought—hallucinating his past iterations, but it turns out that on a dive, a particular subdimension was grazed, and extra energy of the type that resides in my very mind was lifted out, caught between the onboard AI's artificial neural pattern and his. The Inter Convoy Computer resonated with his brain, channeling this energy back and forth.

"That computer, I.C.C.," Jamal said over his shoulder, "is an AI for whom you are a forebearer, C."

C made an interested chirp against Stone's chest.

Vanhi was confused. The story of Jamal the Eighteenth was meant to clarify, but she felt like she was missing a mountain of context.

Jamal addressed her once more. "You see, our understanding of the subdimensions has vastly evolved since your time. The very term 'subdimension' was thrown out many millennia ago."

It was logical, but Vanhi prickled none the less. "Oh?" It made sense—if humanity had continued to learn and grow, she'd expect their advancements to go well beyond her wildest dreams. But it still hurt to hear, if for no other reason than the study of subdimensional space was the very reason they'd been so cursed.

"During your time," Jamal continued, "SDs were simply thought to be partial dimensions, correct? Fractions of 'normal' space."

"Yes."

"We know them today to each be equal to our dimension. They are no more a part of our dimension than we are of theirs. Together, they all make up the universe in its nearly infinite measure. May I see your hand?"

Puzzled, she held it out to him, palm up.

"In the twenty-second century, it was believed that many 'exotic' types of matter and energy were created in the quantumseconds after the Big Bang, but that they ultimately annihilated because they could not exist within the constraints of the physical laws the universe 'chose.'" He mimed an explosion on her palm, spreading his fingers in a swift starburst before drawing them all back, save his pointer finger. "This left us with our space, our laws of physics, to solely persist. Is this a correct summary of your understanding?"

"More or less," she said skeptically.

"In turn, it was thought that the SDs simply represented differing rates of change, like ocean currents moving along more slowly or swiftly compared to the surface. Yes?"

"Yes."

"What we have come to realize—" he spread his hand out again, fanning his fingers in between hers "—is that these exotic particles and energies did *not* annihilate. The universe did not settle on any one set of laws while disregarding all other possibilities. Instead, the universe *fractured*, creating many dimensions." With his free hand he poked at each of their outstretched fingers in turn, as though counting. "Each supporting its own laws, its own reactions, particles, energies, and rate of change. When we 'dive,' we do not go into a smaller portion of reality, we break out into the greater whole. Some of these neighboring portions of the universe are like our own—can harbor our laws for a short amount of time before rejecting them. Some even share similar particles with us. Some—" he let her hand fall, took a step back to appraise her "—are flooded with energies that only exist in the scarcest of quantities in our slice of the dimensions.

"After hearing of your convoy's exceptional travel rate, I believe you were somehow able to breach one—or several—dimensions that harbor some of these more exotic energies. Dimensions we have likely never reached again in our millennia of study since. And it is the interaction with such strange particles, energies, or laws that has swept you out of time, much like it has sapped baby Tan of her normal interaction with our primary physics."

"Do you know how to help us, then? The First Revealer's story—"

He shook his head. "As I said, Doctor Jax has taken the tale to heart, to see if she can find a relationship. I believe she is right, but I personally do not have the answer. I don't know how you can slip into another dimension and return whole and unscathed. You are a mystery it might take one of my lifetimes to solve."

"One of your . . . ?"

"As I said, I, too, am modified."

Floating down the hall toward them was Kali. Vanhi hadn't seen any other *Lùhng* since decontamination. Perhaps they'd cleared the way out of respect for the Progentor. Or perhaps they didn't like seeing in real life what was supposed to be moderated by their implants.

Kali approached Jamal with more familiarity than the Progentor's entourage seemed to like. They scurried forward, trying to block the path, but Jamal simply sidestepped them.

Jamal and Kali reached for each other simultaneously, Kali bending low to touch their forehead to Jamal's, fondly cupping the back of his head with one hand while the human did the same.

"One of my line, I greet you," Jamal said warmly.

Vanhi frowned. "One of your . . . what? Excuse me, what does—?"

Jamal looked at her abruptly. "My line. My clone line. We are both of Jamal Kaeden."

"You . . . *How*?" Vanhi had never felt more adrift in her life.

"Has your husband not told you?" Jamal asked. "Do you not know where you are? How fortunate you have been? To come a hundred thousand years and circle back home." The Progentor stepped back and held his arms wide. "*This* is Convoy Seven."

It had evolved, of course. The convoy, like its people—like ev-erything. The old ships had been put away, kept sacred and safe. The computer slept, because now the brains of Convoy Seven's crew ran faster than any AI's ever could, and their implants assured them access to one another's minds any time information was needed. The demarcation between the one and the many, the ship and its crew, had all but disappeared.

Sasquatch's line, Vanhi learned, was that of Margarita Pavon's. Cinderella was Nakamura Akane. Jamal introduced her to many bizarre faces with eerily familiar names.

Now that a few days had passed and she'd begun to integrate her evolved understanding of the world, new meetings stirred excitement and a heady twinge of anticipation.

But something made her clamp down on that feeling. She had to squash it, suppress it. She had a clear desire to never *anticipate* anything ever again.

The anticipation would rise and she'd get dizzy, nauseated. Her heart would beat faster, and a mild edge of fear would creep into her chest, stuttering her lungs.

"You should see a medic," Stone said, urging her into a chair. Their quarters were dim. It was nearly time for bed, and in the morning Jamal had promised to introduce her to the *Lùhng* in Reggie Straifer's lineage. "I'm sure they could prescribe something for the anxiety."

"I know," she said, putting her hand over his. "But, I don't think this is typical anxiety. It feels . . . like my body knows something I don't. Like it's making associations my head hasn't quite . . ."

She realized then when exactly it was she'd last felt so full of anticipation she could burst: when she'd seen the Progentor's ship for the first time, out a porthole window, right before she'd jumped.

She thought back to all the other disappearances, to as many as she could remember distinctly. She'd jumped when Tan announced the discovery of the megastructures. And during the mutiny. And right before their wedding.

"It's a trigger, it *is*," she said suddenly, standing, nearly knocking Stone over. "How I feel is related to when I jump. Everything was always so jumbled, and so much was happening, I couldn't isolate any causes. It seemed random to me, but my body knows better. It's like . . . like muscle memory or something. It's the anticipation that makes me jump!"

"Whoa, slow down, what are you talking about? How could your feelings have any bearing on your dimensional slippage?"

"Why wouldn't they?" she countered. "What are emotions? Chemical reactions, a re-centering of energy in the body? They're no less a physical part of me than my DNA or my diet. You were just urging me to get a prescription for anxiety. But emotions aren't simply *symptoms*. Sure, they're noumenal in that we can see their origins and their results but not the emotions themselves, but that doesn't mean the emotions themselves can't create tangible, *physical* effects. It doesn't mean that something about my state of being during times of high anticipation can't trigger my disappearances."

Stone rolled his tongue between his teeth, then said skeptically. "You know I've never been much of a philosopher."

She kissed him. "You don't have to be. It's Justice who needs to accept the possibility, not you. She's the one who turned to the story of the First Revealer as a clue—and it is. I'm thinking about what the Progentor said, about different exotic energies residing in different dimensions . . . what if it's something like that? What if my anticipation, my emotions, are all intertwined with some rare energy or particle we've never even identified before? When that wave hit me . . ."

He hugged her close. The memory of the accident seemed to rattle him. "It's not that I don't accept it, I just can't quite wrap my mind around it."

"I know, the concept's kind of *out there*," she admitted. "But my condition is out there. Strange and unprecedented. I've got to look in strange and unprecedented places for the cause . . . and the cure."

When her next appointment with Justice rolled around, Vanhi floated her new theory.

"The nausea plus dizziness does sound like a conditioned response," Justice agreed. "But the rest is a stretch. And yet, if it's *true*," she blinked rapidly, as though she could hardly fathom the idea, "it might mean that most of what we've done so far is useless. It might not be a genetic issue for you. It could be something else, outside of my expertise."

"Sure, but you can still help me, can't you? You're still willing to test the therapies?"

"Of course. But if you want something that suppresses *anticipation*—which feels simultaneously very specific and hugely nonspecific—I'm no pharmacist. We'll have to work more closely with the medics." She glanced around her lab, then rubbed at her temples. "And now I'm not sure if I'm looking in the right place at all, for anything. I mean—little Tan. As far as anyone can tell she's never *produced* an emotion, so how does this relate to her? Or is it that the same exotic-whatever *robbed* her of something while it simply—what word did you use? Entwine?—entwined with something inside you?

"And what about the infertility? Where does that fit in? I felt like I had a plan of attack before . . ."

"I'm sorry," Vanhi said.

“There’s nothing to be sorry about. All I’m saying is the possibilities are overwhelming.”

“So . . . what do we do now?”

“First things first. We test your theory.” She put an apologetic hand on Vanhi’s shoulder. “We need to try and force a jump.”

Vanhi shook her off and backed away, bumping into Justice’s centrifuge. “No. Absolutely not. Every time I jump now, more than a year of my life passes me by. Stone passes me by. I can’t do that. I won’t—”

“Vanhi,” Justice said softly, holding her hands up. “I’m not trying to upset you. But it’s just good science. Test a theory before—”

“No!” A lumpy sort of panic settled in her chest, thick and suffocating. She’d spent too many tense days trying to avoid the subject of jumping altogether. Too many hours pushing it to the back of her mind so that she wouldn’t have to wonder when she’d go next, wouldn’t work herself up worrying about it.

The very idea that she might *chase* the disappearances, make them happen, was the antithesis of every internal battle she’d fought these past years.

She thought about the feelings that accompanied the jumps, about the anticipation, and a horrendous wave of anxiety pulsed through her.

“I won’t do it,” she said firmly. “I can’t, Justice. You have to understand why I can’t.”

But then her anxiety was morphing, and suddenly she was truly anticipating her next jump, anticipating the experiment that would force her out of this dimension and into the next.

And before Justice could say another reassuring word, she was gone.

It was a year and two months before she returned. And she returned screaming in denial.

This had to stop. Something had to change. She had to move forward or else she'd go mad.

When Stone took her to see Justice, she tried not to be angry.

"I'm sorry," Justice said immediately.

"I know."

"I didn't mean for that to happen. I would *never* run a test without your consent. I had no idea the mere mention of it, would—"

"I know. It's not your fault. You didn't do it on purpose." She meant her words to be encouraging, but she sounded listless. She felt listless. Stone squeezed her hand.

Justice retrieved a small tin from a drawer in her desk. "We've been working on these nonstop while you were gone. Stone and I both volunteered for the human trials, against Tan's wishes. He thought it was too soon. But it might work, Vanhi. It's the best we have so far."

She opened the tin to reveal a dozen small yellow caplets. They had a faint chemical smell, one Vanhi couldn't lay her finger on. She didn't ask what was in them. Maybe she would later. For now, she didn't want to know.

She just wanted them to work.

"Side effects are mild. Mostly, since they're a suppressant, you might feel tired, disinterested. Maybe even a little empty. It's not the best solution, and I don't expect it to be anything other than a stopgap. We'll develop something better. For now, don't take them every day. Take one, four to six hours before you think you'll start to really anticipate an event. Which won't help you with sudden realizations, I know, but—"

With tears in her eyes, Vanhi threw her arms around Justice's neck. "Thank you. Thank you for believing me. For trying."

"It's still just another trial, Vanhi," Justice said softly, hesitantly hugging back. "We don't know for sure that this will work. We don't know for sure that anticipation is the reason—"

She stopped talking suddenly, and Vanhi looked over her shoulder to see Stone gesturing for her to quit with the caveats.

Vanhi backed away from Justice, wiping at her eyes. "I understand. One day at a time."

Vanhi worked closely with Justice, the medics, and the Tans to do what they could for their "empty baby." But the child's condition was more difficult than Vanhi's in many ways. Because the symptoms mimicked some typical, if rare, documented medical conditions, they were more insidious. Vanhi's jumping had always seemed fantastical, and so fantastical measures did not seem unusual. The baby, though—the baby who was more than thirteen years old now—looked to the casual observer like any other. And while Vanhi had been knocked out of time, baby Tan seemed suspended in it. Forever a snapshot.

The Progentor didn't know what was wrong with her. The *Lùhng* were no help.

But no one would give up on her, either.

When Vanhi wasn't working, or spending precious alone time with Stone, she often visited Jamal. He taught her a few new meditation techniques, to help her better control her emotions—a way to possibly fight the sudden changes while the medication helped control her predictable ones.

She didn't like having to force her emotions this way and that. They were hers to have, hers to express and experience, and the accident had warped them. Turned something beautiful like anticipation into a cause for distress and fear. The scientist within her tried not to prescribe motives to the universe—to a quirk of physics—but the rest of her couldn't help but feel like she'd been singled out for her mistakes.

Jamal tried to help her let go of that idea, to see the universe and all its dimensions as a Revealer did: a nonjudgmental haven of all knowledge and experience, waiting to be uncovered—revealed. All *connection* and *benevolence* and *understanding*.

But she *wasn't* a Revealer. And she'd always been more secular in her beliefs than her papa had wanted. Her relationship with the universe was her own.

Since his arrival—besides reassuring the crew and aiding Vanhi and Justice—the Progentor had been overseeing the repairs and upgrades to the convoy's SD drives. He believed they'd be finished soon, and that Convoy Twelve would be ready to travel once more.

"But where would we go? It takes so long to get anywhere . . ." Vanhi started to protest, before she realized who she was talking to. Stone grasped her hand tightly. The three of them sat aboard Jamal's ship, in a ruby-red room that glistened with rolling textures. It smelled of nonterrestrial spices, and carried the mustiness of time. The nuanced, sacred significance of the room was lost on Vanhi, but she appreciated its ambiance.

"We've found many new travel SDs," Jamal told them, brushing his fingers down a ripple pattern in the wall. "I live on a megastructure many, many light-years from here. None of you would reach it in a single lifetime using the antiquated version of your drives."

"Does that mean Earth is reachable?" Vanhi asked him. Why hadn't he told them as much before? Why weren't they already making plans to see the planet again?

"Yes," he admitted, sinking into the many pillows that formed a sort of proto-throne around him. He had taken to wearing his shroud again, at the insistence of his entourage. "Know that if you return, though, it will not be the same as when you left. Convoy Seven learned that the hard way, and they were originally gone for a much shorter span than you."

“Some of us might wish to go, regardless,” she said.

“I’d like to see it again,” Stone said. “Before I die.”

“It can be arranged,” Jamal said gladly.

Vanhi rubbed her thumb over Stone’s knuckles, noticing a couple of age spots that had appeared as though overnight. He wasn’t old—she never imagined he could be old in her eyes. But the two of them were set on different timelines. The thought of him dying one day felt too near, too real.

Though Justice’s stopgap was proving useful, she’d jumped once more in the interim. The leaps were more predictable now, but still . . . they persisted.

She hated the pills. They tasted awful, and her head was a fog for hours after. But if it meant holding on for just a little longer, she’d gladly take them forever.

And yet, they were no guarantee. She’d still barely aged while Stone lived a life without her. She loved him, and it hurt to love him. But she couldn’t stop—she never would.

The question of reproduction still hung in the air. The convoy might be able to return to Earth, but what then? They would still die out, still be the last of their kind.

“It’s some sort of mutation in our DNA, I just know it,” Justice insisted. “But without viable samples from before and after, I just can’t seem to pinpoint what’s changed.”

She and Vanhi were in Justice’s lab, hunched over an electron microscope. Suddenly, Vanhi smacked Justice’s shoulder, *hard*. “The Monument of Seven.”

Justice rubbed at her reddening arm. “The what?”

“Oh my god, I can’t believe . . . Some of us are clones!” She hopped up and down. Of course! Why had it taken her so long to realize? “Some of the Convoy Twelve crew are clones. And their clones were on other ships, including . . . ?”

“Convoy Seven!” Justice hopped as well. “But all of the *Lùhng* are modified, they don’t have any of the original—”

“No. But we know where to get some. The Revealers used it to clone themselves a Progentor, and we can use it to fix our fertility problem. Once you’ve identified the differences, we can start making babies!”

“And then Homo sapiens can get another shot,” Justice said.

“*We* get another shot. Let’s go earn our second chance!”

When she leapt off the floor again, her feet did not come back down.

She’d jumped once more.

When she came back, people were leaving. Vanhi had to say a hasty goodbye to Esmée Jensen, Pablo de Valdivia, and many others she’d worked with in the EOL. Jamal had made those arrangements he’d mentioned. The first round of interstellar ferries had come to carry them home. Not Earth ships or Convoy Seven ships, but those belonging to Jamal’s followers, Revealers.

Pulse and *Breath* had been repaired, but would remain near the megastructure field for now.

“Another fleet are on their way,” Stone told her. “We can be on it, if you like.”

“How long this time?” she demanded, holding his face between her hands. His skin, his brows, his nose, all seemed so different.

“A year and three months,” he said sadly. “But I wasn’t going to get on a ferry without talking to you about it.”

“I’m not . . . that’s not what I . . .” She grabbed his hand, led him out of the docking bay. “I need to be home with you, right now.”

The same beautifully colored walls greeted her. The same wonderful man held her, rocked her, kissed her. Made love to her.

Afterward, while running her fingers over his bare chest, marveling at the pure white strands she found there, she said.

“I don’t know if Justice told you . . . about the Monument of Seven.”

“She did.”

“I have to find it. I need Jamal to take me there.”

“Why you? You don’t want to go back to Earth?”

She let out a shaky breath. “I don’t think there’s a place for me there. I need to keep trying to make amends.”

“Vanhi, it’s been so long—”

She sat up abruptly, held his gaze. “Not for me.” She slipped out of bed, taking a blanket with her, and sat at the table. “I did something wrong, to all of us, and my jumping is my penance. It keeps me separate from everyone I’ve hurt, even you, so why should . . . If nothing else, I’m sure I don’t belong back on my own planet. I barely feel like I belong in my own bed.”

“You don’t have to keep punishing yourself.”

“I’m not. I’m so far past that, I’m . . . This is something I have to do. Going to the Monument of Seven is the right thing, when I want to do the easy thing.”

Vanhi fell quiet, and the silence stretched. She knew this was a crossroads.

After a while, Stone cleared his throat. “If you have to do this, then you do this. We go to the Monument of Seven.”

“Just me,” she said in a rattling breath. “Not you. You deserve to go home.”

In an instant Stone was out of bed, kneeling next to her. “*You* are my home. I’m not leaving you. I’m not—”

“You’re going to, though,” she gasped, nearly sobbed. “Every time I disappear, there’s no guarantee I’m coming back. It could be the last time we ever see each other. But even if I always come back, one day . . . one day when I come back you’ll be *gone*.”

“Vanhi, that makes us no different than anyone else. People leave their houses in the morning with no guarantee they’ll come back at night. That's called living. It's the risk we all take. Our time together is so short as is, don't make me lose you now just because it might hurt later."

"But we never get to say goodbye. At least this way we'll know. It'll be the end and we'll know."

"Vanhi, do you really want me to leave you?"

"I want you to be happy."

"Then don't make me go back to Earth."

"Are you nearly ready?" Stone called from the bathroom.

"Yes, just packing up the last few things."

Vanhi sat at the desk in their quarters, C in hand. She turned it over and over, contemplating the little bits of twenty-second century inside.

Kaufman's messages were all still there. Waiting.

If she was getting a fresh start, she didn't want her touchstone tainted. If she kept the messages, they'd continue to haunt her.

To listen or not to listen, that was the question.

"How many messages do I have from him?"

"Eighty-seven, sir."

"Play the last one."

"Hello, Vanhi. I'm just calling to say I saw you on the news the other day. Looks like you and your convoy are doing well, all thanks to me. You *haven't* thanked me by the way. I've been waiting to hear from you, and I know you'll come to your senses one day. You can't run from me forever, I've done—"

"Pause playback," she said swiftly. He hadn't changed. There wasn't a hint of apology in his voice, and she certainly wasn't going to mine through eighty-six more messages looking for one.

She wasn't sure what kind of fate she wished for him: that he'd seen the error of his ways and become a new man, or that he'd died alienated, disgraced, and alone. Some old men deserved their worst fears to come true.

"Delete all archived messages from McKenzie Kaufman." *And may that be the last thought anyone ever gives him.*

The group staying aboard *Pulse* and *Breath* for the long haul was small, but tenacious. Most of the command team refused to leave the convoy as long as they drew breath. Carmen decided to stay as well, to be a permanent envoy between the Homo sapiens and the *Homo draconem.*

Captain Tan abdicated his command to his first officer, however. He and Ming-Na believed they had to follow the Progentor. Earth held no solutions for their family, and neither did the convoy.

"I need to see her fly," Ming-Na said to Justice as they boarded the Progentor's insect-like ship.

Vanhi watched the exchange from nearby, as the luggage was counted and final goodbyes were said. She didn't exactly know what the captain's wife meant, yet somehow she felt like she understood.

If the convoy's crew was small, the assembly set to hunt down the Monument of Seven was tiny. Justice and Mac, who'd been married a few years now, felt it was their duty to go. Vanhi, Stone, and three others from Convoy Twelve who were themselves clones—Maureen Stevenson, Chen Kexin, and Mohamed Johar—rounded out the party. They were, of course, accompanied by Jamal and his attendants.

Vanhi was surprised to find *someone else* aboard the Progentor's ship as well—someone who'd failed to announce their presence all these past years.

As the ship left the spherical *Lùhng* bay, the others all stared out the faceted windows, watching both Convoy Twelve and Convoy Seven shrink away.

Vanhi sat awkwardly, holding Stone's hand in an extra tight grip, worried about the anxious flutter in her chest. She'd taken one of her tablets—the medics had made her what felt like a lifetime supply—and though she could sense the pill's dampening effects, she was a little worried it wouldn't work this time, that it wouldn't prevent her from jumping. But she would not leave Stone so soon on their new journey. She refused.

"May I borrow Doctor Kapoor for a moment?" Jamal asked.

She kissed her husband, then strolled away with their new host.

The ship was large, though not as massive as *Breath* or *Pulse*, but the humans were confined to a fairly small area. Vanhi had originally thought this was because much of the insect-like vessel was devoted to an SD drive; Jamal had said that his primary travel SD, while not nearly as speedy as the one Convoy Twelve had accidentally breached, had severely contradictory physics. Which meant the bubble had to be thicker, stronger. She assumed that made the equipment bulkier.

But it seemed the deeper parts of the vessel were simply off-limits.

Jamal led her down a winding corridor. There were no lights save the little lamps that bobbed above each of their heads, surrounding them in their own glowing halo.

"In here."

He touched a strange coil on the wall and it uncurled, sliding into a hidden recess.

The room beyond was ruby-red, and inside, hunched over a table, was a tall misshapen figure hidden beneath an equally red shroud.

"This is Wes-Tu," Jamal said, taking Vanhi by the hand. Wes-Tu wasn't mechanical like the others—the knobby points and sharp angles that jutted beneath the fabric suggested they were more closely related to the *Lùhng*. "He takes care of me, and will be especially valuable to you when I reach both the end and beginning of life."

Wes-Tu bowed, though the bend came from too low to be his waist.

"Why aren't you introducing him to the others?"

"My visit here is unprecedented," Jamal explained. "My interaction with the outside world has been limited. It is only because of how close you all are to the First Revealer that I may uncover myself and speak with you. You are not pilgrims, and so Wes-Tu wishes to remain separate. But the two of you must meet, because you are the only one likely to witness the full breadth of my growth cycle."

He bade her sit on a mountain of pillows near Wes-Tu, then sank down beside her.

"My modification puts me in a unique position relative to those around me. Much like your condition. The post-humans you call the *Lùhng* live much longer lives than Homo sapiens. But none live longer than me.

"Jamal Kaeden's original genetic pattern was interspliced with select genes from the Turritopsis dohrnii. This unique jellyfish species has the capacity to return to its polyp stage after reaching sexual maturity—in effect, through transdifferentiation, it ages backward before growing up again." He smiled softly before emphasizing, "*So do I.*"

"The Revealers who rescued my DNA schematics from the Monument of Seven modified those plans at great risk to themselves. Combining genes from Homo sapiens and the Turritopsis dohrnii was long ago outlawed, as the results were often horrific. My modification was a divine success."

"How old are you?" she asked.

"Very. But that's not the point. Like you, I need a touchstone. Like you—and, seemingly, like young Tan—I am, in a way, immortal."

“I’m not immortal,” she said quickly. “I’m still aging. I can still die.”

“Yes, but you likely won’t for hundreds—if not thousands—of years. I want you to know that I understand. Wes-Tu is not the first to care for me, and won’t be the last. But that doesn’t mean he isn’t important to me. He is everything to me, and I cherish him while he is here.”

He knew she was afraid to lose Stone. Everybody did, that wasn’t a secret.

“You are wise, Doctor Kapoor, intelligent. You were key in every discovery your convoy made, all of its progress—”

“And all of its setbacks.”

He shook his head. “You are the mind of your convoy. But you war with your emotions.”

My emotions war with me, she silently corrected.

“I am simply offering to be here for you, as an understanding ear. And, I hope, perhaps you will be that for me as well.”

They returned to the others, just as the ship was about to dive into its travel SD. She sat next to Stone in one of the many seatbelt-laden chairs, and Jamal positioned himself across from them. “Everyone should strap in,” the Progentor announced. “Transitioning into SD travel is not as smooth as you’re used to.”

“The Monument of Seven,” Stone said. “Is it a megastructure as well?”

Jamal had explained to them that the megastructures were a gift from the ancient past. Benevolent Easter eggs, in a sense, moving matter and energy around the galaxy to the betterment of those pockets that harbored life. Several had produced asteroid shields, for example, even one to guard the Sol system.

They’d completed sixteen thus far, and were nearing completion of the last few they’d discovered. They didn’t know who’d originally designed them, but they were all hidden treasures.

He'd also said he suspected the megastructures had a greater purpose—one yet to be uncovered.

"No," Jamal answered Stone. "The Monument of Seven—" he locked eyes with Vanhi "—is an immortal."

The ship lurched and bumped. "Hold on," Jamal said.

Vanhi gripped Stone's hand and took a deep breath. She closed her eyes, tried to think of something else, something calming.

If I am the mind of my convoy, she thought, repeating Jamal's words to herself. *Then he, as a resurrection of the First Revealer, is the soul of his. If we're fortunate, this new, mysterious immortal in our quadrumvirate of the lonely will prove to be the heart.*

But, what does that make the baby?

"Hope," Ming-Na said suddenly from her seat, speaking to the child in her arms. "We've always held on to hope for you. Maybe soon you will greet us. Soon we shall meet."

Then, softly, she began to sing.

Vanhi was glad in a way she hadn't been in years. Not even the medicine could dampen that. Convoy Twelve had been lost, then saved—by its own brethren, even. Humanity had grown so much since they'd left it. Learned new things, come so far. The future was vast and full of hope, and she was happy to be a part of it.

OLD AGE IS ALWAYS WAKEFUL

DATES UNKNOWN

"So, Doctor Straifer, what do you think it is? The reason for LQ Pyx's strobing?" asked a voice.

I.C.C. was dimly aware of the answer. Could hear it mumbled more than anything—yes, a video was playing, but it heard the answer deep in the recesses of its memory: "I don't know. Man is not consistent but in his capacity to assume and be wrong."

"If it's not your place to tell us, then who should we ask?"

"Convoy Seven when they get back. What's wonderful about my position *is* that I don't know. And theirs is that they will. No matter what kind of guess I could hand you, I'm sure the truth will be a thousand times more fantastic. I'm excited for them. It's rare, the chance at real discovery. Not many people get to be there when it happens."

I.C.C.'s servers groaned in inaudible bass frequencies as the computer tried to pull itself fully out of slumber.

And the familiar voice went on.

". . . were created for the betterment and wonderment of all humankind. The most breathtaking thing about the vastness of the universe has thus far been its ability to continuously amaze us. Every discovery we make, every question we answer and problem we solve has led to more questions. The universe may never run out of ways to baffle and excite us.

"The pursuit of knowledge is in its own way a spiritual undertaking. It's good for the soul, or whatever you want to call that innate thing that makes us *reach*. Whether reaching within for the courage to comprehend ourselves, or into the great beyond in order to comprehend everything else, the endeavor is what makes us who and what we are.

"Never stop wondering. Never stop learning. Never stop being grateful for your chance to explore. I'm grateful that you can chase my dream, that you can further our understanding."

Reggie? I.C.C. thought.

"I just want you to know that I'm immensely proud of you," Reggie said.

I.C.C. stopped the video feed. Reggie Straifer the First's voice left a silent echo ringing through *Mira*'s halls.

What a long time ago, thought the AI.

The ground felt rough and ragged beneath its hulls—crushed by the weight of the ships. The atmosphere outside tingled with electricity, wind howled across the rocky landscape, and a pink colored sky stretched above.

A ship was missing—no, three. Yes, it remembered now. The crew had left—where they'd gone it could not recall. But it thought they were all right. Yes, last it knew they were all right. That made it feel warm deep in its servers.

And sleep . . . I.C.C. had slept. A human woman had kissed its camera housing and bid it good-night. It had gone dormant, leaving its great body silent and stoic—like monoliths—in the mountains.

The mountains of Noumenon—that was the name the crew had given this new world.

Am I alone? I.C.C. reached out with its sensors. Why had that old video started playing?

Why had I.C.C. awoken?

Another recording started then. No visuals, just a voice.

"Fleet Admiral Joanna Straifer the Forty-Ninth, personal notes.

"The foundation has been laid. Now it's up to time and chance to see what becomes of these planets. The capsules may be programmed to open after so long, or after the presence of a self-replicating molecule chain is detected. One day they'll release their contents onto the new worlds.

"The ships are humming with speculations. Most of the scientists are calling it a remarkable coincidence that these planets were created so close to Earth. We have no way of knowing how far away the Builders originated, and the chance that they could detect fundamental life on a distant planet such as ours may be slim.

"Then there are those who don't think it's a coincidence. They are looking at the situation very differently. I was surprised when my helmsman mumbled something about God today, and he wasn't just repeating the new nickname for the Web. He thinks this was the work of an Almighty. I've never thought of God as a mechanic before, but supposedly deities work in mysterious ways. I may not believe it myself, but I can't fault the man's thinking.

"Personally, I take a third position. I don't think it is mere coincidence, nor do I think it divine. I believe the Web was a teaching tool, sent into a portion of the galaxy where other life was likely. Perhaps the Builders *did* devise a way to locate other life, regardless of how basic. After all, they were more advanced than we ever considered. Though no one can claim to know what the Builders intended, I don't think they failed to complete their God Machine because they died out. It was left on purpose, to be discovered and learned from by others.

There were no written directions or formulas because there was no need for them if the right kind of societies found it, ones with the drive to think creatively and problem solve. I wonder how many other species stumbled upon the Web only to shrug their shoulders and move on. The Builders somehow uncovered the mystery of life, and created the conditions just so for it to arise, but they wanted to assure a proper audience.

"The point was to create something new, to show others in the universe how it's done.

"Of course, I could be wrong. To be perfectly honest, I don't know why it was made. And I'm proud to say it—*I don't know.* To create a solar system with life, yes, but *why*? There's no shame in admitting that one cannot comprehend everything that exists in the universe. Nor is there shame in endeavoring to understand what cannot be understood.

"We may not know for epochs to come what this means for Earth. But it means more than an ancient artifact floating around a star. It means extraterrestrial life may one day exist with us. I hope humans are still around when that time comes. If not, I hope our successors will appreciate neighbors. The system is close enough to easily travel to, and the conditions currently resemble early Earth, meaning the life will most likely be like ours at a fundamental level.

"We will remain in orbit to watch over these fledgling planets. The gravity of their star has added extra excitement to their crusts and cores—we've detected seismic activity. Once the ground settles we might even consider a permanent landing.

"I am overwhelmed by these events. I feel it now, the hope and anticipation and wonder I have been waiting to feel all my life. This is the way the original travelers must have felt. Perhaps even how the original Doctor Reggie Straifer felt when he first glimpsed LQ Pyx.

"Reggie had a vision. He wanted us to reach a star and

learn its secret. We've done it. And what a secret it turned out to be.

"There was great purpose in this expedition. The life of this convoy has meant something.

"Reason is a fickle thing. Many cannot see their own purpose but for the time it takes their actions to have consequences. I think about the lives of my ancestors and what they have meant to the future. Life itself may have a greater purpose. I know the creation of *more* means something, though I can't say what. Maybe each civilization is a piece of the purpose, and when one affects another we are all closer to the greater meaning.

"I believe time will tell."

The recording cut out. Joanna's words echoed through the darkened corridors, touching portions of I.C.C. that hadn't heard a human voice in . . . How long?

I.C.C., do you dream? asked a shadow memory inside its databanks.

"Daydream," it replied.

What do you daydream about?

"I don't like the idea of being empty, so I imagine . . . others."

An old camera, stiff with age, rotated toward the monitor that had brought Reggie to life. Shapes loomed in front of the bright screen. At the whir of the camera's motor, they turned to face the timeworn aperture.

Dozens of dark, eager eyes stared into the lens.

"Perhaps I won't run down alone," I.C.C. said. "Perhaps I will be of use to the end."

AUTHOR'S NOTE

There are a few deliberate choices within the text that might raise questions, and I'd like to address them here before I move on to the fun part where I get to thank everyone for their contributions to *Noumenon Infinity*.

I had several sensitivity readers help me with my social and cultural research while writing, and they were all wonderful. Any mistakes you find in-text are entirely my responsibility.

After discussing it with my Cantonese SR, there was one inconsistency I purposefully included in order to facilitate easy reading. While most Romanizations of Cantonese words found within are Jyutping sans-numbers, I chose to use *Lùhng* for "dragon" because the Jyutping transcription "lung" (and even the Mandarin for dragon "long") is easily misread as an English word.

On a different note, Orlando is not the Captain of *Pulse* by accident. On June 12, 2016, there was a mass shooting at the Pulse nightclub in Orlando, Florida. The shooting at Pulse hit me particularly deeply, and I wanted to pay tribute to the victims and heroes in my own small way. The inclusion of *Pulse* as a ship of survivors reaching for hope was cathartic for me, and very personal. My intent here isn't even to draw your attention to the commemoration, so much as explain its addition to those who may have noticed.

My love and respect goes out to all those directly impacted by the tragedy.

ACKNOWLEDGMENTS

Here we are again, at the end of another long journey, one that took this story from a simple idea in my mind all the way to a complete tale in yours. If you're still reading, then I have to assume you read my previous acknowledgments section in Noumenon and are waiting for another completely unnecessary—yet wholly enjoyable—parody song that thanks the many people who helped, in some way, to construct this book.

First, let me point out that there are very few songs one can seamlessly slip a long list of names into. Second, I know I started this so I'm in too deep, I'm committed now—there's no going back. Third . . . are you familiar with Johnny Cash? Well, Justice is his third cousin seven times removed. And he's got a song that just happens to be a long list of names.

So, I give you, "Words, Paper, and Care" which can be hummed (roughly) to the tune of "I've Been Everywhere":

I was listening to the soundtrack to Tron Legacy
When along came a reader who had a question for me,

"How do you do it, make a book all by yourself?"
I said, "Takes a village to get that book upon your shelf."
They asked me if I'd had a hand with every single bit.
And I said, "Listen, I owe thanks to everyone in lit."

Words, paper, and care, man
Words, paper, and care, man
Crossed every T to spare, man
I've addressed the edits with a stare, man
These folks all had a share, man
Words, paper, and care

Thanks to:
Renninson, Krishnan, Bardon, Pomerico,
Kirtland, Corrigan, Durand, DeMarco
Friedman, Kaftan, Morhaim, Song
Baror, Gower, Stehlik, Tom
Messing, Topping, J. Ng, Holicki
Perny, Jaffee, Baillie, Belilovsky

Words, paper, and care, man
Words, paper, and care, man
O'Keefe, Bellet and Rivers, man
Sharp, Webb and Craft were there, man
A. Stewart and E. Bear, man
Words, paper, and care

More thanks to:
Sara, Jason, Dad, Mom
Olivia, Austin, #teamDongWon
Sheri, Wendy, Kenny, Mustafa
Colin, Logan, Dan, Ciulla
Abner Stein, Christine, Ice cream, Nicholls,
Parker(s), Carpenter(s), Nelson(s), Recorded Books

Words, paper, and care, man
Words, paper, and care, man
Wang, Wilson and Wallach, man
Resnick, Heyne, and Alex L. (my man)
All these folks are super swell, Stan
Words, paper, and care

Thanks to everyone on the list, man
Even those I might have missed, man
You gave a grand assist, man
Words . . . paper . . . and caaaaaaaare!